Praise for #1 *New York Times* bestselling author Linda Lael Miller

"This second-chance romance is set in the perfect setting of Painted Pony Creek. Curl up in your favorite reading chair and get lost in the pages of this book."

—Debbie Macomber,
#1 *New York Times* bestselling author, on *Country Strong*

"Miller's down-home, easy-to-read style keeps the plot moving, and she includes…likable characters, picturesque descriptions and some very sweet pets."

—*Publishers Weekly* on *Big Sky Country*

Praise for *USA TODAY* bestselling author Michelle Major

"A fantastic mix of drama and romance, starring a fragile, belligerent heroine and wounded hero. The innuendos, banter and role-perfect nicknames make it exceptional and genuine."

—*RT Book Reviews* on *A Kiss on Crimson Ranch*, 4.5 stars

"A sweet start to a promising series, perfect for fans of Debbie Macomber." —*Publishers Weekly* (starred review)
on *The Magnolia Sisters*

#1 *NEW YORK TIMES* BESTSELLING AUTHOR

LINDA LAEL MILLER

PART *of the* BARGAIN

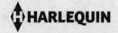

Special thanks and acknowledgment
are given to Michelle Major for her contribution
to The Fortunes of Texas: The Hotel Fortune miniseries.

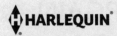

ISBN-13: 978-1-335-66254-5

Part of the Bargain
First published in 1985.
This edition published in 2023.
Copyright © 1985 by Linda Lael Miller

Her Texas New Year's Wish
First published in 2020.
This edition published in 2023.
Copyright © 2020 by Harlequin Enterprises ULC

PLEASE RECYCLE
THIS PRODUCT IS RECYCLABLE

Recycling programs
for this product may
not exist in your area.

For questions and comments about the quality of this book, please contact us at CustomerService@Harlequin.com.

Harlequin Enterprises ULC
22 Adelaide St. West, 41st Floor
Toronto, Ontario M5H 4E3, Canada
www.Harlequin.com

Printed in U.S.A.

CONTENTS

PART OF THE BARGAIN   7
Linda Lael Miller

HER TEXAS NEW YEAR'S WISH   297
Michelle Major

The daughter of a town marshal, **Linda Lael Miller** is the author of more than a hundred historical and contemporary novels. Now living in Spokane, Washington, the "First Lady of the West" hit a career high when all three of her 2011 Creed Cowboy books debuted at #1 on the *New York Times* list. In 2007, the Romance Writers of America presented her their Lifetime Achievement Award. She personally funds her Linda Lael Miller Scholarships for Women. Visit her at lindalaelmiller.com.

Books by Linda Lael Miller

Painted Pony Creek

Country Born
Country Proud
Country Strong

The Carsons of Mustang Creek

A Snow Country Christmas
Forever a Hero
Always a Cowboy
Once a Rancher

The Brides of Bliss County

Christmas in Mustang Creek
The Marriage Season
The Marriage Charm
The Marriage Pact

Visit the Author Profile page
at Harlequin.com for more titles.

PART OF THE BARGAIN

Linda Lael Miller

In loving and grateful memory of Laura Mast.

Chapter 1

The landing gear made an unsettling *ka-thump* sound as it snapped back into place under the small private airplane. Libby Kincaid swallowed her misgivings and tried not to look at the stony, impassive face of the pilot. If he didn't say anything, she wouldn't have to say anything either, and they might get through the short flight to the Circle Bar B ranch without engaging in one of their world-class shouting matches.

It was a pity, Libby thought, that at the ages of thirty-one and thirty-three, respectively, she and Jess still could not communicate on an adult level.

Pondering this, Libby looked down at the ground below and was dizzied by its passing as they swept over the small airport at Kalispell, Montana, and banked eastward, toward the Flathead River. Trees so green that they had a blue cast carpeted the majestic mountains rimming the valley.

Womanhood being what it is, Libby couldn't resist watching Jess Barlowe surreptitiously out of the corner of her eye. He was like a lean, powerful mountain lion waiting to pounce, even though he kept his attention strictly on the controls and the thin air traffic sharing the big Montana sky that spring morning. His eyes were hidden behind a pair of mirrored sunglasses, but Libby knew that they would be dark with the animosity that had marked their relationship for years.

She looked away again, trying to concentrate on the river, which coursed beneath them like a dusty-jade ribbon woven into the fabric of a giant tapestry. Behind those mirrored glasses, Libby knew Jess's eyes were the exact same shade of green as that untamed waterway below.

"So," he said suddenly, gruffly, "New York wasn't all the two-hour TV movies make it out to be."

Libby sighed, closed her eyes in a bid for patience and then opened them again. She wasn't going to miss one bit of that fabulous view—not when her heart had been hungering for it for several bittersweet years.

Besides, Jess had been to New York dozens of times on corporation business. Who did he think he was fooling?

"New York was all right," she said, in the most inflammatory tone she could manage. *Except that Jonathan died*, chided a tiny, ruthless voice in her mind. *Except for that nasty divorce from Aaron.* "Nothing to write home about," she added aloud, realizing her blunder too late.

"So your dad noticed," drawled Jess in an undertone that would have been savage if it hadn't been so carefully modulated. "Every day, when the mail came, he fell on it like it was manna from heaven. He never stopped hoping—I'll give him that."

"Dad knows I hate to write letters," she retorted defensively. But Jess had made his mark, all the same—Libby felt real pain, picturing her father flipping eagerly through the mail and trying to hide his disappointment when there was nothing from his only daughter.

"Funny—that's not what Stace tells me."

Libby bridled at this remark, but she kept her composure. Jess was trying to trap her into making some foolish statement about his older brother, no doubt, one that he could twist out of shape and hold over her head. She raised her chin and choked back the indignant diatribe aching in her throat.

The mirrored sunglasses glinted in the sun as Jess turned to look at her. His powerful shoulders were taut beneath the blue cotton fabric of his workshirt, and his jawline was formidably hard.

"Leave Cathy and Stace alone, Libby," he warned with blunt savagery. "They've had a lot of problems lately, and if you do anything to make the situation worse, I'll see that you regret it. Do I make myself clear?"

Libby would have done almost anything to escape his scrutiny just then, short of thrusting open the door of that small four-passenger Cessna and jumping out, but her choices were undeniably limited. Trembling just a little, she turned away and fixed her attention on the ground again.

Dear heaven, did Jess really think that she would

interfere in Cathy's marriage—or any other, for that matter? Cathy was her *cousin*—they'd been raised like sisters!

With a sigh, Libby faced the fact that there was every chance that Jess and a lot of other people would believe she had been involved with Stacey Barlowe. There had, after all, been that exchange of correspondence, and Stace had even visited her a few times, in the thick of her traumatic divorce, though in actuality he had been in the city on business.

"Libby?" prodded Jess sharply, when the silence grew too long to suit him.

"I'm not planning to vamp your brother!" she snapped. "Could we just drop this, please?"

To her relief and surprise, Jess turned his concentration on piloting the plane. His suntanned jaw worked with suppressed annoyance, but he didn't speak again.

The timbered land below began to give way to occasional patches of prairie—cattle country. Soon they would be landing on the small airstrip serving the prosperous 150,000-acre Circle Bar B, owned by Jess's father and overseen, for the most part, by Libby's.

Libby had grown up on the Circle Bar B, just as Jess had, and her mother, like his, was buried there. Even though she couldn't call the ranch home in the legal sense of the word, it was *still* home to her, and she had every right to go there—especially now, when she needed its beauty and peace and practical routines so desperately.

The airplane began to descend, jolting Libby out of her reflective state. Beside her, Jess guided the craft skillfully toward the paved landing strip stretched out before them.

The landing gear came down with a sharp snap, and Libby drew in her breath in preparation. The wheels of the plane screeched and grabbed as they made contact with the asphalt, and then the Cessna was rolling smoothly along the ground.

When it came to a full stop, Libby wrenched at her seat belt, anxious to put as much distance as possible between herself and Jess Barlowe. But his hand closed over her left wrist in a steel-hard grasp. "Remember, Lib—these people aren't the sophisticated if-it-feels-good-do-it types you're used to. No games."

Games. *Games?* Hot color surged into Libby's face and pounded there in rhythm with the furious beat of her heart. "Let go of me, you bastard!" she breathed.

If anything, Jess's grip tightened. "I'll be watching you," he warned, and then he flung Libby's wrist from his hand and turned away to push open the door on his side and leap nimbly to the ground.

Libby was still tugging impotently at the handle on her own door when her father strode over, climbed deftly onto the wing and opened it for her. She felt such a surge of love and relief at the sight of him that she cried out softly and flung herself into his arms, nearly sending both of them tumbling to the hard ground.

Ken Kincaid hadn't changed in the years since Libby had seen him last—he was still the same handsome, rangy cowboy that she remembered so well, though his hair, while as thick as ever, was iron-gray now, and the limp he'd acquired in a long-ago rodeo accident was more pronounced.

Once they were clear of the plane, he held his daughter at arm's length, laughed gruffly, and then pulled her close again. Over his shoulder she saw Jess drag her suitcases and portable drawing board out of the Cessna's luggage compartment and fling them unceremoniously into the back of a mud-speckled truck.

Nothing if not perceptive, Ken Kincaid turned slightly, assessed Senator Cleave Barlowe's second son, and grinned. There was mischief in his bright blue eyes when he faced Libby again. "Rough trip?"

Libby's throat tightened unaccountably, and she wished she could explain *how* rough. She was still stung by Jess's insulting opinion of her morality, but how could she tell her father that? "You know that it's always rough going where Jess and I are concerned," she said.

Her father's brows lifted speculatively as Jess got behind the wheel of the truck and sped away without so much as a curt nod or a halfhearted so-long. "You two'd better watch out," he mused. "If you ever stop butting heads, you might find out you like each other."

"Now, that," replied Libby with dispatch, "is a horrid thought if I've ever heard one. Tell me, Dad—how have you been?"

He draped one wiry arm over her shoulders and guided her in the direction of a late-model pickup truck. The door on the driver's side was emblazoned with the words CIRCLE BAR B RANCH, and Yosemite Sam glared from both the mud flaps shielding the rear tires. "Never mind how I've been, dumplin'. How've *you* been?"

Libby felt some of the tension drain from her as her father opened the door on the passenger side of the truck and helped her inside. She longed to shed her expensive tailored linen suit for jeans and a T-shirt, and—oh, heaven—her sneakers would be a welcome change from the high heels she was wearing. "I'll be okay," she said in tones that were a bit too energetically cheerful.

Ken climbed behind the wheel and tossed one searching, worried look in his daughter's direction. "Cathy's waiting over at the house, to help you settle in and all that. I was hoping we could talk…"

Libby reached out and patted her father's work-worn hand, resting now on the gearshift knob. "We can talk tonight. Anyway, we've got lots of time."

Ken started the truck's powerful engine, but his wise blue eyes had not strayed from his daughter's face. "You'll stay here awhile, then?" he asked hopefully.

Libby nodded, but she suddenly found that she had to look away. "As long as you'll let me, Dad."

The truck was moving now, jolting and rattling over the rough ranch roads with a pleasantly familiar vigor. "I expected you before this," he said. "Lib…"

She turned an imploring look on him. "Later, Dad—okay? Could we please talk about the heavy stuff later?"

Ken swept off his old cowboy hat and ran a practiced arm across his forehead. "Later it is, dumplin'." Graciously he changed the subject. "Been reading your comic strip in the funny papers, and it seems like every kid in town's wearing one of those T-shirts you designed."

Libby smiled; her career as a syndicated cartoonist was certainly safe conversational ground. And it had all started right here, on this ranch, when she'd sent away the coupon printed on a matchbook and begun taking art lessons by mail. After that, she'd won a scholarship to a prestigious college, graduated, and made her mark, not in portraits or commercial design, as some of her friends had, but in cartooning. Her character, Liberated Lizzie, a cave-girl with modern ideas, had created something of a sensation and was now featured not only in the Sunday newspapers but also on T-shirts, greeting cards, coffee mugs and calendars. There was a deal pending with a poster company, and Libby's bank balance was fat with the advance payment for a projected book.

She would have to work hard to fulfill her obligations—there was the weekly cartoon strip to do, of course, and the panels for the book had to be sketched in. She hoped that between these tasks and the endless allure of the Circle Bar B, she might be able to turn her thoughts from Jonathan and the mess she'd made of her personal life.

"Career-wise, I'm doing fine," Libby said aloud, as much to herself as to her father. "I don't suppose I could use the sunporch for a studio?"

Ken laughed. "Cathy's been working for a month to get it ready, and I had some of the boys put in a skylight. All you've got to do is set up your gear."

Impulsively Libby leaned over and kissed her father's beard-stubbled cheek. "I love you!"

"Good," he retorted. "A husband you can dump—a daddy you're pretty well stuck with."

The word "husband" jarred Libby a little, bringing an unwelcome image of Aaron into her mind as it did, and she didn't speak again until the house came into sight.

Originally the main ranch house, the structure set

aside for the general foreman was an enormous, drafty place with plenty of Victorian scrollwork, gabled windows and porches. It overlooked a sizable spring-fed pond and boasted its own sheltering copse of evergreens and cottonwood trees.

The truck lurched a little as Ken brought it to a stop in the gravel driveway, and through the windshield Libby could see glimmering patches of the silver-blue sparkle that was the pond. She longed to hurry there now, kick off her shoes on the grassy bank and ruin her stockings wading in the cold, clear water.

But her father was getting out of the truck, and Cathy Barlowe, Libby's cousin and cherished friend, was dashing down the driveway, her pretty face alight with greeting.

Libby laughed and stood waiting beside the pickup truck, her arms out wide.

After an energetic hug had been exchanged, Cathy drew back in Libby's arms and lifted a graceful hand to sign the words: "I've missed you so much!"

"And I've missed you," Libby signed back, though she spoke the words aloud, too.

Cathy's green eyes sparkled. "You haven't forgotten how to sign!" she enthused, bringing both hands into play now. She had been deaf since childhood, but she communicated so skillfully that Libby often forgot that they weren't conversing verbally. "Have you been practicing?"

She had. Signing had been a game for her and Jonathan to play during the long, difficult hours she'd spent at his hospital bedside. Libby nodded and tears of love and pride gathered in her dark blue eyes as she surveyed her cousin—physically, she and Cathy bore no resemblance to each other at all.

Cathy was petite, her eyes wide, mischievous emeralds, her hair a glistening profusion of copper and chestnut and gold that reached almost to her waist. Libby was of medium height, and her silver-blond hair fell just short of her shoulders.

"I'll be back later," Ken said quietly, signing the words as he spoke so that Cathy could understand, too. "You two have plenty to say to each other, it looks like."

Cathy nodded and smiled, but there was something sad trembling behind the joy in her green eyes, something that made Libby want to scurry back to the truck and beg to be driven back to the airstrip. From there she could fly to Kalispell and catch a connecting flight to Denver and then New York...

Good Lord—surely Jess hadn't been so heartless as to share his ridiculous suspicions with Cathy!

The interior of the house was cool and airy, and Libby followed along behind Cathy, her thoughts and feelings in an incomprehensible tangle. She was glad to be home, no doubt about it. She'd yearned for the quiet sanity of this place almost from the moment of leaving it.

On the other hand, she wasn't certain that she'd been wise to come back. Jess obviously intended to make her feel less than welcome, and although she had certainly never been intimately involved with Stacey Barlowe, Cathy's husband, sometimes her feelings toward him weren't all that clearly defined.

Unlike his younger brother, Stace was a warm, outgoing person, and through the shattering events of the past year and a half, he had been a tender and steadfast

friend. Adrift in waters of confusion and grief, Libby
had told Stacey things that she had never breathed to
another living soul, and it was true that, as Jess had so
bitterly pointed out, she had written to the man when
she couldn't bring herself to contact her own father.

But she wasn't in love with Stace, Libby told herself
firmly. She had always looked up to him, that was all—
like an older brother. Maybe she'd become a little too
dependent on him in the bargain, but that didn't mean
she cared for him in a romantic way, did it?

She sighed, and Cathy turned to look at her pensively, almost as though she had heard the sound. That
was impossible, of course, but Cathy was as perceptive as anyone Libby had ever known, and she often
felt sounds.

"Glad to be home?" the deaf woman inquired, gesturing gently.

Libby didn't miss the tremor in her cousin's hands,
but she forced a weary smile to her face and nodded in
answer to the question.

Suddenly Cathy's eyes were sparkling again, and she
caught Libby's hand in her own and tugged her through
an archway and into the glassed-in sunporch that overlooked the pond.

Libby drew in a swift, delighted breath. There was
indeed a skylight in the roof—a big one. A drawing
table had been set up in the best light the room offered,
along with a lamp for night work, and there were flow-
ering plants hanging from the exposed beams in the
ceiling. The old wicker furniture that had been stored in
the attic for as long as Libby could remember had been
painted a dazzling white and bedecked with gay floral-

print cushions. Small rugs in complementary shades of pink and green had been scattered about randomly, and there was even a shelving unit built into the wall behind the art table.

"Wow!" cried Libby, overwhelmed, her arms spread out wide in a gesture of wonder. "Cathy, you missed your calling! You should have been an interior decorator."

Though Libby hadn't signed the words, her cousin had read them from her lips. Cathy's green eyes shifted quickly from Libby's face, and she lowered her head. "Instead of what?" she motioned sadly. "Instead of Stacey's wife?"

Libby felt as though she'd been slapped, but she recovered quickly enough to catch one hand under Cathy's chin and force her head up. "Exactly what do you mean by that?" she demanded, and she was never certain afterward whether she had signed the words, shouted them, or simply thought them.

Cathy shrugged in a miserable attempt at nonchalance, and one tear slid down her cheek. "He went to see you in New York," she challenged, her hands moving quickly now, almost angrily. "You wrote to him."

"Cathy, it wasn't what you think—"

"Wasn't it?"

Libby was furious and wounded, and she stomped one foot in frustration. "Of course it wasn't! Do you really think I would do a thing like that? Do you think Stacey would? He *loves* you!" *And so does Jess*, she lamented in silence, without knowing why that should matter.

Stubbornly Cathy averted her eyes again and shoved

her hands into the pockets of her lightweight cotton jacket—a sure signal that as far as she was concerned, the conversation was over.

In desperation, Libby reached out and caught her cousin's shoulders in her hands, only to be swiftly rebuffed by an eloquent shrug. She watched, stricken to silence, as Cathy turned and hurried out of the sunporch-turned-studio and into the kitchen beyond. Just a moment later the back door slammed with a finality that made Libby ache through and through.

She ducked her head and bit her lower lip to keep the tears back. That, too, was something she had learned during Jonathan's final confinement in a children's hospital.

Just then, Jess Barlowe filled the studio doorway. Libby was aware of him in all her strained senses.

He set down her suitcases and drawing board with an unsympathetic thump. "I see you're spreading joy and good cheer as usual," he drawled in acid tones. "What, pray tell, was *that* all about?"

Libby was infuriated, and she glared at him, her hands resting on her trim rounded hips. "As if you didn't know, you heartless bastard! How could you be so mean...so thoughtless..."

The fiery green eyes raked Libby's travel-rumpled form with scorn. Ignoring her aborted question, he offered one of his own. "Did you think your affair with my brother was a secret, princess?"

Libby was fairly choking on her rage and her pain. "What affair, dammit?" she shouted. "We didn't *have* an affair!"

"That isn't what Stacey says," replied Jess with impervious savagery.

Libby felt the high color that had been pounding in her face seep away. *"What?"*

"Stace is wildly in love with you, to hear him tell it. You need him and he needs you, and to hell with minor stumbling blocks like his wife!"

Libby's knees weakened and she groped blindly for the stool at her art table and then sank onto it. "My God…"

Jess's jawline was tight with brutal annoyance. "Spare me the theatrics, princess—I know why you came back here. Dammit, *don't you have a soul?"*

Libby's throat worked painfully, but her mind simply refused to form words for her to utter.

Jess crossed the room like a mountain panther, terrifying in his grace and prowess, and caught both her wrists in a furious, inescapable grasp. With his other hand he captured Libby's chin.

"Listen to me, you predatory little witch, and listen well," he hissed, his jade eyes hard, his flesh pale beneath his deep rancher's tan. "Cathy is good and decent and she loves my brother, though I can't for the life of me think why she condescends to do so. And I'll be *damned* if I'll stand by and watch you and Stacey turn her inside out! Do you understand me?"

Tears of helpless fury and outraged honor burned like fire in Libby's eyes, but she could neither speak nor move. She could only stare into the frightening face looming only inches from her own. It was a devil's face.

When Jess's tightening grasp on her chin made it

clear that he would have an answer of some sort, no matter what, Libby managed a small, frantic nod.

Apparently satisfied, Jess released her with such suddenness that she nearly lost her balance and slipped off the stool.

Then he whirled away from her, his broad back taut, one powerful hand running through his obsidian hair in a typical gesture of frustration. "Damn you for ever coming back here," he said in a voice no less vicious for its softness.

"No problem," Libby said with great effort. "I'll leave."

Jess turned toward her again, this time with an ominous leisure, and his eyes scalded Libby's face, the hollow of her throat, the firm roundness of her high breasts. "It's too late," he said.

Still dazed, Libby sank back against the edge of the drawing table, sighed and covered her eyes with one hand. "Okay," she began with hard-won, shaky reason, "why is that?"

Jess had stalked to the windows; his back was a barrier between them again, and he was looking out at the pond. Libby longed to sprout claws and tear him to quivering shreds.

"Stacey has the bit in his teeth," he said at length, his voice low, speculative. "Wherever you went, he'd follow."

Since Libby didn't believe that Stacey had declared himself to be in love with her, she didn't believe that there was any danger of his following her away from the Circle Bar B, either. "You're crazy," she said.

Jess faced her quickly, some scathing retort brewing in his eyes, but whatever he had meant to say was lost as Ken strode into the room and demanded, "What the hell's going on in here? I just found Cathy running up the road in tears!"

"Ask your daughter!" Jess bit out. "Thanks to her, Cathy has just gotten *started* shedding tears!"

Libby could bear no more; she was like a wild creature goaded to madness, and she flung herself bodily at Jess Barlowe, just as she had in her childhood, fists flying. She would have attacked him gladly if her father hadn't caught hold of her around the waist and forcibly restrained her.

Jess raked her with one last contemptuous look and moved calmly in the direction of the door. "You ought to tame that little spitfire, Ken," he commented in passing. "One of these days she's going to hurt somebody."

Libby trembled in her father's hold, stung by his double meaning, and gave one senseless shriek of fury. This brought a mocking chuckle from a disappearing Jess and caused Ken to turn her firmly to face him.

"Good Lord, Libby, what's the *matter* with you?"

Libby drew a deep, steadying breath and tried to quiet the raging ten-year-old within her, the child that Jess had always been able to infuriate. "I hate Jess Barlowe," she said flatly. "I hate him."

"Why?" Ken broke in, and he didn't look angry anymore. Just honestly puzzled.

"If you knew what he's been saying about me—"

"If it's the same as what Stacey's been mouthing off about, I reckon I do."

Libby stepped back, stunned. "What?"

Ken Kincaid sighed, and suddenly all his fifty-two years showed clearly in his face. "Stacey and Cathy have been having trouble the last year or so. Now he's telling everybody who'll listen that it's over between him and Cathy and he wants you."

"I don't believe it! I—"

"I wanted to warn you, Lib, but you'd been through so much, between losing the boy and then falling out with your husband after that. I thought you needed to be home, but I knew you wouldn't come near the place if you had any idea what was going on."

Libby's chin trembled, and she searched her father's honest, weathered face anxiously. "I... I haven't been fooling around with C-Cathy's husband, Dad."

He smiled gently. "I know that, Lib—knew it all along. Just never mind Jess and all the rest of them—if you don't run away, this thing'll blow over."

Libby swallowed, thinking of Cathy and the pain she had to be feeling. The betrayal. "I can't stay here if Cathy is going to be hurt."

Ken touched her cheek with a work-worn finger. "Cathy doesn't really believe the rumors, Libby—think about it. Why would she work so hard to fix a studio up for you if she did? Why would she be waiting here to see you again?"

"But she was crying just now, Dad! And she as much as accused me of carrying on with her husband!"

"She's been hurt by what's been said, and Stacey's been acting like a spoiled kid. Honey, Cathy's just testing the waters, trying to find out where you stand. You can't leave her now, because except for Stace, there's nobody she needs more."

Despite the fact that all her instincts warned her to put the Circle Bar B behind her as soon as humanly possible, Libby saw the sense in her father's words. As incredible as it seemed, Cathy would need her—if for nothing else than to lay those wretched rumors to rest once and for all.

"These things Stacey's been saying—surely he didn't unload them on Cathy?"

Ken sighed. "I don't think he'd be that low, Libby. But you know how it is with Cathy, how she always knows the score."

Libby shook her head distractedly. "Somebody told her, Dad—and I think I know who it was."

There was disbelief in Ken's discerning blue eyes, and in his voice, too. "*Jess?* Now, wait a minute…"

Jess.

Libby couldn't remember a time when she had gotten along well with him, but she'd been sure that he cared deeply for Cathy. Hadn't he been the one to insist that Stace and Libby learn signing, as he had, so that everyone could talk to the frightened, confused little girl who couldn't hear? Hadn't he gifted Cathy with cherished bullfrogs and clumsily made valentines and even taken her to the high-school prom?

How could Jess, of all people, be the one to hurt Cathy, when he knew as well as anyone how badly she'd been hurt by her disability and the rejection of her own parents? How?

Libby had no answer for any of these questions. She knew only that she had separate scores to settle with both the Barlowe brothers.

And settle them she would.

Chapter 2

Libby sat at the end of the rickety swimming dock, bare feet dangling, shoulders slumped, her gaze fixed on the shimmering waters of the pond. The lines of her long, slender legs were accentuated, rather than disguised, by the old blue jeans she wore. A white eyelet suntop sheltered shapely breasts and a trim stomach and left the rest of her upper body bare.

Jess Barlowe studied her in silence, feeling things that were at wide variance with his personal opinion of the woman. He was certain that he hated Libby, but something inside him wanted, nonetheless, to touch her, to comfort her, to know the scent and texture of her skin.

A reluctant grin tilted one corner of his mouth. One tug at the top of that white eyelet and...

Jess caught his skittering thoughts, marshaled them back into stern order. As innocent and vulnerable as Libby Kincaid looked at the moment, she was a viper, willing to betray her own cousin to get what she wanted.

Jess imagined Libby naked, her glorious breasts free and welcoming. But the man in his mental scenario was not himself—it was Stacey. The thought lay sour in Jess's mind.

"Did you come to apologize, by any chance?"

The question so startled Jess that he flinched; he had not noticed that Libby had turned around and seen him, so caught up had he been in the vision of her giving herself to his brother.

He scowled, as much to recover his wits as to oppose her. It was and always had been his nature to oppose Libby Kincaid, the way electricity opposes water, and it annoyed him that, for all his travels and his education, he didn't know why.

"Why would I want to do that?" he shot back, more ruffled by her presence than he ever would have admitted.

"Maybe because you were a complete ass," she replied in tones as sunny as the big sky stretched out above them.

Jess lifted his hands to his hips and stood fast against whatever it was that was pulling him toward her. *I want to make love to you*, he thought, and the truth of that ground in his spirit as well as in his loins.

There was pain in Libby's navy blue eyes, as well as a cautious mischief. "Well?" she prodded.

Jess found that while he could keep himself from going to her, he could not turn away. Maybe her net reached farther than he'd thought. Maybe, like Stacey and that idiot in New York, he was already caught in it.

"I'm not here to apologize," he said coldly.

"Then why?" she asked with chiming sweetness.

He wondered if she knew what that shoulderless blouse of hers was doing to him. Damn. He hadn't been this tongue-tied since the night of his fifteenth birthday, when Ginny Hillerman had announced that she would show him hers if he would show her his.

Libby's eyes were laughing at him. "Jess?"

"Is your dad here?" he threw out in gruff desperation.

One shapely, gossamer eyebrow arched. "You know perfectly well that he isn't. If Dad were home, his pickup truck would be parked in the driveway."

Against his will, Jess grinned. His taut shoulders rose in a shrug. The shadows of cottonwood leaves moved on the old wooden dock, forming a mystical path—a path that led to Libby Kincaid.

She patted the sun-warmed wood beside her. "Come and sit down."

Before Jess could stop himself, he was striding along that small wharf, sinking down to sit beside Libby and dangle his booted feet over the sparkling water. He was never entirely certain what sorcery made him ask what he did.

"What happened to your marriage, Libby?"

The pain he had glimpsed before leapt in her eyes and then faded away again, subdued. "Are you trying to start another fight?"

Jess shook his head. "No," he answered quietly, "I really want to know."

She looked away from him, gnawing at her lower lip with her front teeth. All around them were ranch sounds—birds conferring in the trees, leaves rustling in the wind, the clear pond water lapping at the mossy pilings of the dock. But no sound came from Libby.

On an impulse, Jess touched her mouth with the tip of one index finger. Water and electricity—the analogy came back to him with a numbing jolt.

"Stop that," he barked, to cover his reactions.

Libby ceased chewing at her lip and stared at him with wide eyes. Again he saw the shadow of that nameless, shifting ache inside her. "Stop what?" she wanted to know.

Stop making me want to hold you, he thought. *Stop making me want to tuck your hair back behind your ears and tell you that everything will be all right.* "Stop biting your lip!" he snapped aloud.

"I'm sorry!" Libby snapped back, her eyes shooting indigo sparks.

Jess sighed and again spoke involuntarily. "Why did you leave your husband, Libby?"

The question jarred them both: Libby paled a little and tried to scramble to her feet; Jess caught her elbow in one hand and pulled her down again.

"Was it because of Stacey?"

She was livid. "No!"

"Someone else?"

Tears sprang up in Libby's dark lashes and made them spiky. She wrenched free of his hand but made no move to rise again and run away. "Sure!" she gasped. "'If it feels good, do it'—that's my motto! By God, I *live* by those words!"

"Shut up," Jess said in a gentle voice.

Incredibly, she fell against him, wept into the shoulder of his blue cotton workshirt. And it was not a delicate, calculating sort of weeping—it was a noisy grief.

Jess drew her close and held her, broken on the shoals of what she was feeling even though he did not know its name. "I'm sorry," he said hoarsely.

Libby trembled beneath his arm and wailed like a wounded calf. The sound solidified into a word usually reserved for stubborn horses and income-tax audits.

Jess laughed and, for a reason he would never understand, kissed her forehead. "I love it when you flatter me," he teased.

Miraculously, Libby laughed, too. But when she tilted her head back to look up at him, and he saw the tear streaks on her beautiful, defiant face, something within him, something that had always been disjointed, was wrenched painfully back into place.

He bent his head and touched his lips to hers, gently, in question. She stiffened, but then, at the cautious bidding of his tongue, her lips parted slightly and her body relaxed against his.

Jess pressed Libby backward until she lay prone on the shifting dock, the kiss unbroken. As she responded to that kiss, it seemed that the sparkling water-light of the pond danced around them both in huge, shimmering chips, that they were floating inside some cosmic prism.

His hand went to the full roundness of her left breast. Beneath his palm and the thin layer of white eyelet, he felt the nipple grow taut in that singular invitation to passion.

Through the back of his shirt, Jess was warmed by the

heat of the spring sun and the tender weight of Libby's hands. He left her mouth to trail soft kisses over her chin, along the sweet, scented lines of her neck.

All the while, he expected her to stiffen again, to thrust him away with her hands and some indignant—and no doubt colorful—outburst. Instead, she was pliant and yielding beneath him.

Enthralled, he dared more and drew downward on the uppermost ruffle of her suntop. Still she did not protest.

Libby arched her back and a low, whimpering sound came from her throat as Jess bared her to the soft spring breeze and the fire of his gaze.

Her breasts were heavy golden-white globes, and their pale rose crests stiffened as Jess perused them. When he offered a whisper-soft kiss to one, Libby moaned and the other peak pouted prettily at his choice. He went to it, soothed it to fury with his tongue.

Libby gave a soft, lusty cry, shuddered and caught her hands in his hair, drawing him closer. He needed more of her and positioned his body accordingly, careful not to let his full weight come to bear. Then, for a few dizzying moments, he took suckle at the straining fount of her breast.

Recovering himself partially, Jess pulled her hands from his hair, gripped them at the wrists, pressed them down above her head in gentle restraint.

Her succulent breasts bore his assessment proudly, rising and falling with the meter of her breathing.

Jess forced himself to meet Libby's eyes. "This is me," he reminded her gruffly. "Jess."

"I know," she whispered, making no move to free her imprisoned hands.

Jess lowered his head, tormented one delectable nipple by drawing at it with his lips. "This is real, Libby," he said, circling the morsel with just the tip of his tongue now. "It's important that you realize that."

"I do...oh, God... Jess, *Jess*."

Reluctantly he left the feast to search her face with disbelieving eyes. "Don't you want me to stop?"

A delicate shade of rose sifted over her high cheekbones. Her hands still stretched above her, her eyes closed, she shook her head.

Jess went back to the breasts that so bewitched him, nipped at their peaks with gentle teeth. "Do you...know how many...times I've wanted...to do this?"

The answer was a soft, strangled cry.

He limited himself to one nipple, worked its surrendering peak into a sweet fervor with his lips and his tongue. "So...many...times. My God, Libby...you're so beautiful..."

Her words were as halting as his had been. "What's happening to us? We h-hate each other."

Jess laughed and began kissing his way softly down over her rib cage, her smooth, firm stomach. The snap on her jeans gave way easily—and was echoed by the sound of car doors slamming in the area of the house.

Instantly the spell was broken. Color surged into Libby's face and she bolted upright, nearly thrusting Jess off the end of the dock in her efforts to wrench on the discarded suntop and close the fastening of her jeans.

"Broad daylight…" she muttered distractedly, talking more to herself than to Jess.

"Lib!" yelled a jovial masculine voice, approaching fast. "Libby?"

Stacey. The voice belonged to Stacey.

Sudden fierce anger surged, white-hot, through Jess's aching, bedazzled system. Standing up, not caring that his thwarted passion still strained against his jeans, visible to anyone who might take the trouble to look, he glared down at Libby and rasped, "I guess reinforcements have arrived."

She gave a primitive, protesting little cry and shot to her feet, her ink-blue eyes flashing with anger and hurt. Before Jess could brace himself, her hands came to his chest like small battering rams and pushed him easily off the end of the dock.

The jolting cold of that spring-fed pond was welcome balm to Jess's passion-heated flesh, if not his pride. When he surfaced and grasped the end of the dock in both hands, he knew there would be no physical evidence that he and Libby had been doing anything other than fighting.

Libby ached with embarrassment as Stacey and Senator Barlowe made their way down over the slight hillside that separated the backyard from the pond.

The older man cast one mischievously baleful look at his younger son, who was lifting himself indignantly onto the dock, and chuckled, "I see things are the same as always," he said.

Libby managed a shaky smile. *Not quite*, she thought, her body remembering the delicious dance Jess's hard frame had choreographed for it. "Hello, Senator," she said, rising on tiptoe to kiss his cheek.

"Welcome home," he replied with gruff affection. Then his wise eyes shifted past her to rest again on Jess. "It's a little cold yet for a swim, isn't it, son?"

Jess's hair hung in dripping ebony strands around his face, and his eyes were jade-green flares, avoiding his father to scald Libby's lips, her throat, her still-pulsing breasts. "We'll finish our...discussion later," he said.

Libby's blood boiled up over her stomach and her breasts to glow in her face. "I wouldn't count on that!"

"I would," Jess replied with a smile that was at once tender and evil. And then, without so much as a word to his father and brother, he walked away.

"What the hell did he mean by that?" barked Stacey, red in the face.

The look Libby gave the boyishly handsome, caramel-eyed man beside her was hardly friendly. "You've got some tall explaining to do, Stacey Barlowe," she said.

The senator, a tall, attractive man with hair as gray as Ken's, cleared his throat in the way of those who have practiced diplomacy long and well. "I believe I'll go up to the house and see if Ken's got any beer on hand," he said. A moment later he was off, following Jess's soggy path.

Libby straightened her shoulders and calmly slapped Stacey across the face. "How dare you?" she raged, her words strangled in her effort to modulate them.

Stacey reddened again, ran one hand through his fashionably cut wheat-colored hair. He turned, as if to follow his father. "I could use a beer myself," he said in distracted, evasive tones.

"Oh, no you don't!" Libby cried, grasping his arm and holding on. The rich leather of his jacket was smooth under her hand. "Don't you *dare* walk away from me, Stacey—not until you explain why you've been lying about me!"

"I haven't been lying!" he protested, his hands on his hips now, his expensively clad body blocking the base of the dock as he faced her.

"You have! You've been telling everyone that I... That we..."

"That we've been doing what you and my brother were doing a few minutes ago?"

If Stacey had shoved Libby into the water, she couldn't have been more shocked. A furious retort rose to the back of her throat but would go no further.

Stacey's tarnished-gold eyes flashed. "Jess was making love to you, wasn't he?"

"What if he was?" managed Libby after a painful struggle with her vocal cords. "It certainly wouldn't be any of your business, would it?"

"Yes, it would. I love you, Libby."

"You love *Cathy*!"

Stacey shook his head. "No. Not anymore."

"Don't say that," Libby pleaded, suddenly deflated. "Oh, Stacey, don't. Don't do this..."

His hands came to her shoulders, fierce and strong. The topaz fever in his eyes made Libby wonder if he was sane. "I love you, Libby Kincaid," he vowed softly but ferociously, "and I mean to have you."

Libby retreated a step, stunned, shaking her head.

The reality of this situation was so different from what she had imagined it would be. In her thoughts, Stacey had laughed when she confronted him, ruffled her hair in that familiar brotherly way of old, and said that it was all a mistake. That he loved Cathy, wanted Cathy, and couldn't anyone around here take a joke?

But here he was declaring himself in a way that was unsettlingly serious.

Libby took another step backward. "Stacey, I need to be here, where my dad is. Where things are familiar and comfortable. Please…don't force me to leave."

Stacey smiled. "There is no point in leaving, Lib. If you do, I'll be right behind you."

She shivered. "You've lost your mind!"

But Stacey looked entirely sane as he shook his handsome head and wedged his hands into the pockets of his jacket. "Just my heart," he said. "Corny, isn't it?"

"It's worse than corny. Stacey, you're unbalanced or something. You're fantasizing. There was never anything between us—"

"No?" The word was crooned.

"No! You need help."

His face had all the innocence of an altar boy's. "If I'm insane, darlin', it's something you could cure."

Libby resisted an urge to slap him again. She wanted to race into the house, but he was still barring her way, so that she could not leave the dock without brushing against him. "Stay away from me, Stacey," she said as he advanced toward her. "I mean it—stay away from me!"

"I can't, Libby."

The sincerity in his voice was chilling; for the first

time in all the years she'd known Stacey Barlowe, Libby was afraid of him. Discretion kept her from screaming, but just barely.

Stacey paled, as though he'd read her thoughts. "Don't look at me like that, Libby—I wouldn't hurt you under any circumstances. And I'm not crazy."

She lifted her chin. "Let me by, Stacey. I want to go into the house."

He tilted his head back, sighed, met her eyes again. "I've frightened you, and I'm sorry. I didn't mean to do that."

Libby couldn't speak. Despite his rational, settling words, she was sick with the knowledge that he meant to pursue her.

"You must know," he said softly, "how good it could be for us. You needed me in New York, Libby, and now I need you."

The third voice, from the base of the hillside, was to Libby as a life preserver to a drowning person. "Let her pass, Stacey."

Libby looked up quickly to see Jess, unlikely rescuer that he was. His hair was towel-rumpled and his jeans clung to muscular thighs—thighs that only minutes ago had pressed against her own in a demand as old as time. His manner was calm as he buttoned a shirt, probably borrowed from Ken, over his broad chest.

Stacey shrugged affably and walked past his brother without a word of argument.

Watching him go, Libby went weak with relief. A lump rose in her throat as she forced herself to meet Jess's gaze. "You were right," she muttered miserably. "You were *right*."

Jess was watching her much the way a mountain cat would watch a cornered rabbit. For the briefest moment there was a look of tenderness in the green eyes, but then his expression turned hard and a muscle flexed in his jaw. "I trust the welcome-home party has been scheduled for later—after Cathy has been tucked into her bed, for instance?"

Libby gaped at him, appalled. Had he interceded only to torment her himself?

Jess's eyes were contemptuous as they swept over her. "What's the matter, Lib? Couldn't you bring yourself to tell your married lover that the welcoming had already been taken care of?"

Rage went through Libby's body like an electric current surging into a wire. "You don't seriously think that I would… That I was—"

"You even managed to be alone with him. Tell me, Lib—how did you get rid of my father?"

"G-get rid…" Libby stopped, tears of shock and mortification aching in her throat and burning behind her eyes. She drew a deep, audible breath, trying to assemble herself, to think clearly.

But the whole world seemed to be tilting and swirling like some out-of-control carnival ride. When Libby closed her eyes against the sensation, she swayed dangerously and would probably have fallen if Jess hadn't reached her in a few strides and caught her shoulders in his hands.

"Libby…" he said, and there was anger in the sound, but there was a hollow quality, too—one that Libby couldn't find a name for.

Her knees were trembling. Too much, it was all too

much. Jonathan's death, the ugly divorce, the trouble that Stacey had caused with his misplaced affections—all of those things weighed on her, but none were so crushing as the blatant contempt of this man. It was apparent to Libby now that the lovemaking they had almost shared, so new and beautiful to her, had been some sort of cruel joke to Jess.

"How could you?" she choked out. "Oh, Jess, how could you?"

His face was grim, seeming to float in a shimmering mist. Instead of answering, Jess lifted Libby into his arms and carried her up the little hill toward the house.

She didn't remember reaching the back door.

"What the devil happened on that dock today, Jess?" Cleave Barlowe demanded, hands grasping the edge of his desk.

His younger son stood at the mahogany bar, his shoulders stiff, his attention carefully fixed on the glass of straight Scotch he meant to consume. "Why don't you ask Stacey?"

"Goddammit, I'm asking *you*!" barked Cleave. "Ken's mad as hell, and I don't blame him—that girl of his was shattered!"

Girl. The word caught in Jess's beleaguered mind. He remembered the way Libby had responded to him, meeting his passion with her own, welcoming the greed he'd shown at her breasts. Had it not been for the arrival of his father and brother, he would have possessed her completely within minutes. "She's no 'girl,'" he said, still aching to bury himself in the depths of her.

The senator swore roundly. "What did you say to

her, Jess?" he pressed, once the spate of unpoliticianly profanity had passed.

Jess lowered his head. He'd meant the things he'd said to Libby, and he couldn't, in all honesty, have taken them back. But he knew some of what she'd been through in New York, her trysts with Stacey notwithstanding, and he was ashamed of the way he'd goaded her. She had come home to heal—the look in her eyes had told him that much—and instead of respecting that, he had made things more difficult for her.

Never one to be thwarted by silence, no matter how eloquent, Senator Barlowe persisted. "Dammit, Jess, I might expect this kind of thing from Stacey, but I thought you had more sense! You were harassing Libby about these blasted rumors your brother has been spreading, weren't you?"

Jess sighed, set aside the drink he had yet to take a sip from, and faced his angry father. "Yes," he said.

"Why?"

Stubbornly, Jess refused to answer. He took an interest in the imposing oak desk where his father sat, the heavy draperies that kept out the sun, the carved ivory of the fireplace.

"All right, mulehead," Cleave muttered furiously, "don't talk! Don't explain! And don't go near Ken Kincaid's daughter again, damn you. That man's the best foreman I've ever had and if he gets riled and quits because of you, Jess, you and I are going to come to time!"

Jess almost smiled, though he didn't quite dare. Not too many years before the phrase "come to time," when used by his father, had presaged a session in the woodshed. He wondered what it meant now that he was thirty-three years old, a member of the Montana State Bar Association, and a full partner in the family corporation. "I care about Cathy," he said evenly. "What was I supposed to do—stand by and watch Libby and Stace grind her up into emotional hamburger?"

Cleave gave a heavy sigh and sank into the richly upholstered swivel chair behind his desk. "I love Cathy, too," he said at length, "but Stacey's behind this whole mess, not Libby. Dammit, that woman has been through hell from what Ken says—she was married to a man who slept in every bed but his own, and she had to watch her nine-year-old stepson die by inches. Now she comes home looking for a little peace, and what does she get? Trouble!"

Jess lowered his head, turned away—ostensibly to take up his glass of Scotch. He'd known about the bad marriage—Ken had cussed the day Aaron Strand was born often enough—but he hadn't heard about the little boy. My God, he hadn't known about the boy.

"Maybe Strand couldn't sleep in his own bed," he said, urged on by some ugliness that had surfaced inside him since Libby's return. "Maybe Stacey was already in it."

"Enough!" boomed the senator in a voice that had made presidents tremble in their shoes. "I like Libby and I'm not going to listen to any more of this, either from you or from your brother! Do I make myself clear?"

"Abundantly clear," replied Jess, realizing that the Scotch was in his hand now and feeling honor-bound to take at least one gulp of the stuff. The taste was reminiscent of scorched rubber, but since the liquor seemed to quiet the raging demons in his mind, he finished the drink and poured another.

He fully intended to get drunk. It was something he hadn't done since high school, but it suddenly seemed appealing. Maybe he would stop hardening every time he thought of Libby, stop craving her.

Too, after the things he'd said to her that afternoon by the pond, he didn't want to remain sober any longer than necessary. "What did you mean," he ventured, after downing his fourth drink, "when you said Libby had to watch her stepson die?"

Papers rustled at the big desk behind him. "Stacey says the child had leukemia."

Jess poured another drink and closed his eyes. *Oh, Libby,* he thought, *I'm sorry. My God, I'm sorry.* "I guess Stacey would know," he said aloud, with bitterness.

There was a short, thunderous silence. Jess expected his father to explode into one of his famous tirades, was genuinely surprised when the man sighed instead. Still, his words dropped on Jess's mind like a bomb.

"The firewater isn't going to change the fact that you love Libby Kincaid, Jess," he said reasonably. "Making her life and your own miserable isn't going to change it, either."

Love Libby Kincaid? Impossible. The strange needs possessing him now were rooted in his libido, not his heart. Once he'd had her—and have her he would, or go crazy—her hold on him would be broken. "I've never loved a woman in my life," he said.

"Fool. You've loved one woman—Libby—since you were seven years old. Exactly seven years old, in fact."

Jess turned, studying his father quizzically. "What the hell are you talking about?"

"Your seventh birthday," recalled Cleave, his eyes far away. "Your mother and I gave you a pony. First time you saw Libby Kincaid, you were out of that saddle and helping her into it."

The memory burst, full-blown, into Jess's mind. A pinto pony. The new foreman arriving. The little girl with dark blue eyes and hair the color of winter moonlight.

He'd spent the whole afternoon squiring Libby around the yard, content to walk while she rode.

"What do you suppose Ken would say if I went over there and asked to see his daughter?" Jess asked.

"I imagine he'd shoot you, after today."

"I imagine he would. But I think I'll risk it."

"You've made enough trouble for one day," argued Cleave, taking obvious note of his son's inebriated state. "Libby needs time, Jess. She needs to be close to Ken. If you're smart, you'll leave her alone until she has a chance to get her emotional bearings again."

Jess didn't want his father to be right, not in this instance, anyway, but he knew that he was. Much as he wanted to go to Libby and try to make things right, the fact was that he was the last person in the world she needed or wanted to see.

"Better?"

Libby smiled at Ken as she came into the kitchen, freshly showered and wrapped in the cozy, familiar chenille robe she'd found in the back of her closet. "Lots better," she answered softly.

Her father was standing at the kitchen stove stirring something in the blackened cast-iron skillet.

Libby scuffled to the table and sat down. It was good to be home, so good. Why hadn't she come sooner? "Whatever you're cooking there smells good," she said.

Ken beamed. In his jeans and his Western shirt, he looked out of place at that stove. He should, Libby decided fancifully, have been crouching at some campfire on the range, stirring beans in a blue enamel pot. "This here's my world-famous red-devil sauce," he grinned, "for which I am known and respected."

Libby laughed, and tears of homecoming filled her eyes. She went to her father and hugged him, needing to be a little girl again, just for a moment.

Chapter 3

Libby nearly choked on her first taste of Ken's taco sauce. "Did you say you were known and respected for this stuff, or known and feared?"

Ken chuckled roguishly at her tear-polished eyes and flaming face. "My calling it 'red devil' should have been a clue, dumplin'."

Libby muttered an exclamation and perversely took another bite from her bulging taco. "From now on," she said, chewing, "I'll do the cooking around this spread."

Her father laughed again and tapped one temple with a calloused index finger, his pale blue eyes twinkling.

"You deliberately tricked me!" cried Libby.

He grinned and shrugged. "Code of the West, sweetheart. Grouse about the chow, and presto—you're the cook!"

"Actually," ventured Libby with cultivated innocence, "this sauce isn't too bad."

"Too late," laughed Ken. "You already broke the code."

Libby lowered her taco to her plate and lifted both hands in a gesture of concession. "All right, all right—but have a little pity on me, will you? I've been living among dudes!"

"That's no excuse."

Libby shrugged and took up her taco again. "I tried. Have you been doing your own cooking and cleaning all this time?"

Ken shook his head and sat back in his chair, his thumbs hooked behind his belt buckle. "Nope. The Barlowes' housekeeper sends her crew down here once in a while."

"What about the food?"

"I eat with the boys most of the time, over at the cook shack." He rose, went to fill two mugs from the coffeepot on the stove. When he turned around again, his face was serious. "Libby, what happened today? What upset you like that?"

Libby averted her eyes. "I don't know," she lied lamely.

"Dammit, you *do* know. You fainted, Libby. When Jess carried you in here, I—"

"I know," Libby broke in gently. "You were scared. I'm sorry."

Carefully, as though he feared he might drop them, Ken set the cups of steaming coffee on the table. "What happened?" he persisted as he sat down in his chair again.

Libby swallowed hard, but the lump that had risen

in her throat wouldn't go down. Knowing that this conversation couldn't be avoided forever, she managed to reply, "It's complicated. Basically, it comes down to the fact that Stacey's been telling those lies."

"And?"

"And Jess believes him. He said…he said some things to me and…well, it must have created some kind of emotional overload. I just gave out."

Ken turned his mug idly between his thumb and index finger, causing the liquid to spill over and make a coffee stain on the tablecloth. "Tell me about Jonathan, Libby," he said in a low, gentle voice.

The tears that sprang into Libby's eyes were not related to the tang of her father's red-devil taco sauce. "He died," she choked miserably.

"I know that. You called me the night it happened, remember? I guess what I'm really asking you is why you didn't want me to fly back there and help you sort things out."

Libby lowered her head. Jonathan hadn't been her son, he'd been Aaron's, by a previous marriage. But the loss of the child was a raw void within her, even though months had passed. "I didn't want you to get a firsthand look at my marriage," she admitted with great difficulty—and the shame she couldn't seem to shake.

"Why not, Libby?"

The sound Libby made might have been either a laugh or a sob. "Because it was terrible," she answered.

"From the first?"

She forced herself to meet her father's steady gaze, knew that he had guessed a lot about her marriage from her rare phone calls and even rarer letters. "Almost," she replied sadly.

"Tell me."

Libby didn't want to think about Aaron, let alone talk about him to this man who wouldn't understand so many things. "He had…he had lovers."

Ken didn't seem surprised. Had he guessed that, too? "Go on."

"I can't!"

"Yes, you can. If it's too much for you right now, I won't press you. But the sooner you talk this out, Libby, the better off you're going to be."

She realized that her hands were clenched in her lap and tried to relax them. There was still a white mark on her finger where Aaron's ostentatious wedding ring had been. "He didn't care," she mourned in a soft, distracted whisper. "He honestly didn't care…"

"About you?"

"About Jonathan. Dad, he didn't care about his own son!"

"How so, sweetheart?"

Libby dashed away tears with the back of one hand. "Th-things were bad between Aaron and me b-before we found out that Jonathan was sick. After the doctors told us, it was a lot worse."

"I don't follow you, Libby."

"Dad, Aaron wouldn't have anything to do with Jonathan from the moment we knew he was dying. He wasn't there for any of the tests and he never once came to visit at the hospital. Dad, that little boy cried for his father, and Aaron wouldn't come to him!"

"Did you talk to Aaron?"

Remembered frustration made Libby's cheeks pound with color. "I *pleaded* with him, Dad. All he'd say was, 'I can't handle this.'"

"It would be a hell of a thing to deal with, Lib. Maybe you're being too hard on the man."

"Too hard? *Too hard?* Jonathan was terrified, Dad, and he was in pain—constant pain. All he asked was that his own father be strong for him!"

"What about the boy's mother? Did she come to the hospital?"

"Ellen died when Jonathan was a baby."

Ken sighed, framing a question he was obviously reluctant to ask. "Did you ever love Aaron Strand, Libby?"

Libby remembered the early infatuation, the excitement that had never deepened into real love and had quickly been quelled by the realities of marriage to a man who was fundamentally self-centered. She tried, but she couldn't even recall her ex-husband's face clearly—all she could see in her mind was a pair of jade-green eyes, dark hair. Jess. "No," she finally said. "I thought I did when I married him, though."

Ken stood up suddenly, took the coffeepot from its back burner on the stove, refilled both their cups. "I don't like asking you this, but—"

"No, Dad," Libby broke in firmly, anticipating the question all too well, "I don't love Stacey!"

"You're sure about that?"

The truth was that Libby *hadn't* been sure, not entirely. But that ill-advised episode with Jess at the end of the swimming dock had brought everything into clear perspective. Just remembering how willingly she had submitted to him made her throb with embarrassment. "I'm sure," she said.

Ken's strong hand came across the table to close over hers. "You're home now," he reminded her, "and things are going to get better, Libby. I promise you that."

Libby sniffled inelegantly. "Know something, cow-boy? I love you very much."

"Bet you say that to all your fathers," Ken quipped. "You planning to work on your comic strip tomorrow?"

The change of subject was welcome. "I'm six or eight weeks ahead of schedule on that, so I'm not worried about my deadline. I think I'll go riding, if I can get Cathy to go with me."

"I was looking forward to watching you work. What's your process?"

Libby smiled, feeling sheltered by the love of this strong and steady man facing her. She explained how her cartoons came into being, thinking it was good to talk about work, to think about work.

Disdainful as he had been about her career, it was the one thing Aaron had not been able to spoil for her.

Nobody's fool, Ken drew her out on the subject as much as he could, and she found herself chattering on and on about cartooning and even her secret hope to branch out into portraits one day.

They talked, father and daughter, far into the night.

"You deserve this," Jess Barlowe said to his reflection in the bathroom mirror. A first-class hangover pounded in his head and roiled in his stomach, and his face looked drawn, as though he'd been hibernat-

ing like one of the bears that sometimes troubled the
range stock.

Grimly he began to shave, and as he wielded his
disposable razor, he wondered if Libby was awake yet.
Should he stop at Ken's and talk to her before going on
to the main house to spend a day with the corporation
accountants?

Jess wanted to go to Libby, to tell her that he was sorry
for baiting her, to try to get their complex relationship—
if it *was* a relationship—onto some kind of sane ground.
However, all his instincts told him that his father had
been right the day before: Libby needed time.

His thoughts strayed to Libby's stepson. What would
it be like to sit by a hospital bed, day after day, watching a child suffer and not being able to help?

Jess shuddered. It was hard to imagine the horror of
something like that. At least Libby had had her husband
to share the nightmare.

He frowned as he nicked his chin with the razor,
blotted the small wound with tissue paper. If Libby had
had her husband during that impossible time, why had
she needed Stacey?

Stacey. Now, there was someone he could talk to.
Granted, Jess had not been on the best of terms with his
older brother of late, but the man had a firsthand knowledge of what was happening inside Libby Kincaid, and
that was reason enough to approach him.

Feeling better for having a plan, Jess finished his
ablutions and got dressed. Normally he spent his days
on the range with Ken and the ranch hands, but today,
because of his meeting with the accountants, he forwent
his customary blue jeans and cotton workshirt for a tai-

lored three-piece suit. He was still struggling with his tie as he made his way down the broad redwood steps that led from the loftlike second floor of his house to the living room.

Here there was a massive fireplace of white limestone, taking up the whole of one wall. The floors were polished oak and boasted a number of brightly colored Indian rugs. Two easy chairs and a deep sofa faced the hearth, and Jess's cluttered desk looked out over the ranchland and the glacial mountains beyond.

Striding toward the front door, in exasperation he gave up his efforts to get the tie right. He was glad he didn't have Stacey's job; not for him the dull task of overseeing the family's nationwide chain of steakhouse franchises.

He smiled. Stacey liked playing the dude, doing television commercials, traveling all over the country.

And taking Libby Kincaid to bed.

Jess stalked across the front lawn to the carport and climbed behind the wheel of the truck he'd driven since law school. One of these times, he was going to have to get another car—something with a little flash, like Stacey's Ferrari.

Stacey, Stacey. He hadn't even seen his brother yet, and already he was sick of him.

The truck's engine made a grinding sound and then huffed to life. Jess patted the dusty dashboard affectionately and grinned. A car was a car was a car, he reflected as he backed the notorious wreck out of his driveway. The function of a car was to transport people, not impress them.

Five minutes later, Jess's truck chortled to an asthmatic stop beside his brother's ice-blue Ferrari. He looked up at the modernistic two-story house that had been the senator's wedding gift to Stacey and Cathy and wondered if Libby would be impressed by the place.

He scowled as he made his way up the curving white-stone walk. What the hell did he care if Libby was impressed?

Irritated, he jabbed one finger at the special doorbell that would turn on a series of blinking lights inside the house. The system had been his own idea, meant to make life easier for Cathy.

His sister-in-law came to the door and smiled at him somewhat wanly, speaking with her hands. "Good morning."

Jess nodded, smiled. The haunted look in the depths of Cathy's eyes made him angry all over again. "Is Stacey here?" he signed, stepping into the house.

Cathy caught his hand in her own and led him through the cavernous living room and the formal dining room beyond. Stacey was in the kitchen, looking more at home in a three-piece suit than Jess ever had.

"You," Stacey said tonelessly, setting down the English muffin he'd been slathering with honey.

Cathy offered coffee and left the room when it was politely declined. Distractedly Jess reflected on the fact that her life had to be boring as hell, centering on Stacey the way it did.

"I want to talk to you," Jess said, scraping back a chrome-and-plastic chair to sit down at the table.

Stacey arched one eyebrow. "I hope it's quick—I'm leaving for the airport in a few minutes. I've got some business to take care of in Kansas City."

Jess was impatient. "What kind of man is Libby's ex-husband?" he asked.

Stacey took up his coffee. "Why do you want to know?"

"I just do. Do I have to have him checked out, or are you going to tell me?"

"He's a bastard," said Stacey, not quite meeting his brother's eyes.

"Rich?"

"Oh, yes. His family is old-money."

"What does he do?"

"Do?"

"Yeah. Does he work, or does he just stand around being rich?"

"He runs the family advertising agency; I think he has a lot of control over their other financial interests, too."

Jess sensed that Stacey was hedging, wondered why. "Any bad habits?"

Stacey was gazing at the toaster now, in a fixed way, as though he expected something alarming to pop out of it. "The man has his share of vices."

Annoyed now, Jess got up, helped himself to the cup of coffee he had refused earlier, sat down again. "Pulling porcupine quills out of a dog's nose would be easier than getting answers out of you. When you say he has vices, do you mean women?"

Stacey swallowed, looked away. "To put it mildly," he said.

Jess settled back in his chair. "What the hell do you mean by that?"

"I mean that he not only liked to run around with other women, he liked to flaunt the fact. The worse he could make Libby feel about herself, the happier he was."

"Jesus," Jess breathed. "What else?" he pressed, sensing, from Stacey's expression, that there was more.

"He was impotent with Libby."

"Why did she stay? Why in God's name did she stay?" Jess mused distractedly, as much to himself as to his brother.

A cautious but smug light flickered in Stacey's topaz eyes. "She had me," he said evenly. "Besides, Jonathan was sick by that time and she felt she had to stay in the marriage for his sake."

The spacious sun-filled kitchen seemed to buckle and shift around Jess. "Why didn't she tell Ken, at least?"

"What would have been the point in that, Jess? He couldn't have made the boy well again or transformed Aaron Strand into a devoted husband."

The things Libby must have endured—the shame, the loneliness, the humiliation and grief, washed over Jess in a dismal, crushing wave. No wonder she had reached out to Stacey the way she had. No wonder. "Thanks," he said gruffly, standing up to leave.

"Jess?"

He paused in the kitchen doorway, his hands clasping the woodwork, his shoulders aching with tension. "What?"

"Don't worry about Libby. I'll take care of her."

Jess felt a despairing sort of anger course through him. "What about Cathy?" he asked, without turning around. "Who is going to take care of her?"

"You've always—"

Jess whirled suddenly, staring at his brother, almost hating him. "I've always *what*?"

"Cared for her." Stacey shrugged, looking only mildly unsettled. "Protected her..."

"Are you suggesting that I sweep up the pieces after you shatter her?" demanded Jess in a dangerous rasp.

Stacey only shrugged again.

Because he feared that he would do his brother lasting harm if he stayed another moment, Jess stormed out of the house. Cathy, dressed in old jeans, boots and a cotton blouse, was waiting beside the truck. The pallor in her face told Jess that she knew much more about the state of her marriage than he would have hoped.

Her hands trembled a little as she spoke with them. "I'm scared, Jess."

He drew her into his arms, held her. "I know, baby," he said, even though he knew she couldn't hear him or see his lips. "I know."

Libby opened her eyes, yawned and stretched. The smells of sunshine and fresh air swept into her bedroom through the open window, ruffling pink eyelet curtains and reminding her that she was home again. She tossed back the covers on the bed and got up, sleepily making her way into the bathroom and starting the water for a shower.

As she took off her short cotton nightshirt, she looked down at herself and remembered the raging sensations Jess Barlowe had ignited in her the day before. She had been stupid and self-indulgent to let that happen, but after several years of celibacy, she supposed it was natural that her passions had been stirred so easily—especially by a man like Jess.

As Libby showered, she felt renewed. Aaron's flagrant infidelities had been painful for her, and they had seriously damaged her self-esteem in the bargain.

Now, even though she had made a fool of herself by being wanton with a man who could barely tolerate her, many of Libby's doubts about herself as a woman had been eased, if not routed. She was not as useless and undesirable as Aaron had made her feel. She had caused Jess Barlowe to want her, hadn't she?

Big deal, she told the image in her mirror as she brushed her teeth. *How do you know Jess wasn't out to prove that his original opinion of you was on target?*

Deflated by this very real possibility, Libby combed her hair, applied the customary lip gloss and light touch of mascara and went back to her room to dress. From her suitcases she selected a short-sleeved turquoise pullover shirt and a pair of trim jeans. Remembering her intention to find Cathy and persuade her to go riding, she ferreted through her closet until she found the worn boots she'd left behind before moving to New York, pulling them on over a pair of thick socks.

Looking down at those disreputable old boots, Libby imagined the scorn they would engender in Aaron's jet-set crowd and laughed. Problems or no problems, Jess or no Jess, it was good to be home.

Not surprisingly, the kitchen was empty. Ken had probably left the house before dawn, but there was coffee on the stove and fruit in the refrigerator, so Libby helped herself to a pear and sat down to eat.

The telephone rang just as she was finishing her

second cup of coffee, and Libby answered cheerfully, thinking that the caller would be Ken or the house- keeper at the main house, relaying some message for Cathy.

She was back at the table, the receiver pressed to her ear, before Aaron spoke.

"When are you coming home?"

"Home?" echoed Libby stupidly, off-balance, unable to believe that he'd actually asked such a question. "I *am* home, Aaron."

"Enough," he replied. "You've made your point, ex- hibited your righteous indignation. Now you've got to get back here because I need you."

Libby wanted to hang up, but it seemed a very long way from her chair to the wall, where the rest of the telephone was. "Aaron, we are divorced," she reminded him calmly, "and I am never coming back."

"You have to," he answered, without missing a beat. "It's crucial."

"Why? What happened to all your...friends?"

Aaron sighed. "You remember Betty, don't you? Miss November? Well, Betty and I had a small disagreement, as it happens, and she went to my family. I am, shall we say, exposed as something less than an ideal spouse.

"In any case, my grandmother believes that a man who cannot run his family—she was in Paris when we divorced, darling—cannot run a company, either. I have six months to bring you back into the fold and start an heir, or the whole shooting match goes to my cousin."

Libby was too stunned to speak or even move; she simply stood in the middle of her father's kitchen, try- ing to absorb what Aaron was saying.

"That," Aaron went on blithely, "is where you come in, sweetheart. You come back, we smile a lot and make a baby, my grandmother's ruffled feathers are smoothed. It's as simple as that."

Sickness boiled into Libby's throat. "I don't believe this!" she whispered.

"You don't believe what, darling? That I can make a baby? May I point out that I sired Jonathan, of whom you were so cloyingly fond?"

Libby swallowed. "Get Miss November pregnant," she managed to suggest. And then she added distractedly, more to herself than Aaron, "I think I'm going to be sick."

"Don't tell me that I've been beaten to the proverbial draw," Aaron remarked in that brutally smooth, caustic way of his. "Did the steak-house king already do the deed?"

"You are disgusting!"

"Yes, but very practical. If I don't hand my grandmother an heir, whether it's mine or the issue of that softheaded cowboy, I stand to lose millions of dollars."

Libby managed to stand up. A few steps, just a few, and she could hang up the telephone, shut out Aaron's voice and his ugly suggestions. "Do you really think that I would turn any child of mine over to someone like you?"

"There is a child, then," he retorted smoothly.

"No!" Five steps to the wall, six at most.

"Be reasonable, sweetness. We're discussing an empire here. If you don't come back and attend to your wifely duties, I'll have to visit that godforsaken ranch and try to persuade you."

"I am not your wife!" screamed Libby. One step. One step and a reach.

"Dear heart, I don't find the idea any more appealing than you do, but there isn't any other way, is there? My grandmother likes you—sees you as sturdy peasant stock—and she wants the baby to be yours."

At last. The wall was close and Libby slammed the receiver into place. Then, dazed, she stumbled back to her chair and fell into it, lowering her head to her arms. She cried hard, for herself, for Jonathan.

"Libby?"

It was the last voice she would have wanted to hear, except for Aaron's. "Go away, Stacey!" she hissed.

Instead of complying, Stacey laid a gentle hand on her shoulder. "What happened, Libby?" he asked softly. "Who was that on the phone?"

Fresh horror washed over Libby at the things Aaron had requested, mixed with anger and revulsion. God, how self-centered and insensitive that man was! And what gall he had, suggesting that she return to that disaster of a marriage, like some unquestioning brood mare, to produce a baby on order!

She gave a shuddering cry and motioned Stacey away with a frantic motion of her arm.

He only drew her up out of the chair and turned her so that he could hold her. She hadn't the strength to resist the intimacy and, in her half-hysterical state, he seemed to be the old Stacey, the strong big brother.

Stacey's hand came to the back of her head, tangling in her freshly washed hair, pressing her to his shoulder.

"Tell me what happened," he urged, just as he had when Libby was a child with a skinned knee or a bee sting.

From habit, she allowed herself to be comforted. For so long there had been no one to confide in except Stacey, and it seemed natural to lean on him now. "Aaron... Aaron called. He wanted me to have his...his baby!"

Before Stacey could respond to that, the door separating the kitchen from the living room swung open. Instinctively Libby drew back from the man who held her.

Jess towered in the doorway, pale, his gaze scorching Libby's flushed, tear-streaked face. "You know," he began in a voice that was no less terrible for being soft, "I almost believed you. I almost had myself convinced that you were above anything this shabby."

"Wait—you don't understand..."

Jess smiled a slow, vicious smile—a smile that took in his startled brother as well as Libby. "Don't I? Oh, princess, I wish I didn't." The searing jade gaze sliced menacingly to Stacey's face. "And it seems I'm going to be an uncle. Tell me, brother—what does that make Cathy?"

To Libby's horror, Stacey said nothing to refute what was obviously a gross misunderstanding. He simply pulled her back into his arms, and her struggle was virtually imperceptible because of his strength.

"Let me go!" she pleaded, frantic.

Stacey released her, but only grudgingly. "I've got a plane to catch," he said.

Libby was incredulous. "Tell him! Tell Jess that he's wrong," she cried, reaching out for Stacey's arm, trying to detain him.

But Stacey simply pulled free and left by the back door.

There was a long, pulsing silence, during which both Libby and Jess seemed to be frozen. He was the first to thaw.

"I know you were hurt, Libby," he said. "Badly hurt. But that didn't give you the right to do something like this to Cathy."

It infuriated Libby that this man's good opinion was so important to her, but it was, and there was no changing that. "Jess, I didn't do anything to Cathy. Please listen to me."

He folded his strong arms and rested against the door jamb with an ease that Libby knew was totally feigned. "I'm listening," he said, and the words had a flippant note.

Libby ignored fresh anger. "I am not expecting Stacey's baby, and this wasn't a romantic tryst. I don't even know why he came here. I was on the phone with Aaron and he—"

A muscle in Jess's neck corded, relaxed again. "I hope you're not going to tell me that your former husband made you pregnant, Libby. That seems unlikely."

Frustration pounded in Libby's temples and tightened the already constricted muscles in her throat. "I am not pregnant!" she choked out. "And if you are going to eavesdrop, Jess Barlowe, you could at least pay attention! Aaron wanted me to come back to New York and have his baby so that he would have an heir to present to his grandmother!"

"You didn't agree to that?"

"Of course I didn't agree! What kind of monster do you think I am?"

Jess shrugged with a nonchalance that was belied by

the leaping green fire in his eyes. "I don't know, princess, but rest assured—I intend to find out."

"I have a better idea!" Libby flared. "Why don't you just leave me the hell alone?"

"In theory that's brilliant," he fired back, "but there is one problem—I want you."

Involuntarily Libby remembered the kisses and caresses exchanged by the pond the day before, relived them. Hot color poured into her face. "Am I supposed to be honored?"

"No," Jess replied flatly, "you're supposed to be kept so busy that you won't have time to screw up Cathy's life any more than you already have."

If Libby could have moved, she would have rushed across that room and slapped Jess Barlowe senseless. Since she couldn't get her muscles to respond to the orders of her mind, she was forced to watch in stricken silence as he gave her a smoldering assessment with his eyes, executed a half salute and left the house.

Chapter 4

When the telephone rang again, immediately after Jess's exit from the kitchen, Libby was almost afraid to answer it. It would be like Aaron to persist, to use pressure to get what he wanted.

On the other hand, the call might be from someone else, and it could be important.

"Hello?" Libby dared, with resolve.

"Ms. Kincaid?" asked a cheerful feminine voice. "This is Marion Bradshaw, and I'm calling for Mrs. Barlowe. She'd like you to meet her at the main house if you can, and she says to dress for riding."

Libby looked down at her jeans and boots and smiled. In one way, at least, she and Cathy were still on the same wavelength. "Please tell her that I'll be there as soon as I can."

There was a brief pause at the other end of the line, followed by, "Mrs. Barlowe wants me to ask if you have a car down there. If not, she'll come and pick you up in a few minutes."

Though there was no car at her disposal, Libby declined the offer. The walk to the main ranch house would give her a chance to think, to prepare herself to face her cousin again.

As Libby started out, striding along the winding tree-lined road, she ached to think that she and Cathy had come to this. Fresh anger at Stacey quickened her step.

For a moment she was mad at Cathy, too. How could she believe such a thing, after all they'd been through together? How?

Firmly Libby brought her ire under control. *You don't get mad at a disabled person*, she scolded herself.

The sun was already high and hot in the domelike sky, and Libby smiled. It was warm for spring, and wasn't it nice to look up and see clouds and mountain-tops instead of tall buildings and smog?

Finally the main house came into view. It was a rambling structure of red brick, and its many windows glistened in the bright sunshine. A porch with marble steps led up to the double doors, and one of them swung open even as Libby reached out to ring the bell.

Mrs. Bradshaw, the housekeeper, stepped out and enfolded Libby in a delighted hug. A slender middle-aged woman with soft brown hair, Marion Bradshaw was as much a part of the Circle Bar B as Senator Barlowe himself. "Welcome home," she said warmly.

Libby smiled and returned the hug. "Thank you, Marion," she replied. "Is Cathy ready to go riding?"

"She's gone ahead to the stables—she'd like you to join her there."

Libby turned to go back down the steps but was stopped by the housekeeper. "Libby?"

She faced Marion, again, feeling wary.

"I don't believe it of you," said Mrs. Bradshaw firmly.

Libby was embarrassed, but there was no point in trying to pretend that she didn't get the woman's meaning. Probably everyone on the ranch was speculating about her supposed involvement with Stacey Barlowe. "Thank you."

"You stay right here on this ranch, Libby Kincaid," Marion Bradshaw rushed on, her own face flushed now. "Don't let Stacey or anybody else run you off."

That morning's unfortunate scene in Ken's kitchen was an indication of how difficult it would be to take the housekeeper's advice. Life on the Circle Bar B could become untenable if both Stacey and Jess didn't back off.

"I'll try," she said softly before stepping down off the porch and making her way around the side of that imposing but gracious house.

Prudently, the stables had been built a good distance away. During the walk, Libby wondered if she shouldn't leave the ranch after all. True, she needed to be there, but Jonathan's death had taught her that sometimes a person had to put her own desires aside for the good of other people.

But would leaving help, in the final analysis? Suppose Stacey did follow her, as he'd threatened to do? What would that do to Cathy?

The stables, like the house, were constructed of red brick. As Libby approached them, she saw Cathy leading two horses out into the sun—a dancing palomino gelding and the considerably less prepossessing pinto mare that had always been Libby's to ride.

Libby hesitated; it had been a long, long time since she'd ridden a horse, and the look in Cathy's eyes was cool. Distant. It was almost as though Libby were a troublesome stranger rather than her cousin and confidante.

As if to break the spell, Cathy lifted one foot to the stirrup of the Palomino's saddle and swung onto its back. Though she gave no sign of greeting, her eyes bade Libby to follow suit.

The elderly pinto was gracious while Libby struggled into the saddle and took the reins in slightly shaky hands. A moment later they were off across the open pastureland behind the stables, Cathy confident in the lead.

Libby jostled and jolted in the now unfamiliar saddle, and she felt a fleeting annoyance with Cathy for setting the brisk pace that she did. Again she berated herself for being angry with someone who couldn't hear.

Cathy rode faster and faster, stopping only when she reached the trees that trimmed the base of a wooded hill. There she turned in the saddle and flung a look back at the disgruntled Libby.

"You're out of practice," she said clearly, though her voice had the slurred meter of those who have not heard another person speak in years.

Libby, red-faced and damp with perspiration, was not surprised that Cathy had spoken aloud. She had learned to talk before the childhood illness that had made her deaf, and when she could be certain that no one else would overhear, she often spoke. It was a secret the two women kept religiously.

"Thanks a lot!" snapped Libby.

Deftly Cathy swung one trim blue-jeaned leg over the neck of her golden gelding and slid to the ground. The fancy bridle jingled musically as the animal bent its great head to graze on the spring grass. "We've got to talk, Libby."

Libby jumped from the pinto's back and the action engendered a piercing ache in the balls of her feet. "You've got that right!" she flared, forgetting for the moment her earlier resolve to respect Cathy's affliction. "Were you trying to get me killed?"

Watching Libby's lips, Cathy grinned. "Killed?" she echoed in her slow, toneless voice. "You're my cousin. That's important, isn't it? That we're cousins, I mean?"

Libby sighed. "Of course it's important."

"It implies a certain loyalty, don't you think?"

Libby braced herself. She'd known this confrontation was coming, of course, but that didn't mean she wanted it or was ready for it. "Yes," she said somewhat lamely.

"Are you having an affair with my husband?"

"No!"

"Do you want to?"

"What the hell kind of person do you think I am, Cathy?" shouted Libby, losing all restraint, flinging her arms out wide and startling the horses, who nickered and danced and tossed their heads.

"I'm trying to find that out," said Cathy in measured

and droning words. Not once since the conversation began had her eyes left Libby's mouth.

"You already know," retorted her cousin.

For the first time, Cathy looked ashamed. But there was uncertainty in her expression, too, along with a great deal of pain. "It's no secret that Stacey wants you, Libby. I've been holding my breath ever since you decided to come back, waiting for him to leave me."

"Whatever problems you and Stacey have, Cathy, I didn't start them."

"What about all his visits to New York?"

Libby's shoulders slumped, and she allowed herself to sink to the fragrant spring-scented ground, where she sat cross-legged, her head down. With her hands she said, "You knew about the divorce, and about Jonathan. Stacey was only trying to help me through—we weren't lovers."

The lush grass moved as Cathy sat down too, facing Libby. There were tears shining in her large green eyes, and her lower lip trembled. Nervously she plied a blade of grass between her fingers.

"I'm sorry about your little boy," she said aloud.

Libby reached out, calmer now, and squeezed Cathy's hands with her own. "Thanks."

A lonely, haunted look rose in Cathy's eyes. "Stacey wanted us to have a baby," she confided.

"Why didn't you?"

Sudden color stained Cathy's lovely cheeks. "I'm deaf!" she cried defensively.

Libby released her cousin's hands to sign, "So what? Lots of deaf people have babies."

"Not me!" Cathy signaled back with spirited despair. "I wouldn't know when it cried!"

Libby spoke slowly, her hands falling back to her lap. "Cathy, there are solutions for that sort of problem. There are trained dogs, electronic devices—"

"Trained dogs!" scoffed Cathy, but there was more anguish in her face than anger. "What kind of woman needs a dog to help her raise her own baby?"

"A deaf woman," Libby answered firmly. "Besides, if you don't want a dog around, you could hire a nurse."

"No!"

Libby was taken aback. "Why not?" she signed after a few moments.

Cathy clearly had no intention of answering. She bolted to her feet and was back in the palomino's saddle before Libby could even rise from the ground.

After that, they rode without communicating at all. Knowing that things were far from settled between herself and her cousin, Libby tried to concentrate on the scenery. A shadow moved across the sun, however, and a feeling of impending disaster unfolded inside her.

Jess glared at the screen of the small computer his father placed so much store in and resisted a caveman urge to strike its side with his fist.

"Here," purred a soft feminine voice, and Monica Summers, the senator's curvaceous assistant, reached down to move the mouse and tap the keyboard in a few strategic places.

Instantly the profit-and-loss statement Jess had been trying to call up was prominently displayed on the screen.

"How did you do that?"

Monica smiled her sultry smile and pulled up a chair to sit down beside Jess. "It's a simple matter of command," she said, and somehow the words sounded wildly suggestive.

Jess's collar seemed to tighten around his throat, but he grinned, appreciating Monica's lithe, inviting body, her profusion of gleaming brown hair, her impudent mouth and soft gray eyes. Her visits to the ranch were usually brief, but the senator's term of office was almost over, and he planned to write a long book—with which Monica was slated to help. Until that project was completed, she would be around a lot.

The fact that the senior senator did not intend to campaign for reelection didn't seem to faze her—it was common knowledge that she had a campaign of her own in mind.

Monica had made it clear, time and time again, that she was available to Jess for more than an occasional dinner date and subsequent sexual skirmish. And before Libby's return, Jess had seriously considered settling down with Monica.

He didn't love her, but she was undeniably beautiful, and the promises she made with her skillfully made-up eyes were not idle ones. In addition to that, they had a lot of ordinary things in common—similar political views, a love of the outdoors, like tastes in music and books.

Now, even with Monica sitting so close to him, her perfume calling up some rather heated memories, Jess Barlowe was patently unmoved.

A shower of anger sifted through him. He *wanted* to be moved, dammit—he wanted everything to be the way it was before Libby's return. Return? It was an invasion! He thought about the little hellion day and night, whether he wanted to or not.

"What's wrong, Jess?" Monica asked softly, perceptively, her hand resting on his shoulder. "It's more than just this computer, isn't it?"

He looked away. The sensible thing to do would be to take Monica by the hand, lead her off somewhere private and make slow, ferocious love to her. Maybe that would exorcise Libby Kincaid from his mind.

He remembered passion-weighted breasts, bared to him on a swimming dock, remembered their nipples blossoming sweetly in his mouth. Libby's breasts.

"Jess?"

He forced himself to look at Monica again. "I'm sorry," he said. "Did you say something?"

Mischief danced in her charcoal eyes. "Yes. I offered you my body."

He laughed.

Instead of laughing herself, Monica gave him a gentle, discerning look. "Mrs. Bradshaw tells me that Libby Kincaid is back," she said. "Could it be that I have some competition?"

Jess cleared his throat and diplomatically fixed his attention on the computer screen. "Show me how you made this monster cough up that profit-and-loss statement," he hedged.

"Jess." The voice was cool, insistent.

He made himself meet Monica's eyes again. "I don't

know what I feel for Libby," he confessed. "She makes me mad as hell, but…"

"But," said Monica with rueful amusement, "you want her very badly, don't you?"

There was no denying that, but neither could Jess bring himself to openly admit to the curious needs that had been plaguing him since the moment he'd seen Libby again at the small airport in Kalispell.

Monica's right index finger traced the outline of his jaw, tenderly. Sensuously. "We've never agreed to be faithful to each other, Jess," she said in the silky voice that had once enthralled him. "There aren't any strings tying you to me. But that doesn't mean that I'm going to step back and let Libby Kincaid have a clear field. I want you myself."

Jess was saved from answering by the sudden appearance of his father in the study doorway.

"Oh, Monica—there you are," Cleave Barlowe said warmly. "Ready to start working on that speech now? We have to have it ready before we fly back to Washington, remember."

Gray eyes swept Jess's face in parting. "More than ready," she replied, and then she was out of her chair and walking across the study to join her employer.

Jess gave the computer an unloving look and switched it off, taking perverse pleasure in the way the images on the screen dissolved. "State of the art," he mocked, and then stood up and strode out of the room.

The accountants would be angry, once they returned from their coffee break, but he didn't give a damn. If he didn't do something physical, he was going to go crazy.

* * *

Back at the stables, Libby surrendered her horse to a ranch hand with relief. Already the muscles in her thighs were aching dully from the ride; by morning they would be in savage little knots.

Cathy, who probably rode almost every day, looked breezy and refreshed, and from her manner no one would have suspected that she harbored any ill feelings toward Libby. "Let's take a swim," she signed, "and then we can have lunch."

Libby would have preferred to soak in the hot tub, but her pride wouldn't allow her to say so. Unless a limp betrayed her, she wasn't going to let Cathy know how sore a simple horseback ride had left her.

"I don't have a swimming suit," she said, somewhat hopefully.

"That's okay," Cathy replied with swift hands. "It's an indoor pool, remember?"

"I hope you're not suggesting that we swim naked," Libby argued aloud.

Cathy's eyes danced. "Why not?" she signed impishly. "No one would see us."

"Are you kidding?" Libby retorted, waving one arm toward the long, wide driveway. "Look at all these cars! There are *people* in that house!"

"Are you so modest?" queried Cathy, one eyebrow arched.

"Yes!" replied Libby, ignoring the subtle sarcasm.

"Then we'll go back to your house and swim in the pond, like we used to."

Libby recalled the blatant way she'd offered herself to Jess Barlowe in that place and winced inwardly. The peaceful solace of that pond had probably been altered forever, and it was going to be some time before she could go there comfortably again. "It's spring, Cathy, not summer. We'd catch pneumonia! Besides, I think it's going to rain."

Cathy shrugged. "All right, all right. I'll borrow a car and we'll drive over and get your swimming suit, then come back here."

"Fine," Libby agreed with a sigh.

She was to regret the decision almost immediately. When she and Cathy reached the house they had both grown up in, there was a florist's truck parked out front.

On the porch stood an affable young man, a long, narrow box in his hands. "Hi, Libby," he said.

Libby recognized Phil Reynolds, who had been her classmate in high school. *Go away, Phil*, she thought, even as she smiled and greeted him.

Cathy's attention was riveted on the silver box he carried, and there was a worried expression on her face.

Phil approached, beaming. "I didn't even know you were back until we got this order this morning. Aren't you coming into town at all? We got a new high school…"

Simmonsville, a dried-up little community just beyond the south border of the Circle Bar B, hadn't even entered Libby's thoughts until she'd seen Phil Reynolds. She ignored his question and stared at the box he held out to her as if it might contain something squirmy and vile.

"Wh-who sent these?" she managed, all too conscious of the suspicious way Cathy was looking at her.

"See for yourself," Phil said brightly, and then he got back into his truck and left.

Libby took the card from beneath the red ribbon that bound the box and opened it with trembling fingers. The flowers couldn't be from Stacey, please God, they couldn't!

The card was typewritten. *Don't be stubborn, sweetness*, the message read. *Regards, Aaron.*

For a moment Libby was too relieved to be angry. "Aaron," she repeated. Then she lifted the lid from the box and saw the dozen pink rosebuds inside.

For one crazy moment she was back in Jonathan's hospital room. There had been roses there, too—along with mums and violets and carnations. Aaron and his family had sent costly bouquets and elaborate toys, but not one of them had come to visit.

Libby heard the echo of Jonathan's purposefully cheerful voice. *Daddy must be busy*, he'd said.

With a cry of fury and pain, Libby flung the roses away, and they scattered over the walk in a profusion of long-stemmed delicacy. The silver box lay with them, catching the waning sunlight.

Cathy knelt and began gathering up the discarded flowers, placing them gently back in their carton. Once or twice she glanced up at Libby's livid face in bewilderment, but she asked no questions and made no comments.

Libby turned away and bounded into the house. By the time she had found a swimming suit and come back downstairs again, Cathy was arranging the rosebuds in a cut-glass vase at the kitchen sink.

She met Libby's angry gaze and held up one hand to

stay the inevitable outburst. "They're beautiful, Libby," she said in a barely audible voice. "You can't throw away something that's beautiful."

"Watch me!" snapped Libby.

Cathy stepped between her cousin and the lush bouquet. "Libby, at least let me give them to Mrs. Bradshaw," she pleaded aloud. "Please?"

Glumly Libby nodded. She supposed she should be grateful that the roses hadn't been sent by Stacey in a fit of ardor, and they *were* too lovely to waste, even if she herself couldn't bear the sight of them.

Libby remembered the words on Aaron's card as she and Cathy drove back to the main house. *Don't be stubborn.* A tremor of dread flitted up and down her spine.

Aaron hadn't been serious when he'd threatened to come to the ranch and "persuade" her to return to New York with him, had he? She shivered.

Surely even Aaron wouldn't have the gall to do that, she tried to reassure herself. After all, he had never come to the apartment she'd taken after Jonathan's death, never so much as called. Even when the divorce had been granted, he had avoided her by sending his lawyer to court alone.

No. Aaron wouldn't actually come to the Circle Bar B. He might call, he might even send more flowers, just to antagonize her, but he wouldn't come in person. Despite his dismissal of Stacey as a "soft-headed cowboy," he was afraid of him.

Cathy was drawing the car to a stop in front of the main house by the time Libby was able to recover herself. To allay the concern in her cousin's eyes, she carried the vase of pink roses into the kitchen and presented them to Mrs. Bradshaw, who was puzzled but clearly pleased.

Inside the gigantic, elegantly tiled room that housed the swimming pool and the spacious hot tub, Libby eyed the latter with longing. Thus, it was a moment before she realized that the pool was already occupied.

Jess was doing a furious racing crawl from one side of the deep end to the other, his tanned, muscular arms cutting through the blue water with a force that said he was trying to work out some fierce inner conflict. Watching him admiringly from the poolside, her slender legs dangling into the water, was a pretty dark-haired woman with beautiful gray eyes.

The woman greeted Cathy with an easy gesture of her hands, though her eyes were fixed on Libby, seeming to assess her in a thorough, if offhand, fashion.

"I'm Monica Summers," she said, as Jess, apparently oblivious of everything other than the furious course he was following through the water, executed an impressive somersault turn at the poolside and raced back the other way.

Monica Summers. The name was familiar to Libby, and so, vaguely, was the perfect fashion-model face.

Of course. Monica was Senator Barlowe's chief assistant. Libby had never actually met the woman, but she had seen her on television newscasts and Ken had mentioned her in passing, on occasion, over long-distance telephone.

"Hello," Libby said. "I'm—"

The gray eyes sparkled. "I know," Monica broke in smoothly. "You're Libby Kincaid. I enjoy your cartoons very much."

Libby felt about as sophisticated, compared to this woman, as a Girl Scout selling cookies door-to-door. And Monica's subtle emphasis on the word "cartoons" had made her feel defensive.

All the same, Libby thanked her and forced herself not to watch Jess's magnificent body moving through the bright blue water of the pool. It didn't bother her that Jess and Monica had been alone in this strangely sensual setting. It didn't.

Cathy had moved away, anxious for her swim.

"I'm sorry if we interrupted something," Libby said, and hated herself instantly for betraying her interest.

Monica smiled. Clearly she had not been in swimming herself, for her expensive black swimsuit was dry, and so was her long, lush hair. Her makeup, of course, was perfect. "There are always interruptions," she said, and then she turned away to take up her adoring-spectator position again, her gaze following the play of the powerful muscles in Jess's naked back.

My thighs are too fat, mourned Libby, in petulant despair. She took a seat on a lounge far removed from Jess and his lovely friend and tried to pretend an interest in Cathy's graceful backstroke.

Was Jess intimate with Monica Summers? It certainly seemed so, and Libby couldn't understand, for the life of her, why she was so brutally surprised by the knowledge. After all, Jess was a handsome, healthy man, well beyond the age of handholding and fantasies-from-afar. Had she really ever believed that he had just been existing on this ranch in some sort of suspended animation?

Cathy roused her from her dismal reflection by flinging a stream of water at her with both hands. Instantly Libby was drenched and stung to an annoyance out of all proportion to the offense. Surprising even herself, she stomped over to the hot tub, flipped the switch that would make the water bubble and churn, and after hurling one scorching look at her unrepenting cousin, slid into the enormous tile-lined tub.

The heat and motion of the water were welcome balm to Libby's muscles, if not to her spirit. She had no right to care who Jess Barlowe slept with, no right at all. It wasn't as though she had ever had any claim on his affections.

Settling herself on a submerged bench, Libby tilted her head back, closed her eyes, and tried to pretend that she was alone in that massive room with its sloping glass roof, lush plants and lounges.

The fact that she was sexually attracted to Jess Barlowe was undeniable, but it was just a physical phenomenon, certainly. It would pass.

All she had to do to accelerate the process was allow herself to remember how very demeaning Aaron's lovemaking had been. And remember she did.

After Libby had caught her husband with the first of his lovers, she had moved out of his bedroom permanently, remaining in his house only because Jonathan, still at home then, had needed her so much.

Before her brutal awakening, however, she had tried hard to make the rapidly failing marriage work. Even then, bedtime had been a horror.

Libby's skin prickled as she recalled the way Aaron would ignore her for long weeks and then pounce on her with a vicious and alarming sort of determination, tearing her clothes, sometimes bruising her.

In retrospect, Libby realized that Aaron must have been trying to prove something to himself concerning his identity as a man, but at the time she had known only that sex, much touted in books and movies, was something to be feared.

Not once had Libby achieved any sort of satisfaction with Aaron—she had only endured. Now, painfully conscious of the blatantly masculine, near-naked cowboy swimming in the pool nearby, Libby wondered if lovemaking would be different with Jess.

The way that her body had blossomed beneath his seemed adequate proof that it would be different indeed, but there was always the possibility that she would be disappointed in the ultimate act. Probably she had been aroused only because Jess had taken the time to offer her at least a taste of pleasure. Aaron had never done that, never shown any sensitivity at all.

Shutting out all sight and sound, Libby mentally decried her lack of experience. If only she'd been with even one man besides Aaron, she would have had some frame of reference, some inkling of whether or not the soaring releases she'd read about really existed.

The knowledge that so many people thought she had been carrying on a torrid affair with Stacey brought a wry smile to her lips. If only they knew.

"What are you smiling about?"

The voice jolted Libby back to the here and now with a thump. Jess had joined her in the hot tub at some point; indeed, he was standing only inches away.

Startled, Libby stared at him for a moment, then

looked wildly around for Cathy and the elegant Ms. Summers.

"They went in to have lunch," Jess informed her, his eyes twinkling. Beads of water sparkled in the dark down that matted his muscular chest, and his hair had been towel-rubbed into an appealing disarray.

"I'll join them," said Libby in a frantic whisper, but the simple mechanics of turning away and climbing out of the hot tub eluded her.

Smelling pleasantly of chlorine, Jess came nearer. "Don't go," he said softly. "Lunch will wait."

Anger at Cathy surged through Libby. Why had she gone off and left her here?

Jess seemed to read the question in her face, and it made him laugh. The sound was soft—sensuously, wholly male. Overhead, spring thunder crashed in a gray sky.

Libby trembled, pressing back against the edge of the hot tub with such force that her shoulder blades ached. "Stay away from me," she breathed.

"Not on your life," he answered, and then he was so near that she could feel the hard length of his thighs against her own. The soft dark hair on his chest tickled her bare shoulders and the suddenly alive flesh above her swimsuit top. "I intend to finish what we started yesterday beside the pond."

Libby gasped as his moist lips came down to taste hers, to tame and finally part them for a tender invasion. Her hands went up, of their own accord, to rest on his hips.

He was naked. The discovery rocked Libby, made her try to twist away from him, but his kiss deepened and subdued her struggles. With his hands, he lifted her legs, draped them around the rock-hard hips she had just explored.

The imposing, heated length of his desire, now pressed intimately against her, was powerful proof that he meant to take her.

Chapter 5

Libby felt as though her body had dissolved, become part of the warm, bubbling water filling the hot tub. When Jess drew back from his soft conquering of her mouth, his hands rose gently to draw down the modest top of her swimsuit, revealing the pulsing fullness of her breasts to his gaze.

It was not in Libby to protest: she was transfixed, caught up in primal responses that had no relation to good sense or even sanity. She let her head fall back, saw through the transparent ceiling that gray clouds had darkened the sky, promising a storm that wouldn't begin to rival the one brewing inside Libby herself.

Jess bent his head, nipped at one exposed, aching nipple with cautious teeth.

Libby drew in a sharp breath as a shaft of searing

pleasure went through her, so powerful that she was nearly convulsed by it. A soft moan escaped her, and she tilted her head even further back, so that her breasts were still more vulnerable to the plundering of his mouth.

Inside Libby's swirling mind, a steady voice chanted a litany of logic: she was behaving in a wanton way—Jess didn't really care for her, he was only trying to prove that he could conquer her whenever he desired—this place was not private, and there was a very real danger that someone would walk in at any moment and see what was happening.

Thunder reverberated in the sky, shaking heaven and earth. And none of the arguments Libby's reason was offering had any effect on her rising need to join herself with this impossible, overbearing man feasting so brazenly on her breast.

With an unerring hand, Jess found the crux of her passion, and through the fabric of her swimsuit he stroked it to a wanting Libby had never experienced before. Then, still greedy at the nipple he was attending, he deftly worked aside the bit of cloth separating Libby's womanhood from total exposure.

She gasped as he caught the hidden nubbin between his fingers and began, rhythmically, to soothe it. Or was he tormenting it? Libby didn't know, didn't care.

Jess left her breast to nibble at her earlobe, chuckled hoarsely when the tender invasion of his fingers elicited a throaty cry of welcome.

"Go with it, Libby," he whispered. "Let it carry you high…higher…"

Libby was already soaring, sightless, mindless, conscious only of the fiery marauding of his fingers and the strange force inside her that was building toward something she had only imagined before. "Oh," she gasped as he worked this new and fierce magic. "Oh, Jess…"

Mercilessly he intensified her pleasure by whispering outrageously erotic promises, by pressing her legs wide of each other with one knee, by caressing her breast with his other hand.

A savage trembling began deep within Libby, causing her breath to quicken to a soft, lusty whine.

"Meet it, Libby," Jess urged. "Rise to meet it."

Suddenly Libby's entire being buckled in some ancient, inescapable response. The thunder in the distant skies covered her final cry of release, and she convulsed again and again, helpless in the throes of her body's savage victory.

When at last the ferocious clenching and unclenching had ceased, Libby's reason gradually returned. Forcing wide eyes to Jess's face, she saw no demand there, no mockery or revulsion. Instead, he was grinning at her, as pleased as if he'd been sated himself.

Wild embarrassment surged through Libby in the wake of her passion. She tried to avert her face, but Jess caught her chin in his hand and made her look at him.

"Don't," he said gruffly. "Don't look that way. It wasn't wrong, Libby."

His ability to read her thoughts so easily was as unsettling as the knowledge that she'd just allowed this man unconscionable liberties in a hot tub. "I suppose you think… I suppose you want…"

Jess withdrew his conquering hand, tugged her swimsuit back into place. "I think you're beautiful," he supplied, "and I want you—that's true. But for now, watching you respond like that was enough."

Libby blushed again. She was still confused by the power of her release, and she had expected Jess to demand his own satisfaction. She was stunned that he could give such fierce fulfillment and ask nothing for himself.

"You've never been with any man besides your husband, have you, Libby?"

The outrageous bluntness of that question solidified Libby's jellylike muscles, and she reached furiously for one of the towels Mrs. Bradshaw had set nearby on a low shelf. "I've been with a thousand men!" she snapped in a harsh whisper. "Why, one word from any man, and I let him… I let him…"

Jess grinned again. "You've never had a climax before," he observed.

How could he guess a thing like that? It was uncanny. Libby knew that the hot color in her face belied her sharp answer. "Of course I have! I've been married—did you think I was celibate?"

The rapid-fire hysteria of her words only served to amuse Jess, it seemed. "We both know, Libby Kincaid, that you are, for all practical intents and purposes, a virgin. You may have lain beneath that ex-husband of yours and wished to God that he would leave you alone, but until a few minutes ago you had never even guessed what it means to be a woman."

Libby wouldn't have thought it possible to be as murderously angry as she was at that moment. "Why, you arrogant, *insufferable*…"

He caught her hand at the wrist before it could make

the intended contact with his face. "You haven't seen anything yet, princess," he vowed with gentle force. "When I take you to bed—and I assure you that I will— I'll prove that everything I've said is true."

While Libby herself was outraged, her traitorous body yearned to lie in his bed, bend to his will. Having reached the edges of passion, it wanted to go beyond, into the molten core. "You egotistical bastard!" Libby hissed, breaking away from him to lift herself out of the hot tub and land on its edge with an inelegant, squishy plop, "You act as if you'd invented sex!"

"As far as you're concerned, little virgin, I did. But have no fear—I intend to deflower you at the first opportunity."

Libby stood up, wrapped her shaky, nerveless form in a towel the size of a bedsheet. "Go to hell!"

Jess rose out of the water, not the least bit self-conscious of his nakedness. The magnitude of his desire for her was all too obvious.

"The next few hours will be just that," he said, reaching for a towel of his own. Naturally, the one he selected barely covered him.

Speechless, Libby imagined the thrust of his manhood, imagined her back arching to receive him, imagined a savage renewal of the passion she had felt only minutes before.

Jess gave her an amused sidelong glance, as though he knew what she was thinking, and intoned, "Don't worry, princess. I'll court you if that's what you want. But I'll have you, too. And thoroughly."

Having made this incredible vow, he calmly walked

out of the room, leaving Libby alone with a clamoring flock of strange emotions and unmet needs.

The moment Jess was gone, she stumbled to the nearest lounge chair and sank onto it, her knees too weak to support her. *Well, Kincaid,* she reflected wryly, *now you know. Satisfied?*

Libby winced at the last word. Though she might have wished otherwise, given the identity of the man involved, she was just that.

With carefully maintained dignity, Jess Barlowe strode into the shower room adjoining the pool and wrenched on one spigot. As he stepped under the biting, sleetlike spray, he gritted his teeth.

Gradually his body stopped screaming and the stubborn evidence of his passion faded. With relief, Jess dived out of the shower stall and grabbed a fresh towel.

A hoarse chuckle escaped him as he dried himself with brisk motions. Good God, if he didn't have Libby Kincaid soon, he was going to die of pneumonia. A man could stand only so many plunges into icy ponds, only so many cold showers.

A spare set of clothes—jeans and a white pullover shirt—awaited Jess in a cupboard. He donned them quickly, casting one disdainful look at the three-piece suit he had shed earlier. His circulation restored, to some degree at least, he toweled his hair and then combed it with the splayed fingers of his left hand.

A sweet anguish swept through him as he remembered the magic he had glimpsed in Libby's beautiful face during that moment of full surrender. *My father was right*, Jess thought as he pulled on socks and old, comfortable boots. *I love you, Libby Kincaid. I love you.*

Jess was not surprised to find that Libby wasn't with Cathy and Monica in the kitchen—she had probably made some excuse to get out of joining them for lunch and gone off to gather her thoughts. God knew, she had to be every bit as undone and confused as he was.

Mostly to avoid the sad speculation in Monica's eyes, Jess glanced toward the kitchen windows. They were already sheeted with rain.

A crash of thunder jolted him out of the strange inertia that had possessed him. He glanced at Cathy, saw an impish light dancing in her eyes.

"You can catch her if you hurry," she signed, cocking her head to one side and grinning at him.

Did she know what had happened in the hot tub? Some of the heat lingering in Jess's loins rose to his face as he bolted out of the room and through the rest of the house.

His truck, an eyesore among the other cars parked in front of the house, patently refused to start. Annoyed, Jess "borrowed" Monica's sleek green Porsche without a moment's hesitation, and his aggravation grew as he left the driveway and pulled out onto the main road.

What the hell did Libby think she was doing, walking in this rain? And why had Cathy let her go?

He found Libby near the mailboxes, slogging despondently along, soaked to the skin.

"Get in!" he barked, furious in his concern.

Libby lifted her chin and kept walking. Her turquoise shirt was plastered to her chest, revealing the outlines of her bra, and her hair hung in dripping tendrils.

"Now!" Jess roared through the window he had rolled down halfway.

She stopped, faced him with indigo fury sparking in her eyes. "Why?" she yelled over the combined roars of the deluge and Monica's car engine. "Is it time to teach me what it means to be a woman?"

"How the hell would I know what it means to be a woman?" he shouted back. "Get in this car!"

Libby told him to do something that was anatomically impossible and then went splashing off down the road again, ignoring the driving rain.

Rasping a swearword, Jess slipped the Porsche out of gear and wrenched the emergency brake into place. Then he shoved open the door and bounded through the downpour to catch up with Libby, grasp her by the shoulders and whirl her around to face him.

"If you don't get your backside into that car *right now*," he bellowed, "I swear to God I'll *throw* you in!"

She assessed the Porsche. "Monica's car?"

Furious, Jess nodded. Christ, it was raining so hard that his clothes were already saturated and she was standing there talking details!

An evil smile curved Libby's lips and she stalked toward the automobile, purposely stepping in every mud puddle along the way. Jess could have sworn that she enjoyed sinking, sopping wet, onto the heretofore spotless suede seat.

"Home, James," she said smugly, folding her arms and grinding her mud-caked boots into the lush carpeting on the floorboard.

Jess had no intention of taking Libby to Ken's place, but he said nothing. Envisioning her lying in some hospital bed, wasted away by a case of rain-induced pneumonia, he ground the car savagely back into gear and gunned the engine.

When they didn't take the road Libby expected, the smug look faded from her face and she stared at Jess with wide, wary eyes. "Wait a minute…"

Jess flung an impudent grin at her and saluted with one hand. "Yes?" he drawled, deliberately baiting her.

"Where are we going?"

"My place," he answered, still angry. "It's the classic situation, isn't it? I'll insist you get out of those wet clothes, then I'll toss you one of my bathrobes and pour brandy for us both. After that, lady, I'll make mad love to you."

Libby paled, though there was a defiant light in her eyes. "On a fur rug in front of your fireplace, no doubt!"

"No doubt," Jess snapped, wondering why he found it impossible to deal with this woman in a sane and reasonable way. It would be so much simpler just to tell her straight out that he loved her, that he needed her. But he couldn't quite bring himself to do that, not just yet, and he was still mad as hell that she would walk in the pouring rain like that.

"Suppose I tell you that I don't want you to 'make mad love' to me, as you so crudely put it? Suppose I tell you that I won't give in to you until the first Tuesday after doomsday, if then, brandy and fur rugs notwithstanding?"

"The way you didn't give in in the hot tub?" he gibed, scowling.

Libby blushed. "That was different!"

"How so?"

"You...you *cornered* me, that's how."

His next words were out of his mouth before he could call them back. "I know about your ex-husband, Libby."

She winced, fixed her attention on the overworked windshield wipers. "What does he have to do with anything?"

Jess shifted to a lower gear as he reached the road leading to his house and turned onto it. "Stacey told me about the women."

The high color drained from Libby's face and she would not look at him. She appeared ready, in fact, to thrust open the door on her side of the car and leap out. "I don't want to talk about this," she said after an interval long enough to bring them to Jess's driveway.

"Why not, Libby?" he asked, and his voice was gentle, if a bit gruff.

One tear rolled over the wet sheen on her defiant rain-polished face, and Libby's chin jutted out in a way that was familiar to him, at once maddening and appealing. "Why do you want to talk about Aaron?" she countered in low, ragged tones. "So you can sit there and feel superior?"

"You know better."

She glared at him, her bruised heart in her eyes, and Jess ached for her. She'd been through so much, and he wished that he could have taken that visible, pounding pain from inside her and borne it himself.

"I don't know better, Jess," she said quietly. "We haven't exactly been kindred spirits, you and I. For all I know, you just want to torture me. To throw all my mistakes in my face and watch me squirm."

Jess's hands tightened on the steering wheel. It took

great effort to reach down and shut off the Porsche's engine. "It's cold out here," he said evenly, "and we're both wet to the skin. Let's go inside."

"You won't take me home?" Her voice was small.

He sighed. "Do you want me to?"

Libby considered, lowered her head. "No," she said after a long time.

The inside of Jess's house was spacious and uncluttered. There were skylights in the ceiling and the second floor appeared to be a loft of some sort. Lifting her eyes to the railing above, Libby imagined that his bed was just beyond it and blushed.

Jess seemed to be ignoring her; he was busy with newspaper and kindling at the hearth. She watched the play of the muscles in his back in weary fascination, longing to feel them beneath her hands.

The knowledge that she loved Jess Barlowe, budding in her subconscious mind since her arrival in Montana, suddenly burst into full flower. But was the feeling really new?

If Libby were to be honest with herself—and she tried to be, always—she had to admit that the chances were good that she had loved Jess for a very long time.

He turned, rose from his crouching position, a small fire blazing and crackling behind him. "How do you like my house?" he asked with a half smile.

Between her newly recognized feelings for this man and the way his jade eyes seemed to see through all her reserve to the hurt and confusion hidden beneath, Libby felt very vulnerable. Trusting in an old trick that had always worked in the past, she looked around in search of something to be angry about.

The skylights, the loft, the view of the mountains from the windows beyond his desk—all of it was appealing. Masculine. Quietly romantic.

"Perfect quarters for a wealthy and irresponsible playboy," she threw out in desperation.

Jess stiffened momentarily, but then an easy grin creased his face. "I think that was a shot, but I'm not going to fire back, Libby, so you might as well relax."

Relax? Was the man insane? Half an hour before, he had blithely brought her to climax in a hot tub, for God's sake, and now they were alone, the condition of their clothes necessitating that they risk further intimacies by stripping them off, taking showers. If they couldn't fight, what *were* they going to do?

Before Libby could think of anything to say in reply, Jess gestured toward the broad redwood stairs leading up to the loft. "The bathroom is up there," he said. "Take a shower. You'll find a robe hanging on the inside of the door." With that, he turned away to crouch before the fire again and add wood.

Because she was cold and there seemed to be no other options, Libby climbed the stairs. It wasn't until she reached the loft that her teeth began to chatter.

There she saw Jess's wide unmade bed. It was banked by a line of floor-to-ceiling windows, giving the impression that the room was open to the outdoors, and the wrinkled sheets probably still bore that subtle, clean scent that was Jess's alone...

Libby took herself in hand, wrenched her attention away from the bed. There was a glass-fronted wood-burning stove in one corner of the large room, and a long bookshelf on the other side was crammed with everything from paperback mysteries to volumes on veterinary medicine.

Libby made her way into the adjoining bathroom and kicked off her muddy boots, peeled away her jeans and shirt, her sodden underwear and socks. Goosebumps leapt out all over her body, and they weren't entirely related to the chill.

The bathtub was enormous, and like the bed, it was framed by tall uncurtained windows. Bathing here would be like bathing in the high limbs of a tree, so sweeping was the view of mountains and grassland beyond the glass.

Trembling a little, Libby knelt to turn on the polished brass spigots and fill the deep tub. The water felt good against her chilled flesh, and she was submerged to her chin before she remembered that she had meant to take a quick shower, not a lingering, dreamy bath.

Libby couldn't help drawing a psychological parallel between this tub and the larger one at the main house, where she had made such a fool of herself. Was there some mysterious significance in the fact that she'd chosen the bathtub over the double-wide shower stall on the other side of the room?

Now you're really getting crazy, Kincaid, she said to herself, settling back to soak.

Somewhere in the house, a telephone rang, was swiftly answered.

Libby relaxed in the big tub and tried to still her roiling thoughts and emotions. She would not consider what might happen later. For now, she wanted to be comforted, pampered. Deliciously warm.

She heard the click of boot heels on the stairs, though, and sat bolt upright in the water. A sense of sweet alarm raced through her system. Jess wouldn't come in, actually *come in,* would he?

Of course he would! Why would a bathroom door stop a man who would make such brazen advances in a hot tub?

With frantic eyes Libby sought the towel shelf. It was entirely too far away, and so was the heavy blue-and-white velour robe hanging on the inside of the door. She sank into the bathwater until it tickled her lower lip, squeezed her eyes shut and waited.

"Lib?"

"Wh-what?" she managed. He was just beyond that heavy wooden panel, and Libby found herself hoping...

Hoping what? That Jess would walk in, or that he would stay out? She honestly didn't know.

"That was Ken on the phone," Jess answered, making no effort to open the door. "I told him you were here and that I'd bring you home after the rain lets up."

Libby reddened, there in the privacy of that unique bathroom, imagining the thoughts that were probably going through her father's mind. "Wh-what did he say?"

Jess chuckled, and the sound was low, rich. "Let me put it this way—I don't think he's going to rush over here and defend your virtue."

Libby was at once pleased and disappointed. Wasn't a father *supposed* to protect his daughter from persuasive lechers like Jess Barlowe?

"Oh," she said, her voice sounding foolish and uncertain. "D-do you want me to hurry? S-so you can take a shower, I mean?"

"Take your time," he said offhandedly. "There's another bathroom downstairs—I can shower there."

Having imparted this conversely comforting and disenchanting information, Jess began opening and closing drawers. Seconds later, Libby again heard his footsteps on the stairs.

Despite the fact that she would have preferred to lounge in that wonderful bathtub for the rest of the day, Libby shot out of the water and raced to the towel bar. This was her chance to get dried off and dressed in something before Jess could incite her to further scandalous behavior.

She was wrapped in his blue-and-white bathrobe, the belt securely tied, and cuddled under a knitted afghan by the time Jess joined her in the living room, looking reprehensibly handsome in fresh jeans and a green turtleneck sweater. His hair, like her own, was still damp, and there was a smile in his eyes, probably inspired by the way she was trying to burrow deeper into her corner of the couch.

"There isn't any brandy after all," he said with a helpless gesture of his hands. "Will you settle for chicken soup?"

Libby would have agreed to anything that would get Jess out of that room, even for a few minutes, and he would have to go to the kitchen for soup, wouldn't he? Unable to speak, she nodded.

She tried to concentrate on the leaping flames in the fireplace, but she could hear the soft thump of cupboard doors, the running of tapwater, the singular whir of a microwave oven. The sharp *ting* of the appliance's timer bell made her flinch.

Too soon, Jess returned, carrying two mugs full of steaming soup. He extended one to Libby and, to her eternal gratitude, settled in a chair nearby instead of on the couch beside her.

Outside, the rain came down in torrents, making a musical, pelting sound on the skylights, sliding down the windows in sheets. The fire snapped and threw out sparks, as if to mock the storm that could not reach it.

Jess took a sip of the hot soup and grinned. "This doesn't exactly fit the scenario I outlined in the car," he said, lifting his cup.

"You got everything else right," Libby quipped, referring to the bath she'd taken and the fact that she was wearing his robe. Instantly she realized how badly she'd slipped, but it was too late to call back her words, and the ironic arch of Jess's brow and the smile on his lips indicated that he wasn't going to let the comment pass.

"Everything?" he teased. "There isn't any fur rug, either."

Libby's cheekbones burned. Unable to say anything, she lowered her eyes and watched the tiny noodles colliding in her mug of soup.

"I'm sorry," Jess said softly.

She swallowed hard and met his eyes. He did look contrite, and there was nothing threatening in his manner. Because of that, Libby dared to ask, "Do you really mean to…to make love to me?"

"Only if you want me to," he replied. "You must know that I wouldn't force you, Libby."

She sensed that he meant this and relaxed a little.

Sooner or later, she was going to have to accept the fact that all men didn't behave in the callous and hurtful way that Aaron had. "You believe me now—don't you? About Stacey, I mean?"

If that off-the-wall question had surprised or nettled Jess, he gave no indication of it. He simply nodded.

Some crazy bravery, carrying her forward like a reckless tide, made Libby put aside her carefully built reserve and blurt out, "Do you think I'm a fool, Jess?"

Jess gaped at her, the mug of soup forgotten in his hands. "A fool?"

Libby lowered her eyes. "I mean...well...because of Aaron."

"Why should I think anything like that?"

Thunder exploded in the world outside the small cocoonlike one that held only Libby and Jess. "He was...he..."

"He was with other women," supplied Jess quietly. Gently.

Libby nodded, managed to look up.

"And you stayed with him." He was setting down the mug, drawing nearer. Finally he crouched before her on his haunches and took the cup from her hands to set it aside. "You couldn't leave Jonathan, Libby. I understand that. Besides, why should the fact that you stuck with the marriage have any bearing on my attitude toward you?"

"I just thought..."

"What?" prodded Jess when her sentence fell away. "What did you think, Libby?"

Tears clogged her throat. "I thought that I couldn't

be very desirable if my o-own husband couldn't...
wouldn't..."

Jess gave a ragged sigh. "My God, Libby, you don't
think that Aaron was unfaithful because of some lack
in you?"

That was exactly what she'd thought, on a subliminal
level at least. Another woman, a stronger, more experienced, more alluring woman, might have been able to
keep her husband happy, make him want her.

Jess's hands came to Libby's shoulders, gentle and
insistent. "Lib, talk to me."

"Just how terrific could I be?" she erupted suddenly,
in the anguish that would be hidden no longer. "Just how
desirable? My husband needed other women because he
couldn't bring himself to make love to me!"

Jess drew her close, held her as the sobs she had
restrained at last broke free. "That wasn't your fault,
Libby," he breathed, his hand in her hair now, soothing and strong. "Oh, sweetheart, it wasn't your fault."

"Of course it was!" she wailed into the soft green knit
of his sweater, the hard strength of the shoulder beneath.
"If I'd been better...if I'd known how..."

"Shhh. Baby, don't. Don't do this to yourself."

Once freed, Libby's emotions seemed impossible to
check. They ran as deep and wild as any river, swirling in senseless currents and eddies, causing her pride
to founder.

Jess caught her trembling hands in his, squeezed
them reassuringly. "Listen to me, princess," he said.
"These doubts that you're having about yourself are
understandable, under the circumstances, but they're

not valid. You are desirable." He paused, searched her face with tender, reproving eyes. "I can swear to that."

Libby still felt broken, and she hadn't forgotten the terrible things Aaron had said to her during their marriage—that she was cold and unresponsive, that he hadn't been impotent before he'd married her. Time and time again he had held up Jonathan as proof that he had been virile with his first wife, taken cruel pleasure in pointing out that none of his many girlfriends found him wanting.

Wrenching herself back to the less traumatic present, Libby blurted out, "Make love to me, Jess. Let me prove to myself—"

"No," he said with cold, flat finality. And then he released her hands, stood up and turned away as if in disgust.

Chapter 6

"I thought you wanted me," Libby said in a small, broken voice.

Jess's broad back stiffened, and he did not turn around to face her. "I do."

"Then, why…?"

He went to the fireplace, took up a poker, stoked the blazing logs within to burn faster, hotter. "When I make love to you, Libby, it won't be because either one of us wants to prove anything."

Libby lowered her head, ashamed. As if to scold her, the wind and rain lashed at the windows and the lightning flashed, filling the room with its eerie blue-gold light. She began to cry again, this time softly, wretchedly.

And Jess came to her, lifted her easily into his arms. Without a word, he carried her up the stairs, across the storm-shadowed loft room to the bed. After pulling back the covers with one hand, he lowered her to the sheets. "Rest," he said, tucking the blankets around her.

Libby gaped at him, amazed and stricken. She couldn't help thinking that he wouldn't have tucked Monica Summers into bed this way, kissed *her* forehead as though she were some overwrought child needing a nap.

"I don't want to rest," Libby said, insulted. And her hands moved to pull the covers down.

Jess stopped her by clasping her wrists. A muscle knotted in his jaw, and his jade-green eyes flashed, their light as elemental as that of the electrical storm outside. "Don't Libby. Don't tempt me."

She *had* been tempting him—if he hadn't stopped her when he did, she would have opened the robe, wantonly displayed her breasts. Now, she was mortally embarrassed. What on earth was making her act this way?

"I'm sorry," she whispered. "I don't know what's the matter with me."

Jess sat down on the edge of the bed, his magnificent face etched in shadows, his expression unreadable. "Do we have to go into that again, princess? Nothing is wrong with you."

"But—"

Jess laid one index finger to her lips to silence her. "It would be wrong if we made love now, Libby—don't you see that? Afterward, you'd be telling yourself what a creep I was for taking advantage of you when you were so vulnerable."

His logic was unassailable. To lighten the mood, Libby summoned up a shaky grin. "Some playboy you are. Chicken soup. Patience. Have you no passion?"

He laughed. "More than I know what to do with," he said, standing up, walking away from the bed. At the top of the stairs he paused. "Am I crazy?"

Libby didn't answer. Smiling, she snuggled down under the covers—she was just a bit tired—and placidly watched the natural light show beyond the windows. Maybe later there would be fireworks of another sort.

Downstairs, Jess resisted a fundamental urge to beat his head against the wall. Libby Kincaid was up there in his bed, for God's sake, warm and lush and wanting him.

He ached to go back up the stairs and finish what they'd begun that morning in the hot tub. He couldn't, of course, because Libby was in no condition, emotionally, for that kind of heavy scene. If he did the wrong thing, said the wrong thing, she could break, and the pieces might not fit together again.

In a fit of neatness, Jess gathered up the cups of cold chicken soup and carried them into the kitchen. There he dumped their contents into the sink, rinsed them, and stacked them neatly in the dishwasher.

The task was done too quickly. What could he do? He didn't like the idea of leaving Libby alone, but he didn't dare go near her again, either. The scent of her, the soft disarray of her hair, the way her breasts seemed to draw at his mouth and the palms of his hands—all those things combined to make his grasp on reason tenuous.

Jess groaned, lifted his eyes to the ceiling and wondered if he was going to have to endure another ice-cold shower. The telephone rang, startling him, and he reached for it quickly. Libby might already be asleep, and he didn't want her to be disturbed.

"Hello?"

"Jess?" Monica's voice was calm, but there was an undercurrent of cold fury. "Did you take my car?"

He sighed, leaning back against the kitchen counter. "Yeah. Sorry. I should have called you before this, but—"

"But you were busy."

Jess flinched. Exactly what could he say to that? "Monica—"

"Never mind, Jess." She sighed the words. "I didn't have any right to say that. And if you helped yourself to my car, you must have had a good reason."

Why the hell did she have to be so reasonable? Why didn't Monica yell at him or something, so that he could get mad in good conscience and stop feeling like such an idiot? "I'm afraid the seats are a little muddy," he said.

"Muddy? Oh, yes—the rain. Was Libby okay?"

Again Jess's gaze lifted to the ceiling. Libby was not okay, thanks to him and Stacey and her charming ex-husband. But then, Monica was just making polite conversation, not asking for an in-depth account of Libby's emotional state. "She was drenched."

"So you brought her there, got her out of her wet clothes, built a fire—"

The anger Jess had wished for was suddenly there. "Monica."

She drew in a sharp breath. "All right, all right—I'm sorry. I take it our dinner date is off?"

"Yeah," Jess answered, turning the phone cord between his fingers. "I guess it is."

Monica was nothing if not persistent—probably that

quality accounted for her impressive success in political circles. "Tomorrow night?"

Jess sighed. "I don't know."

There was a short, uncomfortable silence. "We'll talk later," Monica finally said brightly. "Listen, is it okay if I send somebody over there to get my car?"

"I'll bring it to you," Jess said. It was, after stealing it, the least he could do. He'd check first, to make sure that Libby really was sleeping, and with luck, he could be back before she woke up.

"Thanks," sang Monica in parting.

Jess hung up the phone and climbed the stairs, pausing at the edge of the bedroom. He dared go no farther, wanting that rumple-haired little hellion the way he did. "Libby?"

When there was no answer, Jess turned and went back down the stairs again, almost grateful that he had somewhere to go, something to do.

Monica hid her annoyance well as she inspected the muddy splotches on her car's upholstery. Overhead, the incessant rain pummeled the garage roof.

"I'm sorry," Jess said. It seemed that he was always apologizing for one thing or another lately. "My truck wouldn't start, and I was in a hurry…"

Monica allowed a flicker of anger to show in her gray eyes. "Right. When there is a damsel to be rescued, a knight has to grab the first available charger."

Having no answer for that, Jess shrugged. "I'll have your car cleaned," he offered when the silence grew too long, and then he turned to walk back out of the garage and down the driveway to his own car, which refused to start.

He got out and slammed the door. "Damn!" he bellowed, kicking yet another dent into the fender.

"Problems?"

Jess hadn't been aware of Ken until that moment, hadn't noticed the familiar truck parked nearby. "It would take all day to list them," he replied ruefully.

Ken grinned a typical sideways grin, and his blue eyes twinkled. He seemed oblivious of the rain pouring off the brim of his ancient hat and soaking through his denim jacket and jeans. "I think maybe my daughter might be at the top of the list. Is she all right?"

"She's…" Jess faltered, suddenly feeling like a high-school kid. "She's sleeping."

Ken laughed. "Must have been real hard to say that," he observed, "me being her daddy and all."

"It isn't… I didn't…"

Again Ken laughed. "Maybe you should," he said.

Jess was shocked—so shocked that he was speechless.

"Take my truck if you need it," Ken offered calmly, his hand coming to rest on Jess's shoulder. "I'll get a ride home from somebody here. And, Jess?"

"What?"

"Don't hurt Libby. She's had enough trouble and grief as it is."

"I know that," Jess replied, as the rain plastered his hair to his neck and forehead and made his clothes cling to his flesh in sodden, clammy patches. "I swear I won't hurt her."

"That's good enough for me," replied Libby's father, and then he pried the truck keys out of his pocket and tossed them to Jess.

"Ken…"

The foreman paused, looking back, his eyes wise and patient. How the hell was Jess going to ask this man what he had to ask, for Libby's sake?

"Spit it out, son," Ken urged. "I'm getting wet."

"Clothes—she was… Libby was caught in the rain, and she needs dry clothes."

Ken chuckled and shrugged his shoulders. "Stop at our place and get some of her things then," he said indulgently.

Jess was suddenly as confused by this man as he was by his daughter. What the hell was Ken doing, standing there taking this whole thing so calmly? Didn't it bother him, knowing what might happen when Jess got back to that house?

"See ya," said Ken in parting.

Completely confused, Jess got into Ken's truck and drove away. It wasn't until he'd gotten a set of dry clothes for Libby and reached his own house again that he understood. Ken trusted him.

Jess let his forehead rest on the truck's steering wheel and groaned. He couldn't stand another cold shower, dammit. He just couldn't.

But Ken trusted him. Libby was lying upstairs in his bed, and even if she was, by some miracle, ready to handle what was destined to happen, Jess couldn't make love to her. To do so would be to betray a man who had, in so many ways, been as much a father to him as Cleave Barlowe had.

The problem was that Jess couldn't think of Libby as a sister.

* * *

Jess sat glumly at the little table in the kitchen, making patterns in his omelet with a fork. Tiring of that, he flung Libby a beleaguered look and sneezed.

She felt a surge of tenderness. "Aren't you hungry?"

He shook his head. "Libby…"

It took all of her forbearance not to stand up, round the table, and touch Jess's forehead to see if he had a fever. "What?" she prompted softly.

"I think I should take you home."

Libby was hurt, but she smiled brightly. "Well, it *has* stopped raining," she reasoned.

"And I've got your dad's truck," added Jess.

"Um-hmm. Thanks for stopping and getting my clothes, by the way."

Outside, the wind howled and the night was dark. Jess gave the jeans and loose pink sweater he had picked up for Libby a distracted look and sneezed again. "You're welcome."

"And you, my friend, are sick."

Jess shook his head, went to the counter to pour coffee from the coffeemaker there. "Want some?" he asked, lifting the glass pot.

Libby declined. "Were you taking another shower when I got up?" she ventured cautiously. The peace between them, for all its sweet glow, was still new and fragile.

Libby would have sworn that he winced, and his face was unreadable. "I'm a clean person," he said, averting his eyes.

Libby bit the inside of her lower lip, suddenly possessed by an untimely urge to laugh. Jess had been shivering when he came out of that bathroom and unexpectedly encountered his newly awakened houseguest.

"Right," she said.

Jess sneezed again, violently. Somehow, the sound unchained Libby's amusement and she shrieked with laughter.

"What is so goddamn funny?" Jess demanded, setting his coffee cup down with an irritated thump and scowling.

"N-nothing," cried Libby.

Suddenly Jess was laughing, too. He pulled Libby out of her chair and into his arms, and she deliberately pressed herself close to him, delighting in the evidence of his desire, in the scent and substance and strength of him.

She almost said that she loved him.

"You wanted my body!" she accused instead, teasing.

Jess groaned and tilted his head back, ostensibly to study the ceiling. Libby saw a muscle leap beneath his chin and wanted to kiss it, but she refrained.

"You were taking a cold shower, weren't you, Jess?"

"Yes," he admitted with a martyrly sigh. "Woman, if I die of pneumonia, it will be your fault."

"On the contrary. I've done everything but throw myself at your feet, mister, and you haven't wanted any part of me."

"Wrong." Jess grinned wickedly, touching the tip of her breast with an index finger. "I want this part..." The finger trailed away, following an erotic path. "And this part..."

It took all of Libby's courage to say the words again, after his brisk rejection earlier. "Make love to me, Jess."

"My God, Libby—"

She silenced him by laying two fingers to his lips. Remembering the words he had flung at her in the Cessna the day of her arrival, she said saucily, "If it feels good, do it."

Jess gave her a mock scowl, but his arms were around her now, holding her against him. "You were a very mean little kid," he muttered, "and now you're a mean adult. Do you know what you're doing to me, Kincaid?"

Libby moved her hips slightly, delighting in the contact and the guttural groan the motion brought from Jess. "I have some vague idea, yes."

"Your father trusts me."

"My father!" Libby stared up at him, amazed. "Is that what you've been worried about? What my father will think?"

Jess shrugged, and his eyes moved away from hers. Clearly he was embarrassed. "Yes."

Libby laughed, though she was not amused. "You're not serious!"

His eyes came back to meet hers and the expression in their green depths was nothing if not serious. "Ken is my best friend," he said.

"Shall I call him up and ask for permission? Better yet, I could drive over there and get a note!"

The taunts caused Jess to draw back a little, though their thighs and hips were still touching, still piping primitive messages one to the other. "Very funny!" he snapped, and a muscle bunched in his neck, went smooth again.

Libby was quietly furious. "You're right—it isn't funny. This is my body, Jess—mine. I'm thirty-one years old and I make my own living and I *damned well* don't need my daddy's permission to go to bed with a man!"

The green eyes were twinkling with mischief. "That's a healthy attitude if I've ever heard one," he broke in. "However, before we go up those stairs, there is one more thing I want to know. Are you using me, Libby?"

"Using you?"

"Yes. Do I really mean something to you, or would any man do?"

Libby felt as though she'd just grabbed hold of a high-voltage wire; in a few spinning seconds she was hurled from pain to rage to humiliation.

Jess held her firmly. "I see the question wasn't received in the spirit in which it was intended," he said, his eyes serious now, searching her burning, defiant face. "What I meant to ask was, are we going to be making love, Libby, or just proving that you can go the whole route and respond accordingly?"

Libby met his gaze bravely, though inside she was still shaken and angry. "Why would I go to all this trouble, Jess, if I didn't want you? After all, I could have just stopped someone on the street and said, 'Excuse me, sir, but would you mind making love to me? I'd like to find out if I'm frigid or not.'"

Jess sighed heavily, but his hands were sliding up under the back of Libby's pink sweater, gently kneading the firm flesh there. The only sign that her sarcasm had rankled him was the almost imperceptible leaping of the pulsepoint beneath his right ear.

"I guess I'm having a little trouble understanding your sudden change of heart, Libby. For years you've hated my guts. Now, after confiding that your ex-husband put you through some kind of emotional wringer and left you feeling about as attractive as a sink drain, you want to share my bed."

Libby closed her eyes. The motion of his hands on her back was hypnotic, making it hard for her to breathe, let alone think. When she felt the catch of her bra give way, she shivered.

She should tell him that she loved him, that maybe, despite outward appearances, she'd always loved him, but she didn't dare. This was a man who had thought the worst of her at every turn, who had never missed a chance to get under her skin. Allowing him inside the fortress where her innermost emotions were stored could prove disastrous.

His hands came slowly around from her back to the aching roundness of her breasts, sliding easily, brazenly under the loosened bra.

"Answer me, Libby," he drawled, his voice a sleepy rumble.

She was dazed; his fingers came to play a searing symphony at her nipples, plying them, drawing at them. "I… I want you. I'm not trying to p-prove anything."

"Let me look at you, Libby."

Libby pulled the pink sweater off over her head, stood perfectly still as Jess dispensed with her bra and then stepped back a little way to admire her.

He outlined one blushing nipple with the tip of his finger, progressed to wreak the same havoc on the other. Then, with strong hands, he lifted Libby up onto a counter, so that her breasts were on a level with his face.

She gasped as he took languid, tentative suckle at

one peak, then trailed a path with the tip of his tongue to the other, conquering it with lazy ease.

She was desperate now. "Make love to me," she whispered again in broken tones.

"Make love to me, *Jess*," he prompted, nibbling now, driving her half-wild with the need of him.

Libby swallowed hard, closed her eyes. His teeth were scraping gently at her nipple now, rousing it to obedience. "Make love to me, Jess," she repeated breathlessly.

He withdrew his mouth, cupping her in his hands, letting his thumbs do the work his lips and teeth had done before. "Open your eyes," he commanded in a hoarse rumble. "Look at me, Libby."

Dazed, her very soul spinning within her, Libby obeyed.

"Tell me," he insisted raggedly, "that you're not seeing Stacey or your misguided ex-husband. Tell me that you see *me*, Libby."

"I do, Jess."

He lifted her off the counter and into his arms, and his mouth came down on hers, cautious at first, then almost harshly demanding. Libby was electrified by the kiss, by the searching fierceness of his tongue, by the moan of need that came from somewhere deep inside him. Finally he ended the kiss, and his eyes were smiling into hers.

Feeling strangely giddy, Libby laughed. "Is this the part where you make love to me?"

"This is it," he replied, and then they were moving through the house toward the stairs. Lightning crackled and flashed above the skylights, while thunder struck a booming accompaniment.

"The earth is moving already," said Libby into the Jess-scented wool of his sweater.

Jess took the stairs two at a time. "Just wait," he replied.

In the bedroom, which was lit only by the lightning that was sundering the night sky, he set Libby on her feet. For a moment they just stood still, looking at each other. Libby felt as though she had become a part of the terrible storm that was pounding at the tall windows, and she grasped Jess's arms so that she wouldn't be blown away to the mountaintops or flung beyond the angry clouds.

"Touch me, Libby," Jess said, and somehow, even over the renewed rage of the storm, she heard him.

Cautiously she slid her hands beneath his sweater, splaying her fingers so that she could feel as much of him as possible. His chest was hard and broad and softly furred, and he groaned as she found masculine nipples and explored them.

Libby moved her hands down over his rib cage to the sides of his waist, up his warm, granite-muscled back. *I love you*, she thought, and then she bit her lower lip lest she actually say the words.

At some unspoken urging from Jess, she caught his sweater in bunched fists and drew it up over his head. Silver-blue lightning scored the sky and danced on the planes of his bare chest, his magnificent face.

Libby was drawn to him, tasting one masculine nipple with a cautious tongue, suckling the other. He moaned and tangled his fingers in her hair, pressing her close, and she knew that he was experiencing the same keen pleasure she had known.

Presently he caught her shoulders in his hands and held her at arm's length, boldly admiring her bare breasts. "Beautiful," he rasped. "So beautiful."

Libby had long been ashamed of her body, thinking it inadequate. Now, in this moment of storm and fury, she was proud of every curve and hollow, every pore and freckle. She removed her jeans and panties with graceful motions.

Jess's reaction was a low, rumbling groan, followed by a gasp of admiration. He stood still, a Western Adonis, as she undid his jeans, felt the hollows of his narrow hips, the firmness of his buttocks. Within seconds he was as naked as Libby.

She caught his hands in her own, drew him toward the bed. But instead of reclining with her there, he knelt at the side, positioned Libby so that her hips rested on the edge of the mattress.

His hands moved over every part of her—her breasts, her shoulders, her flat, smooth stomach, the insides of her trembling thighs.

"Jess..."

"Shh, it's all right."

"But..." Libby's back arched and a spasm of delight racked her as he touched the curls sheltering the core of her passion, first with his fingers, then with his lips. "Oh...wait...oh, Jess, no..."

"Yes," he said, his breath warm against her. And then he parted her and took her fully into his mouth, following the instinctive rising and falling of her hips, chuckling at the soft cry she gave.

A violent shudder went through Libby's already throbbing body, and her knees moved wide of each other, shaking, made of no solid substance.

Frantic, she found his head, tangled her fingers in his hair. "Stop," she whimpered, even as she held him fast.

Jess chuckled again and then went right on consuming her, his hands catching under her knees, lifting them higher, pressing them farther apart.

Libby was writhing now, her breath harsh and burning, her vision blurred. The storm came inside the room and swept her up, up, up, beyond the splitting skies. She cried out in wonder as she collided with the moon and bounced off, to be enfolded by a waiting sun.

When she came back inside herself, Jess was beside her on the bed, soothing her with soft words, stroking away the tears that had somehow gathered on her face.

"I've never read..." she whispered stupidly. "I didn't know..."

Jess was drawing her up, so that she lay full on the bed, naked and sated at his side. "Look it up," he teased, kissing her briefly, tenderly. "I think it would be under O."

Libby laughed, and the sound was a warm, soft contrast to the tumult of the storm. "What an ego!"

With an index finger, Jess traced her lips, her chin, the moist length of her neck. Small novas flashed and flared within her as her pulsing senses began to make new demands.

When his mouth came to her breast again, Libby arched her back and whimpered. "Jess... Jess..."

He circled the straining nipple with a warm tongue. "What, babe?"

No coherent words would come to Libby's beleaguered mind. "I don't know," she managed finally. "I
don't know!"

"I do," Jess answered, and then he suckled in earnest.

Powerless under the tyranny of her own body, Libby
gave herself up to sensation. It seemed that no part of
her was left untouched, unconquered or unworshiped.

When at last Jess poised himself above her, strong
and fully a man, his face reflected the flashing lightning that seemed to seek them both.

"I'm Jess," he warned again in a husky whisper that
betrayed his own fierce need.

Libby drew him to her with quick, fevered hands. "I
know," she gasped, and then she repeated his name like
some crazy litany, whispering it first, sobbing it when
he thrust his searing magnificence inside her.

He moved slowly at first, and the finely sculptured
planes of his face showed the cost of his restraint, the
conflicting force of his need. "Libby," he pleaded. "Oh,
God… Libby…"

She thrust her hips upward in an instinctive, un-
planned motion that shattered Jess's containment and
caused his great muscular body to convulse once and
then assert its dominance in a way that was at once
fierce and tender. It seemed that he sought some treasure within her, so deeply did he delve, some shimmering thing that he would perish without.

His groans rose above the sound of thunder, and as
his pace accelerated and his passion was unleashed,
Libby moved in rhythm with him, one with him, his.

Their bodies moved faster, agile in their quest, each

glistening with the sheen of sweet exertion, each straining toward the sun that, this time, would consume them both.

The tumult flung them high, tore them asunder, fused them together again. Libby sobbed in the hot glory of her release and heard an answering cry from Jess.

They clung together, struggling for breath, for a long time after the slow, treacherous descent had been made. Twice, on the way, Libby's body had paused to greedily claim what had been denied it before.

She was flushed, reckless in her triumph. "I did it," she exalted, her hands moving on the slackened muscles in Jess's back. "I did it… I responded…"

Instantly she felt those muscles go taut, and Jess's head shot up from its resting place in the curve where her neck and shoulder met.

"What?"

Libby stiffened, knowing now, too late, how grave her mistake had been. "I mean, *we* did it…" she stumbled lamely.

But Jess was wrenching himself away from her, searching for his clothes, pulling them on. "Congratulations!" he yelled.

Libby sat up, confused, wildly afraid. Dear God, was he going to walk out now? Was he going to hate her for a few thoughtless words?

"Jess, wait!" she pleaded, clutching the sheet to her chest. "Please!"

"For what, Libby?" he snapped from the top of the stairs. "Exhibit B? Is there something else you want to prove?"

"Jess!"

But he was storming down the stairs, silent in his rage, bent on escaping her.

"Jess!" Libby cried out again in fear, tears pouring down her face, her hands aching where they grasped the covers.

The only answer was the slamming of the front door.

Chapter 7

Ken Kincaid looked up from the cards in his hand as the lights flickered, went out, came on again. Damn, this was a hell of a storm—if the rain didn't let up soon, the creeks would overflow and they'd have range calves drowning right and left.

Across the table, Cleave Barlowe laid down his own hand of cards. "Quite a storm, eh?" he asked companionably. "Jess bring your truck back yet?"

"I don't need it," said Ken, still feeling uneasy.

Lightning creased the sky beyond the kitchen window, and thunder shook the old house on its sturdy foundations. Cleave grinned. "He's with Libby, then?"

"Yup," said Ken, smiling himself.

"Think they know the sky's turning itself inside out?"

There was an easing in Ken; he laughed outright. "Doubt it," he replied, looking at his cards again.

For a while the two men played the two-handed poker they had enjoyed for years, but it did seem that luck wasn't running with either one of them. Finally they gave up the effort and Cleave went home.

With his old friend gone, Ken felt apprehensive again. He went around the house making sure all the windows were closed against the rain, and wondered why one storm should bother him that way, when he'd seen a thousand and never found them anything more than a nuisance.

He was about to shut off the lamp in the front room when he saw the headlights of his own truck swing into the driveway. Seconds later, there was an anxious knock at the door.

"Jess?" Ken marveled, staring at the haggard, rain-drenched man standing on the front porch. "What the hell...?"

Jess looked as though he'd just taken a first-rate gut punch. "Could I come in?"

"That's a stupid question," retorted Ken, stepping back to admit his unexpected and obviously distraught visitor. "Is Libby okay?"

Jess's haunted eyes wouldn't quite link up with Ken's. "She's fine," he said, his hands wedged into the pockets of his jeans, his hair and sweater dripping rainwater.

Ken arched an eyebrow. "What'd you do, anyway—ride on the running board of that truck and steer from outside?"

Jess didn't answer; he didn't seem to realize that he

was wet to the skin. There was a distracted look about him that made Ken ache inside.

In silence Ken led the way into the kitchen, poured a dose of straight whiskey into a mug, added strong coffee.

"You look like you've been dragged backward through a knothole," he observed when Jess was settled at the table. "What happened?"

Jess closed his hands around the mug. "I'm in love with your daughter," he said after a long time.

Ken sat down, allowed himself a cautious grin. "If you drove over here in this rain just to tell me that, friend, you got wet for nothing."

"You knew?" Jess seemed honestly surprised.

"Everybody knew. Except maybe you and Libby."

Jess downed the coffee and the potent whiskey almost in a single gulp. There was a struggle going on in his face, as though he might be fighting hard to hold himself together.

Ken rose to put more coffee into Jess's mug, along with a lot more whiskey. If ever a man needed a drink, this one did.

"Maybe you'd better put on some dry clothes," the older man ventured.

Jess only shook his head.

Ken sat back in his chair and waited. When Jess was ready to talk, he would. There was, Ken had learned, no sense in pushing before that point was reached.

"Libby's beautiful, you know," Jess remarked presently, as he started on his third drink.

Ken smiled. "Yeah. I've noticed."

Simple and ordinary though they were, the words

triggered some kind of emotional reaction in Jess, broke down the barriers he had been maintaining so carefully. His face crumbled, he lowered his head to his arms, and he cried. The sobs were deep and dry and ragged.

Hurting because Jess hurt, Ken waited.

Soon enough, his patience was rewarded. Jess began to talk, brokenly at first, and then with stone-cold reason.

Ken didn't react openly to anything he said; much of what Jess told him about Libby's marriage to Aaron Strand came as no real surprise. He was wounded, all the same, for his daughter and for the devastated young man sitting across the table from him.

The level of whiskey in Ken's bottle went down as the hour grew later. Finally, when Jess was so drunk that his words started getting all tangled up with each other, Ken half led, half carried him up the stairs to Libby's room.

In the hallway, he paused, reflecting. Life was a hell of a thing, he decided. Here was Jess, sleeping fitfully in Libby's bed, all alone. And just up the hill, chances were, Libby was tossing and turning in Jess's bed, just as lonely.

Not for the first time, Ken Kincaid felt a profound desire to get them both by the hair and knock their heads together.

Libby cried until far into the night and then, exhausted, she slept. When she awakened, shocked to find herself in Jess Barlowe's bed, she saw that the world beyond the windows had been washed to a clean sparkle.

The world inside her seemed tawdry by comparison.

Her face feeling achy and swollen, Libby got out of bed, stumbled across the room to the bathroom. Jess was nowhere in the house; she would have sensed it if he were.

As Libby filled the tub with hot water, she wondered whether she was relieved that he wasn't close by, or disappointed. A little of both, she concluded as she slid into her bath and sat there in miserable reverie.

Facing Jess now would have been quite beyond her. Why, why had she said such a foolish thing, when she might have known how Jess would react? On the other hand, why had *he* made such a big deal out of a relatively innocuous remark?

More confused than ever, Libby finished her bath and climbed out to dry herself with a towel. In short order she was dressed and her hair was combed. Because she had no toothbrush—Jess had forgotten that when he picked up her things—she had to be content with rinsing her mouth.

Downstairs, Libby stood staring at the telephone, willing herself to call her father and confess that she needed a ride home. Pride wouldn't allow that, however, and she had made up her mind to walk the distance when she heard a familiar engine outside, the slam of a truck door.

Jess was back, she thought wildly. Where had he been all night? With Monica? What would she say to him?

The questions were pointless, for when Libby forced herself to go to the front door and open it, she saw her father striding up the walk, not Jess.

Fresh embarrassment stained Libby's cheeks, though

there was no condemnation in Ken's weathered face, no anger in his understanding eyes. "Ride home?" he said.

Unable to speak, Libby only nodded.

"Pretty bad night?" he ventured in his concise way when they were both settled in the truck and driving away.

"Dismal," replied Libby, fixing her eyes on the red Hereford cattle grazing in the green, rain-washed distance.

"Jess isn't in very good shape, either," commented Ken after an interval.

Libby's eyes were instantly trained on her father's profile. "You've seen him?"

"Seen him?" Ken laughed gruffly. "I poured him into bed at three this morning."

"He was drunk?" Libby was amazed.

"He had a nip or two."

"How is he now?"

Ken glanced at her, turned his eyes back to the rutted, winding country road ahead. "Jess is hurting," he said, and there was a finality in his tone that kept Libby from asking so much as one more question.

Jess is hurting. What the devil did that mean? Was he hung over? Had the night been as miserable for him as it had been for her?

Presently the truck came to a stop in front of the big Victorian house that had been "home" to Libby for as long as she could remember. Ken made no move to shut off the engine, and she got out without saying goodbye. For all her brave words of the night before, about not needing her father's approval, she felt estranged from him now, subdued.

After forcing down a glass of orange juice and a slice of toast in the kitchen, Libby went into the studio Cathy and her father had improvised for her and did her best to work. Even during the worst days in New York, she had been able to find solace in the mechanics of drawing her cartoon strip, forgetting her own troubles to create comical dilemmas for Liberated Lizzie.

Today was different.

The panels Libby sketched were awkward, requiring too many erasures, and even if she had been able to get the drawings right, she couldn't have come up with a funny thought for the life of her.

At midmorning, Libby decided that her career was over and paced from one end of the studio to the other, haunted by thoughts of the night before.

Jess had made it clear, in his kitchen, that he didn't want to make love just to let Libby prove that she was "normal." And what had she done? She'd *gloated*.

Shame ached in Libby's cheeks as she walked. *I did it*, she'd crowed, as though she were Edison and the first electric light had just been lit. God, how could she have been so stupid? So insensitive?

"You did have a little help, you know," she scolded herself out loud. And then she covered her face with both hands and cried. It had been partly Jess's fault, that scene—he had definitely overreacted, and on top of that, he had been unreasonable. He had stormed out without giving Libby a chance to make things right.

Still, it was all too easy to imagine how he'd felt. Used. And the truth was that, without intending to, Libby had used him.

Small, strong hands were suddenly pulling Libby's

hands away from her face. Through the blur, she saw Cathy watching her, puzzled and sad.

"What's wrong?" her cousin asked. "Please, Libby, tell me what's wrong."

"Everything!" wailed Libby, who was beyond trying to maintain her dignity now.

Gently Cathy drew her close, hugged her. For a moment they were two motherless little girls again, clinging to each other because there were some pains that even Ken, with his gruff, unswerving devotion, couldn't ease.

The embrace was comforting, and after a minute or two Libby recovered enough to step back and offer Cathy a shaky smile. "I've missed you so much, Cathy," she said.

"Don't get sloppy," teased Cathy, using her face to give the toneless words expression.

Libby laughed. "What are you doing today, besides being one of the idle rich?"

Cathy tilted her head to one side. "Did you really stay with Jess last night?" she asked with swift hands.

"Aren't we blunt today?" Libby shot back, both speaking and signing. "I suppose the whole ranch is talking about it!"

Cathy nodded.

"Damn!"

"Then it's true!" exalted Cathy aloud, her eyes sparkling.

Some of Libby's earlier remorse drained away, pushed aside by feelings of anger and betrayal. "Has Jess been bragging?" she demanded, her hands on her hips, her indignation warm and thick in her throat.

"He isn't the type to do that," Cathy answered in slow, carefully formed words, "and you know it."

Libby wasn't so certain—Jess had been very angry, and his pride had been stung. Besides, the only other person who had known was Ken, and he was notoriously tight-lipped when it came to other people's business. "Who told you?" she persisted, narrowing her eyes.

"Nobody had to," Cathy answered aloud. "I was down at the stables, saddling Banjo, and one of the range crews was there—ten or twelve men, I guess. Anyway, there was a fight out front—Jess punched out one of the cowboys."

Libby could only gape.

Cathy gave the story a stirring finale. "I think Jess would have killed that guy if Ken hadn't hauled him off."

Libby found her voice. "Was Jess hurt? Cathy, did you see if he was hurt?"

Cathy grinned at her cousin's undisguised concern. "Not a scratch. He got into an argument with Ken and left."

Libby felt a strong need to find her father and ask him exactly what had happened, but she knew that the effort would be wasted. Even if she could find Ken, which was unlikely considering the size of the ranch and all the places he could be, he wouldn't explain.

Cathy was studying the messy piece of drawing paper affixed to the art board. "You're not going to work?" she signed.

"I gave up," Libby confessed. "I couldn't keep my mind on it."

"After a night with Jess Barlowe, who could?"

Libby suddenly felt challenged, defensive. She even thought that, perhaps, there was more to the deep closeness between Jess and Cathy than she had guessed. "What do you know about spending the night with Jess?" she snapped before she could stop herself.

Cathy rolled her beautiful green eyes. "*Nothing.* For better or worse, and mostly it's been better, I'm married to Jess's brother—remember?"

Libby swallowed, feeling foolish. "Where is Stacey, anyway?" she asked, more to make conversation than because she wanted to know.

The question brought a shadow of sadness to Cathy's face. "He's away on one of his business trips."

Libby sat down on her art stool, folded her hands. "Maybe you should have gone with him, Cathy. You used to do that a lot, didn't you? Maybe if you two could be alone...talk..."

The air suddenly crackled with Cathy's anger and hurt. "*He* talks!" she raged aloud. "I just move my hands!"

Libby spoke softly, gently. "You could talk to Stacey, Cathy—really talk, the way you do with me."

"No."

"Why not?"

"I know I sound like a record playing on the wrong speed, that's why!"

"Even if that were so, would it matter?" signed Libby, frowning. "Stacey knew you were deaf before he married you, for heaven's sake."

Cathy's head went down. "He must have felt sorry for me or something."

Instantly Libby was off her stool, gripping Cathy's shoulders in firm, angry hands. "He loves you!"

Tears misted the emerald-green eyes and Cathy's lower lip trembled. "No doubt that's why he intends to divorce me and marry you, Libby."

"No," insisted Libby, giving her cousin a slight shake. "No, that isn't true. I think Stacey is confused, Cathy. Upset. Maybe it's this thing about your not wanting to have a baby. Or maybe he feels that you don't need him, you're so independent."

"Independent? Don't look now, Libby Kincaid, but *you're* the independent one! You have a career...you can hear—"

"Will you stop feeling sorry for yourself, dammit!" Libby almost screamed. "I'm so tired of hearing how you suffer! For God's sake, stop whining and fight for the man you love!"

Cathy broke free of Libby's grasp, furious, tears pouring down her face. "It's too late!" she cried. "You're here now, and it's too late!"

Libby sighed, stepped back, stricken by her own outburst and by Cathy's, too. "You're forgetting one thing," she reasoned quietly. "I'm not in love with Stacey. And it would take two of us to start anything, wouldn't it?"

Cathy went to the windows and stared out at the pond, her chin high. Knowing that her cousin needed this interval to restore her dignity and assemble her thoughts, Libby did not approach her.

Finally Cathy sniffled and turned back to offer a shaky smile. "I didn't come over here to fight with you," she said clearly. "I'm going to Kalispell, and I wanted to know if you would like to come with me."

Libby agreed readily, and after changing her clothes and leaving a quick note for Ken, she joined Cathy in the shiny blue Ferrari.

The ride to Kalispell was a fairly long one, and by the time Cathy and Libby reached the small city, they had reestablished their old, easy relationship.

They spent the day shopping, had lunch in a rustic steak house bearing the Circle Bar B brand, and then started home again.

"Are you really going to give that to Jess?" Cathy asked, her eyes twinkling when she cast a look at the bag in Libby's lap.

"I may lose my courage." Libby frowned, wondering what had possessed her to buy a T-shirt with such an outlandish saying printed on it. She supposed she'd hoped that the gesture would penetrate the barrier between herself and Jess, enabling them to talk.

"Take my advice," said Cathy, guiding the powerful car off the highway and onto the road that led to the heart of the ranch. "Give him the shirt."

"Maybe," said Libby, looking off into the sweeping, endless blue sky. A small airplane was making a graceful descent toward the Circle Bar B landing strip.

"Who do you suppose that is?" Libby asked, catching Cathy's attention with a touch on her arm.

The question was a mistake. Cathy, who had not, of course, heard the plane's engine, scanned the sky and saw it. "Why don't we find out?"

Libby scrunched down in her seat, sorry that she had pointed out the airplane now. Suppose Stacey was aboard, returning from his business trip, and there was another uncomfortable scene at the airstrip? Suppose it was Jess, and he either yelled at Libby or, worse yet, pretended that she wasn't there?

"I'd rather go home," she muttered.

But Cathy's course was set, and the Ferrari bumped and jostled over the road to the landing strip as though it were a pickup truck.

The plane came to a smooth stop as Cathy parked at one side of the road and got out of the car, shading her eyes with one hand, watching. Libby remained in her seat.

She had, it seemed, imagined only part of the possible scenario. The pilot was Jess, and his passenger was a wan, tight-lipped Stacey.

"Oh, God," said Libby, sinking even farther into the car seat. She would have kept her face hidden in her hand forever, probably, if it hadn't been for the crisp, insistent tap at her window.

Having no other choice, she rolled the glass down and squinted into Jess Barlowe's unreadable, hard-lined face. "Come with me," he said flatly.

Libby looked through the Ferrari's windshield, saw Stacey and Cathy standing nearby, a disturbing distance between them. Cathy was glaring angrily into Stacey's face, and Stacey was casting determined looks in Libby's direction.

"They need some time alone," Jess said, his eyes linking fiercely, warningly, with Libby's as he opened the car door for her.

Anxious not to make an obviously unpleasant situation any worse, Libby gathered up her bags and her purse and got out of the car, following along behind

Jess's long strides. His truck, which she hadn't noticed before, was parked close by.

Without looking back at Stacey and Cathy, Libby slid gratefully into the dusty front seat and closed her eyes. Not until the truck was moving did she open them, and even then she couldn't quite bring herself to look at the man behind the wheel.

"That was touching," he said in a vicious rasp.

Libby stiffened in the seat, staring at Jess's rock-hard profile now. "What did you say?"

The powerful shoulders moved in an annoying shrug. "Your wanting to meet Stacey on his triumphant return."

It took Libby a moment to absorb what he was implying. When she had, she slammed him with the paper bag that contained the T-shirt she'd bought for him in Kalispell and hissed, "You bastard! I didn't know Stacey was going to be on that plane, and if I had, I certainly wouldn't have been there at all!"

"Sure," he drawled, and even though he was grinning and looking straight ahead at the road, there was contempt in his tone and a muscle pulsing at the base of his jaw.

Libby felt tears of frustration rise in her eyes. "I thought you believed me," she said.

"I thought I did, too," Jess retorted with acid amusement. "But that was before you showed up at the landing strip at such an opportune moment."

"It was Cathy's idea to meet the plane!"

"Right."

The paper bag crackled as Libby lifted it, prepared to swing.

"Do that again and I'll stop this car and raise blisters on your backside," Jess warned, without so much as looking in her direction.

Libby lowered the bag back to her lap, swallowed miserably, and turned her attention to the road. She did not believe Jess's threat for one moment, but she felt childish for trying to hit him with the bag. "Cathy told me there was a fight at the stables this morning," she dared after a long time. "What happened?"

Another shrug, as insolent as the first, preceded his reply. "One of Ken's men said something I didn't like."

"Like what?"

"Like didn't it bother me to sleep with my brother's mistress."

Libby winced, sorry for pressing the point. "Oh, God," she said, and she was suddenly so tired, so broken, and so frustrated that she couldn't hold back her tears anymore. She covered her face with both hands and turned her head as far away from Jess as she could, but the effort was useless.

Jess stopped the truck at the side of the road, turned Libby easily toward him. Through a blur, she saw the Ferrari race past.

"Let go of me!"

Jess not only didn't let go, he pulled her close. "I'm sorry," he muttered into her hair. "God, Libby, I don't know what comes over me, what makes me say things to hurt you."

"Garden-variety hatred!" sniffled Libby, who was already forgiving him even though it was against her better judgment.

He chuckled. "No. I couldn't ever hate you, Libby."

She looked up at him, confused and hopeful. Before she could think of anything to say, however, there was a loud *pop* from beneath the hood of the truck, followed by a sizzle and clouds of steam.

"Goddammit!" rasped Jess.

Libby laughed, drunk on the scent of him, the closeness of him, the crazy paradox of him. "This crate doesn't exactly fit your image, you know," she taunted. "Why don't you get yourself a decent car?"

He turned from glowering at the hood of the truck to smile down into her face. "If I do, Kincaid, will you let me make love to you in the backseat?"

She shoved at his immovable chest with both hands, laughing again. "No, no, a thousand times no!"

Jess nibbled at her jawline, at the lobe of her ear, chuckled huskily as she tensed. "How many times no?"

"Maybe," said Libby.

Just when she thought she would surely go crazy, Jess drew back from his brazen pursuits and smiled lazily. "It is time I got a new car," he conceded, with an evil light glistening in his jade eyes. "Will you come to Kalispell and help me pick it out, Libby?"

A thrill skittered through Libby's body and flamed in her face. "I was just there," she protested, clutching at straws.

"It shouldn't—" Jess bent, nipped at the side of her neck with gentle teeth "—take long. A couple of days at the most."

"A couple of days!"

"And nights." Jess's lips were scorching their way across the tender hollow of her throat. "Think about it,

Lib. Just you and me. No Stacey. No Cathy. No problems."

Libby shivered as a knowledgeable hand closed over
one of her breasts, urging, reawakening. "No p-prob-
lems?" she echoed.

Jess undid the top button of her blouse.

Libby's breath caught in her throat; she felt heat
billowing up inside her, foaming out, just as it was
foaming out of the station wagon's radiator. "Wh-where
would we s-stay?"

Another button came undone.

Jess chuckled, his mouth on Libby's collarbone now,
tasting it, doing nothing to cool the heat that was pounding within her. "How about—" the third button gave
way, and Libby's bra was displaced by a gentle hand
"—one of those motels…with the…vibrating beds?"

"Tacky," gasped Libby, and her eyes closed languidly
and her head fell back as Jess stroked the nipple he'd
just found to pebble-hard response.

"My condo, then," he said, and his lips were sliding
down from her collarbone, soft, soft, over the upper
rounding of her bare breast.

Libby gasped and arched her back as his lips claimed
the distended, hurting peak. "Jess…oh, God…this is a
p-public road!"

"Umm," Jess said, lapping at her now with the tip of
his tongue. "Will you go with me, Libby?"

Wild need went through her as he stroked the insides
of her thighs, forcing her blue-jeaned legs apart. And
all the while he plied her nipple into a panic of need.
"Yes!" she gasped finally.

Jess undid the snap of her jeans, slid his hand inside, beneath the scanty lace of her panties.

"Damn you," Libby whispered hoarsely, "s-stop that! I said I'd go—"

He told her what else she was about to do. And one glorious, soul-scoring minute later, she did.

Red in the face, still breathing heavily, Libby closed her jeans, tugged her bra back into place, buttoned her blouse. God, what if someone had come along and seen her letting Jess…letting him play with her like that?

All during the ride home, she mentally rehearsed the blistering diatribe he deserved to hear. He could just go to Kalispell by *himself*, she would tell him. If he thought for one damned minute that he was going to take her to his condo and make love to her, he was sadly mistaken, she would say.

"Be ready in half an hour," Jess told her at her father's front door.

"Okay," Libby replied.

After landing the Cessna in Kalispell and making arrangements to rent a car, which turned out to be a temperamental cousin to Jess's truck, they drove through the small city to an isolated tree-dense property beyond. There were at least a million stars in the sky, and as the modest rental rattled over a narrow wooden bridge spanning a creek, Libby couldn't help giving in a little to the romance of it all.

Beyond the bridge, there were more trees—towering ponderosa pines; whispering, shiny-leaved birches. They stopped in the driveway of a condominium that stood apart from several others. Jess got out of the car, came around to open Libby's door for her.

"Let's get rid of the suitcases and go out for something to eat," he said.

Libby's stomach rumbled inelegantly, and Jess laughed as he caught her hand in his and drew her up the darkened walk to the front door of the condominium. "That shoots my plans for a little fun before dinner," he teased.

"There's always after," replied Libby, lifting her chin.

Chapter 8

The inside of the condominium was amazingly like Jess's house on the ranch. There was a loft, for instance, this one accessible by both stairs and, of all things, a built-in ladder. Too, the general layout of the rooms was much the same.

The exceptions were that the floors were carpeted rather than bare oak, and the entire roof was made of heavy glass. *When we make love here, I'll be able to look up and see the stars*, Libby mused.

"Like it?" Jess asked, setting the suitcases down and watching her with discerning, mirthful green eyes.

Libby was uncomfortable again, doubting the wisdom of coming here now that she was faced with the realities of the situation. "Is this where you bring all your conquests?"

Jess smiled, shrugged.

"Well?" prodded Libby, annoyed because he hadn't even had the common decency to offer a denial.

He sat down on the stone ledge fronting the fire-place, wrapped his hands around one knee. "The place does happen to be something of a love nest, as a matter of fact."

Libby was stung. Dammit, how unchivalrous could one man be? "Oh," she said loftily.

"It's my father's place," Jess said, clearly delighting in her obvious curiosity and the look of relief she couldn't quite hide.

"Your father's?"

Jess grinned. "He entertains his mistress here, from time to time. In his position, he has to be discreet."

Libby was gaping now, trying to imagine the sedate, dignified Senator Barlowe cavorting with a woman beneath slanted glass roofs, climbing ladders to star-dappled lofts.

Jess's amused gaze had strayed to the ladder. "It probably puts him in mind of the good old days—climbing into the hayloft, and all that."

Libby blushed. She was still quite disturbed by that ladder, among other things. "You did ask the senator's permission to come here, didn't you?"

Jess seemed to know that she had visions of Cleave Barlowe carrying some laughing woman over the threshold and finding the place already occupied. "Yes," he assured her in a teasing tone, rising and coming toward her. "I said, 'Mind if I take Libby to your condo, dear old dad, and take her to bed?' And he said—"

"Jess!" Libby howled, in protest.

He laughed, caught her elbows in his hands, kissed her playfully, his lips sampling hers, tugging at them in soft entreaty. "My father is in Washington," he said. "Stop worrying."

Libby pulled back, her face hot, her mind spinning. "I'm hungry!"

"Umm," replied Jess, "so am I."

Why did she feel like a sixteen-year-old on the verge of big trouble? "Please...let's go now."

Jess sighed.

They went, but they were back, arms burdened with cartons of Chinese food, in less than half an hour.

While Jess set the boxes out on the coffee table, Libby went to the kitchen for plates and silverware. Scribbled on a blackboard near the sink, she saw the surprising words: "Thanks, Ken. See you next week. B."

A soft chuckle simmered up into Libby's throat and emerged as a giggle. Could it be that her father, her serious, hardworking father, had a ladyfriend who visited him here in this romantic hideaway? Tilting her head to one side, she considered, grinned again. "Naaaah!"

But Libby's grin wouldn't fade as she carried plates, forks, spoons and paper napkins back into the living room.

"What's so funny?" Jess asked, trying to hide the hunk of sweet-and-sour chicken he had just purloined from one of the steaming cartons.

"Nothing," said Libby, catching his hand and raising it to his mouth. Sheepishly he popped the tidbit of chicken onto his tongue and chewed.

"You lie," Jess replied, "but I'm too hungry to press the point."

While they ate, Libby tried to envision what sort of woman her father would be drawn to—tall, short? Quiet, talkative?

"You're mulling over more than the chow mein," accused Jess presently in a good-natured voice. "Tell me, what's going on in that gifted little head?"

Libby shrugged. "Romance."

He grinned. "That's what I like to hear."

But Libby was thinking seriously, following her thoughts through new channels. In all the years since her mother's death, just before Cathy had come to live on the ranch, she had never imagined Ken Kincaid caring about another woman. "It isn't as though he's old," she muttered, "or unattractive."

Jess set down his plate with a mockingly forceful thump. "That does it. Who are you talking about, Kincaid?" he demanded archly, his wonderful mouth twitching in the effort to suppress a grin.

She perused him with lofty disdain. "Am I correct in assuming that you are jealous?"

"Jealous as hell," came the immediate and not-so-jovial response.

Libby laughed, laid a hand on his knee. "If you must know, I was thinking about my father. I've always kept him in this neat little cubicle in my mind, marked 'Dad.' If you can believe it, it has just now occurred to me that he's a man, with a life, and maybe even a love, of his own."

Mirth danced in Jess's jade eyes, but if he knew anything about Ken's personal life, he clearly wasn't going to speak of it. "Pass the eggroll," he said diplomatically.

When the meal was over, Libby's reflections began to shift to matters nearer the situation at hand.

"I don't know what I'm doing here," she said pensively as she and Jess cleared the coffee table and started toward the kitchen with the debris. "I must be out of my mind."

Jess dropped the cartons and the crumpled napkins into the trash compactor. "Thanks a lot," he said, watching her attentively as she rinsed the plates and silverware and put them into the dishwasher.

Wearing tailored gray slacks and a lightweight teal-blue sweater, he was devastatingly attractive. Still, the look Libby gave him was a serious, questioning one. "What is it with us, Jess? What makes us behave the way we do? One minute, we're yelling at each other, or not speaking at all, and the next we're alone in a place like this."

"Chemistry?"

Libby laughed ruefully. "More like voodoo. So what kind of car are you planning to buy?"

Jess drew her to him; his fingertips were butterfly-light on the small of her back. "Car?" he echoed, as though the word were foreign.

There was a soft, quivering ache in one corner of Libby's heart. Why couldn't things always be like this between them? Why did they have to wrangle so fiercely before achieving this quiet accord? "Stop teasing me," she said softly. "We did come here to buy a car, you know."

Jess's hands pulled her blouse up and out of her slacks, made slow-moving, sensuous circles on her bare back. "Yes," he said in a throaty rumble. "A car. But there are lots of different kinds of cars, aren't there, Libby? And a decision like this can't be made in haste."

Libby closed her eyes, almost hypnotized by the slow, languid meter of his words, the depth of his voice. "N-no," she agreed.

"Definitely not," he said, his mouth almost upon hers. "It could take two—or three—days to decide."

"Ummm," agreed Libby, slipping deeper and deeper under his spell.

Jess had pressed her back against a counter, and his body formed an impassable barricade, leaning, hard and fragrant, into hers. He was tracing the length of her neck with soft, searing lips, tasting the hollow beneath her ear.

Finally he kissed her, first with tenderness, then with fervor, his tongue seeking and being granted sweet entry. This preliminary joining made Libby's whole entity pulse with an awareness of the primitive differences between his body and her own. Where she was soft and yielding, he was fiercely hard. Her nipples pouted into tiny peaks, crying out for his attention.

Seeming to sense that, Jess unbuttoned her blouse with deft, brazen fingers that felt warm against her skin. He opened the front catch on her bra, admired the pink-tipped lushness that seemed to grow richer and rounder under his gaze.

Idly he bent to kiss one peak into ferocious submission, and Libby groaned, her head falling back. Etched against the clear roof, she saw the long needles of ponderosa pines splintering the spring moonlight into shards of silver.

After almost a minute of pleasure so keen that Libby

was certain she couldn't bear it, Jess turned to the other breast, kissing, suckling, nipping softly with his teeth. And all the while, he worked the opposite nipple skillfully with his fingers, putting it through delicious paces.

Libby was almost mindless by the time she felt the snap and zipper of her jeans give way, and her hands were still tangled in his dark hair as he knelt. Down came the jeans, her panties with them.

She could manage no more than a throaty gasp as his hands stroked the smooth skin of her thighs, the V of curls at their junction. She felt his breath there, warm, promising to cherish.

Libby trembled as he sought entrance with a questioning kiss, unveiled her with fingers that would not await permission.

As his tongue first touched the tenderness that had been hidden, his hands came to Libby's hips, pressing her down onto this fiery, inescapable glory. Only when she pleaded did he tug her fully into his mouth and partake of her.

Jess enjoyed Libby at his leisure, demanding her essence, showing no mercy even when she cried out and shuddered upon him in a final, soaring triumph. When her own chants of passion had ceased, she was conscious of his.

Jess still knelt before her, his every touch saying that he was worshiping, but there was sweet mastery in his manner, too. After one kiss of farewell, he gently drew her jeans and panties back into place and stood.

Libby stared at him, amazed at his power over her. He smiled at her wonder, though there was a spark of that same emotion deep in his eyes, and then lifted her off her feet and into his arms.

Say "I love you," Libby thought with prayerful fervor.

"I need you," he said instead.

And, for the moment, it was enough.

Stars peeked through the endlessly varied patterns the fallen pine needles made on the glass roof, as if to see and assess the glory that glowed beneath. Libby preened under their celestial jealousy and cuddled closer to Jess's hard, sheet-entangled frame.

"Why didn't you ever marry, Jess?" she asked, tracing a soft path across his chest with her fingers.

The mattress shifted as he moved to put one arm around Libby and draw her nearer still. "I don't know. It always seemed that marriage could wait."

"Didn't you even come close?"

Jess sighed, his fingers moving idly in her hair. "A couple of times I seriously considered it, yes. I guess it bothered me, subliminally, that I was looking these women over as though they were livestock or something. This one would have beautiful children, that one would like living on the ranch—that sort of thing."

"I see."

Jess stiffened slightly beneath the patterns she was making in the soft swirls of hair on his chest, and she felt the question coming long before he uttered it.

"What attracted you to Aaron Strand?"

Libby had been pondering that mystery herself, ever since her marriage to Aaron had begun to dissolve. Now, suddenly, she was certain that she understood.

Weak though he might be, Aaron Strand was tall, dark-haired, broad in the shoulders. He had given the impression of strength and self-assurance, qualities that any woman would find appealing.

"I guess I thought he was strong, like Dad," she said, because she couldn't quite amend the sentence to a full truth and admit that she had probably superimposed Jess's image over Aaron's in the first place.

"Ummm," said Jess noncommittally.

"Of course, he is actually very weak."

Jess offered no comment.

"I guess my mistake," Libby went on quietly, "was in seeing myself through Aaron's eyes. He made me feel so worthless…"

"Maybe that made him feel better about himself."

"Maybe. But I still hate him, Jess—isn't that awful? I still hate him for leaving Jonathan in the lurch like that, especially."

"It isn't awful, it's human. It appears that you and Jonathan needed more than he had to give. Unconsciously, you probably measured him against Ken, and whatever else he is, your dad is a hard act to follow, Libby."

"Yes," said Libby, but she was thinking: *I didn't measure Aaron against Dad. God help me, Jess, I measured him against you.*

Jess turned over in a graceful, rolling motion, so that he was above her, his head and shoulders blocking out the light of the stars. "Enough heavy talk, woman. I came here to—"

"Buy a car?" broke in Libby, her tone teasing and full of love.

He nuzzled his face between her warm, welcoming breasts. "My God," he said, his voice muffled by her satin flesh, "what an innocent you are, Libby Kincaid!" One of his hands came down, gentle and mischievous, to squeeze her bottom. "Nice upholstery."

Libby gasped and arched her back as his mouth slid up over the rounding of her breast to claim its peak. "Not much mileage," she choked out.

Jess laughed against the nipple he was tormenting so methodically. "A definite plus." His hand moved between her thighs to assert an ancient mastery, and his breath quickened at Libby's immediate response. "Starts easily," he muttered, sipping at her nipple now, tugging it into an obedient little point.

Libby was beyond the game now, rising and falling on the velvet swells of need he was stirring within her. "I... Oh, God, Jess...what are you...ooooh!"

Somehow, Jess managed to turn on the bedside lamp without interrupting the searing pace his right hand was setting for Libby's body. "You are a goddess," he said.

The fevered dance continued, even though Libby willed herself to lie still. Damn him, he was watching her, taking pleasure from the unbridled response she could not help giving. Her heart raced with exertion, blood boiled in every vein, and Jess's lazy smile was lost in a silver haze.

She sobbed out his name, groping for his shoulders with her hands, holding on. Then, shuddering violently, she tumbled into some chasm where there was no sound but the beat of her own heart.

"You like doing that, don't you?" she snapped when she could see again, breathe again.

"Yes," replied Jess without hesitation.

Libby scrambled into a sitting position, blue eyes shooting flames. "Bastard," she said.

He met her gaze placidly. "What's the matter with you?"

Libby wasn't quite sure of the answer to that question. "It just…it just bothers me that you were…you were looking at me," she faltered, covering her still-pulsing breasts with the bedclothes.

With a deliberate motion of his hands, Jess removed the covers again, and Libby's traitorous nipples puckered in response to his brazen perusal. "Why?" he asked.

Libby's cheeks ached with color, and she lowered her eyes. Instantly Jess caught her chin in a gentle grasp, made her look at him again.

"Sweetheart, you're not ashamed, are you?"

Libby couldn't reply, she was so confused.

His hand slid, soothing, from Libby's chin to the side of her face. "You were giving yourself to me, Libby, trusting me. Is there shame in that?"

She realized that there wasn't, not the way she loved this brazen, tender, outlandish man. If only she dared to tell him verbally what her body already had.

He kissed her softly, sensing her need for greater reassurance. "Exquisite," he said. "Even ordinarily, you are exquisite. But when you let me love you, you go beyond that. You move me on a level where I've never even been touched before."

Say it now, Libby urged silently, *say you love me.*

But she had to be satisfied with what he had already said, for it was immediately clear that there would be no poetic avowals of devotion forthcoming. He'd said she was exquisite, that she moved him, but he'd made no declaration.

For this reason, there was a measure of sadness in the lovemaking that followed.

Long after Jess slept, exhausted, beside her, Libby lay awake, aching. She wanted, needed more from Jess than his readily admitted lust. So much more.

And yet, if a commitment were offered, would Libby want to accept it? Weren't there already too many conflicts complicating their lives? Though she tried to shut out the memory, Libby couldn't forget that Jess had believed her capable of carrying on with his brother and hurting her cousin and dearest friend in the process. Nor could she forget the wedge that had been driven between them the first time they'd made love, when she'd slipped and uttered words that had made him feel as though she'd used him to prove herself as a woman.

Of course, they had come together again, despite these things, but that was of no comfort to Libby. If they were to achieve any real closeness, more than just their bodies would have to be in accord.

After several hours, Libby fell into a fitful, dream-ridden sleep. When morning came, casting bright sunlight through the expanse of glass overhead, she was alone in the tousled bed.

"Lib!"

She went to the edge of the loft, peering down over the side. "What?" she retorted, petulant in the face of Jess's freshly showered, bright-and-shiny good cheer.

He waved a cooking spatula with a flourish. "One egg or two?"

"Drop dead," she replied flatly, frowning at the ladder.

Jess laughed. "Watch it. You'll get my hopes up with such tender words."

"What's this damned ladder for, anyway?"

"Are you this grouchy every morning?" he countered.

"Only when I've engaged in illicit sex the night before!" Libby snapped, scowling. "I believe I asked you about the ladder?"

"It's for climbing up and down." Jess shrugged.

Libby's head throbbed, and her eyes felt puffy and sore. "Given time, I probably could have figured out that much!"

Jess chuckled and shook his head, as if in sympathy.

Libby grasped the top of the peculiar ladder in question and gave it a vigorous shake. It was immovable. Her puzzlement made her feel even more irritable and, for no consciously conceived reason, she put out her tongue at Jess Barlowe and whirled away from the edge of the loft, out of his view.

His laughter rang out as she stumbled into the bathroom and turned on the water in the shower stall.

Once she had showered and brushed her teeth, Libby began to feel semihuman. With this came contrition for the snappish way she had greeted Jess minutes before. It wasn't his fault, after all, that he was so nauseatingly happy in the mornings.

Grinning a mischievous grin, Libby rummaged through the suitcase she had so hastily packed and found the T-shirt she had bought for Jess the day before, when she'd come to Kalispell with Cathy. She pulled the garment on over her head and, in a flash of daring, swung over the loft to climb down the ladder.

Her reward was a low, appreciative whistle.

"Now I know why that ladder was built," Jess said. "The view from down here is great."

Libby was embarrassed; she'd thought Jess was in the kitchen and thus unable to see her novel descent from the loft. Reaching the floor, she whirled, her face crimson, to glare at him.

Jess read the legend printed on the front of the T-shirt, which was so big that it reached almost to her knees, and laughed explosively. "'If it feels good, do it'?" he marveled.

Libby's glare simply would not stay in place, no matter how hard she tried to sustain it. Her mouth twitched and a chuckle escaped her and then she was laughing as hard as Jess was.

Given the situation, his words came as a shock.

"Libby, will you marry me?"

She stared at him, bewildered, afraid to hope. "What?"

The jade eyes were gentle now, still glistening with residual laughter. "Don't make me repeat it, princess."

"I think the eggs are burning," said Libby in tones made wooden by surprise.

"Wrong. I've already eaten mine, and yours are congealing on your plate. What's your answer, Kincaid?"

Libby's throat ached; something about the size of her heart was caught in it. "I... What..."

"I thought you only talked in broken sentences at the height of passion. Are you really as surprised as all that?"

"Yes!" croaked Libby after a struggle.

The broad shoulders, accentuated rather than hidden by a soft yellow sweater, moved in a shrug. "It seemed like a good solution to me."

"A solution? To what?"

"All our separate and combined problems," answered Jess airily. Persuasively. "Think about it, Lib. Stacey couldn't very well hassle you anymore, could he? And you could stay on the ranch."

Despite the companionable delivery, Jess's words made Libby's soul ache. "Those are solutions for me. What problems would marriage solve for you?"

"We're good in bed," he offered, shattering Libby with what he seemed to mean as a compliment.

"It takes more than that!"

"Does it?"

Libby was speechless, though a voice inside her kept screaming silly, sentimental things. *What about love? What about babies and leftover meatloaf and filing joint tax returns?*

"You dad would be happy," Jess added, and he couldn't have hurt Libby more if he'd raised his hand and slapped her.

"My dad? My *dad*?"

Jess turned away, seemingly unaware of the effect his convoluted proposal was having on Libby. He looked like exactly what he was: a trained, skillful attorney pleading a weak case. "You want children, don't you? And I know you like living on the ranch."

Libby broke in coldly. "I guess I meet all the qual-ifications. I do want children. I do like living on the

Circle Bar B. So why don't you just hog-tie me and brand me a Barlowe?"

Every muscle in Jess's body seemed to tense, but he did not turn around to face her. "There is one other reason," he offered.

For all her fury and hurt, hope sang through Libby's system like the wind unleashed on a wide prairie. "What's that?"

He drew a deep breath, his hands clasped behind him, courtroom style. "There would be no chance, for now at least, of Cathy being hurt."

Cathy. Libby's knees weakened; she groped for the sofa behind her, fell into it. Good God, was his devotion to Cathy so deep that he would marry the woman he considered a threat to her happiness, just to protect her?

"I am so damned tired of hearing about Cathy," she said evenly, tugging the end of the T-shirt down over her knees for something to do.

Now Jess turned, looked at her with unreadable eyes.

Even though Libby felt the guilt she always did whenever she was even mildly annoyed with Cathy, she stood her ground. "A person doesn't have to be disabled to hurt, you know," she said in a small and rather uncertain voice.

Jess folded his arms and the sunlight streaming in through the glass ceiling glittered in his dark hair. "I know that," he said softly. "And we all have challenges, don't we?"

She couldn't tell whether he was reprimanding her or offering an olive branch. Huddling on the couch, feeling foolish in the T-shirt she had put on as a joke,

Libby knotted her hands together in her lap. "I suppose that remark was intended as a barb."

Jess came to sit beside her on the couch, careful not to touch her. "Libby, it wasn't. I'm tired of exchanging verbal shots with you—that was fine when we had to ride the same school bus every day, but we're adults now. Let's try to act as such."

Libby looked into Jess's face and was thunderstruck by how much she cared for him, needed him. And yet, even a week before, she would have said she despised Jess and meant it. All that rancor they'd borne each other—had it really been passion instead?

"I don't understand any of this."

Jess took one of her hands into both of his. "Do you want to marry me or not?"

Both fear and joy rose within Libby. In order to look inward at her own feelings, she was forced to look away from him. She did love Jess, there was absolutely no doubt of that, and she wanted, above all things, to be his wife. She wanted children and, at thirty-one, she often had the feeling that time was getting short. Dammit, why couldn't he say he loved her?

"Would you be faithful to me, Jess?"

He touched her cheek, turning her face without apparent effort, so that she was again looking into those bewitching green eyes. "I would never betray you."

Aaron had said those words, too. Aaron had been so very good with words.

But this was Jess, Libby reminded herself. Jess, not Aaron. "I couldn't give up my career," she said. "It's a crazy business, Jess, and sometimes there are long stretches of time when I don't do much of anything.

Other times, I have to work ten- or twelve-hour days to meet a deadline."

Jess did not seem to be dissuaded.

Libby drew a deep breath. "Of course, I'd go on being known as Libby Kincaid. I never took Aaron's name and I don't see any sense in taking yours—should I agree to marry you, that is."

He seemed amused, but she had definitely touched a sore spot. That became immediately obvious. "Wait a minute, lady. Professionally, you can be known by any name you want. Privately, however, you'll be Libby Barlowe."

Libby was secretly pleased, but because she was angry and hurt that he didn't love her, she lifted her chin and snapped, "You have to have that Circle Bar B brand on everything you consider yours, don't you?"

"You are not a thing, Libby," he replied rationally, "but I want at least that much of a commitment. Call it male ego if you must, but I want my wife to be Mrs. Barlowe."

Libby swallowed. "Fair enough," she said.

Jess sat back on the sofa, folded his arms again. "I'm waiting," he said, and the mischievous glint was back in his eyes.

"For what?"

"An answer to my original question."

Fool, fool! Don't you ever learn, Libby Kincaid? Don't you ever learn? Libby quieted the voice in her mind and lifted her chin. Life was short, and unpredictable in the bargain. Maybe Jess would learn to love her the way she loved him. Wasn't that kind of happiness worth a risk?

"I'll marry you," she said.

Jess kissed her with an exuberance that soon turned to desire.

Jess frowned at the sleek showroom sports car, his tongue making one cheek protrude. "What do you think?" he asked.

Libby assessed the car again. "It isn't you."

He grinned, ignoring the salesman's quiet disappointment. "You're right."

Neither, of course, had the last ten cars they had looked at been "him." The sports cars seemed to cramp his long legs, while the big luxury vehicles were too showy.

"How about another truck?" Libby suggested.

"Do you know how many trucks there already are on the ranch?" he countered. "Besides, some yokel would probably paint on the family logo when I wasn't looking."

Libby deliberately widened her eyes. "That would be truly terrible!"

He made a face at her, but when he spoke, his words were delivered in a touchingly serious way. "We could get a van and fill the seats with kids and dogs."

Libby smiled at the image. "A grungy sort of heaven," she mused.

Jess laughed. "And of course there would be lots of room to make love."

The salesman cleared his throat and discreetly walked away.

Chapter 9

"I think you shocked that salesman," observed Libby, snapping the seat belt into place as Jess settled behind the wheel of their rental car.

Jess shrugged. "By wanting a van?" he teased.

"By wanting *me* in the van," clarified Libby.

Jess turned the key in the ignition and shifted gears. "He's lucky I didn't list all the other places I'd like to have you. The hood, for instance. And then there's the roof…"

Libby colored richly as they pulled into the slow traffic. "Jess!"

He frowned speculatively. "And, of course, on the ladder at the condo."

"The ladder?"

Jess flung her a brazen grin. "Yeah. About halfway up."

"Don't you think about anything but sex?"

"I seem to have developed a fixation, Kincaid—just since you came back, of course."

She couldn't help smiling. "Of course."

Nothing more was said until they'd driven through the quiet, well-kept streets to the courthouse. Jess parked the car and turned to Libby with a comical leer. "Are you up to a blood test and a little small-town bureaucracy, Kincaid?"

Libby felt a wild, twisting thrill in the pit of her stomach. A marriage license. He wanted to get a marriage license. In three short days, she could be bound to Jess Barlowe for life. At least, she *hoped* it would be for life.

After drawing a deep breath, Libby unsnapped her seat belt and got out of the car.

Twenty minutes later, the ordeal was over. The fact that the wedding itself wouldn't take nearly as long struck Libby as an irony.

On the sidewalk, Jess caught her elbow in one hand and helped her back into the car. While he must have noticed that she was preoccupied, he was chivalrous enough not to say so.

"Stop at that supermarket!" Libby blurted when they'd been driving for some minutes.

Jess gave her a quizzical look. "Supermarket?"

"Yes. They sell food there, among other necessary items."

Jess frowned. "Why can't we just eat in restaurants? There are several good ones—"

"Restaurants?" Libby cried with mock disdain. "How can I prove what a great catch I am if I don't cook something for you?"

Jess's right hand left the steering wheel to slide languorously up and down Libby's linen-skirted thigh. "Relax, sweetheart," he said in a rather good imitation of Humphrey Bogart. "I already know you're good in the kitchen."

The obvious reference to last night's episode in that room unsettled Libby. "You delight in saying outrageous things, don't you?" she snapped.

"I delight in *doing* outrageous things."

"You'll get no argument on that score, fella," she retorted acidly.

The car came to a stop in front of the supermarket, which was in the center of a small shopping mall. Libby noticed that Jess's gaze strayed to a jewelry store down the way.

"I'll meet you inside," he said, and then he was gone.

Though Libby told herself that she was being silly and sentimental, she was pleased to think that Jess might be shopping for a ring.

The giddy, romantic feeling faded when she selected a shopping cart inside the supermarket, however. She was wallowing in gushy dreams, behaving like a seventeen-year-old virgin. Of *course* Jess would buy a ring, but only because it would be expected of him.

Glumly Libby went about selecting items from a mental grocery list she had been composing since she'd checked the refrigerator and cupboards at the condominium and found them all but empty.

Taking refuge in practical matters, she frowned at a display of cabbage and wondered how much food to buy. Jess hadn't said how long they would be staying in Kalispell, beyond the time it would take to find the car he wanted.

Shrugging slightly, Libby decided to buy provisions for three days. Because that was the required waiting period for a marriage license, they would probably be in town at least that long.

She looked down at her slacks and brightly colored top. The wedding ceremony was going to be an informal one, obviously, but she would still need a new dress, and she wanted to buy a wedding band for Jess, too.

She pushed her cart along the produce aisle, woodenly selecting bean sprouts, fresh broccoli, onions. Her first wedding had been a quiet one, too, devoid of lace and flowers and music, and something within her mourned those things.

They hadn't even discussed a honeymoon, and what kind of ceremony would this be, without Ken, without Cathy, without Senator Barlowe and Marion Bradshaw, the housekeeper?

A box seemed to float up out of the cart, but Libby soon saw that it was clasped in a strong sun-browned hand.

"I hate cereals that crunch," Jess said, and his eyes seemed to be looking inside Libby, seeing the dull ache she would rather have kept hidden. "What's wrong, love?"

Libby fought back the sudden silly tears that ached in her throat and throbbed behind her eyes. "Nothing," she lied.

Jess was not fooled. "You want Ken to come to the wedding," he guessed.

Libby lowered her head slightly. "He was hurt when

Aaron and I got married without even telling him first," she said.

There was a short silence before a housewife, tagged by two preschoolers, gave Libby's cart a surreptitious bump with her own, tacitly demanding access to the cereal display. Libby wrestled her groceries out of the way and looked up at Jess, waiting for his response.

He smiled, touched her cheek. "Tell you what. We'll call the ranch and let everybody know we're getting married. That way, if they want to be there, they can. And if you want frills and flash, princess, we can have a formal wedding later."

The idea of a second wedding, complete with the trimmings, appealed to Libby's romantic soul. She smiled at the thought. "You would do that? You would go through it all over again, just for show?"

"Not for show, princess. For you."

The housewife made an appreciative sound and Libby started a little, having completely forgotten their surroundings.

Jess laughed and the subject was dropped. They walked up one aisle and down another, dropping the occasional pertinent item into the cart, arguing good-naturedly about who would do the cooking after they were married.

The telephone was ringing as Libby unlocked the front door of the condo, so she left Jess to carry in their bags of groceries and ran to answer it, expecting to hear Ken's voice, or Marion Bradshaw's, relaying some message from Cathy.

A cruel wave of déjà vu washed over her when she heard Aaron's smooth, confident greeting. "Hello, Libby."

"What do you want?" Libby rasped, too stunned to hang up. How on earth had he gotten that number?

"I told you before, dear heart," said Aaron smoothly. "I want a child."

Libby was conscious of Jess standing at her elbow, the shopping bags clasped in his arms. "You're insane!" she cried into the receiver.

"Maybe so, but not insane enough to let my grandmother hand over an empire to someone else. She has doubts, you know, about my dependability."

"I wonder why!"

"Don't be sarcastic, sugarplum. My request isn't really all that unreasonable, considering all I stand to lose."

"It is unreasonable, Aaron! In fact, it's sick!" At this point Libby slammed down the receiver with a vengeance. She was trembling so hard that Jess hastily shunted the grocery bags onto a side table and took her into his arms.

"What was that all about?" he asked when Libby had recovered herself a little.

"He's horrible," Libby answered, distracted and very much afraid. "Oh, Jess, he's a monster—"

"What did he say?" Jess pressed quietly.

"Aaron wants me to have his baby! Jess, he actually had the gall to ask me to come back, just so he can produce an heir and please his grandmother!"

Jess's hand was entangled in her hair now, comforting her. "It's all right, Lib. Everything will be all right."

Then why am I so damned scared? Libby asked herself, but she put on a brave face for Jess and even managed a smile. "Let's call my dad," she said.

Jess nodded, kissed her forehead. And then he took up the grocery bags again and carried them into the kitchen while Libby dialed her father's telephone number.

There was no answer, which was not surprising, considering that it was still early. Ken would be working, and because of the wide range of his responsibilities, he could be anywhere on the 150,000 acres that made up the Circle Bar B.

Sounds from the kitchen indicated that Jess was putting the food away, and Libby wandered in, needing to be near him.

"No answer?" he asked, tossing a package of frozen egg rolls into the freezer.

"No answer," confirmed Libby. "I should have known, I guess."

Jess turned, gave her a gentle grin. "You did know, Libby. But you needed to touch base just then, and going through the motions was better than nothing."

"When did you get so smart?"

"Last Tuesday, I think," he answered ponderously. "Know something? You look a little tired. Why don't you climb up that ladder that bugs you so much and take a nap?"

Libby arched one eyebrow. "While you do what?"

His answer was somewhat disappointing. "While I go back to town for a few hours," he said. "I have some things to do."

"Like what?"

He grinned. "Like picking up some travel brochures, so we can decide where to take our honeymoon."

Libby felt a rush of pleasure despite the weariness

she was suddenly very aware of. Had it been there all along, or was she tired simply because this subtle hypnotist had suggested it to her? "Does it matter where we honeymoon?"

"Not really," Jess replied, coming disturbingly close, kissing Libby's forehead. "But I like having you all to myself. I can't help thinking that the farther we get from home right now, the better off we're going to be."

A tremor of fear brushed against Libby's heart, but it was quickly stilled when Jess caught her right earlobe between gentle teeth and then told her in bluntly erotic terms what he had wanted to do to her on the supermarket checkout counter.

When he'd finished, Libby was wildly aroused and, at the same time, resigned to the fact that when she crawled into that sun-washed bed up in the loft, she would be alone. "Rat," she said.

Jess swatted her backside playfully. "Later," he promised, and then calmly left the condo to attend to his errands.

Libby went obediently up to the bedroom, using the stairs rather than the ladder, and yawned as she stripped down to her lacy camisole and panties. She shouldn't be having a nap now, she told herself, when she had things of her own to do—choosing Jess's ring, for one thing, and buying a special dress, for another...

She was asleep only seconds after slipping beneath the covers.

Libby stirred, indulged in a deliciously lazy stretch. Someone was trailing soft, warm kisses across her collarbone—or was she dreaming? Just in case she was, she did not open her eyes.

Cool air washed over her breasts as the camisole was gently displaced. "Ummm," she said.

"Good dream?" asked Jess, moistening one pulsing nipple to crisp attention with his tongue.

"Oooooh," answered Libby, arching her back slightly, her eyes still closed, her head pressed into the silken pillow in eager, soft surrender. "Very good."

Jess left that nipple to subject its twin to a tender plundering that caused Libby to moan with delight. Her hips writhed slightly, calling to their powerful counterpart.

Jess heard their silent plea, slid the satiny panties down, down, away. "You're so warm, Libby," he said in a ragged whisper. "So soft and delicious." The camisole was unlaced, laid aside reverently, like the wrapping on some splendid gift. Kisses rained down on Libby's sleep-warmed, swollen breasts, her stomach, her thighs.

At last she opened her eyes, saw Jess's wondrous nakedness through a haze of sweet, sleepy need. As he ventured nearer and nearer to the silk-sheltered sanction of her womanhood, she instinctively reached up to clasp the brass railings on the headboard of the bed, anchoring herself to earth.

Jess parted the soft veil, admired its secret with a throaty exclamation of desire and a searing kiss.

A plea was wrenched from Libby, and she tightened her grasp on the headboard.

For a few mind-sundering minutes Jess enjoyed the swelling morsel with his tongue. "More?" he asked, teasing her, knowing that she was already half-mad with the need of him.

"More," she whimpered as his fingers strayed to the pebblelike peaks of her breasts, plying them, sending an exquisite lacelike net of passion knitting its way through her body.

Another tormenting flick of his tongue. "Sweet," he said. And then he lifted Libby's legs, placing one over each of his shoulders, making her totally, beautifully vulnerable to him.

She cried out in senseless delirium as he took his pleasure, and she was certain that she would have been flung beyond the dark sky if not for her desperate grasp on the headboard.

Even after the highest peak had been scaled, Libby's sated body convulsed again and again, caught in the throes of other, smaller releases.

Still dazed, Libby felt Jess's length stretch out upon her, seeking that sweetest and most intimate solace. In a burst of tender rebellion, she thrust him off and demanded loving revenge.

Soon enough, it was Jess who grasped the gleaming brass railings lest he soar away, Jess who chanted a desperate litany.

Wickedly, Libby took her time, savoring him, taking outrageous liberties with him. Finally she conquered him, and his cry of joyous surrender filled her with love almost beyond bearing.

His breathing still ragged, his face full of wonder, Jess drew Libby down, so that she lay beside him. With his hands he explored her, igniting tiny silver fires in every curve and hollow of her body.

This time, when he came to her, she welcomed him with a ferocious thrust of her hips, alternately setting the pace and following Jess's lead. When the pinnacle was reached, each was lost in the echoing, triumphant cry of the other, and bits of a broken rainbow showered down around them.

Sitting cross-legged on the living-room sofa, Libby twisted the telephone cord between her fingers and waited for her father's response to her announcement.

It was a soft chuckle.

"You aren't the least bit surprised!" Libby accused, marveling.

"I figured anybody that fought and jawed as much as you two did had to end up hitched," replied Ken Kincaid in his colorful way. "Did you let Cleave know yet?"

"Jess will, in a few minutes. Will you tell Cathy for me, please?"

Ken promised that he would.

Libby swallowed hard, gave Jess a warning glare as he moved to slide an exploring hand inside the top of her bathrobe. "Aren't you going to say that we're rushing into this or something like that? Some people will think it's too soon—"

"It was damned near too late," quipped Ken. "What time is the ceremony again?"

There were tears in Libby's eyes, though she had never been happier. "Two o'clock on Friday, at the courthouse."

"I'll be there, dumplin'. Be happy."

The whole room was distorted into a joyous blur. "I will, Dad. I love you."

"I love you, too," he answered with an ease that was typical of him. "Take care and I'll see you Friday."

"Right," said Libby, sniffling as she gently replaced the receiver.

Jess chuckled, touched her chin. "Tears? I'm insulted."

Libby made a face and shoved the telephone into his lap. "Call your father," she said.

Jess settled back in the sofa as he dialed the number of the senator's house in Washington, balancing the telephone on one blue-jeaned knee. While he tried to talk to his father in normal tones, Libby ran impudent fingertips over his bare chest, twining dark hair into tight curls, making hard buttons of deliciously vulnerable nipples.

With a mock-glare and a motion of his free arm, Jess tried to field her blatant advances. She simply knelt astraddle of his lap and had her way with him, her fingers tracing a path of fire around his mouth, along his neck, over his nipples.

Jess caught the errant hand in a desperate hold, only to be immediately assaulted by the other. Mischief flashed in his jade eyes, followed by an I'll-get-you-for-this look. "See you then," he said to his father, his voice a little deeper than usual and very carefully modulated. There was a pause, and then he added, "Oh, don't worry, I will. In about five seconds, I'm going to lay Libby on the coffee table and kiss her in all the best places. Yes, sir, by the time I get through with her, she'll be—"

Falling into the trap, Libby colored, snatched the receiver out of Jess's hand and pressed it to her ear. The line was, of course, dead.

Jess laughed as she assessed him murderously. "You deserved that," he said.

Libby moved to struggle off his lap, still crimson in the face, her heart pounding with embarrassment. But Jess's hands were strong on her upper arms, holding her in place.

"Oh, no you don't, princess. You're not getting out of this so easily."

"What—"

Jess smiled languidly, still holding her fast with one hand, undoing his jeans with the other. "You let this horse out of the barn, lady. Now you're going to ride it."

Libby gasped as she felt him prod her, hard and insistent, and fierce needs surged through her even as she raged at the affront. She was powerless, both physically and emotionally, to break away from him.

Just barely inside her, Jess reached out and calmly untied her bathrobe, baring her breasts, her stomach, her captured hips. His green eyes glittered as he stroked each satiny expanse in turn, allowing Libby more and more of him until she was fully his.

Seemingly unmoved himself, Jess took wicked delight in Libby's capture and began guiding her soft, trim hips up and down, endlessly up and down, upon him. All the while, he used soft words to lead her through flurries of silver snow to the tumultuous release beyond.

When her vision cleared, Libby saw that Jess had been caught in his own treachery. She watched in love and wonder as he gave himself up to raging sensation—

his head fell back, his throat worked, his eyes were sightless.

Gruffly Jess pleaded with Libby, and she accelerated the up-and-down motion of her hips until he shuddered violently beneath her, stiffened and growled her name.

"Mess with me, will you?" she mocked, grinning down at him.

Jess began to laugh, between rasping breaths. When his mirth had subsided and he didn't have to drag air into his lungs, he caressed her with his eyes. In fact, it was almost as though he'd said he loved her.

Libby was still incredibly moved by the sweet spectacle she had seen played out in his face as he submitted to her, and she understood then why he so loved to watch her respond while pleasuring her.

Jess reached up, touched away the tear that tickled on her cheek. It would have been a perfect time for those three special words she so wanted to hear, but he did not say them.

Hurt and disappointed, Libby wrenched her bathrobe closed and tried to rise from his lap, only to be easily thwarted. Jess's hands opened the robe again, his eyes perused her and then came back to her face, silently daring her to hide any part of her body or soul from him.

With an insolent finger he brushed the pink buttons at the tips of her full breasts, smiled as they instantly obeyed him. Apparently satisfied with their pert allegiance, Jess moved on to trace patterns of fire on Libby's stomach, the rounding of her hips, the sensitive hollow at the base of her throat.

Jess seemed determined to prove that he could subdue Libby at will, and he only smiled at the startled gasp she gave when it became apparent that all his prowess had returned in full and glorious force.

He slid her robe off her shoulders then and removed it entirely. They were still joined, and Libby shivered as he toyed idly with her breasts, weighing them in his hands, pressing them together, thumbing their aching tips until they performed for him.

Presently Jess left his sumptuous playthings to tamper elsewhere, wreaking still more havoc, eliciting little anxious cries from a bedazzled Libby.

"What do you want, princess?" he asked in a voice of liquid steel.

Libby was wild upon him, her hands clutching desperately at his shoulders, her knees wide. "I want to be…under you. Oh, Jess…under you…"

In a swift and graceful motion, he turned her, was upon her. The movement unleashed the passion Jess had been able to contain until then, and he began to move over her and within her, his thrusts deep and powerful, his words ragged and incoherent.

As their very souls collided and then fused together, imitating their bodies, it was impossible to tell who had prevailed over whom.

Libby awakened first, entangled with Jess, amazed that they could have slept the whole night on that narrow couch.

A smile lifted one corner of her mouth as she kissed Jess's temple tenderly and then disengaged herself, careful not to disturb him. Heaven knew, he had a right to be tired.

Twenty minutes later, when Libby returned from her

shower, dressed in sandals, white slacks and a light-weight yellow sweater, Jess was still sleeping. She could empathize, for her own slumber had been fathomless.

"I love you," she said, and then she went to the kitchen and wrote a quick note on the blackboard there, explaining that she had gone shopping and would be back within a few hours.

Getting into the rented car, which was parked in the gravel driveway near the front door, Libby spotted a cluster of colorful travel brochures fanned out on the opposite seat. Each one touted a different paradise: Acapulco, the Bahamas, Maui.

As Libby slid the key into the ignition and started the car, she grinned. She had it on good authority that paradise was only a few yards away, on the couch where Jess lay sleeping.

The day was a rich mixture of blue and green, set off by the fierce green of pine trees and the riotous blooms of crocuses and daffodils in quiet front yards. Downtown, Libby found a parking place immediately, locked the car and hurried on about her business.

Her first stop was a jewelry store, and while she had anticipated a great quandary, the decision of which wedding band to buy for Jess proved an easy one. Her eyes were immediately drawn to one particular ring, forged of silver, inset with polished chips of turquoise.

Once the jeweler had assured her the band could be resized if it didn't fit Jess's finger, Libby bought it.

In an art-supply store she purchased a sketching pad and a gum eraser and some charcoal pencils. Sweet as this interlude with Jess had been, Libby missed her work and her fingers itched to draw. Too, there were all sorts of new ideas for the comic strip bubbling in her mind.

From the art store, Libby pressed on to a good-sized department store. None of the dresses there quite struck her fancy, and she moved on to one boutique and then another.

Finally, in a small and wickedly expensive shop, she found that special dress, that dress of dresses, the one she would wear when she married Jess Barlowe.

It was a clingy creation of burgundy silk, showing off her figure, bringing a glow of color to her cheeks. There were no ruffles of lace or fancy buttons—only a narrow belt made of the same fabric as the dress itself. It was the last word in elegant simplicity, that garment, and Libby adored it.

Carrying the dress box and the heavy bag of art supplies, she hurried back to the car and locked her purchases inside. It was only a little after ten, and Libby wanted to find shoes that would match her dress.

The shoes proved very elusive, and only after almost an hour of searching did she find a pair that would do. Tired of shopping and anxious to see Jess again, Libby started home.

Some intuitive feeling made her uneasy as she drove toward the elegant condominium hidden in the tall trees. After crossing the wooden bridge and making the last turn, she knew why—Stacey's ice-blue Ferrari was parked in the driveway.

Don't be silly, Libby reprimanded herself, but she still felt alarmed. What if Stacey had come to try to talk her out of marrying Jess? What if Cathy was with him, and there was an unpleasant scene?

Determined not to let her imagination get the upper hand, Libby gathered up her loot from the shopping trip and got out of the car. As she approached the house, she caught sight of a familiar face at the window and was surprised all over again. Monica! What on earth was she doing here? Hadn't she left for Washington, D.C., with the senator?

Now Libby really hesitated. She remembered the proprietary looks the woman had given Jess as he swam that day in the pool at the main ranch house. Looks that had implied intimacy.

Libby sighed. So what if Jess and Monica had slept together? She could hardly have expected a man like him to live like a monk, and it wasn't as if Libby hadn't had a prior relationship herself, however unsatisfactory.

Despite the cool sanity of this logic, it hurt to imagine Jess making love with Monica—or with any other woman, for that matter.

Libby grappled with her purchases at the front door, reached for the knob. Before she could clasp it, the door opened.

Jess was standing there, shirtless, wearing jeans, his hair and suntanned chest still damp from a recent shower. Instead of greeting Libby with a smile, let alone a kiss, he scowled at her and stepped back almost grudgingly, as though he had considered refusing her entrance.

Bewildered and hurt, Libby resisted a primal instinct urging her to flee and walked in.

Monica had left the window and was now seated comfortably on the couch, her shapely legs crossed at the knee, a cocktail in her hand.

Libby took in the woman's sleek designer suit and felt shabby by comparison in her casual attire. "Hello, Monica."

"Libby," replied Monica with a polite nod.

The formalities dispensed with, Libby flung a hesitant look at Jess. Why was he glaring at her like that, as though he wanted to do her bodily harm? Why was his jawline so tight, and why was it that he clenched the towel draped around his neck in white-knuckled hands?

Before Libby could voice any of her questions, Stacey came out of the kitchen, raked her with guileless caramel eyes and smiled.

"Hello," he said, as though his very presence, under the circumstances, was not an outrage.

Libby only stared at him. She was very conscious of Jess, seething somewhere on the periphery of her vision, and of Monica, taking in the whole scene with detached amusement.

Suddenly Stacey was coming toward Libby, speaking words she couldn't seem to hear. Then he had the outright gall to kiss her, and Libby's inertia was broken.

She drew back her hand and slapped him, her dress box, purse and bag of art supplies falling to the floor.

Stacey reached out for her, caught her waist in his hands. She squirmed and flung one appealing look in Jess's direction.

Though he looked anything but chivalrous, he did intercede. "Leave Libby alone, Stacey."

Stacey paled. "I've left Cathy," he said, as though that settled everything. "Libby, we can be together now!"

Libby stumbled backward, stunned. Only when she came up against the hard barrier of Jess's soap-scented body did she stop. Wild relief went through her as he enclosed her in a steel-like protective embrace.

"Get out," he said flatly, addressing his brother.

Stacey hesitated, but then he reddened and left the condo in a huff, pulling Monica Summers behind him.

Chapter 10

Furious and shaken, Libby turned to glare at Jess. It was all too clear what had happened—Stacey had been telling more of his outrageous lies and Jess had believed them.

For a few moments he stubbornly returned her angry regard, but then he spread his hands in a gesture of concession and said, "I'm sorry."

Libby was trembling now, but she stooped to pick up her dress box, and the art-store bag. She couldn't look at Jess or he would see the tears that had clouded her eyes. "After all we've done and planned, how could you, Jess? How could you believe Stacey?"

He was near, very near—Libby was conscious of him in every sense. He moved to touch her, instantly stopped himself. "I said I was sorry."

Libby forgot that she'd meant to hide her tears and looked him full in the face. Her voice shook with anger when she spoke. "Sometimes being sorry isn't enough, Jess!" She carried the things she'd bought across the room, tossed them onto the couch. "Is this what our marriage is going to be like? Are we going to do just fine as long as we aren't around Stacey?"

Jess was standing behind her; his hands came to rest on her shoulders. "What can I say, Libby? I was jealous. That may not be right, but it's human."

Perhaps because she wanted so desperately to believe that everything would turn out all right, that a marriage to this wonderful, contradictory man would succeed, Libby set aside her doubts and turned to face Jess. The depth of her love for this erstwhile enemy still staggered her. "What did Stacey tell you?"

Jess drew in an audible breath, and for a moment there was a tightness in his jaw. Then he sighed and said, "He was sharing the glorious details of your supposed affair. And he had a remarkable grasp on what you like in bed, Libby."

The words were wounding, but Libby was strong. "Did it ever occur to you that maybe all women like essentially the same things?"

Jess didn't answer, but Libby could see that she had made her mark, and she rushed on.

"Exactly what was Monica's part in all this?" she demanded hotly. "Was she here to moderate your sexual discussion? Why the hell isn't she in Washington, where she belongs?"

Jess shrugged, obviously puzzled. "I'm not sure why she was here."

"I am! Once you were diverted from your disastrous course—marrying me—she was going to take you by the hand and lead you home!"

One side of Jess's mouth lifted in a grin. "I'm not the only one who is prone to jealousy, it appears."

"You were involved with her, weren't you?"

"Yes."

The bluntness of the answer took Libby unawares, but only for a moment. After all, had Jess said no, she would have known he was lying and that would have been devastating. "Did you love Monica?"

"No. If I had, I would have married her."

The possible portent of those words buoyed Libby's flagging spirits. "Passion wouldn't be enough?" she ventured.

"To base a marriage on? Never. Now, let's see what you bought today."

Let's see what you bought today. Libby's frustration knew no bounds, but she was damned if she was going to pry those three longed-for words out of him—she'd fished enough as it was. "I bought a wedding dress, for your information. And you're not going to see it until tomorrow, so don't pester me about it."

He laughed. "I like a woman who is loyal to her superstitions. What else did you purchase, milady?"

Libby's sense of financial independence, nurtured during the insecure days with Aaron, chafed under the question. "I didn't use your money, so what do you care?" she snapped.

Jess arched one eyebrow. "Another touchy subject rears its ugly head. I was merely curious, my love—I didn't ask for a meeting with your accountant."

Feeling foolish, Libby made a great project of opening the art-store bag and spreading its contents out on
the couch.

Jess was grinning as he assessed the array of pencils, the large sketchbook. "Have I been boring you,
princess?"

Libby pulled a face at him. "You could be called
many things, Jess Barlowe, but you are definitely not
boring."

"Thank you—I think. Shall we brave the car dealers
of Kalispell again, or are you going to be busy?" The
question was guileless, indicating that Jess would have
understood if she wanted to stay and block out some of
the ideas that had come to her.

After Aaron, who had viewed her cartooning as a
childish hobby, Jess's attitude was a luxury. "I think I'd
rather go with you," she said with a teasing smile. "If I
don't you might come home with some motorized horror that has horns on its hood."

"Your faith in my good taste is positively under-
whelming," he replied, walking toward the ladder,
climbing its rungs to the loft in search of a shirt.

"You were right!" Libby called after him. "The view
from down here is marvelous!"

During that foray into the jungle of car salesmen and
gasoline-fed beasts, Libby spent most of her time in the
passenger seat of Jess's rented car, sketching. Instead of
drawing Liberated Lizzie, her cartoon character, however, she found herself reproducing Jess's image.

She imagined him looking out over the stunning
view of prairies and mountains at home and drew him
in profile, the wind ruffling his hair, a pensive look to

his eyes and the set of his face. Another sketch showed him laughing, and still another, hidden away in the middle of the drawing pad, not meant for anyone else to see, mirrored the way Jess looked when he wanted her.

To field the responses the drawing evoked in her, Libby quickly sketched Cathy's portrait, and then Ken's. After that, strictly from memory, she drew a picture of Jonathan, full face, as he'd looked before his illness, then, on the same piece of paper, in a profile that revealed the full ravages of his disease.

She supposed it was morbid, including this aspect of the child, but to leave out his pain would have meant leaving out his courage, and Jonathan deserved better.

Touching his charcoal image with gentle, remembering fingers, Libby heard the echo of his voice in her mind. *Naturally I'm brave*, he'd told her once, at the end of a particularly difficult day. *I'm a Jedi knight, like Luke Skywalker.*

Smiling through a mist of tears, Libby added another touch to the sketch—a tiny figure of Jonathan, well and strong, wielding a light saber in valiant defense of the Rebel Alliance.

"That's terrific," observed a gentle voice.

Libby looked up quickly, surprised that she hadn't heard Jess get into the car, hadn't sensed his presence somehow. Because she couldn't speak just yet, she bit her lower lip and nodded an acknowledgment of the compliment.

"Could I take a closer look? Please?"

Libby extended the notebook and it was a gesture of trust, for these sketches were different from the panels for her comic strip. They were large pieces of her soul.

Jess was pensive as he examined the portraits of himself, Cathy, Ken. But the study of Jonathan was clearly his favorite, and he returned to it at intervals, taking in each line, each bit of shading, each unspoken cry of grief.

Finally, with a tenderness that made Libby love him even more than she had before, Jess handed the sketchbook back to her. "You are remarkably talented," he said, and then he had the good grace to look away while Libby recomposed herself.

"D-did you find a car you like?" she asked finally.

Jess smiled at her. "Actually, yes. That's why I came back—to get you."

"Me? Why?"

"Well, I don't want to buy the thing without your checking it out first. Suppose you hated it?"

It amazed Libby that such a thing mattered to him. She set the sketchbook carefully in the backseat and opened her car door to get out. "Lead on," she said, and the clean spring breeze braced her as it touched her face.

The vehicle in question was neither car nor truck, but a Land Rover. It was perfectly suited to the kind of life Jess led, and Libby approved of it with enthusiasm.

The deal was made, much to the relief of a salesman they had been plaguing, on and off, since the day before.

After some discussion, it was decided that they would keep the rental car until after the wedding, in case Libby needed it. Over a luncheon of steak and salad, which did much to settle her shaky nerves, Jess suggested that they start shopping all over again, for a second car.

Practical as it was, the thought exhausted Libby.

"You'll need transportation," Jess argued.

"I don't think I could face all those plaid sport jackets and test drives again," Libby replied with a sigh.

Jess laughed. "But you would like to have a car, wouldn't you?"

Libby shrugged. In New York, she had depended on taxis for transportation, but the ranch was different, of course. "I suppose."

"Aren't you choosy about the make, model—all that?"

"Wheels are wheels," she answered with another shrug.

"Hmmmm," Jess said speculatively, and then the subject was changed. "What about our honeymoon? Any place in particular you'd like to go?"

"Your couch," Libby said, shocked at her own audacity.

Again Jess laughed. "That is patently unimaginative."

"Hardly, considering the things we did there," Libby replied, immediately lifting a hand to her mouth. What was wrong with her? Why was she suddenly spouting these outlandish remarks?

Jess bent forward, conjured up a comical leer. "I wish we were on the ranch," he said in a low voice. "I'd take you somewhere private and make violent love to you."

Libby felt a familiar heat simmering inside her, melting through her pelvis. "Jess."

He drew some bills from his wallet, tossed them onto the table. "Let's get out of here while I can still walk," he muttered.

Libby laughed. "I think it's a good thing we're driving separate cars today," she teased, though secretly she was just as anxious for privacy as Jess was.

He groaned. "One more word, lady, and I'll spread you out on this table."

Libby's heart thudded at the bold suggestion and pumped color over her breasts and into her face. She tried to look indignant, but the fact was that she had been aroused by the remark and Jess knew it—his grin was proof of that.

As they left the restaurant, he bent close to her and described the fantasy in vivid detail, sparing nothing. And later, on the table in the condo's kitchen, he turned it into a wildly satisfying reality.

That afternoon, Libby took another nap. Due to the episode just past, her dreams were deliciously erotic.

As he had before, Jess awakened her with strategic kisses. "Hi," he said when she opened her eyes.

She touched his hair, noted that he was wearing his brown leather jacket. "You've been out." She yawned.

Jess kissed the tip of her nose. "I have indeed. Bought you a present or two, as a matter of fact."

The glee in Jess's eyes made Libby's heart twist in a spasm of tenderness; whatever he'd purchased, he was very pleased with. She slipped languid arms around his neck. "I like presents," she said.

Jess drew back, tugged her camisole down so that her breasts were bared to him. Almost idly he kissed each dusty-rose peak and then covered them again. "Sorry," he muttered, his mouth a fraction of an inch from hers. "I couldn't resist."

That strange, magical heat was surging from Libby's just-greeted breasts to her middle, down into her thighs and even her knees. She felt as though every muscle and bone in her body had melted. "You m-mentioned presents?"

He chuckled, kissed her softly, groaned under his breath. "I was momentarily distracted. Get out of bed, princess. Said presents await."

"Can't you just...bring them here?"

"Hardly." Jess withdrew from the bed to stand at its side and wrench back the covers. His green eyes smoldered as he took in the sleep-pinkened glow of her curves, and he bent to swat her satin-covered backside. "Get up," he repeated.

Libby obeyed, curious about the gifts but disappointed that Jess hadn't joined her in the bed, too. She found a floaty cotton caftan and slipped it on.

Jess looked at her, made a low growling sound in his throat, and caught her hand in his. "Come on, before I give in to my baser instincts," he said, pulling her down the stairs.

Libby looked around curiously as he dragged her across the living room but saw nothing out of the ordinary.

Jess opened the front door, pulled her outside. There, beside his maroon Land Rover, sat a sleek yellow Corvette with a huge rosette of silver ribbon affixed to its windshield.

Libby gaped at the car, her eyes wide.

"Like it?" Jess asked softly, his mouth close to her ear.

"Like it?" Libby bounded toward the car, heedless of her bare feet. "I love it!"

Jess followed, opened the door on the driver's side so that Libby could slide behind the wheel. When she did that, she got a second surprise. Taped to the gear-shift knob was a ring of white gold, and the diamond setting formed the Circle Bar B brand.

"I'll hog-tie you later," Jess said.

Libby's hand trembled as she reached for the ring; it blurred and shifted before her eyes as she looked at it. "Oh, Jess."

"Listen, if you hate it…"

Libby ripped away the strip of tape, slid the ring onto her finger. "Hate it? Sacrilege! It's the most beautiful thing I've ever seen."

"Does it fit?"

The ring was a little loose, but Libby wasn't ready to part with it, not even to let a jeweler size it. "No," she said, overwhelmed, "but I don't care."

Gently Jess lifted her chin with his hand, bent to sample her mouth with his. Beneath the hastily donned caftan and her camisole, Libby's nipples hardened in pert response.

"There's only one drawback to this car," Jess breathed, his lips teasing Libby's, shaping them. "It would be impossible to make love in it."

Libby laughed and pretended to shove him. "Scoundrel!"

"You don't know the half of it," he replied hoarsely, drawing Libby out of the beautiful car and back inside the house.

There she gravitated toward the front windows, where she could alternately admire her new car and watch the late-afternoon sun catch in the very special ring on her finger. Standing behind her, Jess wrapped his arms around her waist and held her close, bending to nip at her earlobe.

"Thank you, Jess," Libby said.

He laughed, and his breath moved in Libby's hair and sent warm tingles through her body. "No need for thanks. I'll nibble on your ears anytime."

"You know what I meant!"

His hands had risen to close over her breasts, fully possessing them. "What? What did you mean?" he teased in a throaty whisper.

Libby could barely breathe. "The car...the ring..."

Letting his hands slip from her breasts to her elbows, Jess ushered Libby over to face the mirror above the fireplace. As she watched his reflection in wonder, he undid the caftan's few buttons and slid it slowly down over her shoulders. Then he drew the camisole up over her head and tossed it away.

Libby saw a pink glow rise over her breasts to shine in her face, saw the passion sparking in her dark blue eyes, saw Jess's hands brush upward over her rib cage toward her breasts. The novelty of watching her own reactions to the sensations he was stirring inside her was erotic.

She groaned as she saw—and felt—masculine fingers rise to her waiting nipples and pluck then gently to attention.

"See?" Jess whispered at her ear. "See how beautiful you are, Libby? Especially when I'm loving you."

Libby had never thought of herself as beautiful, but now, looking at her image in the mirror, seeing how passion darkened her eyes to indigo and painted her cheeks with its own special apricot shade, she felt ravishing.

She tilted her head back against the hard breadth of Jess's shoulder, moaned as he softly plundered her nipples.

He spoke with a gruff, choked sort of sternness. "Don't close your eyes, Libby. Watch. You're beautiful— so beautiful—and I want you to know it."

It was hard for Libby not to close her eyes and give herself up to the incredible sensations that were raging through her, but she managed it even as Jess came from behind her to bend his head and take suckle at one breast.

Watching him do this, watching the heightened color in her own face, gave a new intensity to the searing needs that were like storm winds within Libby. Her eyes were fires of ink-blue, and there was a proud, even regal lift to her chin as she watched herself pleasing the man she loved.

Jess drank deeply of one breast, turned to the other. It was an earthy communion between one man and one woman, each one giving and taking.

Presently Jess's mouth slid down over Libby's slightly damp stomach, and then he was kneeling, no longer visible in the magic mirror. "Don't close your eyes," he repeated, and Libby felt her satiny panties sliding slowly down over her hips, her knees, her ankles.

The wide-eyed sprite in the mirror gasped, and Libby was forced to brace herself with both hands against the mantelpiece, just to keep from falling. Her breathing quickened to a rasp as Jess ran skilled hands over her bare bottom, her thighs, the backs of her knees. He heightened her pleasure by telling her precisely what he meant to do.

And then he did it.

Libby's release was a maelstrom of soft sobs that finally melded together into one lusty cry of pleasure. Jess was right, she thought, in the midst of all this and during the silvery descent that followed: she *was* beautiful.

Standing again, Jess lifted Libby up into his arms. Still feeling like some wanton Gypsy princess, she let her head fall back and gloried in the liberties his mouth took with the breasts that were thrust into easy reach.

Libby was conscious of an otherworldly floating sensation as she and Jess glided downward, together, to the floor.

Rain pattered and danced on the glass ceiling above the bed, a dismal heralding of what promised to be the happiest day of Libby Kincaid's life.

Jess slept beside her, beautifully naked, his breathing deep and even. If he hadn't actually spoken of his love, he had shown it in a dozen ways. So why did the pit of Libby's stomach jiggle, as though something awful was about to happen?

The insistent ringing of the doorbell brought Jess up from his stomach, push-up style, grumbling. His dark hair hopelessly rumpled, his eyes glazed, he stumbled around the bedroom until he found his robe and managed to struggle into it.

Libby laughed at him as he started down the stairs. "So much for being happy in the mornings, Barlowe," she taunted.

His answer was a terse word that Libby couldn't quite make out.

She heard the door open downstairs, heard Senator Barlowe's deep laugh and exuberant greeting. The sounds eased the feeling of dread that had plagued Libby earlier, and she got out of bed and hurried to the bathroom for a shower.

Periodically, as Libby shampooed her hair and washed, she laughed. Having his father arrive unexpectedly from Washington, probably with Ken and Cathy soon to follow, would certainly throw cold water on any plans the groom might have had for prenuptial frolicking.

When Libby went downstairs, her hair blown dry, her makeup in place, she was delighted to see that Cathy was with the senator. They were both, in fact, seated comfortably on the couch, drinking coffee.

"Where's Dad?" Libby asked when hugs and kisses had been exchanged.

Cleave Barlowe, with his elegant, old-fashioned manners, waited for Libby to sit down before returning to his own seat near Cathy. "He'll be here in time for the ceremony," he said. "When we left the ranch, he was heading out with that bear patrol of his."

Libby frowned and fussed with her crisp pink sundress, feeling uneasy again. Jess had gone upstairs, and she could hear the water running in the shower. "Bear patrol?"

"We've lost a few calves to a rogue grizzly," Cleave said easily, as though such a thing were an everyday occurrence. "Ken and half a dozen of his best men have been tracking him, but they haven't had any luck so far."

Cathy, sitting at her father-in-law's elbow, seemed to sense her cousin's apprehension and signed that she wanted a better look at Libby's ring.

The tactic worked, but as Libby offered her hand, she at last looked into Cathy's face and saw the ravages of her marital problems. There were dark smudges under the green eyes, and a hollow ache pulsed inside them.

Libby reprimanded herself for being so caught up in her own tumultuous romance with Jess as to forget that during his visit the day before, Stacey had said he'd left Cathy. It shamed Libby that she hadn't thought more about her cousin, made it a point to find out how she was.

"Are you all right?" she signed, knowing that Cathy was always more comfortable with this form of communication than with lip reading.

Cathy's responding smile was real, if wan. She nodded and with mischievous interest assessed the ring Jess had had specially designed.

Cleave demanded a look at this piece of jewelry that was causing such an "all-fired" stir and laughed with appreciation when he saw his own brand in the setting.

Cathy lifted her hands. "I want to see your dress."

After Jess had come downstairs, dressed in jeans and the scandalous T-shirt Libby had given him, the two women went up to look at the new burgundy dress.

The haunted look was back in Cathy's eyes as she approved the garment. "I can hardly believe you're marrying Jess," she said in the halting, hesitant voice she would allow only Libby to hear.

Libby sat down on the rumpled bed beside her cousin. "That should settle any doubts you might have had about my relationship with Stacey," she said gently.

Cathy's pain was a visible spasm in her face. "He's

living at the main house now," she confessed. "Libby, Stacey says he wants a divorce."

Libby's anger with Stacey was equal only to her sympathy for his wife. "I'm sure he doesn't mean any of the things he's been saying, Cathy. If only you would talk to him…"

The emerald eyes flashed. "So Stacey could laugh at me, Libby? No, thanks!"

Libby drew a deep breath. "I can't help thinking that this problem stems from a lack of communication and trust," she persisted, careful to face toward her cousin. "Stacey loves you. I know he does."

"How can you be so sure?" whispered Cathy. "How, Libby? Marriages end every day of the week."

"No one knows that better than I do. But some things are a matter of instinct, and mine tells me that Stacey is doing this to make you notice him, Cathy. And maybe because you won't risk having a baby."

"Having a baby would be pretty stupid, wouldn't it? Even if I wanted to take the risk, as you call it. After all, my husband moved out of our house!"

"I'm not saying that you should rush back to the ranch and get yourself pregnant, Cathy. But couldn't you just talk to Stacey, the way you talk to me?"

"I told you—I'd be embarrassed!"

"Embarrassed! You are married to the man, Cathy— you share his bed! How can you be embarrassed to let him hear your voice?"

Cathy knotted her fingers together in her lap and lowered her head. From downstairs Libby could hear Jess and the senator talking quietly about the vote

Cleave had cast before coming back to Montana for the wedding.

Finally Cathy looked up again. "I couldn't talk to anyone but you, Libby. I don't even talk to Jess or Ken."

"That's your own fault," Libby said, still angry. "Have you kept your silence all this time—all during the years I've been away?"

Cathy shook her head. "I ride up into the foothills sometimes and talk to the wind and the trees, for practice. Do you think that's silly?"

"No, and stop being so afraid that someone is going to think you're silly, dammit! So what if they do? What do you suppose people thought about me when I stayed with a man who had girlfriends?"

Cathy's mouth fell open. "Girlfriends?"

"Yes," snapped Libby, stung by the memory. "And don't tell my dad. He'd faint."

"I doubt it," replied Cathy. "But it must have hurt terribly. I'm so sorry, Libby."

"And I'm sorry if I was harsh with you," Libby answered. "I just want you to be happy, Cathy—that's all. Will you promise me that you'll talk to Stacey? Please?"

"I... I'll try."

Libby hugged her cousin. "That's good enough for me."

There was again a flash of delight in Cathy's eyes, indicating an imminent change of subject. "Is that car outside yours?"

Libby's answer was a nod. "Isn't it beautiful?"

"Will you take me for a ride in it? When the wedding is over and you're home on the ranch?"

"You know I will. We'll be the terror of the back roads—legends in our own time!"

Cathy laughed. "Legends? We'll be memories if we aren't careful."

Libby rose from her seat on the bed, taking up the pretty burgundy dress, slipping it carefully onto a hanger, hanging it in the back of the closet.

When that was done, the two women went downstairs together. By this time Jess and his father were embroiled in one of their famous political arguments.

Feeling uneasy again, Libby went to the telephone with as much nonchalance as she could and dialed Ken's number. There was no answer, of course—she had been almost certain that there wouldn't be—but the effort itself comforted her a little.

"Try the main house," Jess suggested softly from just behind her.

Libby glanced back at him, touched by his perception. Consoled by it. "How is it," she teased in a whisper, "that you managed to look elegant in jeans and a T-shirt that says 'If it feels good, do it'?"

Jess laughed and went back to his father and Cathy.

Libby called the main house and got a somewhat flustered Marion Bradshaw. "Hello!" barked the woman.

"Mrs. Bradshaw, this is Libby. Have you seen my father this morning?"

There was a long sigh, as though the woman was relieved to learn that the caller was not someone else. "No, dear, I haven't. He and the crew are out looking for that darned bear. Don't you worry, though—Ken told me he'd be in town for your wedding in plenty of time."

Libby knew that her father's word was good. If he

said he'd be there, he would, come hell or high water. Still, something in Mrs. Bradshaw's manner was disturbing. "Is something the matter, Marion?"

Another sigh, this one full of chagrin. "Libby, one of the maids told me that a Mr. Aaron Strand called here, asking where you could be reached. Without so much as a by-your-leave, that woman came right out and told him you were in Kalispell and gave him the number. I'm so sorry."

So that was how Aaron had known where to call. Libby sighed. "It's all right, Marion—it wasn't your fault."

"I feel responsible all the same," said the woman firmly, "but I'll kick myself on my own time. I just wanted to let you know what happened. Did Miss Cathy and the senator get there all right?"

Libby smiled. "Yes, they're here. Any messages?"

"No, but I'd like a word with Jess, if it's all right."

Libby turned and gestured to the man in question. He came to the phone, took the receiver, greeted Marion Bradshaw warmly. Their conversation was a brief one, and when Jess hung up, he was laughing.

"What's so funny?" the senator wanted to know.

Jess slid an arm around Libby and gave her a quick squeeze. "Dare I say it in front of the creator of Liberated Lizzie, cartoon cave-woman? I just got Marion's blessing—she says I branded the right heifer."

Chapter 11

Libby stood at a window overlooking the courthouse parking lot, peering through the gray drizzle, anxiously scanning each vehicle that pulled in.

"He'll be here," Cathy assured her, joining Libby at the rain-sheeted window.

Libby sighed. She knew that Ken would come if he possibly could, but the rain would make the roads hazardous, and there was the matter of that rogue grizzly bear. "I hope so," she said.

Cathy stood back a little to admire the flowing silken lines of Libby's dress. "You look wonderful. Here—let's see if the flowers match."

"Flowers?" Libby hadn't thought about flowers, hadn't thought about much at all, beyond contemplating the wondrous event about to take place. Her reason said that it was insanity to marry again, especially to marry Jess Barlowe, but her heart sang a very different song.

Cathy beamed and indicated a cardboard box sitting on a nearby table.

At last Libby left her post at the window, bemused. "But I didn't…"

Cathy was already removing a cellophane-wrapped corsage, several boutonnieres, an enormous bouquet made up of burgundy rosebuds, baby's breath, and white carnations. "This is yours, of course."

Libby reached out for her bridal bouquet, pleased and very surprised. "Did you order these, Cathy?"

"No," replied Cathy, "but I did nudge Jess in the florist's direction, after seeing what color your dress was."

Moved that such a detail had been taken into consideration, Libby hugged her cousin. "Thank you."

"Thank Jess. He's the one that browbeat the florist into filling a last-minute order." Cathy found a corsage labeled with her name. "Pin this on, will you?"

Libby happily complied. There were boutonnieres for Jess and the senator and Ken, too, and she turned this last one wistfully in her hands. It was almost time for the ceremony to begin—where was her father?

A light tap at the door made Libby's heart do a jittery flip. "Yes?"

"It's me," Jess said in a low, teasing voice. "Are the flowers in there?"

Cathy gathered up the boutonnieres, white carnations wrapped in clear, crackly paper, made her way to the door. Opening it just far enough to reach through, she held out the requested flowers.

Jess chuckled but made no move to step past the barrier and see his bride before the designated moment. "Five minutes, Libby," he said, and then she heard him walking away, his heels clicking on the marble courthouse floor.

Libby went back to the window, spotted a familiar truck racing into the parking lot, lurching to a stop. Two men in rain slickers got out and hurried toward the building.

Ken had arrived, and at last Libby was prepared to join Jess in Judge Henderson's office down the hall. She saw that august room through a haze of happiness, noticing a desk, a flag, a portrait of George Washington. In front of the rain-beaded windows, with their heavy, threadbare velvet draperies, stood Jess and his father.

Everyone seemed to move in slow motion. The judge took his place, and Jess, looking quietly magnificent in a tailored three-piece suit of dark blue, took his. His eyes caressed Libby, even from that distance, and somehow drew her toward him. At his side stood the senator, clearly tired from his unexpected cross-country trip, but proud and pleased, too.

Like a person strolling through a sweet dream, Libby let Jess draw her to him. At her side was Cathy, standing up very straight, her green eyes glistening with joyous tears.

Libby's sense of her father's presence was so strong that she did not need to look back and confirm it with her eyes. She tucked her arm through Jess's and the ceremony began.

When all the familiar words had been said, Jess bent toward Libby and kissed her tenderly. The haze lifted and the bride and groom turned, arm in arm, to face their few but much-loved guests.

Instead of congratulations, they met the pain-filled stares of two cowboys dressed in muddy jeans, sodden shirts and raincoats.

Suddenly frantic, Libby scanned the small chamber for her father's face. She'd been so sure that he was there; he had seemed near enough to touch.

"Where—" she began, but her question was broken off because Jess left her side to stride toward the emissaries from the ranch, the senator close behind him.

"The bear…" said one of them in answer to Jess's clipped question. "We had him cornered and—" the cowboy's Adam's apple moved up and down in his throat "—and he was a mean one, Mr. Barlowe. Meaner'n the devil's kid brother."

Libby knew what was coming and the worn courthouse carpeting seemed to buckle and shift beneath her high-heeled burgundy sandals. Had it not been for Cathy, who gripped her elbow and maneuvered her into a nearby chair, she would have fallen.

"Just tell us what happened!" Jess rasped.

"The bear worked Ken over pretty good," the second cowboy confessed.

Libby gave a strangled cry and felt Cathy's arm slide around her shoulders.

"Is Ken dead?" demanded Cleave Barlowe, and as far as Libby was concerned, the whole universe hinged on the answer to that question.

"No, sir—we got Mr. Kincaid to the hospital fast as we could. But…but."

"But what?" hissed Jess.

"The bear got away, Mr. Barlowe."

Jess came slowly toward Libby, or at least it seemed so to her. As he crouched before her chair and took her chilled hands into his, his words were gentle. "Are you all right?"

Libby was too frightened and sick to speak, but she did manage a nod. Jess helped her to her feet, supported her as they left the room.

She was conscious of the cowboys, behind her, babbling an account of the incident with the bear to Senator Barlowe, of Cathy's quiet sobs, of Jess's steel arm around her waist. The trip to the hospital, made in the senator's limousine, seemed hellishly long.

At the hospital's admissions desk, they were told by a harried, soft-voiced nurse that there was no news yet and directed to the nearest waiting room.

Stacey was there, and Cathy ran to him. He embraced her without hesitation, crooning to her, smoothing her hair with one hand.

"Ken?" barked the senator, his eyes anxious on his elder son's pale face.

"He's in surgery," replied Stacey. And though he still held Cathy, his gaze shifted, full of pain and disbelief, to Libby. "It's bad," he said.

Libby shuddered, more afraid than she'd ever been in her life, her arms and legs useless. Jess was holding her up—Jess and some instinct that had lain dormant within her since Jonathan's death. "Were you there when it happened, Stacey?" she asked dully.

Stacey was rocking Cathy gently in his arms, his chin propped in her hair. "Yes," he replied.

Suddenly rage surged through Libby—a senseless, shrieking tornado of rage. "You had guns!" she screamed. "I know you had guns! Why didn't you stop the bear? Why didn't you kill it?"

Jess's arm tightened around her. "Libby—"

Stacey broke in calmly, his voice full of compassion even in the face of Libby's verbal attack. "There was too much chance that Ken would be hit," he answered. "We hollered and fired shots in the air and that finally scared the grizzly off." There was a hollow look in Stacey's eyes as they moved to his father's face and then Jess's, looking for the same understanding he had just given to Libby.

"What about the bear?" the senator wanted to know.

Stacey averted his eyes for a moment. "He got away," he breathed, confirming what one of the cowboys had said earlier at the courthouse. "Jenkins got him in the hind flank, but he got away. Ran like a racehorse, that son of a bitch. Anyway, we were more concerned with Ken at the moment."

The senator nodded, but Jess tensed beside Libby, his gaze fierce. "You sent men after the grizzly, didn't you?"

Stacey looked pained and his hold on Cathy tightened as her sobs ebbed to terrified little sniffles. "I... I didn't think—"

"You didn't think?" growled Jess. "Goddammit, Stacey, now we've got a wounded bear on the loose—"

The senator interceded. "I'll call the ranch and make sure the grizzly is tracked down," he said reasonably. "Stacey got Ken to the hospital, Jess, and that was the most important thing."

An uncomfortable silence settled over the waiting

room then. The senator went to the window to stand, hands clasped behind his back, looking out. The cowboys went back to the ranch, and Stacey and Jess maneuvered their stricken wives into chairs.

The sounds and smells peculiar to a hospital were a torment to Libby, who had endured the worst minutes, hours, days, and weeks of her life in just such a place. She had lost Jonathan in an institution like this one—would she lose Ken, too?

"I can't stand it," she whispered, breaking the awful silence.

Jess took her chin in his hand, his eyes locking with hers, sharing badly needed strength. "Whatever happens, Libby, we'll deal with it together."

Libby shivered violently, looked at Jess's tailored suit, her own dress, the formal garb of Cathy and the senator. Only Stacey, in his muddy jeans, boots, shirt and sodden denim jacket, seemed dressed for the horrible occasion. The rest of the party was at ludicrous variance with the situation.

My father may be dying, she thought in quiet hysteria, *and we're wearing flowers*. The smell of her bouquet suddenly sickened Libby, bringing back memories of Jonathan's funeral, and she flung it away. It slid under a couch upholstered in green plastic and cowered there against the wall.

Jess's grip tightened on her hand, but no one made a comment.

Presently the senator wandered out, returning some minutes later with cups of vending-machine coffee balanced on a small tray. "Ken is my best friend," he announced in befuddled tones to the group in general.

The words brought a startling cry of grief from Cathy, who had been huddled in her chair until that moment, behind a curtain of tangled, rain-dampened hair. "I won't let him die!" she shrieked, to the open-mouthed amazement of everyone except Libby.

Stacey, draped over the arm and back of Cathy's chair, stared down at her, his throat working. "Cathy?" he choked out.

Because Cathy was not looking at him, could not see her name on his lips, she did not answer. Her small hands flew to cover her face and she wept for the man who had loved her as his own child, raised her as his own, been her strength as well as Libby's.

"She can't hear you," Libby said woodenly.

"But she talked!" gasped Jess.

Libby lifted one shoulder in a broken shrug. "Cathy has been talking for years. To me, anyway."

"Good God," breathed the senator, his gaze sweeping over his shattered daughter-in-law. "Why didn't she speak to any of us?"

Libby was sorry for Stacey, reading the pain in his face, the shock. Of course, it was a blow to him to realize that his own wife had kept such a secret for so long.

"Cathy was afraid," Libby explained quietly. "She is very self-conscious about the way her voice sounds to hearing people."

"That's ridiculous!" barked Stacey, looking angry now, paler than before. He bolted away from Cathy's chair to stand at the windows, his back to the room. "For God's sake, I'm her husband!"

"Some of us had a few doubts about that," remarked Jess in an acid undertone.

Stacey whirled, full of fury, but the senator stepped between his two sons before the situation could get out of hand. "This is no time for arguments," he said evenly but firmly. "Libby and Cathy don't need it, and neither do I."

Both brothers receded, Stacey lowering his head a little, Jess averting a gaze that was still bright with anger. Libby watched a muscle leap in her husband's jaw and stifled a crazy urge to touch it with her finger, to still it.

"Was Dad conscious when you brought him here?" she asked of Stacey in a voice too calm and rational to be her own.

Stacey nodded, remembering. "He said that bear was almost as tough as a Mexican he fought once, down in Juarez."

The tears Libby had not been able to cry before suddenly came to the surface, and Jess held her until they passed. "Ken is strong," he reminded her. "Have faith in him."

Libby tried to believe the best, but the fact remained that Ken Kincaid was a mortal man, strong or not. And he'd been mauled viciously by a bear. Even if he survived, he might be crippled.

It seemed that Jess was reading her mind, as he so often did. His hand came up to stroke away her tears, smooth her hair back from her face. "Don't borrow trouble," he said gently. "We've got enough now."

Trying to follow this advice, Libby deliberately reviewed pleasant memories: Ken cursing a tangle of Christmas-tree lights; Ken sitting proudly in the audience while Cathy and Libby accepted their high school diplomas; Ken trying, and somehow managing, to be both mother and father.

More than two hours went by before a doctor appeared in the waiting room doorway, still wearing a surgical cap, his mask hanging from his neck. "Are you people here for Ken Kincaid?" he asked, and the simple words had the electrifying effect of a cattle prod on everyone there.

Both Libby and Cathy stiffened in their chairs, unable to speak. It was Jess who answered the doctor's question.

"Mr. Kincaid was severely injured," the surgeon said, "but we think he'll be all right, if he rests."

Libby was all but convulsed by relief. "I'm his daughter," she managed to say finally. "Do you think I could see him, just for a few minutes?"

The middle-aged physician smiled reluctantly. "He'll be in Recovery for some time," he said. "Perhaps it would be better if you visited your father tomorrow."

Libby was steadfast. It didn't matter that Ken was still under anesthetic; if she could touch his hand or speak to him, he would know that she was near. Another vigil had taught her the value of that. "I must see him," she insisted.

"She won't leave you alone until you say yes," Jess put in, his arm tight around Libby's shoulders.

Before the doctor could answer, Cathy was gripping Libby's hands, searching her cousin's face. "Libby?" she pleaded desperately. "Libby?"

It was clear that Cathy hadn't discerned the verdict on Ken's condition, and Libby's heart ached for her cousin as she freed her hands, quickly motioned the reassurances needed.

When that was done, Libby turned back to the doctor. "My cousin will want to see my father, too."

"Now, just a minute…"

Stubbornly Libby lifted her chin.

Three hours later, Ken Kincaid was moved from the recovery room to a bed in the intensive-care unit. As soon as he had been settled there, Cathy and Libby were allowed into his room.

Ken was unconscious, and there were tubes going into his nostrils, an IV needle in one of his hands. His chest and right shoulder were heavily bandaged, and there were stitches running from his right temple to his neck in a crooked, gruesome line.

"Oh, God," whimpered Cathy.

Libby caught her cousin's arm firmly in her hand and faced her. "Don't you *dare* fall apart in here, Cathy Barlowe," she ordered. "He would sense how upset you are, and that would be bad for him."

Cathy trembled, but she squared her shoulders, drew a deep breath and then nodded. "We'll be strong," she said.

Libby went to the bedside, barely able to reach her father for all the equipment that was monitoring and sustaining him. "I hear you beat up on a bear," she whispered.

There was no sign that Ken had heard her, of course, but Libby knew that humor reached this man as nothing else could, and she went on talking, berating him softly for cruelty to animals, informing him that the next time he wanted to waltz, he ought to choose a partner that didn't have fur.

Before an insistent nurse came to collect Ken's visitors, both Libby and Cathy planted tender kisses on his forehead.

Stacey, Jess and Cleave were waiting anxiously when they reached the waiting room again.

"He's going to live," Libby said, and then the room danced and her knees buckled and everything went dark.

She awakened to find herself on a table in one of the hospital examining rooms, Jess holding her hand.

"Thanks for scaring the hell out of me," he said softly, a relieved grin tilting one corner of his mouth. "I needed that."

"Sorry," Libby managed, touching the wilting boutonniere that was still pinned to the lapel of his suit jacket. "Some wedding day, huh, handsome?"

"That's the wild west for you. We like excitement out here. How do you feel, princess?"

Libby tried to sit up, but the room began to swirl, so she fell back down. "I'm okay," she insisted. "Or I will be in a few minutes. How is Cathy?"

Jess smiled, kissed her forehead. "Cathy reacted a little differently to the good news than you did."

Libby frowned, still worried. "How do you mean?"

"After she'd been assured that you had fainted and not dropped dead of a coronary, she lit into Stacey like a whirlwind. It seems that my timid little sister-in-law is through being mute—once and for all."

Libby's eyes rounded. "You mean she was yelling at him?"

"Was she ever. When they left, he was yelling back."

Despite everything, Libby smiled. "In this case, I think a good loud argument might be just what the doctor ordered."

"I agree. But the condo will probably be a war zone by the time we get there."

Libby remembered that this was her wedding night, and with a little help from Jess, managed to sit up. "The condo? They're staying there?"

"Yes. The couch makes out into a bed, and Cathy wants to be near the hospital."

Libby reached out, touched Jess's strong face. "I'm sorry," she said.

"About what?"

"About everything. Especially about tonight."

Jess's green eyes laughed at her, gentle, bright with understanding. "Don't worry about tonight, princess. There will be plenty of other nights."

"But—"

He stilled her protests with an index finger. "You are in no condition to consummate a marriage, Mrs. Barlowe. You need to sleep. So let's go home and get you tucked into bed—with a little luck, Stacey and Cathy won't keep us awake all night while they throw pots and pans at each other."

Jess's remark turned out to be remarkably apt, for when they reached the condo, Stacey and his wife were bellowing at each other and the floor was littered with sofa pillows and bric-a-brac.

"Don't mind us," Jess said with a companionable smile as he ushered his exhausted bride across the war-torn living room. "We're just mild-mannered honey-mooners, passing through."

Jess and Libby might have been invisible, for all the notice they got.

"Maybe we should have stayed in a motel," Libby yawned as she snuggled into Jess's strong shoulder, minutes later, in the loft bed.

Something shattered downstairs, and Jess laughed. "And miss this? No chance."

Cathy and Stacey were yelling again, and Libby winced. "You don't think they'll hurt each other, do you?"

"They'll be all right, princess. Rest."

Too tired to discuss the matter further, Libby sighed and fell asleep, lulled by Jess's nearness and the soft sound of rain on the glass roof overhead. She awakened once, in the depths of the night, and heard the sounds of another kind of passion from the darkened living room. A smile curved her lips as she closed her eyes.

Cathy was blushing as she tried to neaten up the demolished living room and avoid Libby's gaze at the same time. Stacey, dead to the world, was sprawled out on the sofa bed, a silly smile shaping his mouth.

Libby made her way to the telephone in silence, called the hospital for a report on her father. He was still unconscious, the nurse on duty told her, but his vital signs were strong and stable.

Cathy was waiting, wide-eyed, when Libby turned away from the telephone.

Gently Libby repeated what the nurse had told her.

After that, the two women went into the kitchen and began preparing a quick breakfast.

"I'm sorry about last night," Cathy said.

Standing at the stove, spatula in hand, Libby waited for her cousin to look at her and then asked, "Did you settle anything?"

Cathy's cheeks were a glorious shade of hot pink. "You heard!" she moaned.

Libby had been referring to the fight, not the love-making that had obviously followed, but there was no way she could clarify this without embarrassing her cousin further. She bit her lower lip and concentrated on the eggs she was scrambling.

"It was crazy," Cathy blurted, remembering. "I was *yelling* at Stacey! I wanted to hurt him, Libby—I really wanted to hurt him!"

Libby was putting slices of bread into the toaster and she offered no comment, knowing that Cathy needed to talk.

"I even threw things at him," confessed Cathy, taking orange juice from the refrigerator and putting it in the middle of the table. "I can't believe I acted like that, especially when Ken had just been hurt so badly."

Libby met her cousin's gaze and smiled. "I don't see what one thing has to do with the other, Cathy. You were angry with your husband—justifiably so, I'd say—and you couldn't hold it in any longer."

"I wasn't even worried about the way I sounded," Cathy reflected, shaking her head. "I suppose what happened to Ken triggered something inside me—I don't know."

"The important thing is that you stood up for yourself," Libby said, scraping the scrambled eggs out of the pan and onto a platter. "I was proud of you, Cathy."

"Proud? I acted like a fool!"

"You acted like an angry woman. How about calling those lazy husbands of ours to breakfast while I butter the toast?"

Cathy hesitated, wrestling with her old fear of being ridiculed, and then squared her shoulders and left the kitchen to do Libby's bidding.

Tears filled Libby's eyes at the sound of her cousin's voice. However ordinary the task was, it was a big step forward for Cathy.

The men came to the table, Stacey wearing only jeans and looking sheepish, Jess clad in slacks and a neatly pressed shirt, his green eyes full of mischief.

"Any word about Ken?" he asked.

Libby told him what the report had been and loved him the more for the relief in his face. He nodded and then executed a theatrical yawn.

Cathy blushed and looked down at her plate, while Stacey glared at his brother. "Didn't you sleep well, Jess?" he drawled.

Jess rolled his eyes.

Stacey looked like an angry little boy; Libby had forgotten how he hated to be teased. "I'll fight with my wife if I want to!" he snapped.

Both Libby and Jess laughed.

"Fight?" gibed Jess good-naturedly. "Was that what you two were doing? Fighting?"

"*Somebody* had to celebrate your wedding night," Stacey retorted, but then he gave in and laughed, too.

When the meal was over, Cathy and Libby left the

dirty dishes to their husbands and went off to get ready for the day.

They were allowed only a brief visit with Ken, and even though his doctor assured them that he was steadily gaining ground, they were both disheartened as they returned to the waiting room.

Senator Barlowe was there, with Jess and Stacey, looking as wan and worried as either of his daughters-in-law. Unaware of their approach, he was saying, "We've got every available man tracking that bear, plus hands from the Three Star and the Rocking C. All we've found so far is paw-prints and dead calves."

Libby was brought up short, not by the mention of the bear but by the look on Jess's face. He muttered something she couldn't hear.

Stacey sliced an ironic look in his brother's direction. "I suppose you think you can find that son of Satan when the hands from three of the biggest ranches in the state can't turn up a trace?"

"I know I can," Jess answered coldly.

"Dammit, we scoured the foothills, the ranges…"

Jess's voice was low, thick with contempt. "And when you had the chance to bring the bastard down, you let him trot away instead—wounded."

"What was I supposed to do? Ken was bleeding to death!"

"Somebody should have gone after the bear," Jess insisted relentlessly. "There were more than enough people around to see that Ken got to the hospital."

Stacey swore.

"Were you scared?" Jess taunted. "Did the big bad bear scare away our steak-house cowboy?"

At this, Stacey lunged toward Jess and Jess bolted out of his chair, clearly spoiling for a fight.

Again, as he had before, the senator averted disaster. "Stop it!" he hissed. "If you two have to brawl, kindly do it somewhere else!"

"You can bank on that," Jess said bitterly, his green gaze moving over Stacey and then dismissing him.

"What's gotten into the two of you?" Senator Barlowe rasped in quiet frustration. "This is a hospital! And have you forgotten that you're brothers?"

Libby cleared her throat discreetly, to let the men know that she and Cathy had returned. She was disturbed by the barely controlled hostility between Jess and his brother, but with Ken in the condition that he was, she had no inclination to pursue the issue.

It was later, in the Land Rover, when she and Jess were alone, that Libby voiced a subject that had been bothering her. "You plan to go looking for that bear, don't you?"

Jess appeared to be concentrating on the traffic, but a muscle in his cheek twitched. "Yes."

"You're going back to the ranch and track him down," Libby went on woodenly.

"That's right."

She sank back against the seat and closed her eyes. "Let the others do it."

There was a short, ominous silence. "No way."

Libby swallowed the sickness and fear that roiled in her throat. God in heaven, wasn't it enough that she'd nearly lost her father to that vicious beast? Did she have to risk losing her husband, too? "Why?" she whispered miserably. "Why do you want to do this?"

"It's my job," he answered flatly, and Libby knew that there was no point in trying to dissuade him.

She squeezed her eyes even more tightly shut, but the tears escaped anyway. When they reached the condo again, Stacey's car and Cleave's pulling in behind them, Jess turned to her, brushed the evidence of her fear from her cheeks with gentle thumbs and kissed her.

"I promise not to get killed," he said softly.

Libby stiffened in his arms, furious and full of terror. "That's comforting!"

He kissed the tip of her nose. "You can handle this alone, can't you? Going to the hospital, I mean?"

Libby bit her lower lip. Here was her chance. She could say that she needed Jess now, she could keep him from hunting that bear. She did need him, especially now, but in the end, she couldn't use weakness to hold him close. "I can handle it."

An hour later, when Stacey and the senator left for the ranch, Jess went with them. Libby was now keeping two vigils instead of one.

Understanding Libby's feelings but unable to help, Cathy built a fire in the fireplace, brewed cocoa, and tried to interest her cousin in a closed-caption movie on television.

Libby watched for a while, then got out her sketchbook and began to draw with furious, angry strokes: Jess on horseback, a rifle in the scabbard of his saddle; a full-grown grizzly, towering on its hind legs, ominous muscles rolling beneath its hide, teeth bared. Try though she did, Libby could not bring herself to put Jess and that bear in the same picture, either mentally or on paper.

That evening, when Libby and Cathy went to the hospital, Ken was awake. He managed a weak smile as they came to his bedside to bestow tearful kisses.

"Sorry about missin' the wedding," he said, and for all his obvious pain, there was mirth in his blue eyes.

Libby dashed away the mist from her own eyes and smiled a shaky smile, shrugging. "You've seen one, cowboy, you've seen them all."

Ken laughed and the sound was beautiful.

Chapter 12

Having assured herself that Ken was indeed recovering, Cathy slipped out to allow Libby a few minutes alone with her father.

"Thanks for scaring me half to death," she said.

Ken tried to shrug, winced instead. "You must have known I was too mean to go under," he answered. "Libby, did they get the bear?"

Libby stiffened. The bear, the bear—she was so damned sick of hearing about the bear! "No," she said after several moments, averting her eyes.

Ken sighed. He was pale and obviously tired. "Jess went after him, didn't he?"

Libby fought back tears of fear. Was Jess face to face with that creature even now? Was he suffering injuries like Ken's, or even worse? "Yes," she admitted.

"Jess will be all right, Libby."

"Like you were?" Libby retorted sharply, without thinking.

Ken studied her for a moment, managed a partial grin. "He's younger than I am. Tougher. No grizzly in his right mind would tangle with him."

"But this grizzly isn't in his right mind, is he?" Libby whispered, numb. "He's wounded, Dad."

"All the more reason to find him," Ken answered firmly. "That bear was dangerous before, Libby. He's deadly now."

Libby shuddered. "You'd think the beast would just crawl off and die somewhere."

"That would be real handy, but he won't do it, Lib. Grizzlies have nasty dispositions as it is—their eyesight is poor and their teeth hurt all the time. When they're wounded, they can rampage for days before they finally give out."

"The Barlowes can afford to lose a few cows!"

"Yes, but they can't afford to lose people, Lib, and that's what'll happen if that animal isn't found."

There was no arguing that; Ken was proof of how dangerous a bear could be. "The men from the Three Star and the Rocking C are helping with the hunt, anyway," Libby said, taking little if any consolation from the knowledge.

"That's good," Ken said, closing his eyes.

Libby bent, kissed his forehead and left the room.

Cathy was pacing the hallway, her lower lip caught in her teeth, her eyes wide. Libby chastised herself for not realizing that Stacey was probably hunting the bear too, and that her cousin was as worried as she was.

When Libby suggested a trip to the Circle Bar B, Cathy agreed immediately.

During the long drive, Libby made excuses to herself. She wasn't going just to check on Jess—she absolutely was not. She needed her drawing board, her pens and inks, jeans and blouses.

The fact that she could have bought any or all of these items in Kalispell was carefully ignored.

By the time Libby and Cathy drew the Corvette to a stop in the wide driveway of the main ranch house, the sun was starting to go down. There must have been fifty horsemen converging on the stables, all of them looking tired and discouraged.

Libby's heart wedged itself into her throat when she spotted Jess. He was dismounting, wrenching a high-powered rifle from the scabbard on his saddle.

She literally ran to him, but then she stopped short, her shoes encased in the thick, gooey mud Montanans call gumbo, her vocal cords no more mobile than her feet.

"Ken?" he asked in a hoarse whisper.

Libby was quick to reassure him. "Dad's doing very well."

"Then what are you doing here?"

Libby smiled, pried one of her feet out of the mud, only to have it succumb again when she set it down. "I had to see if you were all right," she admitted. "May I say that you look terrible?"

Jess chuckled, rubbed the stubble of beard on his chin, assessed the dirty clothes he wore in one downward glance. "You should have stayed in town."

Libby lifted her chin. "I'll go back in the morning," she said, daring him to argue.

Jess surrendered his horse to one of the ranch hands, but the rifle swung at his side as he started toward the big, well-lighted house. Libby slogged along at his side.

"Is that gun loaded?" she demanded.

"No," he replied. "Any more questions?"

"Yes. Did you see the bear?"

They had reached the spacious screened-in porch, where Mrs. Bradshaw had prudently laid out newspapers to accommodate dozens of mud-caked boots.

"No," Jess rasped, lifting his eyes to some distant thing that Libby could not see. "That sucker might as well be invisible."

Libby watched as Jess kicked off his boots, flung his sodden denim jacket aside, dispensed with his hat. "Maybe he's dead, Jess," she blurted out hopefully, resorting to the optimism her father had tacitly warned her against. "Maybe he collapsed somewhere—"

"Wrong," Jess bit out. "We found more cattle."

"Calves?"

"A bull and two heifers," Jess answered. "And the hell of it is, he didn't even kill them to eat. He just ripped them apart."

Libby shivered. "He must be enormous!"

"The men that were with Stacey and Ken said he stood over eight feet," Jess replied, and his green eyes moved wearily over Libby's face. "I don't suppose I need to say this, but I will. I don't like having you here, not now. For God's sake, don't go wandering off by yourself—not even to walk down to the mailboxes. The same goes for Cathy."

It seemed ludicrous that one beast could restrict the normal activities of human beings—in fact, the bear didn't seem real to Libby, even after what had happened to Ken. Instead, it was as though Jess was telling one of the delicious, scary stories he'd loved to terrify Libby with when they were children.

"That means, little one," he went on sternly, "that you don't go out to the barn and you don't go over to Ken's to sit and moon by that pond. Am I making myself clear?"

"Too clear," snapped Libby, following him as he carried the rifle through the kitchen, down a long hallway and into the massive billiard room where the gun cabinets were.

Jess locked the weapon away and turned to his wife. "I'm a little bit glad you're here," he confessed with a weary grin.

"Even tough cowboys need a little spoiling now and then," she replied, "so hie thyself to an upstairs bathroom, husband of mine, and get yourself a shower. I'll bring dinner to your room."

"And how do you know where my room is, Mrs. Barlowe?"

Libby colored a little. "I used to help Marion Bradshaw with the cleaning sometimes, remember?"

"I remember. I used to watch you bending over to tuck in sheets and smooth pillows and think what a great rear end you had."

She arched one eyebrow. "Had?"

Jess caught her bottom in strong hands, pressed her close to him. "Have," he clarified.

"Go take your shower!" Libby huffed, suddenly conscious of all the cowboys that would be gathering in the house for supper that night.

"Join me?" drawled Jess, persistent to the end.

"Absolutely not. You're exhausted." Libby broke away, headed toward the kitchen.

"Not *that* exhausted," Jess called after her.

Libby did not respond, but as she went in to prepare a dinner tray for her husband, she was smiling.

Minutes later, entering Jess's boyhood bedroom, she set the tray down on a long table under a line of windows. The door of the adjoining bathroom was open and steam billowed out like the mist in a spooky movie.

Presently Libby heard the shower shut off, the rustling sound of a towel being pulled from a rack. She sat down on the edge of Jess's bed and then bounded up again.

"Libby?"

She went cautiously to the doorway, looked in. Jess was peering into a steamy mirror, trying to shave. "Your dinner is getting cold," she said.

After flinging one devilish look at his wife, Jess grabbed the towel that had been wrapped around his hips and calmly used it to wipe the mirror. "I'll hurry," he replied.

Libby swallowed hard, as stunned by the splendor of his naked, muscle-corded frame as she had been on that first mantelpiece night when they'd made love in the bedroom at Jess's house, the fevered motions of their bodies metered by the raging elements outside.

Jess finished shaving, rinsed his face, turned toward Libby like a proud savage. She could not look away, even though she wanted to. Her eyes were fixed on the rising, swelling shaft of his manhood.

Jess laughed. "I used to fantasize about this."

"What?" Libby croaked, her throat tight.

"Bringing the foreman's pretty daughter up here and having my way with her."

Libby's eyes were, at last, freed, and they shot upward to his face. "Oh, yeah?"

"Yeah."

"I thought you liked Cathy then."

He nodded. "I did. But even before she married Stacey, I thought of her as a sister."

"And what, pray tell, did you think of me as?"

"A hellion. But I wanted to be your lover, all the same. Since I didn't dare, I settled for making your life miserable."

"How very chivalrous of you!"

Jess was walking toward her now, holding her with the scorching assessment of those jade-green eyes even before his hands touched her. "Teenage boys are not chivalrous, Libby."

Libby closed her eyes as he reached her, drew her close. "Neither are men," she managed to say.

Her blouse was coming untucked from her jeans, rising until she felt the steamy air on her stomach and back. Finally it was bunched under her arms and Jess was tracing a brazen finger over the lines of her scanty lace bra. Beneath the fabric, her nipples sprang into full bloom, coy flowers offering their nectar.

"Y-your dinner," she reminded Jess, floating on the sensations he was stirring within her, too bedazzled even to open her eyes.

The bra slipped down, just on one side, freeing a hard-peaked, eager breast. "Yes," Jess breathed evilly, "my dinner."

"Not that. I mean—"

His mouth closed over the delicate morsel, drawing at it softly. With a pleased and somewhat triumphant chuckle, Jess drew back from the tender treat and Libby's eyes flew open as he began removing her blouse and then her bra, leaving her jeans as they were.

He led her slowly to the bed, but instead of laying her down there, as she had expected, Jess stretched out on his back and positioned her so that she was sitting up, astraddle of his hips.

Gripping her waist, he pulled her forward and lifted, so that her breasts were suspended within easy reach of his mouth.

"The age-old quandary," he breathed.

Libby was dazed. "What qu-quandary?"

"Which one," Jess mused. "How like nature to offer two when a man has only one mouth."

Libby blushed hotly as Jess nuzzled a knotted peak, a peak that ached to nourish him. "Oh, God, Jess," she whispered. "Take it...take it!"

He chuckled, flicked the nipple in question with an impertinent tongue. "I love it when you beg."

Both rage and passion moved inside Libby. "I'm... not...begging!" she gasped, but even as she spoke she was bracing herself with her hands, brushing her breast back and forth across Jess's lips, seeking admission.

"You will," he said, and then he caught the pulsing nipple between careful teeth, raking it to an almost un-endurable state of wanting.

"Not on your wretched life!" moaned Libby.

"We'll see," he replied.

The opposite breast was found and thoroughly teased and Libby had to bite her lower lip to keep from giving in and pleading senselessly for the suckling Jess promised but would not give. He played with her, using his tongue and his lips, delighting in the rocking motion of her body and the soft whimpers that came from her throat.

The sweet torment became keener, and Libby both loved and hated Jess for being able to drive her to such lengths. "Make love to me…oh, Jess…make love…to me."

The concession elicited a hoarse growl from Jess, and Libby found herself spinning down to lie flat on the bed. Her remaining clothes were soon stripped away, her legs were parted.

Libby gasped and arched her back as he entered her in one ferocious, needing thrust. After gaining this warm and hidden place, Jess paused, his hard frame shuddering with restraint.

As bedazzled as she was, Libby saw her chance to set the pace, to take command, and she took it. Acting on an age-old instinct, she wrapped her legs around his hips in a fierce claiming and muttered, "Give me all of you, Jess—all of you."

He groaned in lusty surrender and plunged deep within her, seeking solace in the velvety heat of her womanhood. They were locked together for several glittering moments, each afraid to move. Soon enough, however, their bodies demanded more and began a desperate, swift rhythm.

Straining together, both moaning in fevered need, Libby and Jess reached their shattering pinnacle at the same moment, crying out as their two souls flared as one golden fire.

Twice after Jess lay still upon her, his broad back moist beneath her hands, Libby convulsed softly, whimpering.

"Some people are really greedy," he teased when, at last, her body had ceased its spasmodic clenching and unclenching.

Libby stretched, sated, cosseted in delicious appeasement. "More," she purred.

"What did I tell you?" Jess sighed. "The lady is greedy."

"Very."

He rolled, still joined with Libby, bringing her with him so that she once again sat astraddle of him. They talked, in hushed and gentle voices, of very ordinary things.

After some minutes had passed, however, Libby began to trace his nipples with feather-light fingertips. "I've always wanted to have my way with the boss's son," she crooned, teasing him as he had teased her earlier.

She bent forward, tasted those hardening nipples, each in turn, with only the merest flick of her tongue. Jess groaned and grew hard within her, by degrees, as she continued to torment him.

"How like nature," she gibed tenderly, "to offer two when a woman has only one mouth."

Jess grasped her hips in inescapable hands and thrust his own upward in a savage demand.

Libby's release came swiftly; it was soft and warm, rather than violent, and its passing left her free to bring Jess to exquisite heights. She set a slow pace for him, delighting in the look in his eyes, the back-and-forth motion of his head on the pillow, the obvious effort it took for him to lie still beneath her.

He pleaded for release, but Libby was impervious, guiding him gently, reveling in the sweet power she held over this man she so completely loved. "I'm going to love you in my own way," she told him. "And in my own time."

His head pressed back into the pillows in magnificent surrender, Jess closed his eyes and moaned. His control was awesome, but soon enough it slipped and he began to move beneath Libby, slowly at first and then quickly. Finally, his hands tangling in her hair, he cried out and his body spasmed as she purposely intensified his pleasure. His triumph seemed endless.

When Jess was still at last, his eyes closed, his body glistening with perspiration, Libby tenderly stroked a lock of hair back from his forehead and whispered, "Some people are really greedy."

Jess chuckled and was asleep before Libby withdrew from him to make her way into the bathroom for a shower of her own.

The dream was very sexy. In it, a blue-gray dawn was swelling at the bedroom windows and Libby's breast was full in Jess's hand, the nipple stroked to a pleading state.

She groaned as she felt his hard length upon her, his manhood seeking to sheathe itself in her warmth.

Jess entered her, and his strokes were slow and gentle, evoking an immediate series of tremulous, velvet-smooth responses.

"Good," she sighed, giving herself up to the dream. "So good…"

The easy strokes became demanding thrusts. "Yes," said the dream Jess gruffly. "Good."

"Ooooooh," moaned Libby, as a sudden and piercing release rocked her, thrusting her into wakefulness.

And Jess was there, upon her, his face inches from her own. She watched in wonder and in love as his features grew taut and his splendid body flexed, more rapidly now. She thrust herself up to receive the fullness of his love.

Libby's hands clasped Jess's taut buttocks as he shuddered and delved deep, his manhood rippling powerfully within her, his rasping moan filling Libby's heart.

Minutes later, a languid, hazy sleep overtook Libby and she rolled over onto her stomach and settled back into her dreams. She stirred only slightly when Jess patted her derriere and left the bed.

Hours later, when she awakened fully, Libby was not entirely certain that she hadn't dreamed the whole gratifying episode. As she got out of bed, though, to take a bath and get dressed, Libby knew that Jess had loved her—the feeling of lush well-being she enjoyed was proof of that.

The pampered sensation was short-lived. When Libby went downstairs to search out a light breakfast, she found Monica Summers sitting in the kitchen, sipping coffee and reading a weekly newsmagazine.

Even though Monica smiled, her dark gray eyes betrayed her malice. "Hello... Mrs. Barlowe."

Libby nodded uneasily and opened the refrigerator to take out an apple and a carton of yogurt. "Good morning," she said.

"I was very sorry to hear about your father," Monica went on, the tone of her voice totally belying her expression. "Is he recovering?"

Libby got a spoon for her yogurt and sat down at the table. "Yes, thank you, he is."

"Will you be staying here with us, or going back to Kalispell?"

There was something annoyingly proprietary in the way Monica said the word "us," as though Libby were somehow invading territory where she didn't belong. She lifted her chin and met the woman's stormy-sky gaze directly. "I'll be going back to Kalispell," she said.

"You must hate leaving Jess."

The pit of Libby's stomach developed an unsettling twitch. She took a forceful bite from her apple and said nothing.

"Of course, I'll be happy to...look after him," sighed Monica, striking a flame to the fuse she had been uncoiling. "It's an old habit, you know."

Libby suppressed an unladylike urge to fly over the table, teeth bared, fists flying. "Sometimes old habits have to be broken," she said, sitting very still, reminding herself that she was a grown woman now, not the foreman's little brat. Furthermore, she was Jess's wife and she didn't have to take this kind of subtle abuse in any case.

Monica arched one perfect eyebrow. "Do they?"

Libby leaned forward. "Oh, yes. You see, Ms. Summers, if you mess with my husband, I'll not only break the habit for you, I'll break a few of your bones for good measure."

Monica paled, muttered something about country girls.

"I am not a girl," Libby pointed out. "I'm a woman, and you'd better remember it."

"Oh, I will," blustered Monica, recovering quickly. "But will Jess? That's the question, isn't it?"

If there was one thing in the world Libby had absolutely no doubts about, at that moment anyway, it was her ability to please her husband in the way Monica was referring to. "I don't see how he could possibly forget," she said, and then she finished her apple and her yogurt, dropped the remnants into the trash, and left the room.

Marion Bradshaw was sweeping away residual dried mud when Libby reached the screened porch, hoping for one glimpse of Jess before she had to go back to Kalispell.

He was nowhere in sight, of course—Libby had not really expected him to be.

"How's Ken getting on?" Marion asked.

Libby smiled. "He's doing very well."

The housekeeper sighed, leaning on her broom. "Thank the good Lord for that. Me and Ken Kincaid run this place, and I sure couldn't manage it alone!"

Libby laughed and asked if Cathy was around.

Sheer delight danced in Mrs. Bradshaw's eyes. "She's where she belongs—upstairs in her husband's bed."

Libby blushed. She had forgotten how much this astute woman knew about the goings-on on the ranch.

Did she know, too, why Jess had never gotten around to eating his dinner the night before?

"No shame in loving your man," Mrs. Bradshaw twinkled.

Libby swallowed. "Do you know if Stacey went with the others this morning?"

"He did. You go ahead and wake Miss Cathy right now, if you want to."

Libby was grateful for an excuse to hurry away.

Finding Stacey's room from memory, in just the way she'd found Jess's, she knocked briskly at the closed door, realized the foolishness of that, and turned the knob.

Cathy was curled up like a kitten in the middle of a bed as mussed and tangled as the one Libby had shared with Jess.

Libby bent to give Cathy's bare shoulder a gentle shake. Her cousin sat up, mumbling, her face lost behind a glistening profusion of tangled hair. "Libby? What…?"

Libby laughed and signed, "I'm going back to town as soon as I pick up some of my things at the other house. Do you want to go with me?"

Cathy's full lips curved into a mischievous smile and she shook her head.

"Things are going well between you and Stacey, then?"

Cathy's hands moved in a scandalously explicit answer.

"I'm shocked!" Libby signed, beaming. And then she gave her cousin a quick kiss on the forehead, promised to call Mrs. Bradshaw if there was any sort of change in Ken's condition, and left the room.

In Jess's room she found paper and a pen, and probably because of the tempestuous night spent in his bed, dared to write, "Jess. I love you. Sorry I couldn't stay for a proper goodbye, but I've got to get back to Dad. Take care and come to me if you can. Smiles and sunshine, Libby."

On the way downstairs, Libby almost lost her courage and ran back to rip up the note. Telling Jess outright that she loved him! What if he laughed? What if he was derisive or, even worse, pitying?

Libby denied herself the cowardice of hiding her feelings any longer. It was time she took responsibility for her own emotions, wasn't it?

The weather was crisp and bright that day, and Libby hummed as she drove the relatively short distance to her father's house, parked her car behind his truck and went in to get the things she needed.

Fitting extra clothes and her special set of pens and inks into the back of the Corvette proved easy enough, but the drawing board was another matter. She turned it this way and that way and it just wouldn't fit.

Finally Libby took it back inside the house and left it there. She would just have to make do with the kitchen table at the condo for the time being.

Libby was just passing the passenger side of Ken's truck when she heard the sound; it was a sort of shifting rustle, coming from the direction of the lilac hedge on the far side of the yard. There followed a low, ominous grunt.

Instinctively Libby froze, the hair tingling on the

nape of her neck. Dear God, it couldn't be… Not here—not when there were men with rifles searching every inch of the ranch…

She turned slowly, and her heart leapt into her throat and then spun back down into the pit of her stomach. The bear stood within ten feet of her, on its hind legs.

The beast growled and lolled its massive head to one side. Its mangy, lusterless hide seemed loose over the rolling muscles beneath, and on its flank was a blood-crusted, seeping wound.

In that moment, it was as though Libby became two people, one hysterically afraid, one calm and in control. Fortunately, it was this second Libby that took command. Slowly, ever so slowly, she eased her hand back behind her, to the door handle, opened it. Just as the bear lunged toward her, making a sound more horrifying than she could ever have imagined, she leapt inside the truck and slammed the door after her.

The raging beast shook the whole vehicle as it flung its great bulk against its side, and Libby allowed herself the luxury of one high-pitched scream before reaching for Ken's CB radio under the dashboard.

Again and again, the furious bear pummeled the side of the truck, while Libby tried frantically to make the CB radio work. She knew that the cowboys would be carrying receivers, in order to communicate with each other, and they were her only hope.

Fingers trembling, Libby finally managed to lift the microphone to her mouth and press the button. Her mind skittered over a series of movies she'd seen, books she'd read. *Mayday*, she thought with triumphant terror. *Mayday!* But the magic word would not come past her tight throat.

Suddenly a giant claw thundered across the windshield, shattering it into a glittering cobweb of cracks. One more blow, just one, and the bear would reach her easily, even though she was now crouching on the floorboard.

At last she found her voice. "Cujo!" she screamed into the radio receiver. "Cujo!" She closed her eyes, gasping, tried to get a hold on herself. *This is not a Stephen King movie*, she reminded herself. *This is reality. And that bear out there is going to tear you apart if you don't do something!*

"Libby!" the radio squawked suddenly. "Libby, come in!"

The voice was Jess's. "Th-the bear," she croaked, remembering to hold in the button on the receiver when she talked. "Jess, the bear!"

"Where are you?"

Libby closed her eyes as the beast again threw itself against the truck. "My dad's house—in his truck."

"Hold on. Please, baby, hold on. We're not far away."

"Hurry!" Libby cried, as the bear battered the windshield again and tiny bits of glass rained down on her head.

Another voice came in over the radio, this one belonging to Stacey. "Libby," he said evenly, "honk the horn. Can you do that?"

Libby couldn't speak. There were tears pouring down her face and every muscle in her body seemed inert, but she did reach up to the center of the wheel and press the truck's horn.

The bear bellowed with rage, as though the sound had hurt him, but he stopped striking the truck and withdrew a little way. Libby knew he wasn't gone, for she could hear him lumbering nearby, growling in frustration.

Jess's men converged with Stacey's at the end of the rutted country road leading to Ken's house. When the pickup truck was in sight, they reined in their horses.

"He's mine," Jess breathed, reaching for the rifle in his scabbard, drawing it out, cocking it. He was conscious of the other men and their nervous, nickering horses, but only vaguely. Libby was inside that truck—his whole being seemed to focus on that one fact.

The bear rose up in full view suddenly, its enormous head visible even over the top of the pickup's cab. Even over the repeated honking of the truck's horn, the beast's hideous, echoing growl was audible.

"Sweet Jesus," Stacey whispered.

"Easy," said Jess, to himself more than the men around him, as he lifted the rifle, sighted in carefully, pulled back the trigger.

The thunderous shot struck the bear in the center of its nose, and the animal shrieked as it went down. The impact of its body was so solid that it seemed to shake the ground.

Instantly Jess was out of the saddle. "Make sure he's dead," he called over one shoulder as he ran toward the truck.

Stacey and several of his men reached the bear just as Jess wrenched open the door on the driver's side.

Libby scrambled out from under the steering wheel,

her hair a wild, glass-spattered tangle, to fling herself, sobbing, into his arms. Jess cradled her in his arms, carried her away from the demolished truck and inside the house. His own knees suddenly weak, he fell into the first available chair and buried his face in Libby's neck.

"It's over, sweetheart," he said. "It's over."

Libby shuddered and wailed with terror.

When she was calmer, Jess caught her chin in his hand and lifted it. "What the hell did you mean, yelling 'Cujo! Cujo!'"

Libby sniffled, and the fight was back in her eyes, a glorious, snapping blue. "There was this book about a mad dog…and then there was a movie…"

Jess lifted his eyebrows and grinned.

"Oh, never mind!" hissed Libby.

Chapter 13

Libby froze in the doorway of Ken's room in the intensive-care unit, her mouth open, her heart racing as fast as it had earlier, when she'd been trapped by the bear.

"Where is he?" she finally managed to whisper. "Oh, Jess, where is my father?"

Standing behind Libby, Jess lifted his hands to her shoulders and gently ushered her back into the hallway, out of sight of the empty bed. "Don't panic," he said quietly.

Libby trembled, looked frantically toward the nurses' station. "Jess, what if he…?"

There was a gentle lecture forming in Jess's features, but before he could deliver it, an attractive red-headed nurse approached, trim in her uniform. "Mrs. Barlowe?"

Libby nodded, holding her breath.

"Your father is fine. We moved Mr. Kincaid to another floor earlier today, since he no longer needs such careful monitoring. If you will just come back to the desk with me, I'll be happy to find out which room he's in."

Libby's breath escaped in one long sigh. What with spending perilous minutes cowering inside a truck, with a rogue bear doing its best to get inside and tear her to bits, and then rushing to the hospital to find her father's bed empty, she had had more than enough stress for one day. "Thank you," she said, giving Jess a relieved look.

He got rather familiar during the elevator ride down to the second floor, but desisted when the doors opened again.

"You're incorrigible," Libby whispered, only half in anger.

"Snatching my wife from the jaws of death has that effect on me," he whispered back. "I keep thinking that I might never have gotten the chance to touch you like that again."

Libby paused, in the quest for Room 223, to search Jess's face. "Were you scared?"

"Scared? Sweet thing, I was *terrified.*"

"You seemed so calm!"

He lifted one eyebrow. "Somebody had to be."

Libby considered that and then sighed. "I don't suppose we should tell Dad what actually happened. Not yet, at least."

Jess chuckled. "We'll tell a partial truth—that the bear is dead. The rest had better wait until he's stronger."

"Right," agreed Libby.

When they reached Ken's new room, another surprise was in store. A good-looking dark-haired woman was there plumping the patient's pillows, fussing with his covers. She wore well-cut jeans and a Western shirt trimmed with a rippling snow-white fringe, and the way she laughed, low in her throat, said more about her relationship with Ken Kincaid than all her other attentions combined.

"Hello, Becky," said Jess, smiling.

Becky was one of those people, it seemed, who smile not just with the mouth but with the whole face. "Jess Barlowe," she crowed, "you black-hearted son-of-a-gun! Where ya been?"

Libby drew a deep breath and worked up a smile of her own. Was this the woman who had written that intriguing farewell on the condo's kitchen blackboard?

Deliberately she turned her attention on her father, who looked downright rakish as he favored his startled daughter with a slow grin and a wink.

"Who's this pretty little gal?" demanded Becky, giving Libby a friendly once-over.

For the first time, Ken spoke. "This is my daughter, Libby. Libby, Becky Stafford."

"I'll be!" cried Becky, clearly delighted. "Glad to meet ya!"

Libby found the woman's boisterous good nature appealing, and despite a few lingering twinges of surprise, she responded warmly.

"Did you get that bear?" Ken asked of Jess, once the women had made their exchange.

"Yes," Jess replied, after one glance at Libby.

Ken gave a hoot of delight and triumph. "Nail that

son-of-a…nail that devil's hide to the barn door for me, will you?"

"Done," answered Jess with a grin.

A few minutes later, Jess and the energetic Becky left the room to have coffee in the hospital cafeteria. Libby lifted her hands to her hips, fixed her father with a loving glare and demanded, "Is there something you haven't told me?"

Ken laughed. "Maybe. But I'll wager that there are a few things you haven't told me, either, dumplin'."

"Who is Becky, exactly?"

Ken thought for a moment before speaking. "She's a good friend of mine, Libby. An old friend."

For some reason, Libby was determined to find something to dislike about Becky Stafford, difficult as it was. "Why does she dress like that? Is she a rodeo performer or something?"

"She's a cocktail waitress," Ken replied patiently.

"Oh," said Libby. And then she couldn't sustain her petty jealousy any longer, because Becky Stafford was a nice person and Ken had a right to like her. He was more than just her father, after all, more than just Senator Barlowe's general foreman. He was a man.

There was a brief silence, which Ken broke with a very direct question. "Do you like Becky, Lib?"

Like her? The warmth and humor of the woman still lingered in that otherwise dreary room, as did the earthy, unpretentious scent of her perfume. "Sure I do," said Libby. "Anybody with the perception to call Jess Barlowe a 'black-hearted son-of-a-gun' is okay in my book!"

Ken chuckled, but there was relief in his face, and

his expression revealed that he knew how much Libby loved her husband. "How's Cathy?" he asked.

Remembering that morning's brief conversation with her cousin, Libby grinned. "She's doing fine, as far as I can tell. Bad as it was, your tussle with that bear seems to have brought Cathy and Stacey both to a point where they can open up to each other. Cathy actually talked to him."

Ken did not seem surprised by this last; perhaps he'd known all along that Cathy still had use of her voice. "I don't imagine it was peaceable," he observed drily.

"Not in the least," confirmed Libby, "but they're communicating and…and, well, let's just say they're closer."

"That's good," answered Ken, smiling at his daughter's words. "That's real good."

Seeing that her father was getting very tired, Libby quickly kissed him and took her leave. When she reached the cafeteria, Becky was sitting alone at a table, staring sadly into her coffee cup.

Libby scanned the large room for Jess and failed to see him, but she wasn't worried. Probably he had gone back to Ken's room and missed seeing Libby on the way. Noticing the pensive look on Becky's face, she was glad for a few minutes alone with the woman her father obviously liked and perhaps even loved.

"May I sit down?" she asked, standing behind the chair that had probably been Jess's.

Becky looked up, smiled. "Sure," she said, and there was surprise in her dark eyes.

Libby sat down with a sigh. "I hate hospitals," she

said, filled to aching with the memory of Jonathan's confinement.

"Me too," answered Becky, but her eyes were watchful. Hopeful, in a touchingly open way.

Libby swallowed. "My...my father has been very lonely, and I'm glad you're his friend."

Becky's smile was almost cosmic in scope. "That's good to hear," she answered. "Lordy, that man did scare the life out of me, going a round with that damned bear that way."

Libby thought of her own chance meeting with the creature and shivered. She hoped that she would never know that kind of numbing fear again.

Becky's hand came to pat hers. "It's all right now, though, isn't it? That hairy booger is dead, thanks to Jess."

Libby laughed. Indeed, that "hairy booger" was dead, and she did have Jess to thank for her life. When she'd tried to voice her gratitude earlier, he had brushed away her words and said that she was his wife and, therefore, saving her from bears, fire-breathing dragons and the like was just part of the bargain.

As if conjured by her thoughts of him, Jess appeared to take Libby home.

The coming days were happy ones for Libby, if hectic. She visited her father morning and evening and worked on her cartoon strip and the panels for the book between times, her drawing board having been transported from the ranch by Jess and set up in the middle of the condo's living room.

Jess commuted between Kalispell and the ranch;

many of Ken's duties had fallen to him. Instead of being exhausted by the crazy pace, however, he seemed to thrive on it and his reports on the stormy reconciliation taking place between Cathy and Stacey were encouraging. It appeared that, with the help of the marriage counselor they were seeing, their problems might be worked out.

The irrepressible Becky Stafford rapidly became Libby's friend. Vastly different, the two women nevertheless enjoyed each other—Libby found that Becky could draw her out when she became too burrowed down in her work, and just as quickly drive her back if she tried to neglect it.

"You did what?" Jess demanded archly one early-summer evening as he and Libby sat on the living-room floor consuming the take-out Chinese food they both loved.

Libby laughed with glee and a measure of pride. "I rode the mechanical bull at the bar where Becky works," she repeated.

Jess worked up an unconvincing scowl. "Hanging around bars these days, are you?" he demanded, waving a fortune cookie for emphasis.

Libby batted her eyelashes demurely. "Don't you worry one little bit," she said, feigning a musical Southern drawl. "Becky guards mah virtue, y'all."

Jess's green eyes slipped to the V neck of Libby's white sweater, which left a generous portion of cleavage in full and enticing view. "Does she now? And where is she, at this very moment, when said virtue is in immediate peril?"

An anticipatory thrill gyrated in the pit of Libby's

stomach and warmed her breasts, which were bare beneath her lightweight sweater. Jess had loved her often, and well, but he could still stir that sweet, needing tension with remarkable ease. "What sort of peril am I in, exactly?"

Jess grinned and hooked one finger in the V of her sweater, slid it downward into the warmth between her breasts. "Oh, the most scandalous sort, Mrs. Barlowe."

Libby's breath quickened, despite stubborn efforts to keep it even. "Your attentions are quite unseemly, Mr. Barlowe," she replied.

He moved the wanton finger up and down between the swelling softness that was Libby, and sharp responses ached in other parts of her. "Absolutely," he said. "I mean to do several unseemly things to you."

Libby tensed with delicious sensation as Jess's exploring finger slid aside, explored a still-hidden nipple.

"I want to see your breast, Libby. This breast. Show it to me."

The outrageous request made Libby color slightly, but she knew she would comply. She was a strong, independent person, but now, in this sweet, aching moment, she was Jess's woman. With one motion of her hand, she tugged the sweater's neckline down and to one side, so that it made a sort of sling for the breast that had been softly demanded.

Not touching the rounded pink-tipped treasure in any way, Jess admired it, rewarding it with an approving smile when the confectionlike peak tightened into an enticing point.

Libby was kneeling now, resting on her heels, the cartons littering the coffee table completely forgotten.

She was at once too proud to plead for Jess's mouth and too needing of it to cover herself.

Knowing that, Jess chuckled hoarsely and bent to flick at the exposed nipple with just the tip of his tongue. Libby moaned and let her head fall back, making the captured breast even more vulnerable.

"Unseemly," breathed Jess, nibbling, drawing at the straining morsel with his lips.

Libby felt the universe sway in time with his tender plundering, but she bit down hard on the garbled pleas that were rising in her throat. They escaped through her parted lips, all the same, as small gasps.

Her heartbeat grew louder and louder as Jess finally took suckle; it muffled the sounds of his greed, of the cartons being swept from the surface of the coffee table in a motion of one of his arms.

The coolness of the air battled with the heat of Libby's flesh as she was stripped of her sweater, her white slacks, her panties. Gently he placed her on the coffee table.

Entranced, Libby allowed him to position her legs wide of each other, one on one side of the low table, one on the other. Beyond the glass roof, in the dark, dark sky, a million silvery stars surged toward her and then melted back into the folds of heaven, becoming pinpoints.

Jess found the silken nest of her passion and attended it lovingly, stroking, kissing, finding, losing. Libby's hips moved wildly, struggling even as she gave herself up.

And when she had to have this singular gratification or die, Jess understood and feasted unreservedly, his hands firm under her bottom, lifting her, the breadth of his shoulders making it impossible for her to deny him what he would have from her.

At last, when the tumult broke on a lusty cry of triumph from Libby, she saw the stars above plummet toward her—or had she risen to meet them?

"Of course you're going to the powwow!" cried Becky, folding her arms and leaning over the platter of french fries in front of her. "You can't miss that and call yourself a Barlowe!"

Libby shrank down a little in the benchlike steakhouse seat. As this restaurant was a part of the Barlowe chain, the name drew immediate attention from all the waiters and a number of the other diners, too. "Becky," she began patiently, "even though Dad's getting out of the hospital this afternoon, he won't be up to something like that, and I wouldn't feel right about leaving him behind."

"Leaving Ken behind?" scoffed Becky in a more discreet tone of voice. "You just try keeping him away—he hasn't missed a powwow in fifteen years."

Libby's memories of the last powwow and all-day rodeo she had attended were hardly conducive to nostalgia. She remembered the dust, the hot glare of the summer sun, the seemingly endless rodeo events, the revelers draped over the hoods of parked cars and sprawled on the sidewalks. She sighed.

"Jess'll go," Becky prodded.

Libby had no doubt of that, and having spent so much time away from Jess of late, what with him running the ranch while she stayed in Kalispell, she was inclined to attend the powwow after all.

Becky saw that she had relented and beamed. "Wait'll you see the Sioux doing their war dances," she enthused. "There'll be Blackfoot, too, and Flathead."

Libby consoled herself with the thought of the dances and the powwow finery of feathers and buckskin and beads. She could take her sketchbook along and draw, at least.

Becky wasn't through with her conversation. "Did you tell Jess how you rode that electric bull over at the Golden Buckle?"

Libby tried to look dignified in the wake of several molten memories. "I told him," she said shyly.

Her friend laughed. "If that wasn't a sight! I wish I woulda took your picture. Maybe you should enter some of the events at the powwow, Libby." Her face took on a disturbingly serious expression. "Maybe barrel racing, or women's calf roping—"

"Hold it," Libby interceded with a grin. "Riding a mechanical bull is one thing and calf roping is quite another. The only sport I'm going to take part in is stepping over drunks."

"Stepping over what?" inquired a third voice, masculine and amused, from the table side.

Libby looked and saw Stacey. "What are you doing here?"

He laughed, turning his expensive silver-banded cowboy hat in both hands. "I own the place, remember?"

"Where's Cathy?" Becky wanted to know. As she had become Libby's friend, she had also become Cathy's—she was even learning to sign.

Stacey slid into the bench seat beside Libby. "She's

seeing the doctor," he said, and for all his smiling good manners, he seemed nervous.

Libby elbowed her brother-in-law lightly. "Why didn't you stay there and wait for her?"

"She wouldn't let me."

Just then Becky stood up, saying that she had to get to work. A moment later, eyes twinkling over some secret, she left.

Libby felt self-conscious with Stacey, though he hadn't made any more advances or disturbing comments. She wished that Becky had been able to stay a little longer. "What's going on? Is Cathy sick?"

"She's just having a checkup. Libby..."

Libby braced herself inwardly and moved a little closer to the wall of the enclosed booth, so that Stacey's thigh wasn't touching hers. "Yes?" she prompted when he hesitated to go on.

"I owe you an apology," he said, meeting her eyes. "I acted like a damned fool and I'm sorry."

Knowing that he was referring to the rumors he'd started about their friendship in New York, Libby chafed a little. "I accept your apology, Stacey, but I truly don't understand why you said what you did in the first place."

He sighed heavily. "I love Cathy very much, Libby," he said. "But we do have our problems. At that time, things were a lot worse, and I started thinking about the way you'd leaned on me when you were going through all that trouble in New York. I liked having somebody need me like that, and I guess I worked the whole thing up into more than it was."

Tentatively Libby touched his hand. "Cathy needs you, Stacey."

"No," he answered gruffly, looking at the flickering bowl candle in the center of the table. "She won't allow herself to need me. After some of the things I've put her through, I can't say I blame her."

"She'll trust you again, if you're worthy of it," Libby ventured. "Just be there for Cathy, Stace. The way you were there for me when my whole life seemed to be falling apart. I don't think I could have gotten through those days without you."

At that moment Jess appeared out of nowhere and slid into the seat Becky had occupied before. "Now, that," he drawled acidly, "is really touching."

Libby stared at him, stunned by his presence and by the angry set of his face. Then she realized that both she and Stacey were sitting on the same side of the booth and knew that it gave an impression of intimacy. "Jess…"

He looked down at his watch, a muscle dancing furiously in his jaw. "Are you going to pick your father up at the hospital, or do you have more interesting things to do?"

Stacey, who had been as shocked by his brother's arrival as Libby had, was suddenly, angrily vocal. The candle leapt a little when he slammed one fist down on the tabletop and hissed, "Dammit, Jess, you're deliberately misunderstanding this!"

"Am I?"

"Yes!" Libby put in, on the verge of tears. "Becky and I were having lunch and then Stacey came in and—"

"Stop it, Libby," Stacey broke in. "You didn't do anything wrong. Jess is the one who's out of line here."

The long muscle in Jess's neck corded, and his lips were edged with white, but his voice was still low, still controlled. "I came here, Libby, because I wanted to be with you when you brought Ken home," he said, and his green eyes, dark with passion only the night before, were coldly indifferent now. "Are we going to collect him or would you rather stay here and carry on?"

Libby was shaking. "Carry on? *Carry on?*"

Stacey groaned, probably considering the scandal a scene in this particular restaurant would cause. "Couldn't we settle this somewhere else?"

"We'll settle it, all right," Jess replied.

Stacey's jaw was rock-hard as he stood up to let a shaken Libby out of the booth. "I'll be on the ranch," he said.

"So will I," replied Jess, rising, taking a firm grip on Libby's arm. "See you there."

"Count on it."

Jess nodded and calmly propelled Libby out of the restaurant and into the bright sunlight, where her shiny Corvette was parked. Probably he had seen the car from the highway and known that she was inside the steak house.

Now, completely ignoring her protests, he dragged her past her car and thrust her into the Land Rover beside it.

"Jess—damn you—will you *listen* to me?"

Jess started the engine, shifted it into Reverse with a swift motion of his hand. "I'm afraid storytime will have to wait," he informed her. "We've got to go and get Ken, and I don't want him upset."

"Do you think I do?"

Jess sliced one menacing look in her direction but said nothing.

Libby felt a need to reach him, even though, the way he was acting, he didn't deserve reassurances. "Jess, how can you…after last night, how could you…"

"Last night," he bit out. "Yes. Tell me, Libby, do you do that trick for everybody, or just a favored few?"

It took all her determination not to physically attack him. "Take me back to my car, Jess," she said evenly. "Right now. I'll pick Dad up myself, and we'll go back to his house—"

"Correction, Mrs. Barlowe. *He* will go to his house. You, my little vixen, will go to mine."

"I will not!"

"Oh, but you will. Despite your obvious attraction to my brother, you are still my wife."

"I am not attracted to your brother!"

They had reached the hospital parking lot, and the Land Rover lurched to a stop. Jess smiled insolently and patted Libby's cheek in a way so patronizing that it made her screaming mad. "That's the spirit, Mrs. Barlowe. Walk in there and show your daddy what a pillar of morality you are."

Going into that hospital and pretending that nothing was wrong was one of the hardest things Libby had ever had to do.

Preparations for Ken's return had obviously been going on for some time. As Libby pulled her reclaimed Corvette in behind Jess's Land Rover, she saw that the front lawn had been mowed and the truck had been repaired.

Ken, still not knowing the story of his daughter, his truck, and the bear, paused after stepping out of Jess's Land Rover, his arm still in a sling. He looked his own vehicle over quizzically. "Looks different," he reflected.

Jess rose to the occasion promptly, smoothly. "The boys washed and waxed it," he said.

To say the very least, thought Libby, who would never forget, try though she might, how that truck had looked before the repair people in Kalispell had fixed and painted it. She opened her mouth to tell her father what had happened, but Jess stopped her with a look and a shake of his head.

The inside of the house had been cleaned by Mrs. Bradshaw and her band of elves; every floor and stick of furniture had been either dusted or polished or both. The refrigerator had been stocked and a supply of the paperback Westerns Ken loved to read had been laid in.

As if all this wasn't enough to make Libby's services completely superfluous, it turned out that Becky was there, too. She had strung streamers and dozens of brightly colored balloons from the ceiling of Ken's bedroom.

Her father was obviously pleased, and Libby's last hopes of drumming up an excuse to stay the night, at least, were dashed. Becky, however, was delighted with her surprise.

"I thought you were working!" Libby accused.

"I lied," replied Becky, undaunted. "After I left you and Stacey at the steak house, I got a friend to bring me out here."

Libby shot a glance in Jess's direction, knew sweet triumph as she saw that Becky's words had registered with him. After only a moment's chagrin, however, he tightened his jaw and looked away.

While Becky was getting Ken settled in his room and generally spoiling him rotten, Libby edged over to her husband. "You heard her," she whispered tersely, "so where's my apology?"

"Apology?" Jess whispered back, and there was nothing in his face to indicate that he felt any remorse at all. "Why should I apologize?"

"Because I was obviously telling the truth! Becky said—"

"Becky said that she left you and Stacey at the steak house. It must have been a big relief when she did."

Heedless of everything but the brutal effect of Jess's unfair words, Libby raised one hand and slapped him, hard.

Stubbornly, he refused her the satisfaction of any response at all, beyond an imperious glare, which she returned.

"Hey, do you guys…?" Becky's voice fell away when she became aware of the charged atmosphere of the living room. She swallowed and began again. "I was going to ask if you wanted to stay for supper, but maybe that wouldn't be such a good idea."

"You can say that again," rasped Jess, catching Libby's arm in a grasp she couldn't have broken without making an even more embarrassing scene. "Make our excuses to Ken, will you, please?"

After a moment's hesitation and a concerned look at Libby, Becky nodded.

"You overbearing bastard!" Libby hissed as her husband squired her out of the house and toward his Land Rover.

Jess opened the door, helped her inside, met her fiery blue gaze with one of molten green. Neither spoke to the other, but the messages flashing between them were all too clear anyway.

Jess still believed that Libby had been either planning or carrying on a romantic tryst with Stacey, and Libby was too proud and too angry to try to convince him otherwise. She was also too smart to get out of his vehicle and make a run for hers.

Jess would never hurt her, she knew that. But he would not allow her a dramatic exit, either. And she couldn't risk a screaming fight in the driveway of her father's house.

Because she was helpless and she hated that, she began to cry.

Jess ignored her tears, but he too was considerate of Ken—he did not gun the Land Rover's engine or back out at a speed that would fling gravel in every direction, as he might have at another time.

When they passed his house, with its window walls, and started up a steep road leading into the foothills beyond, Libby was still not afraid. For all his fury, this man was too tender a lover to touch her in anger.

"Where are we going?" she demanded.

He ground the Land Rover into a low gear and left the road, now little more than a cow path, for the rugged hillside. "On our honeymoon, Mrs. Barlowe."

Libby swallowed, unnerved by his quiet rage and the jostling, jolting ascent of the Land Rover itself. "If you take me in anger, Jess Barlowe, I'll never forgive you. Never. That would be rape."

The word "rape" got through Jess's hard armor and stung him visibly. He paled as he stopped the Land Rover with a lurch and wrenched on the emergency brake. "Goddammit, you *know* I wouldn't do anything like that!"

"Do I?" They were parked at an almost vertical angle, it seemed to Libby. Didn't he realize that they were almost straight up and down? "You've been acting like a maniac all afternoon!"

Jess's face contorted and he raised his fists and brought them down hard on the steering wheel. "Dammit it all to hell," he raged, "you drive me crazy! Why the devil do I love you so much when *you drive me crazy*?"

Libby stared at him, almost unable to believe what she had heard. Not even in their wildest moments of passion had he said he loved her, and if he had found that note she'd left for him, betraying her own feelings, the day the bear was killed, he'd never mentioned it.

"What did you say?"

Jess sighed, tilted his head back, closed his eyes. "That you drive me crazy."

"Before that."

"I said I loved you," he breathed, as though there was nothing out of the ordinary in that.

"Do you?"

"Hell, yes." The muscles in his sun-browned neck corded as he swallowed, his head still back, his eyes still closed. "Isn't that a joke?"

The words tore at Libby's heart. "A joke?"

"Yes." The word came, raw, from deep within him, like a sob.

"You idiot!" yelled Libby, struggling with the door, climbing out of the Land Rover to stalk up the steep hillside. She trembled, and tears poured down her face, and for once she didn't care who saw them.

At the top of the rise, she sat down on a huge log, her vision too blurred to take in the breathtaking view of mountains and prairies and an endless, sweeping sky.

She sensed Jess's approach, tried to ignore him.

"Why am I an idiot, Libby?"

Though the day was warm, Libby shivered. "You're too stupid to know when a woman loves you, that's why!" she blurted out, sobbing now. "Damn! You've had me every way but hanging from a chandelier, and you still don't know!"

Jess straddled the log, drew Libby into his arms and held her. Suddenly he laughed, and the sound was a shout of joy.

Chapter 14

The powwow of the Sioux, Flathead and Blackfoot was a spectacle to remember. Held annually in the same small and otherwise unremarkable town, the meeting of these three tribes was a tradition that reached back to days of mist and shadow, days recorded on no calendar.

Now, on a hot July morning, the erstwhile cow pasture and ramshackle grandstands were churning with activity, and Libby Barlowe's fingers ached to make use of the sketchbook and pencils she carried.

Craning her neck to see the authentic tepees and their colorfully clad inhabitants, she could hardly stand still long enough for the plump woman at the admission gate to stamp her hand.

There was so much noise—laughter, the tinkle of change in the coin box, the neighing and nickering of horses that would be part of the rodeo. Underlying all this was the steady beat of tom-toms and guttural chants of the singers.

"Enjoy yourself now, honey," enjoined the woman tending the cashbox, and Libby jumped, realizing that she was holding up the line behind her. After one questioning look at the hat the woman wore, which consisted of panels cut from various beer cans and crocheted together, she hurried through the gate.

Jess chuckled at the absorbed expression on Libby's face. There was so much to see that a person didn't know where to look first.

"I think I see a fit of creativity coming on," he said.

Libby was already gravitating toward the tepees, plotting light angles and shading techniques as she went. In her heart was a dream, growing bigger with every beat of the tom-toms. "I want to see, Jess," she answered distractedly. "I've got to *see*."

There was love in the sound of Jess's laughter, but no disdain. "All right, all right—but at least let me get you a hat. This sun is too hot for you to go around bareheaded."

"Get me a hat, get me a hat," babbled Libby, zeroing in on a group of small children as they sat watching fathers, uncles and elder brothers perform the ancient rites for rain or success in warfare or hunting.

Libby was taken with the flash of their coppery skin, the midnight black of their hair, the solemn, stalwart expressions in their dark eyes. Flipping open her sketchbook, she squatted in the lush summer grass and began to rough in the image of one particular little boy.

Her pencil flew, as did her mind. She was thinking

in terms of oil paints—vivid shades that would do jus-
tice to the child's coloring and the peacock splendor of
his headdress.

"Hello," she said when the dark eyes turned to her
in dour question. "My name is Libby, what's yours?"

"Jimmy," the little boy responded, but then he must
have remembered the majesty of his ancestry, for he
squared his small shoulders and amended, "Jim Little
Eagle."

Libby made a hasty note in the corner of his sketch.
"I wish I had a name like that," she said.

"You'll have to settle for 'Barlowe,'" put in a familiar voice from behind her, and a lightweight hat landed
on the top of her head.

Libby looked up into Jess's face and smiled. "I guess
I can make do with that," she answered.

Jess dropped to his haunches, assessed the sketch
she'd just finished with admiring eyes. "Wow," he said.

Libby laughed. "I love it when you're profound," she
teased. And then she took off the hat he'd given her and
inspected it thoroughly. It was a standard Western hat,
made of straw, and it boasted a trailing tangle of turquoise feathers and crystal beads.

Jess took the hat and put it firmly back on, then
arranged the feathers so that they rested on her right
shoulder, tickling the bare, sun-gilded flesh there in a
pleasant way. "Did you wear that blouse to drive me
insane, or are you trying to set a world record for blistering sunburns?" he asked unromantically.

Libby looked down at the brief white eyelet suntop
and wondered if she shouldn't have worn a Western
shirt, the way Becky and Cathy had. The garment she

had on had no shoulders or sleeves; it was just a series of ruffles falling from an elasticized band that fit-
ted around her chest, just beneath her collarbone. Not
even wanting to think about the tortures of a sunburn,
she had liberally applied sunblock to her exposed skin.
Not wanting to give Jess the satisfaction, though, she
crinkled her nose and said, "I wore it to drive you insane, of course."

Jess was going to insist on being practical; she saw it
in his face. "They're selling T-shirts on the fairway—
buy one."

"Now?" complained Libby, not wanting to leave the
splendors of the recreated Native American village even
for a few minutes.

Jess looked down at his watch. "Within half an hour,"
he said flatly. "I'm going to find Ken and the others in
the grandstands, Rembrandt. I'll see you later."

Libby squinted as he rose against the sun, towering
and magnificent even in his ordinary jeans and worn
cowboy shirt. "No kiss?"

Jess crouched again, kissed her. "Remember. Half
an hour."

"Half an hour," promised Libby, turning to a fresh
page in her sketchbook and pondering a little girl with
coal-black braids and a fringed buckskin shift. She took
a new pencil from the case inside her purse and began
to draw again, her hand racing to keep up with the pace
set by her heart.

When the sketch was finished, Libby thought about
what she meant to do and how the syndicate that carried her cartoon strip would react. No doubt they would
be furious.

"Portraits!" her agent would cry. "Libby, Libby, there is no *money* in portraits."

Libby sighed, biting her lower lip. Money wasn't a factor really, since she had plenty of that as it was, not only because she had married a wealthy man but also because of prior successes in her career.

She was tired of doing cartoons, yearning to delve into other mediums—especially oils. She wanted color, depth, nuance—she wanted and needed to grow.

"Where the hell is that T-shirt I asked you to buy?"

Libby started, but the dream was still glowing in her face when she looked up to meet Jess's gaze. "Still on the fairway, I would imagine," she said.

His mouth looked very stern, but Jess's eyes were dancing beneath the brim of his battered Western hat. "I don't know why I let you out of my sight," he teased. And then he extended a hand. "Come on, woman. Let's get you properly dressed."

Libby allowed herself to be pulled through the crowd to one of the concession stands. Here there were such thrilling offerings as ashtrays shaped like the state of Montana and gaudy scarves commemorating the pow-wow itself.

"Your secret is out," she told Jess out of the corner of her mouth, gesturing toward a display of hats exactly like her own. The colors of their feather-and-bead plum-age ranged from a pastel yellow to deep, rich purple. "This hat is not a designer original!"

Jess worked up an expression of horrified chagrin and then laughed and began rifling through a stack of colorful T-shirts. "What size do you wear?"

Libby stood on tiptoe, letting her breath fan against

his ear, delighting as that appendage reddened visibly. "About the size of the palm of your hand, cowboy."

"Damn," Jess chuckled, and the red moved out from his ear to churn under his suntan. "Unless you want me to drag you off somewhere and make love to you right now, you'd better not make any more remarks like that."

Suddenly Libby was as pink as the T-shirt he was measuring against her chest. Coming from Jess, this was no idle threat—since their new understanding, reached several weeks before on the top of the hill behind his house, they had made love in some very unconventional places. It would be like him to take her to one of the small trailers brought by some of the cowboys from the Circle Bar B and follow through.

Having apparently deemed the pink T-shirt appropriate, Jess bought it and gripped Libby's hand, fairly dragging her across the sawdust-covered fairgrounds. From the grandstands came the deafening shouts and boot-stompings of more than a thousand excited rodeo fans.

Reaching the rest rooms, which were housed in a building of their own, Jess gave an exasperated sigh. There must have been a hundred women waiting to use the facilities, and he clearly didn't want to stand around in the sun just so Libby could exchange her suntop for a T-shirt.

Before she could offer to wait alone so that Jess could go back and watch the rodeo, he was hauling her toward the nest of Circle Bar B trailers at such a fast pace that she had to scramble to keep up with him.

Thrusting her inside the smallest, which was littered with boots, beer cans and dirty clothes, he ordered, "Put on the shirt."

Libby's color was so high that she was sure he could see it, even in the cool darkness of that camper-trailer. "This is Jake Peterson's camper, isn't it? What if he comes back?"

"He won't come back—he's entered in the bull-riding competition. Just change, will you?"

Libby knew only too well what would happen if she removed that suntop. "Jess…"

He closed the camper door, flipped the inadequate-looking lock. Then he reached out, collected her be-feathered hat, her sketchbook, her purse. He laid all these items on a small, messy table and waited.

In the distance, over the loudspeaker system, the rodeo announcer exalted, "This cowboy, folks, has been riding bulls longer'n he's been tying his shoes."

There was a thunderous communal cry as the cow-boy and his bull apparently came out of their chute, but it was strangely quiet in that tiny trailer where Jess and Libby stood staring at each other.

Finally, in one defiant motion of her hands, Libby wrenched the suntop off over the top of her head and stood still before her husband, her breasts high and proud and completely bare. "Are you satisfied?" she snapped.

"Not yet," Jess retorted.

He came to stand very close, his hands gentle on her breasts. "You were right," he said into her hair. "You just fit the palms of my hands."

"Oh," said Libby in sweet despair.

Jess's hands continued their tender work, lulling her. It was so cool inside that trailer, so intimate and shadowy.

Presently Libby felt the snap on her jeans, and then

the zipper, give way. She was conscious of a shivering heat as the fabric glided downward. Protesting was quite beyond her powers now; she was bewitched.

Jess laid her on the narrow camper bed, joining her within moments. Stretched out upon her, he entered her with one deft thrust.

Their triumph was a simultaneous one, reached after they'd both traveled through a glittering mine field of physical and spiritual sensation, and it was of such dizzying scope that it seemed natural for the unknowing crowd in the grandstands to cheer.

Furiously Libby fastened her jeans and pulled on the T-shirt that had caused this situation in the first place. She gathered up her things, plopped her hat onto her head, and glared into Jess's amused face.

He dressed at a leisurely pace, as though they weren't trespassing.

"If Jake Peterson ever finds out about his, I'll die," Libby said, casting anxious, impatient looks at the locked door.

Jess pulled on one boot, then the other, ran a hand through his rumpled hair. His eyes smoldering with mischief and lingering pleasure, he stood up, pulled Libby into his arms and kissed her. "I love you," he said. "And your shameful secret is safe with me, Mrs. Barlowe."

Libby's natural good nature was overcoming her anger. "Sure," she retorted tartly. "All the same, I think you should know that every man who had ever compromised me in a ranch hand's trailer has said that self-same thing."

Jess laughed, kissed her again, and then released her. "Go back to your drawing, you little hellion. I'll find you later."

"That's what I'm afraid of," Libby tossed back over one shoulder as she stepped out of the camper into the bright July sunshine. Almost before her eyes had adjusted to the change, she was sketching again.

Libby hardly noticed the passing of the hours, so intent was she on recording the scenes that so fascinated her: men festooned with colorful feathers, doing their war and rain dances; women in their worn buckskin dresses, demonstrating the grinding of corn or making their beaded belts and moccasins; children playing games that were almost as old as the distant mountains and the big sky.

Between the residual effects of that scandalous bout of lovemaking in the trailer and the feast of color and sound assaulting her now, Libby's senses were reeling. She was almost relieved when Cathy came and signed that it was time to leave.

As they walked back to find the others in the still-dense crowd, Libby studied her cousin out of the corner of her eye. Cathy and Stacey were living together again, but there was a wistfulness about Cathy that was disturbing.

There would be no chance to talk with her now—there were too many distractions for that—but Libby made a mental vow to get Cathy alone later, perhaps during the birthday party that was being held on the ranch for Senator Barlowe that evening, and find out what was bothering her.

As the group made plans to stop at a favorite café

for an early supper, Libby grew more and more uneasy about Cathy. What was it about her that was different, besides her obviously downhearted mood?

Before Libby could even begin to work out that complex question, Ken and Becky were off to their truck, Stacey and Cathy to their car. Libby was still staring into space when Jess gently tugged at her hand.

She got into the Land Rover, feeling pensive, and laid her sketchbook and purse on the seat.

"Another fit of creativity?" Jess asked quietly, driving carefully through a maze of other cars, staggering cowboys and beleaguered sheriff's deputies.

"I was thinking about Cathy," Libby replied. "Have you noticed a change in her?"

He thought, shook his head. "Not really."

"She doesn't talk to me anymore, Jess."

"Did you have an argument?"

Libby sighed. "No. I've been so busy lately, what with finishing the book and everything, I haven't spent much time with her. I'm ashamed to say that I didn't even notice the change in her until just a little while ago."

Jess gave her a gentle look. "Don't start beating yourself up Libby. You're not responsible for Cathy's happiness or unhappiness."

Surprised, Libby stared at him. "That sounds strange, coming from you."

They were pulling out onto the main highway, which was narrow and almost as choked with cars as the parking area had been. "I'm beginning to think it was a mistake, our being so protective of Cathy. We all meant well, but I wonder sometimes if we didn't hurt her instead."

"Hurt her?"

One of Jess's shoulders lifted in a shrug. "In a lot of ways, Cathy's still a little girl. She's never had to be a grown-up, Libby, because one of us was always there to fight her battles for her. I think she uses her deafness as an excuse not to take risks."

Libby was silent, reflecting on Cathy's fear of being a mother.

As though he'd looked into her mind, Jess went on to say, "Both Cathy and Stacey want children—did you know that? But Cathy won't take the chance."

"I knew she was scared—she told me that. She's scared of so many things, Jess—especially of losing Stacey."

"She loves him."

"I know. I just wish she had something more—something of her own so that her security as a person wouldn't hinge entirely on what Stacey does."

"You mean the way your security doesn't hinge on what I do?" Jess ventured, his tone devoid of any challenge or rancor.

Libby turned, took off her hat and set it down between them with the other things. "I love you very, very much, Jess, but I could live without you. It would hurt unbearably, but I could do it."

He looked away from the traffic only long enough to flash her one devilish grin. "Who would take shameful liberties with your body, if it weren't for me?"

"I guess I would have to do without shameful liberties," she said primly.

"Thank you for sidestepping my delicate male ego," he replied, "but the fact of the matter is, there's no way a woman as beautiful and talented as you are would be alone for very long."

"Don't say that!"

Jess glanced at her in surprise. "Don't say what?"

It was his meaning that had concerned Libby, not his exact words. "I don't even want to think about another man touching me the way you do."

Jess's attention was firmly fixed on the road ahead. "If you're trying to make me feel secure, princess, it's working."

"I'm not trying to make you feel anything. Jess, before we made love that first time, when you said I was really a virgin, you were right. Even the books I've read couldn't have prepared me for the things I feel when you love me."

"It might interest you to know, Mrs. Barlowe, that my feelings toward you are quite similar. Before we made love, sex was just something my body demanded, like food or exercise. Now it's magic."

She stretched to plant a noisy kiss on her husband's cheek. "Magic, is it? Well, you're something of a sorcerer yourself, Jess Barlowe. You cast spells over me and make me behave like a wanton."

He gave an exaggerated evil chuckle. "I hope I can remember the hex that made you give in to me back there at the fairgrounds."

Libby moved the things that were between them into the backseat and slid closer, taking a mischievous nip at his earlobe. "I'm sure you can," she whispered.

Jess shuddered involuntarily and snapped, "Dammit, Libby, I'm driving."

She was exploring the sensitive place just beneath

his ear with the tip of her tongue. "Umm. You like getting me into situations where I'm really vulnerable, don't you, Jess?" she breathed, sliding one hand inside his shirt. "Like today, for instance."

"Libby…"

"Revenge is sweet."

And it was.

Shyly Libby extended the carefully wrapped package that contained her personal birthday gift to Senator Barlowe. She had not shown it to anyone else, not even Jess, and now she was uncertain. After all, Monica had given Cleave gold cufflinks and Stacey and Cathy planned to present him with a bottle of rare wine. By comparison, would her offering seem tacky and homemade?

With the gentle smile that had won him so many hearts and so many votes over the years, he took the parcel, which was revealingly large and flat, and turned it in his hands. "May I?" he asked softly, his kind eyes twinkling with affection.

"Please do," replied Libby.

It seemed to take Cleave forever to remove the ribbons and wrapping paper and lift the lid from the box inside, but there was genuine emotion in his face when he saw the framed pen-and-ink drawing Libby had been working on, in secret, for days. "My sons," he said.

"That's us, all right," commented Jess, who had appeared at the senator's side. "Personally, I think I'm considerably handsomer than that."

Cleave was examining the drawing closely. It showed Jess looking forward, Stacey in profile. When the senator looked up, Libby saw the love he bore his two sons in his eyes. "Thank you," he said. "This is one of the finest gifts I've ever received." He assessed the drawing again, and when his gaze came back to meet hers, it was full of mischief. "But where are my daughters? Where are you and Cathy?"

Libby smiled and kissed his cheek. "I guess you'll have to wait until your *next* birthday for that."

"In that case," rejoined the senator, "why not throw in a couple of grandchildren for good measure?"

Libby grinned. "I might be able to come up with one, but a couple?"

"Cathy will just have to do her part," came the immediate reply. "Now, if you'll excuse me, I want to take this picture around and show all my guests what a talented daughter-in-law I have."

Once his father had gone, Jess lifted his champagne glass and one eyebrow. "*Talented* is definitely the word," he said.

Libby knew that he was not referring to her artwork and hastily changed the subject. "You look so splendid in that tuxedo that I think I'd like to dance with you."

Jess worked one index finger under the tight collar of his formal shirt, obviously uncomfortable. "Dance?" he echoed drily. "Lead me to the organ grinder and we're in business."

Laughing, Libby caught at his free hand and dragged him into the spacious living room, which had been prepared for dancing. There was a small string band to provide the music.

Libby took Jess's champagne glass and set it aside, then rested both hands on his elegant satin lapels. The other guests—and there were dozens—might not have existed at all.

"Dance with me," she said.

Jess took her into his arms, his eyes never leaving hers. "You know," he said softly, "you look so wonderful in that silvery dress that I'm tempted to take you home and make damned sure my father gets that grandchild he wants."

"When we start a baby," she replied seriously, "I want it to be for us."

Jess's mouth quirked into a grin and his eyes were alight with love. "I wasn't going to tape a bow to the little stinker's head and hand it over to him, Libby."

Libby giggled at the picture this prompted in her mind. "Babies are so funny," she dreamed aloud.

"I know," Jess replied. "I love that look of drunken wonder they get when you lift them up high and talk to them. About that time, they usually barf in your hair."

Before she could answer, Ken and Becky came into the magical mist that had heretofore surrounded Libby and Jess.

"All right if I cut in?" Ken asked.

"How soon do you want a grandchild?" Jess countered.

"Sooner the better," retorted Ken. "And, Jess?"

"What?" demanded his son-in-law, eyes still locked with Libby's.

"The music stopped."

Jess and Libby both came to a startled halt, and Becky was so delighted by their expressions that her laughter pealed through the large room.

When the band started playing again, Libby found

herself dancing with her father, while Jess and Becky waltzed nearby.

"You look real pretty," Ken said, beaming down at her.

"You're pretty fancy yourself," Libby answered. "In fact, you look downright handsome in that tuxedo."

"She says that to everybody," put in Jess, who happened to be whirling past with Becky.

Ken's laugh was low and throaty. "He never gets too far away from you, does he?"

"About as far as white gets from rice. And I like it that way."

"That's what I figured. Libby…"

The serious, tentative way he'd said her name gave Libby pause. "Yes?"

"Becky and I are going to get married," he blurted out, without taking a single breath.

Libby felt her eyes fill. "You were afraid to tell me that? Afraid to tell me something wonderful?"

Ken stopped, his arms still around his daughter, his blue eyes bright with relief and delight. Then, with a raucous shout that was far more typical of him than tuxedos and fancy parties, her father lifted her so high that she was afraid she would fall out of the top of her dress.

"That was certainly rustic," remarked Monica, five minutes later, at the refreshment table.

Libby saw Jess approaching through the crowd of guests and smiled down at the buttery crab puff in her fingers. "Are you making fun of my father, Ms. Summers?"

Monica sighed in exasperation. "This *is* a formal

party, after all—not a kegger at the Golden Buckle. I don't know why the senator insists on inviting the help to important affairs."

Slowly, and with great deliberation, Libby tucked her crab puff into Monica's artfully displayed cleavage. "Will you hold this, please?" she trilled, and then walked toward her husband.

"The foreman's brat strikes again," Jess chuckled, pulling her into another waltz.

Cathy was sitting alone in the dimly lit kitchen, her eyes fixed on something far in the distance. Libby was careful to let her cousin see her, rather than startle her with a touch.

"Hi," she said.

Cathy replied listlessly.

Libby took a chair opposite Cathy's and signed, "I'd like to help if I can."

Cathy's face crumbled suddenly and she gave a soft cry that tore at Libby's heart. Her hands flew as she replied, "Nobody can help me!"

"Don't I even get to try?"

A tendril of Cathy's hair fell from the soft knot at the back of her head and danced against a shoulder left bare by her Grecian evening gown. "I'm pregnant," she whispered. "Oh, Libby, I'm pregnant!"

Libby felt confusion and just a touch of envy. "Is that so terrible? I know you were scared before, but—"

"I'm still scared!" Cathy broke in, her voice unusually loud.

Libby drew a deep breath. "Why, Cathy? You're strong and healthy. And your deafness won't be the problem you think it will—you and Stacey can afford to hire help, if you feel it's necessary."

"All of that is so easy for you to say, Libby!" Cathy flared with sudden and startling anger. "You can hear! You're a whole person!"

Libby felt her own temper, always suppressed when dealing with her cousin, surge into life. "You know something?" she said furiously. "I'm sick of your 'Poor Cathy' number! A child is just about the best thing that can happen to a person and instead of rejoicing, you're standing here complaining!"

"I have a reason to complain!"

Libby's arms flew out from her side in a gesture of wild annoyance. "All right! You're deaf, you can't hear! Poor, poor Cathy! Now, can we get past singing your sad song? Dammit, Cathy, I know how hard it must be to live in silence, but can't you look on the positive side for once? You're married to a successful, gentle-hearted man who loves you very much. You have everything!"

"Said the woman who could hear!" shouted Cathy.

Libby sighed and sat back in her chair. "We all have challenges—Jess told me that once, and I think it's true."

Cathy was not going to be placated. "What's your disability, Libby?" she snapped. "Your short fingernails? The fact that you freckle in the summer instead of getting tan?"

The derisive sarcasm of her cousin's words stung Libby. "I'm as uncertain of myself at times as you are, Cathy," she said softly. "Aaron—"

"Aaron!" spouted Cathy with contempt. "Don't hand me that, Libby! So he ran around a little—I had to stand by and watch my husband adore my own cousin for months! And I'll bet Jess has made any traumas you had about going to bed with a man all better!"

"Cathy, please..."

Cathy gave a guttural, furious cry of frustration. "I'm so damned tired of you, Libby, with your career and your loving father and your..."

Libby was mad again, and she bounded to her feet. "And my what?" she cried. "I can't help that you don't have a father—Dad tried to make up for that and I think he did a damned good job! As for a career—don't you dare hassle me about that! I worked like a slave to get where I am! If you want a career, Cathy, get off your backside and start one!"

Cathy stared at her, stunned, and then burst into tears. And, of course, Jess chose exactly that moment to walk in.

Giving Libby one scalding, reproachful look, he gathered Cathy into his arms and held her.

Chapter 15

After one moment of feeling absolutely shattered, Libby lifted her chin and turned from Jess's annoyance and Cathy's veiled triumph to walk out of the kitchen with dignity.

She encountered a worried-looking Marion Bradshaw just on the other side of the door. "Libby... Mrs. Barlowe...that man is here!"

Libby drew a deep breath. "What man?" she managed to ask halfheartedly.

"Mr. Aaron Strand, that's who!" whispered Marion. "He had the nerve to walk right up and ring the bell..."

Libby was instantly alert, alive in every part of her being, like a creature being stalked in the wilds. "Where is he now?"

"He's in the senator's study," answered the flushed,

quietly outraged housekeeper. "He says he won't leave till he talks with you, Libby. I didn't want a scene, what with all these people here, so I didn't argue."

Wearily Libby patted Marion's shoulder. Facing Aaron Strand, especially now, was the last thing in the world she wanted to do. But she knew that he would create an awful fuss if his request was denied, and besides, what real harm could he do with so many people in the house? "I'll talk to him," she said.

"I'll get Jess," mused Mrs. Bradshaw, "and your daddy, too."

Libby shook her head quickly, and warm color surged up over her face. Jess was busy lending a strong shoulder to Cathy, and she was damned if she was going to ask for his help now, even indirectly. And though Ken was almost fully recovered from his confrontation with the bear, Libby had no intention of subjecting him to the stress that could result from a verbal round with his former son-in-law. "I'll handle this myself," she said firmly, and then, without waiting for a reply, she started for the senator's study.

Aaron was there, tall and handsome in his formal clothes.

"At least when you crash a party, you dress for it," observed Libby drily from the doorway.

Aaron set down the paperweight he had been examining and smiled. His eyes moved over her in a way that made her want to stride across the room and slap him with all her might. "That dress is classy, sugarplum," he said in acid tones. "You're definitely bunkhouse-calendar material."

Libby bit her lower lip, counted mentally until the

urge to scream passed. "What do you want, Aaron?" she asked finally.

"Want?" he echoed, pretending pleasant confusion.

"Yes!" hissed Libby. "You flew two thousand miles—you must want something."

He sighed, leaned back against the senator's desk, folded his arms. "Are you happy?"

"Yes," answered Libby with a lift of her chin.

Again he assessed her shiny silver dress, the hint of cleavage it revealed. "I imagine the cowboy is pretty happy with you, too," he said. "Which Barlowe is it, Libby? The steak-house king or the lawyer?"

Libby's head began to ache; she sighed and closed her eyes for just a moment. "What do you want?" she asked again insistently.

His shoulders moved in a shrug. "A baby," he answered, as though he was asking for a cup of coffee or the time of day. "I know you're not going to give me that, so relax."

"Why did you come here, then?"

"I just wanted a look at this ranch. Pretty fancy spread, Lib. You do know how to land on your feet, don't you?"

"Get out, Aaron."

"Without meeting your husband? Your paragon of a father? I wouldn't think of it, Mrs. Barlowe."

Libby was off balance, trying to figure out what reason Aaron could have for coming all the way to Montana besides causing her added grief. Incredible as it seemed, he had apparently done just that. "You can't hurt me anymore, Aaron," she said. "I won't let you. Now, get out of here, please."

"Oh, no. I lost everything because of you—everything. And I'll have my pound of flesh, Libby—you can be sure of that."

"If your grandmother relieved you of your company responsibilities, Aaron, that's your fault, not mine. I should think you would be glad—now you won't have anything to keep you from your wine, women and song."

Aaron's face was tense. Gone was his easy, gentlemanly manner. "With the company went most of my money, Libby. And let's not pretend, sweetness—I can make your bright, shiny new life miserable, and we both know it."

"How?" asked Libby, poised to turn and walk out of the study.

"By generating shame and scandal, of course. Your father-in-law is a prominent United States senator, isn't he? I should think negative publicity could hurt him very badly—and you know how good I am at stirring that up."

Rage made Libby tremble. "You can't hurt Cleave Barlowe, Aaron. You can't hurt me. Now, get out before I have you thrown out!"

He crossed the room at an alarming speed, had a hold on Libby's upper arms before she could grasp what was happening. He thrust her back against the heavy door of the study and covered her mouth with his own.

Libby squirmed, shocked and repulsed. She tried to push Aaron away, but he had trapped her hands between his chest and her own. And the kiss went on, ugly and wet, obscene because it was forced upon her, because it was Aaron's.

Finally he drew back, smirking down at her, grasping her wrists in both hands when she tried to wriggle away from him. And suddenly Libby was oddly detached, calm even. Mrs. Bradshaw had been right when she'd wanted to let Jess know that Aaron was here, so very right.

Libby had demurred because of her pride, because she was mad at Jess; she'd thought she could handle Aaron Strand. Pride be damned, she thought, and then she threw back her head and gave a piercing, defiant scream.

Aaron chuckled. "Do you think I'm afraid of your husband, Libby?" he drawled. Incredibly, he was about to kiss her again, it appeared, when he was suddenly wrenched away.

Libby dared one look at Jess's green eyes and saw murder flashing there. She reached for his arm, but he shook her hand away.

"Strand," he said, his gaze fixed on a startled but affably recovering Aaron.

Aaron gave a mocking half-bow. It didn't seem to bother him that Jess was coldly furious, that half the guests at the senator's party, Ken Kincaid included, were jammed into the study doorway.

"Is this the part," Aaron drawled, "where we fight over the fair lady?"

"This is the part," Jess confirmed icily.

Aaron shrugged. "I feel honor-bound to warn you," he said smugly, "that I am a fifth-degree black belt."

Jess spared him an evil smile, but said nothing.

Libby was afraid; again she grasped at Jess's arm. "Jess, he really is a black belt."

Jess did not so much as look at Libby; he was out of
her reach, and not just physically. She felt terror thick
in her throat, and flung an appealing look at Ken, who
was standing beside her, one arm around her waist.

Reading the plea in his daughter's eyes, he denied it
with an almost imperceptible shake of his head.

Libby was frantic. As Jess and Aaron drew closer
to each other, circling like powerful beasts, she struggled to free herself from her father's restraining arm.
For all his weaknesses of character, Aaron Strand was
agile and strong, and if he could hurt Jess, he would,
without qualms of any kind.

"Jess, no!" she cried.

Jess turned toward her, his jaw tight with cold annoyance, and Aaron struck in that moment. His foot
came up in a graceful arc and caught Jess in the side
of the neck. Too sick to stand by herself or run away,
Libby buried her face in Ken's tuxedo jacket in horror.

There were sounds—terrible sounds. Why didn't
someone stop the fight? Why were they all standing
around like Romans thrilling to the exploits of gladi-
ators? Why?

When the sounds ceased and Libby dared to look, Jess
was still standing. Aaron was sitting on the floor, groan-
ing theatrically, one corner of his lip bleeding. It was obvious that he wasn't badly hurt, for all his carrying on.

Rage and relief mingled within Libby in one dizzying sweep. "Animals!" she screamed, and when she
whirled to flee the ugliness, no one moved to stop her.

Libby sat on the couch in the condo's living room, her
arms wrapped around her knees, stubbornly ignoring the

ringing of the telephone. She had turned off the answering machine, but she couldn't help counting the rings— that had become something of a game in the two days since she'd left the ranch to take refuge here. Twenty-six rings. It was a record.

She stood up shakily, made her way into the kitchen, where she had been trying to sketch out the panels for her cartoon strip. "Back to the old drawing board," she said to the empty room, and the stale joke fell flat because there was no one there to laugh.

The telephone rang again and, worn down, Libby reached out for the receiver affixed to the kitchen wall and snapped, "Hello!"

"Lib?" The voice belonged to her father, and it was full of concern. "Libby, are you all right?"

"No," she answered honestly, letting a sigh carry the word. "As a matter of fact, I'm not all right. How are you?"

"Never mind me—why did you run off like that?"

"You know why."

"Are you coming back to the ranch?"

"Why?" countered Libby, annoyed. "Am I missing some bloody spectacle?"

Ken gave a gruff sigh. "Dammit, Libby, do you love Jess Barlowe or not?"

Tears stung her eyes. Love him? These two days away from him had been hell, but she wasn't about to admit that. "What does it matter?" she shot back. "He's probably so busy holding Cathy's hand that he hasn't even noticed I'm gone."

"That's it. Cathy. Standing up for her is a habit with Jess, Lib—you know that."

Libby did know; in two days she'd had plenty of time to come to the conclusion that she had overreacted in the kitchen the night of the party when Jess had seemed to take Cathy's part against her. She shouldn't have walked out that way. "There is still the fight—"

"You screamed, Libby. What would you have done, if you'd been in Jess's place?" Without waiting for an answer, her father went on, "You're just being stubborn, and so is Jess. Do you love him enough to make the first move, Lib? Do you have the gumption?"

Libby reached out for a kitchen chair, sank into it. "Where is he?"

There was a smile in her father's voice. "Up on that ridge behind your place," he answered. "He's got a camp up there."

Libby knew mild disappointment; if Jess was camping, he hadn't been calling. She had been ignoring the telephone for two days for nothing. "It's nice to know he misses me so much," she muttered petulantly.

Having said his piece, Ken was silent.

"He does miss me, doesn't he?" demanded Libby.

"He misses you," chuckled Ken. "He wouldn't be doing his hermit routine if he didn't."

Libby sighed. "The ridge, huh?"

"The ridge," confirmed Ken with amusement. And then he hung up.

I shouldn't be doing this in my condition, Libby complained to herself as she made her way up the steep hillside. *But since the mountain won't come to me...*

She stopped, looked up. The smoke from Jess's campfire was curling toward the sky; the sun was hot and bright. What the devil did he need with a fire, anyway? It was broad daylight, for heaven's sake.

Muttering, holding on to her waning courage tenaciously, Libby made her way up over the rise to the top of the ridge. Jess was standing with his back to her, looking in the opposite direction, but the stiffness of his shoulders revealed that he knew she was there.

And suddenly she was furious. Hadn't she climbed up this cursed mountain, her heart in her throat, her pride God-only-knew-where? Wasn't the current situation as much his fault as her own? Hadn't she found out, the very day after she'd left him, that she was going to have his baby?

"Damn you, Jess Barlowe," she hissed, "don't you dare ignore me!"

He turned very slowly to face her. "I'm sorry," he said stiffly and with annoying effort.

"For what?" pressed Libby. Damned if she was going to make it easy!

Jess sighed, idly kicked dirt over his campfire with one booted foot. There was a small tent pitched a few feet away, and a coffeepot sat on a fallen log, along with a paperback book and a half-eaten sandwich. "For assuming that the scene with Cathy was your fault," he said.

Libby huffed over to the log, which was a fair distance from Jess, and sat down, folding her arms. "Well, praise be!" she murmured. "What about that stupid fistfight in your father's study?"

His green eyes shot to her face. "You'll grow horns, lady, before you hear me apologize for that!"

Libby bit her lower lip. Fighting wasn't the ideal

way to settle things, it was true, but she couldn't help recalling the pleasure she herself had taken in stuffing that crab puff down the front of Monica Summers's dress at the party. If Monica had made one move to retaliate, she would have gladly tangled with her. "Fair enough," she said.

There was an uncomfortable silence, which Libby finally felt compelled to break. "Why did you have a fire going in the middle of the day?"

Jess laughed. "I wanted to make damned sure you found my camp," he replied.

"Dad told you I was coming!"

He came to sit beside her on the log and even though he didn't touch her, she was conscious of his nearness in every fiber of her flesh and spirit. "Yeah," he admitted, and he looked so sad that Libby wanted to cry.

She eased closer to him. "Jess?"

"What?" he asked, looking her squarely in the eyes now.

"I'm sorry."

He said nothing.

Libby drew a deep breath. "I'm not only sorry," she went on bravely, "I'm pregnant, too."

He was quiet for so long that Libby feared she'd been wrong to tell him about their child—at least for now. It was possible that he wanted to ask for a separation or even a divorce, but he might stay with her out of duty now that he knew. To hold him in that manner would break Libby's heart.

"When did you find out?" he asked finally, and the lack of emotion in his face and in his voice made Libby feel bereft.

"Day before yesterday. After Cathy said she was pregnant, I got to thinking and realized that I had a few symptoms myself."

Jess was silent, looking out over the trees, the ranges, the far mountains. After what seemed like an eternity, he turned to her again, his green eyes full of pain. "You weren't going to tell me?"

"Of course I was going to tell you, Jess. But, well, the time didn't seem to be right."

"You're not going to leave, are you?"

"Would I have climbed a stupid mountain, for pity's sake, if I wanted to leave you?"

A slow grin spread across Jess's face, and then he gave a startling hoot of delight and shot to his feet, his hands gripping Libby's and pulling her with him. If he hadn't caught her in his arms and held her, she would probably have fallen into the lush summer grass.

"Is it safe to assume you're happy about this announcement?" Libby teased, looking up at him and loving him all the more because there were tears on his face.

He lifted her into his arms, kissed her deeply in reply.

"Excuse me, sir," she said when he drew back, "but I was wondering if you would mind making love to me. You see, I'd like to find out if I'm welcome here."

In answer, Jess carried her to the tent, set her on her feet. "My tent is your tent," he said.

Libby blushed a little and bent to go inside the small canvas shelter. Since there wasn't room enough to stand, she sat on the rumpled sleeping bag and waited as Jess joined her.

She was never sure exactly how it came about, but

within moments they were both lying down, facing each other. The weight of his hand was bliss on her breast, and so were the hoarse words he said.

"I love you, Libby. I need you. No matter how mad I make you, please don't leave me again."

Libby traced the strong lines of his jaw with a fingertip. "I won't, Jess. I might scream and yell, but I won't leave. I love you too much to be away from you—if I learned anything in the last two days, it was that."

He was propped up on one elbow now, very close, and he was idly unbuttoning her blouse. "I want you."

Libby feigned shock. "In a tent, sir?"

"And other novel places." He paused, undid the front catch of her bra.

Libby sighed, then gasped as the warmth of his mouth closed over the straining peak of her breast. The sensation was exquisite, sweeping through her, pushing away the weariness and confusion and pain. She tangled her fingers in his rumpled hair, holding him close.

Jess finally left the breast he had so gently plundered to remove his clothes, and then, more slowly, Libby's. When she lay naked before him in the cool shadows of the tiny tent, he took in her waiting body with a look of rapt wonder. "Little enchantress," he breathed, "let me worship you."

Libby could not bear to be separate from him any longer. "Be close to me, Jess," she pleaded softly, "be part of me."

With a groan, he fell to her, his mouth moist and commanding upon hers. His tongue mated with Libby's and his manhood touched her with fire, prodding, taking only partial shelter inside her.

At last Jess broke the kiss and lifted his head, and Libby saw, through a shifting haze, that he was savoring her passion as well as his own. She was aware of every muscle in his body as he struggled to defy forces that do not brook the rebellion of mere mortals.

Finally these forces prevailed, and Jess was thrust, with a raspy cry, into Libby's depths. They moved together wildly, seeking and reaching and finally breaking through the barriers that divide this world from the glories of the next.

Cathy assessed the large oil painting of Jim Little Eagle, the child Libby had seen at the powwow months before, her hands resting on her protruding stomach.

Libby, whose stomach was as large as Cathy's, was wiping her hands on a rag reserved for the purpose. The painting was a personal triumph, and she was proud of it. "What do you think?" she signed, after setting aside the cloth.

Cathy grinned. "What do I think?" she asked aloud, sitting down on the tall stool behind Libby's drawing board. "I'll tell you what I think. I think you should sell it to me instead of letting that gallery in Great Falls handle it. After all, they've got your pen-and-ink drawings and the other paintings you did."

Libby tried to look stern. "Are you asking for special favors, Cathy Barlowe?"

Cathy laughed. "Yes!" Her sparkling green eyes fell to the sketch affixed to Libby's drawing board and she exclaimed in delighted surprise. "This is great!"

Libby came to stand behind her, but her gaze touched only briefly on the drawing. Instead, she was looking out at the snow through the windows of her studio in Ken and Becky's house.

"What are you going to do with this?" Cathy demanded, tugging at Libby's arm.

Libby smiled, looking at the drawing. It showed her cartoon character, given over to the care of another artist now. Liberated Lizzie was in an advanced state of pregnancy, and the blurb read, "If it feels good, do it."

"I'm going to give it to Jess," she said with a slight blush. "It's a private joke."

Cathy laughed again, then assessed the spacious, well-equipped studio with happy eyes. "I'm surprised you work down here at your dad's place. Especially with Jess home almost every day, doing paperwork and things."

Libby's mouth quirked in a grin. "That's *why* I work down here. If I tried to paint there, I wouldn't get anything done."

"You're really happy, aren't you?"

"Completely."

Cathy enfolded her in a hug. "Me, too," she said. And when her eyes came to Libby's face, they were dancing with mischief. "Of course, you and Jess have to understand that you will never win the Race. Stacey and I are ahead by at least a nose."

Libby stood straight and tried to look imperious. "We will not concede defeat," she said.

Before Cathy could reply to this, Stacey came into the room, pretending to see only Libby. "Pardon me, pudgy person," he began, "but has my wife waddled by lately?"

"Is she kind of short, with long, pretty hair and big

green eyes and a stomach shaped rather like a water-melon?"

Stacey snapped his fingers and a light seemed to go on in his face. "That's a pretty good description."

"Haven't seen her," said Libby.

Cathy gave her a delighted shove and flung herself at her husband, laughing. A moment later they were on their way out, loudly vowing to win what Jess and Stacey had dubbed the Great Barlowe Baby Race.

Through with her work for the day and eager to get home to Jess, Libby cleaned her brushes and put them away, washed her hands again, and went out to find her coat. The first pain struck just as she was getting into the car.

At home, Jess was standing pensively in the kitchen, staring out at the heavy layer of snow blanketing the hillside behind the house. Libby came up as close behind him as her stomach would allow and wrapped her arms around his lean waist.

"I've just had a pretty good tip on the Baby Race," she said.

The muscles beneath his bulky woolen sweater tightened, and he turned to look down at her, his jade eyes dark with wonder. "What did you say?"

"We're on the homestretch, Jess. I need to go to the hospital. Soon."

He paled, this man who had hunted wounded bears and fire-breathing dragons. "My God!" he yelled, and suddenly they were both caught up in a whirlwind of activity. Phone calls were made, suitcases were snatched from the coat-closet floor, and then Jess was dragging Libby toward his Land Rover.

"Wait, I'm sure we have time—"

"I'm not taking any chances!" barked Jess, hoisting her pear-shaped and unwieldy form into the car seat.

"Jess," Libby scolded, grasping at his arm. "You're panicking!"

"You're damned right I'm panicking!" he cried, and then they were driving over the snowy, rutted roads of the ranch at the fastest pace he dared.

When they reached the airstrip, the Cessna had been brought out of the small hangar where it was kept and fuel was being pumped into it. After wrestling Libby into the front passenger seat, Jess quickly checked the engine and the landing gear. These were tasks, she had learned, that he never trusted to anyone else.

"Jess, this is ridiculous!" she protested when he scrambled into the pilot's seat and began a preflight test there. "We have plenty of time to drive to the hospital."

Jess ignored her, and less than a minute later the plane was taxiing down the runway. Out of the corner of one eye Libby saw a flash of ice blue.

"Jess, wait!" she cried. "The Ferrari!"

The plane braked and Jess craned his neck to see around Libby. Sure enough, Stacey and Cathy were running toward them, if Cathy's peculiar gait could be called a run.

Stacey leapt up onto the wing and opened the door. "Going our way?" he quipped, but his eyes were wide and his face was white.

"Get in," replied Jess impatiently, but his eyes were gentle as they touched Cathy and then Libby. "The race is on," he added.

Cathy was the first to deliver, streaking over the finish line with a healthy baby girl, but Libby produced twin sons soon after. Following much discussion, the Great Barlowe Baby Race was declared a draw.

* * * * *

Michelle Major grew up in Ohio but dreamed of living in the mountains. Soon after graduating with a degree in journalism, she pointed her car west and settled in Colorado. Her life and house are filled with one great husband, two beautiful kids, a few furry pets and several well-behaved reptiles. She's grateful to have found her passion writing stories with happy endings. Michelle loves to hear from her readers at michellemajor.com.

Books by Michelle Major

Harlequin Special Edition

Welcome to Starlight

The Best Intentions
The Last Man She Expected
His Secret Starlight Baby
Starlight and the Single Dad
A Starlight Summer
Starlight and the Christmas Dare

Crimson, Colorado

Anything for His Baby
A Baby and a Betrothal
Always the Best Man
Christmas on Crimson Mountain
Romancing the Wallflower
Sleigh Bells in Crimson
Coming Home to Crimson

Visit the Author Profile page
at Harlequin.com for more titles.

HER TEXAS
NEW YEAR'S WISH

Michelle Major

To the Fortunes of Texas team—
thanks for making this journey so much fun.

Chapter 1

"**I** wouldn't drink that if I were you."

Wiley Fortune plucked the glass from his sister's hand and placed it back on the polished mahogany bar.

Nicole gave him a funny look. "It's water, Wi. Roja is providing the food for this party. I may be a guest, but I'm also still on the clock."

"I know it's water." Wiley tugged on the end of Nicole's long blond hair, the way he used to do when they were kids. "That's my point."

Nicole, Ashley and Megan Fortune—the triplets—had been born seven years after Wiley, miracle babies in every sense of the word. Their parents, David and Marci, had married after a whirlwind courtship, blending four sons from their respective first marriages in a way that would have made Carol Brady's head spin back in the day.

The boys had gotten off to a bit of a rocky start as they attempted to figure out their roles in the new family. Everything had changed when his mom gave birth to Stephanie five years later. One thing all four boys could agree on was how much they adored their baby sister. Mom had hoped to add another sibling to the mix right away, but she'd had trouble conceiving. Although she'd tried to hide her emotional pain and physical exhaustion, Wiley knew that season of loss had taken a toll on her.

Wiley loved every member of his family, but he'd been a quiet, introverted kid and it was a lot to grow up in such a big, boisterous family. Maybe that fact had something to do with the distance that had seemed to grow between him and the rest of his siblings.

He was the only one who hadn't migrated to the quaint town of Rambling Rose, Texas, although they'd convinced him to visit over Christmas and return for his cousin Adam Fortune's son's first birthday party.

"What's wrong with the water in Rambling Rose?" Nicole asked, scrunching her perfect nose.

"It's obviously tainted," Wiley said, keeping his features neutral and using the same tone with her that he did for contract negotiations in his law firm back in Chicago. "Look around at all the nauseatingly happy couples here tonight. Something happens when a Fortune drinks the Rambling Rose water. They lose all sense and succumb to Cupid's arrow."

Nicole rolled her bright blue eyes toward the tile ceiling that had just been installed in the restaurant. "I guess that explains why you're on your second whiskey of the night."

He lifted the etched-glass tumbler in her direction. "Much safer. Can I buy you a drink?"

"I'm running the restaurant and bar tonight," Nicole said with a delicate sniff. "I don't need you to buy me a drink."

She swatted his arm, then grabbed the water and made a show of drinking down half of it in a few gulps. "Besides—" she delicately dabbed at the corner of her mouth with the flowing sleeve of her batik-print dress "—what's wrong with love?"

"It's a distraction," he answered without hesitation.

"That's cynical, Wiley, even for you." Nicole climbed onto the bar stool next to him and swiveled so that they were both facing out toward the crowd. "Look at how happy Callum and Dillon are."

She pointed toward their brothers, who stood near the front of the banquet room greeting guests. Dillon stood close to Hailey Miller, his fiancée, whom he'd met because she worked at the local spa the family had opened in town last year, while Callum and his wife, Becky, held hands. They'd met and quickly married after Callum moved to Rambling Rose and fell in love with the sweet nurse and her adorable twin toddlers, Sasha and Luna.

"It's the water," he repeated. "Or they've all been stricken by the Texas heat. Even Steven is all googly-eyed for his lady. I barely recognize my own brothers."

A second sister, Megan, let out a mild laugh as she approached from the other side of him and helped herself to a sip of his drink. "If you don't recognize your brothers, it's because you spend too much time on your own."

"I'm here now," Wiley muttered.

"Because Mom guilted you into it," Megan reminded him. She, Nicole and Ashley looked almost identical with their shiny hair and delicate features. They'd followed their brothers to Rambling Rose and opened a farm-to-table restaurant, Provisions, to a great deal of success. Megan was the most serious of the trio and handled the finances for both Provisions and Roja, located inside the Hotel Fortune, which was due to open in just over a month. Nicole was the more flamboyantly creative and was using her culinary skills to create an innovative menu for Roja as the restaurant's executive chef. Ashley took on the role of bossy micromanager in the best way possible, and as the general manager for Provisions.

"Wiley thinks Rambling Rose is a bad influence on all of us because the Fortunes are falling in love here."

"You could use some more love in your life." Megan poked a finger into his biceps. "You work too much."

"How would you know? I live in Chicago. Don't tell me you're keeping tabs on my life from halfway across the country." Wiley felt heat prick the back of his neck as his sisters exchanged a knowing glance. He didn't think he'd sounded defensive, but this was the reason he skipped so many family gatherings. There was no privacy to be had once his brothers and sisters got involved.

"All you talk about is work," Megan answered, smoothing a hand over her cream-colored sweater.

"I like my job." Wiley took a long drink of whiskey,

welcoming the burn of the liquor in his throat. "It's fascinating."

"Contract law isn't fascinating." Nicole laughed. "The restaurant business is fascinating. It's always evolving."

"Not to mention there's no shortage of yummy food to taste," Megan added.

"Being an attorney is fascinating to me," Wiley grumbled.

"Because you need more excitement in your life." Nicole turned to him. "Don't you long for a change, Wi? For years, you've been at the same firm in the same position—"

"And living in the same condo." Megan fist-bumped her sister.

"I'm stable and consistent," Wiley told them.

"Boring," Nicole countered.

"When was the last time you did something spontaneous?" Megan demanded, placing a hand on his knee and pinching like she used to when they were kids.

"What the hell?" Wiley squirmed and then shooed away her hand.

"You're still girl-crazy," Megan told him with a laugh. "You always have been."

"You just need to improve your taste," Nicole advised.

Megan nodded. "Maybe then it will last beyond a couple of months."

Wiley resisted the urge to growl or to stomp away the way he had when his baby sisters bothered him when they were younger. He pointed to their cousin, Kane, who'd joined Callum's construction company last year once Callum moved the operation to Rambling Rose. "Go bother Kane with your meddling," he said.

Nicole laughed. "What are we, the Scooby-Doo gang?"

"Those meddling sisters," Megan said, making her voice low like a cartoon villain's.

"You have so many choices of Fortunes to annoy here tonight."

"But you're our current favorite." Megan leaned in and placed a smacking kiss on Wiley's cheek.

"The rest of them aren't half as much fun now that they've found love," Nicole admitted, resting her head on his shoulder as her tone turned wistful. "They're all so blissed out from true love."

"You're still an easy target." Megan smiled at him, but it didn't quite reach her blue eyes.

"Why doesn't that sound like a compliment?"

"We want you to be happy," Megan told him, but Wiley wasn't sure if she was truly talking about him or thinking of herself. He wasn't about to point out that neither Nicole nor Megan had found love in Rambling Rose.

Nicole handed him her nearly empty glass of water. "You should have some of this. If there really is something in the water, it will be good for you."

"You know that was a joke." He took the water from her and finished it in one swallow. "First, I don't believe in true love. It isn't pragmatic, and the odds of it being successful are ridiculously bad. Besides, whatever my future holds, I'm pretty sure it doesn't include finding my perfect match in a town that's no more than a tiny speck on the Texas map. I'm here temporarily to support all of you. Nothing more."

"You have to keep your heart open," Megan told him. "You never know when love will find you." She gestured toward Callum, who lifted one of the twins into the air. "When Callum and Becky met, he wasn't looking for love."

"Now he'd tell you he couldn't imagine his life without Becky, Sasha and Luna."

Wiley sighed. His sisters were right about Callum. It still felt strange that his brother had taken on the role of father figure to the pretty widow's daughters so seamlessly. Not that Callum wasn't great with kids. He'd had plenty of experience with Stephanie and the triplets. But up until he'd met Becky, Wiley had been certain Callum didn't want kids. The same went for Dillon and Steven. In fact, it had been the change in each of his brothers that made him feel like even more of an odd man out in his family.

He glanced between Nicole and Megan, at the similar wistful expressions as they surveyed the crowd. No way would he rain on their romantic parade, even if he knew their unwavering belief in true love might have more to do with youth and inexperience than anything else. Wiley had been around the dating block enough to know that some people weren't cut out for love. People like him.

His siblings had a lot to be proud of. They'd accomplished so much in their time in Rambling Rose. He'd watched from a distance with fascination over the past year and half as they'd transformed the sleepy community into a thriving small town.

Wiley smiled as Ashley, the third triplet, approached, wagging her finger. "You three need to mingle."

Ashley had always been the bossiest. Now that she was settled in Rambling Rose and happy with her fiancé, Rodrigo Mendoza, and the success of Provisions, she was even more confident in her ability to order her siblings around.

"We're doing important work here," Megan told Ashley with an arched brow. "Convincing Wiley to move to Rambling Rose."

"He's about to agree." Nicole nodded.

"That's wonderful." Ashley gave Wiley a tight hug.

"And a total lie." He extricated himself from her embrace and held up his empty glass toward the bartender, silently requesting a refill. He was staying out at the Fame and Fortune Ranch where several of his siblings lived, so Nicole had given him a ride to the hotel tonight. Might as well take advantage, especially with his sisters on a mission.

"Larkin is a cute baby," he said casually, then smiled to himself as the triplets began to talk over one another, extolling the virtues of the birthday boy.

Nothing distracted them like an adorable kid.

He thanked the bartender when the man brought him a fresh glass and took a step away from the triplets. Time to make a quick exit from that conversation.

Steven waved to him, and Wiley started in that direction, then paused when a flash of blue caught his attention. A beautiful woman wearing a tailored cerulean sheath dress.

The party was being held on the second floor of Roja, the signature restaurant that was part of the Hotel Fortune. The boutique hotel, with its Spanish architecture and Western decor that was a nod to the town's history, was the crowning achievement for his brothers. Callum, Dillon and Steven had successfully opened various businesses in town over the past year, from the medical clinic to a spa to several upscale retail shops. He knew they'd received the most pushback from the community about the initial plan for the hotel, and it had been Kane who'd smoothed over the waters in town, convincing Callum to rescale the project to be smaller and more intimate.

The Hotel Fortune was set to open in just over a month, and Wiley had no doubt it would be a huge success. His brothers and sisters wouldn't settle for anything less.

There were at least fifty people in attendance for Larkin's birthday. In addition to his parents, Adam and Laurel, and his immediate and extended family, the private banquet room on the restaurant's second floor was filled with friends and hotel employees. The community had banded together last year to support the baby when he needed a bone marrow transplant. Everyone was thrilled to celebrate the little boy who'd overcome so much. And to Wiley's surprise, based on how his siblings had talked about the celebration, all the different Fortune factions seemed to be getting along.

He turned toward the wall of windows and patio doors that had been opened for the evening. It was unseasonably warm for this time of year, even by Texas standards. In the center of the exterior wall was a stamped concrete balcony with wrought iron railings that overlooked the patio and pool below.

His gaze snagged on the same woman who'd caught his attention a few moments earlier. She had long, bourbon-colored hair, a slender build and creamy skin from what he could see of her arms in the sleeveless dress she wore. She spoke to Callum and Mariana, one of the town's most illustrious residents, who was working with Nicole as the sous chef in the Roja kitchen. For years, Mariana had run a successful outdoor market in downtown Rambling Rose, with vendors selling all kinds of food and wares. And her food stall had been one of the most—if not the most—popular stand of all. It was in no small part thanks to her influence with the local vendors that the Fortune family had been able to go ahead with some of their most successful new projects, all because Mariana understood that they would bring new life to her hometown.

Wiley didn't recognize the woman in blue, although he couldn't help but think they'd met before. There was nothing else that would explain the strange connection when he hadn't even fully seen her face.

Then she turned, and the breath whooshed out of him on a long exhale. It was like a piece of a puzzle snapping together with its perfect match. His heart seemed to skip a beat. No, that couldn't be right. The woman was a stranger. There was no question, because he would never forget his reaction to her.

She might be a stranger, but he had to meet her.

He made his way through the crowd. Mariana walked away, but Callum remained in conversation with the woman as Wiley stopped just behind his brother.

"Hey, Wi." Callum glanced over his shoulder. "Have you met Grace Williams? She's one of our management trainees. Grace, this is my brother Wiley. He's our big-shot family attorney visiting from Chicago."

Wiley barely registered the introduction as Grace smiled at him. Her eyes, the same bright blue of a clear summer sky, crinkled at the corners.

"Hi." He struggled to regain control over the rapid cadence of his breathing. If he didn't know better, Wiley would think he was having some sort of heart attack. There was no logical explanation for his reaction. He'd met countless beautiful women over the years and dated his fair share of them. But Grace Williams leveled him with just a smile.

Callum cleared his throat, and Wiley realized Grace had offered her hand to shake.

"It's nice to meet you," she said softly, a blush staining her cheeks.

He took her hand, almost expecting to feel the zap of an electric current when he touched her. No literal shock, which he realized was a ridiculous expectation in the first place.

"Hey, Wiley," Steven called from a few feet away. "Come over here for a second. I have a couple hotel employees I want you to meet."

Wiley had already met a dozen new people tonight, employees, local business owners and members of the extended Fortune family. He'd enjoyed the various introductions until this moment. Now he was done talking to people other than Grace.

"It's fine," Callum told him with a dismissive pat on the shoulder. "Grace and I are discussing some hotel business, anyway."

Wiley wanted to argue, but that would be rude. He looked toward Grace once more and her breath hitched.

"I'll be around all night," she told him, darting a quick glance toward Callum before her gaze returned to Wiley. "I hope we can chat some more."

"Definitely," he told her, the band around his heart loosening slightly. He had all night to talk to Grace.

That thought calmed Wiley enough so that he could shift his attention to Steven as he walked away. He wasn't about to lose his chance with Grace when they'd only just met.

Wiley Fortune was quite possibly the most handsome man Grace had ever seen. And in his family, that was saying something.

He shared the same tall, lean build as Steven and that innate Fortune spark, but Grace's reaction to Wiley had been unexpected. As he walked away, she worked to regain control. The last thing she needed was to make a spectacle of herself in front of Callum.

She did her best not to fidget as she gave an update on the water heater that had leaked in one of the hotel's main-floor utility rooms. She hated relaying anything that seemed like bad news, especially in the middle of a first birthday party, but hoped the fact that she had a solution for the potential dilemma would help.

"It sounds like you handled it perfectly," Callum told her, and she let out a small sigh of relief. "Just like tonight. Larkin's celebration has gone off without a hitch."

"I can't take all the credit," Grace admitted because that was her way. "The Roja staff has done an amazing job. Everyone's pitched in where they were supposed to. And a roomful of Fortunes isn't as intimidating as you led me to believe."

Callum grinned. "We're on our best behavior." He leaned closer. "It's a bit of a surprise, I'll admit. This night makes me feel like we're actually on track for the grand opening next month."

"Definitely," Grace agreed. "By then, all the details will be ironed out. Everyone in Rambling Rose is going to be talking about the Hotel Fortune."

"I hope you're right. This venture has definitely given us the most headaches, although it will all be worth it when we have a full slate of guests."

"You and your brothers and sisters have made sure every step of the redevelopment plan for the town has been thoughtfully crafted and executed. I'm honored to be a part of it." Grace inwardly cringed, hoping she didn't sound like a total suck-up, but Callum smiled.

"We're glad to have you on the team. I'm sorry things at Cowboy Country didn't work out, but their loss is our gain."

Grace forced a smile, although mention of her previous job had her stomach tightening painfully. She didn't think anyone in Rambling Rose knew the full truth of why she'd left the cowboy theme park run by another branch of the Fortune family in the town of Horseback Hollow. There was no way she was going to share her heartbreak and humiliation, not when her life was finally getting back on track.

"Take a break." Callum gestured to the row of food tables. "Have a piece of cake or a drink or just enjoy the beautiful night. You've earned it, Grace."

She nodded. "Thanks. I'll have a piece of birthday

cake. I'm glad things are going so well and Larkin's enjoying the attention."

Someone called to Callum, and she turned for the cake table but first detoured toward the empty balcony overlooking the hotel's impeccably landscaped pool area. She needed to cool off as she could still feel her cheeks burning from the way Wiley had looked at her.

She wouldn't jeopardize her future for any man, no matter how attractive. In some ways, she still felt like pinching herself, because despite all the things that had gone wrong in her life, the three and half months she'd spent in the Hotel Fortune management training program seemed to make all the trouble worth it.

Yes, she'd had to drop out of college to help take care of her older brother after he'd been seriously injured in a car accident almost a decade earlier. Yes, she'd struggled to fit in when she'd finally returned to school, unable to enjoy life in the way regular college students did. She'd been too serious and too focused, determined to get her degree but always guilty that she was able to have a life Jake couldn't due to his recovery. After finally graduating with a degree in hospitality management, she'd landed a job in the Cowboy Country front office. At that point, Grace thought she was finally on her way. She'd had a good job, a handsome boyfriend and a fresh start in life.

Discovering that Craig had been cheating on her with a fellow employee—and that pretty much everyone at Cowboy Country knew it except Grace—had been a blow she hadn't expected. One that brought her to her knees, literally and figuratively.

But she was leaving the past behind for her new

future with the Hotel Fortune. Although members of the family had been taking the lead on running things during construction, they planned to promote someone from within the training program to the role of general manager as part of the grand opening. There might be other employees vying for the coveted position, but Grace was determined to earn it.

She stepped to the edge of the balcony, running her palms across the smooth wrought iron railing. She couldn't remember ever feeling such a sense of anticipation as she did at this moment.

Drawing in a long pull of the fresh air from the open patio doors, she turned back toward the party. Pride swelled in her chest at the crowd of happy people. She'd had a lot to do with making this evening a success.

Her gaze snagged on Wiley once again as he moved away from the group where he stood. One corner of his full mouth tugged into a sexy smirk, like he could feel the way her body went on high alert from across the room. Grace felt like she was on a roller coaster, climbing the track of the first giant hill. Her heart raced as she thought about the free fall to come.

When he started toward her, she turned and leaned forward, gripping the railing with rigid fingers. It wasn't that she didn't want to meet him. In fact, her body practically yearned to get close to him.

But she'd given herself to a man once before with disastrous results. No way would she fall again.

A loud crack split the air, and she stumbled as the balcony pitched forward. Then she was falling so fast she didn't even have time to scream.

Chapter 2

"This doesn't make any sense." Callum dashed a hand through his hair as he paced the small waiting room in the Rambling Rose Medical Center emergency room. "In all my years of construction, I've never had something like that happen on one of our projects."

"We'll figure out what caused it," Wiley said from where he sat on a patterned chair situated against the far wall. "But first we need to make sure Grace is okay. She's the priority right now."

Callum nodded. "You're right. But what if it had been a hotel guest or one of the kids on that balcony when it collapsed? Can you imagine if there were people on the patio below?"

Wiley understood his brother's train of thought but felt oddly defensive at the subtle suggestion that the accident wasn't as catastrophic because a mere employee had been injured.

As if sensing his irritation, Callum held up a hand. He wore dark slacks and a button-down shirt that was covered with dust from the rubble of the mess that had been made when the balcony collapsed. "I'm not insinuating that Grace is disposable. I would never put her or any employee at risk. You know that, Wi."

"She was unconscious," Wiley muttered, his nerve endings pulling tight at the memory of the EMTs lifting her limp body onto a stretcher. "She could have died in that fall."

The thought of losing her before he got to know her felt like a punch to the gut.

"But she woke up in the ambulance." Callum continued to pace back and forth. "She was obviously in shock but seemed lucid. Her ankle was in bad shape, but I have to believe that's the worst of her injuries. We need to believe Grace will be okay."

Grace Williams.

Callum had shared the woman's name with the first responders when they arrived at the hotel mere minutes after Nicole made the 911 call.

In the chaos that ensued after the balcony's collapse, Callum had been designated to accompany Grace to the hospital while his brothers and sisters dealt with things on-site. Wiley couldn't explain why he'd stalked to his car and followed the emergency vehicle, but he couldn't seem to release the impulse to be near Grace, even if she didn't want or need him there.

"You better hope she's okay," Wiley muttered.

Callum stopped directly in front of him, his eyes narrowing. "What's that supposed to mean?"

Wiley drew in a breath. How was he supposed to explain the fierce protectiveness he felt toward a woman he'd only just met? He didn't understand it, so there was no way his brother would.

"The hotel bears a responsibility for the accident. If the construction was faulty or the building materials subpar—"

"Are you kidding?" Callum's jaw tightened. "You know I don't cut corners, Wiley. Everything I build is rock solid."

"Other than the balcony that just collapsed with a woman standing on it." Wiley rose from his chair to stand toe-to-toe with his brother.

"I'm going to assume you're playing devil's advocate because you're an attorney and concerned about the family's liability. I sure as hell hope you aren't suggesting that we didn't take all the necessary steps to ensure proper construction." Temper flared between them, and Wiley wanted to kick himself in the family jewels for goading his brother at a time like this. The thought of Grace's injuries made him want to lash out at anyone and everyone.

He gave a tight nod. "I'm sorry, Callum. You're right. I'm worried about your employee and I'm concerned about the hotel's responsibility and the potential negative press of this kind of accident. There's no doubt about the quality of the work you do. I don't want a single incident to tarnish your track record in town."

Callum eyed him for a moment longer, then stepped away and began to pace again. "We won't let it. Of course we'll take care of any medical bills that aren't covered by Grace's insurance and continue to pay her salary while she's recovering. Once she returns to work—"

"You don't even know the extent of her injuries," Wiley felt compelled to point out.

"I can help with that."

They both turned as a tall man in light blue scrubs entered the waiting room. Callum strode forward and shook the man's hand, reminding Wiley of his brother's ties to the town.

"Mark, how is she?"

The man threw a glance in Wiley's direction.

"This is my brother Wiley. He's in town for Larkin's party."

"Quite an event," the other man murmured, which to Wiley's mind was the understatement of the new year.

"Wiley, this is Dr. Mark Matthews." Callum gestured to the doctor. "Becky says he's one of the best emergency room physicians she knows." He turned his attention fully to Mark. "I'm glad you're on duty tonight. How is Grace?"

"Good, given what she's been through." The doctor looked past Callum and Wiley to the empty waiting room. "Have you called her family?"

Callum nodded. "Ashley tracked down her parents' number and spoke to her mom. They're on their way here."

"Can we see her?" Wiley demanded, crossing his arms over his chest when both men gave him a strange look.

"I suppose that would be all right," Mark agreed almost reluctantly. "We've moved her to a room on the third floor for the night."

"How bad are the injuries?" Callum asked as Dr. Matthews turned toward a bank of elevators.

"You're not family, so I can't share any details." Mark jabbed at the elevator's button. "Grace will decide what she wants to tell you. She was awake when I left, but if she's fallen back asleep I don't want you to wake her. She's in room three sixty-five. I need to check on another patient, and then I'll be up."

Callum nodded. "Thanks, Mark. We won't disturb her if she's resting."

The elevator doors swished open as the doctor turned away. Wiley followed his brother into the small space.

"I appreciate you being here," Callum said as he pushed the button for the third floor. "But you don't have to go with me to see her."

Wiley kept his gaze on the carpeted floor. "I'll stay."

He could feel Callum studying him but didn't answer. Let his brother think that his interest in Grace Williams was due to concern over the hotel's liability for the accident.

It made sense, and not only because of Wiley's career as an attorney. He'd never gotten particularly involved in the details of the lives of his siblings, at least as much as he could help it. After years of being part of such a large family, his identity as a separate individual meant the world to him.

He couldn't figure out why Grace had changed that in a split second, and he wasn't ready to examine it now.

Grace glanced up at the soft knock on the hospital door. Her head felt heavy and somewhat muddled, but now that the pain medicine had kicked in, at least her entire body no longer throbbed in agony.

She expected to see her parents' familiar faces. Shock rippled through her as Callum Fortune entered. She couldn't imagine that the man responsible for the construction of most of the new buildings in Rambling Rose would be too happy that one of his employees had managed to get herself practically killed in the middle of an important family event.

"Hey there," Callum said gently as he came closer to the bed. "Are you up for a couple of visitors?"

Her gaze moved beyond his broad frame and shivers erupted along her skin as she met the intense gaze of the man who'd captured her attention just before the balcony collapsed. Grace stifled a giggle that she knew must be caused by the pain medicine at the thought that her body's overwhelming reaction to Wiley might have caused the earth to move under her feet.

"Grace?" Callum gave her a strange look, and for an instant she worried she'd been singing the words to the classic tune out loud.

She swallowed and tried to pull together her tangled musings. "Thanks for stopping by," she said, and immediately thought she sounded ridiculous. As if Callum Fortune had come to her hospital room for some kind of social call. "I'm sorry I broke your balcony." Her voice sounded strange to her ears, thick and garbled.

Callum shook his head. "You didn't do anything wrong," he assured her. "There's no reason to be sorry. I'm the one who owes you an apology, Grace. I don't understand how or why that balcony collapsed. The county building inspector was out before the holidays and we passed everything."

Wiley stepped forward, clearing his throat. "We're glad you're okay."

The gentle gleam in Wiley's brown eyes made her stomach flutter once again. When they'd been introduced, his eyes had appeared regular brown, but as he approached the bed she could see flecks of gold in their depths. His lashes were also outrageously long for a man. Cosmetics companies could build entire ad campaigns around the promise of achieving lashes like his.

She blinked and tried to focus, realizing she was staring at him like some cow-eyed teenager. "Hi," she breathed, unable to form a more coherent greeting.

"Hello, Grace," he said, lifting her hand and squeezing her fingers with what felt like something close to admiration.

She'd always hated her plain, one-syllable name, but on Wiley's lips it sounded like a poem.

"Hi," she repeated and felt color heating her cheeks. Too bad she couldn't blame the pain medicine for her reaction to him.

"How are you?" he asked, like he truly cared about her answer and not just her physical injuries.

"Did you two know each other before the party?" Callum interrupted before she could answer, sounding both confused and irritated.

Oh, I know this man, Grace thought to herself. At least she wanted to know him.

Wiley abruptly released Grace's hand. Immediately she wanted to reach for him again. Something flashed in his eyes, and she had the thought that he might feel the same as her.

He broke eye contact with her to glance at his brother. "No. You introduced us."

"That's what I thought," Callum said, his voice flat.

Grace forced herself to focus on Callum. "I know the accident wasn't your fault, Callum. I—"

"Someone is sure as hell to blame."

She winced and brought a hand to her head at her brother's overly loud words. Jake and her parents hurried into the room, crowding around her bedside as the Fortune brothers stepped back.

Grace closed her eyes and wished for everyone to disappear other than Wiley. She wanted him to hold her hand again and ask how she was. She wanted to tell him she felt better when he was with her, even though that didn't make any sense. Still, it felt totally justifiable to her heart.

"Jake, this isn't the time." Grace opened her eyes as her mother placed a gentle hand on her brother's arm. "Our focus right now is Grace."

Her brother, older by two years, crossed his arms over his chest. "We can all agree that she wouldn't be fighting for her life in this hospital bed if it weren't for the shoddy construction at the hotel."

"I'm not fighting for my life," Grace said, lifting a hand to cover her mouth when another bubble of laughter threatened to escape. Her brother had always had a quick temper, but she sobered as she noted the look of consternation that crossed Callum's features.

"Oh, sweetheart." Her mother let out a soft sob, and

regret pricked at the hazy fog filling Grace's mind. The last thing she wanted was to upset her mother. "We were so worried when that Fortune woman called."

Grace searched her brain for the details the doctor had shared about the extent of her injuries. "I'm okay, Mom. I broke my ankle and have a minor concussion."

Barbara Williams gasped. "A head injury?"

"Minor," Grace assured her, remembering the weeks after Jake's car accident when he'd lain in a medically induced coma while they waited for the brain swelling to subside. "Plus a few bruises and scrapes. Everything else came back clear."

"Are you sure?" her father asked, his tone gruff. Grace knew that rough exterior hid the heart of a teddy bear.

Her parents turned as Dr. Matthews entered the room. "She's sure. Grace was incredibly lucky that her injuries weren't worse. We're going to keep her overnight for observation due to the concussion, but we anticipate a straightforward recovery."

"Thank God." Her mother leaned forward to brush a kiss across Grace's forehead. "My sweet baby."

"I'm not a baby," Grace muttered. Even the cloud of fogginess from the pain medicine couldn't dull the annoyance at her mother's pronouncement, especially in front of Callum and Wiley.

Despite the caregiver role Grace had taken on during Jake's convalescence and the fact that she'd been managing her own life for years, her mom and dad continued to treat her like a dependent little girl. She tried to be patient with them, because she knew how much

Jake's accident had made them aware of the mortality of their children.

Things had only been exacerbated when Grace moved back to Rambling Rose after the debacle at Cowboy Country. But her duties at the hotel gave her a sense of purpose and a feeling of independence once again. Now it felt like everything was in jeopardy.

Dr. Matthews frowned as she swiped a hand across her cheek, obviously misinterpreting the reason for her unwelcome tears. Grace didn't care what had caused the balcony's collapse, assuming nothing like that happened again. She did worry about what her recovery might mean for her future.

"That doesn't change the fact that someone is responsible for my sister being hurt." Jake shifted his glare between Callum and Wiley.

Callum's mouth thinned. "The hotel will take care of any medical expenses not covered by insurance. Our priority is that she feels better as quickly as possible."

"To cover your assets," Jake muttered.

"Not at all," Callum countered.

"Do you really need to have this discussion in front of Grace?" the doctor asked impatiently.

"Or at all?" Grace added. She sent a beseeching glance toward her brother, silently pleading with him to give it a rest, but Jake only shook his head.

"You want to step out into the hall for a moment?" he asked Callum.

"Good idea," Callum agreed, and turned for the door.

Grace reached for her father's hand. "Don't let Jake be rude, Dad. This wasn't Callum's fault. The Fortunes aren't to blame. I know it."

A muscle ticked in Mike Williams's bearded jaw. Her father retained the stocky build he'd had as younger man, and added a few inches of girth around the waist. "I'll try to keep him calm." He patted the top of Grace's hand. "We're glad you're okay, baby girl."

Her stomach knotted as she watched her father follow the two younger men out into the hall.

Dr. Matthews gave her an encouraging smile. "You doing okay?"

"Fine," she murmured.

Her mom began to pepper the doctor with a litany of questions about her injuries and a recovery plan. Grace hated that she was causing her family this kind of worry or that she could be seen as a burden to the hotel.

"That 'fine' didn't seem convincing," Wiley said as he lowered himself into the chair next to her bed and scooted closer. "You're going to be okay, Grace. I promise."

She automatically smoothed a hand over her hair as if she had a reason to worry about looking pretty for Wiley Fortune. He was so close she could reach out and touch him. The urge was both overwhelming and nonsensical.

"You don't owe me any promises," she said instead, working to keep her wits about her despite the pounding of her heart and the effects of the pain medicine.

"I get that." He offered a tentative smile. "I can't seem to help myself."

She blinked and then looked away, wondering if he was truly as sincere as he seemed. Her mother was still talking with the doctor, nodding furiously and taking notes on a small pad of paper she'd pulled from her purse as he spoke in hushed tones. Her father had closed the door behind him when he'd ventured into the hallway. Grace had a feeling Jake was giving Callum all kinds of trouble, and she wished she could make it stop.

"My brother is protective," she told Wiley. "I'm sure he'll realize that the balcony collapse was an unfortunate accident. Not anyone's fault."

"It's good that you have people to look out for you," he said.

"I guess you're right." She ran a finger along the edge of the thin blanket that covered her. "Although at the moment, I wish Jake would back off. I do want you to know that his accusations aren't personal. He doesn't have it in for your family or anything like that."

"Good to know." Wiley studied her for a long moment and then lifted his hand like he might touch her. With a shake of his head he drew it back again, and disappointment pounded through Grace.

"Do you have any other brothers or sisters?" he asked.

She got the impression he was trying to distract her from worrying about what kind of scene might be unfolding in the hall.

"No." She flashed a smile. "We're a small family compared to yours."

"Nothing wrong with that." He returned her smile. "What about a boyfriend?"

She felt her mouth drop open, and he immediately rose from the chair. He scrubbed a hand over his jaw, looking uncomfortable. "I'm sorry. Forget I asked that. It's none of my business."

"No boyfriend," she told him quietly, feeling heat

rise to her cheeks. "My focus right now is the training program at the hotel." She wiggled her toes, which stuck out of the cast on her left leg that stopped just below her knee. "This couldn't have come at a worse time."

"Is there ever a good time to be standing on a balcony when it collapses?" Wiley asked, smiling again. Teasing her. Possibly even flirting with her?

Before Grace had a chance to process that, her father and Callum reentered the room.

Her mother took a step away from the doctor and frowned. "Where's Jake?"

"I sent him home," Grace's father said with a small shake of his head.

Callum's cheeks were flushed, his jaw taut. He motioned to Wiley. "We should go."

Grace sat up straighter on the bed. She wanted to protest Wiley leaving, but that would be stupid.

"Thank you for being here with me." She looked to Callum first before turning her attention to Wiley. "It helped a lot."

"I'm glad," he said, and the intensity in his gaze made it feel like they were the only two people in the room.

"Grace, I can't tell you how sorry we are that you were hurt tonight." Callum's commanding tone forced her to return her gaze to him. "Like I said earlier, anything you need, our family will take care of it. Just focus on getting well again."

"And back to work," she added quickly. "I want to get back to work as soon as possible. Please let everyone know that."

Callum smiled tightly. "Of course."

"Work is the last thing you need to be concerned with right now," her father said with a sniff. He gave Callum a sidelong glass. "I want confirmation that your hotel is safe before I let my little girl go back there."

Grace bit back a frustrated groan. Was her father trying to make the Fortunes angry? Her potential future at the hotel meant everything. She wouldn't let anything—not even a collapsing balcony—jeopardize that.

"I understand, sir," Callum answered, but she could see by the set of his shoulders that it bothered him to have his workmanship called into question.

"It's fine." Wiley said, moving close to her again. His fingers brushed the top of her cast and despite the layers of plaster, she felt the touch like he was caressing her skin. "Callum understands that your family is upset. I'll talk to him."

"Thank you," she whispered, and bit down on the inside of her cheek to stem her tears. She didn't want to start sobbing in front of the two Fortunes on top of everything else.

Wiley thanked the doctor and offered a heartfelt reassurance to her parents, then followed Callum out of the room.

"I'll give you all a few minutes," Dr. Matthews said, "and then we can talk about next steps."

When the door closed behind the doctor, Grace let the tears flow.

"Oh, sweetie." Barbara was at her bedside in an instant. "You must have been terrified."

Grace took the tissue her mother handed her and blew her nose. "It happened so fast I barely had time to be scared."

"The point is it never should have happened in the first place," her father said, crossing his arms over his meaty chest. "What the hell kind of karma are we saddled with, Gracie, that we almost lose your brother and now you?"

"You didn't almost lose me, Dad."

"A second-floor balcony collapsed with you standing on it," Mike reminded her—as if she needed reminding. "You're very lucky."

"I know." Grace crumpled the tissue. "My injuries aren't anywhere near what Jake went through. I don't want either of you to worry about my recovery process. I'm going to get back to normal sooner than later."

"You can't rush it," her mother said, smoothing the hair from her forehead. "Let me get you a mirror and a wet towel. I'm sure you want to fix your face a bit."

Grace lifted a hand to her cheek. Fix her face? What was wrong with her face?

"You'll move home, of course." Her father's tone brooked no argument.

Grace argued, anyway. "I love my apartment, Dad. I can recover there just as easily." In truth, she didn't exactly love the cramped walk-up she'd rented when she returned to Rambling Rose, but it was better than moving back in with her parents.

Her father snorted. "You live on the second floor of a building with a staircase so narrow I can't believe it's even up to code. No way can you manage that with a cast."

"I could try," she insisted, even though she knew her dad was right.

"Grace Elizabeth."

She resisted the urge to roll her eyes but knew she had little chance of winning an argument when he used her middle name, as well.

"I appreciate the offer," she said instead. "It would make things easier until I'm out of the cast." Her parents lived in a quiet section of Rambling Rose in the same house Grace had grown up in. The house, a rancher, wasn't big, but it did have plenty of space for her.

"We'll take care of packing your things," her mother said, returning from the bathroom with a small hand-held mirror and a stack of wet paper towels. "All you need to focus on is resting."

And returning to work, Grace thought to herself. No point in saying the words out loud and engaging in another argument with her parents.

She took the mirror and a paper towel from her mom. "Oh, no." She glanced up and met her mother's concerned gaze. "Why didn't you tell me?"

"You'll clean up in a jiffy," Barbara said brightly.

All Grace could think about was Wiley seeing her like this. The cast was one thing, but her face was a mess. It wasn't injured—for that she was grateful—but she looked like she'd been on a three-day bender. Her hair hung limp around her shoulders and stuck to her head in several places. Her skin was pasty and pale, and the mascara she'd carefully applied before the event was puddled under her eyes.

If she had any question as to whether Wiley Fortune had been interested in her or simply concerned about her being injured at his family's hotel, she was fairly certain her appearance answered it.

Her ruined makeup and the ruined evening seemed

to be par for the course in Grace's life. Finally things had been turning around for her, and then something had to happen to send her veering off her chosen path once again.

She began to wipe her face as she listened to her parents make plans for her unexpected homecoming. Grace couldn't help but wonder if she'd ever truly attain the future she wanted so badly.

Chapter 3

"That was sure as hell a shock."

Wiley turned as Steven approached from one of the hotel's patio doors. His brother kicked a small piece of terra-cotta-colored stone as he walked toward Wiley.

It was nearly nine on the morning after the party. Wiley wanted to survey the balcony rubble in the daylight and had held out an odd kind of hope that things wouldn't seem as bad in the aftermath of the accident.

Instead, they were worse.

The balcony's deck had ripped off the exterior wall, sending thousands of pounds of concrete and metal plummeting to the ground. Grace had fallen a good twenty-five feet, and it was truly a miracle she hadn't been hurt worse.

He said as much to his brother, who nodded. "Callum said she was in good spirits at the hospital. You were there with him, right?"

Wiley nodded. "She was also doped up on painkillers," he muttered. "I'm not sure we should judge her feelings about the accident based on last night, especially not if her family has any influence on her opinion."

Steven nodded. The two of them had an unspoken language. Wiley had been a toddler when their mother married David Fortune, who'd quickly adopted both of his new wife's young sons and given them his name. Wiley was close to all of his siblings, but he and Steven had a special bond.

Steven had been a committed bachelor until he'd met and fallen for Ellie Hernandez, the mayor of Rambling Rose. Things had started off rocky between them, but they'd quickly fallen deeply in love. Another Fortune who found his perfect future in this small Texas town. "That's to be expected, but we're all committed to doing the right thing by Grace. She's been a huge asset to the hotel. I know Nicole and Mariana feel the same."

"She's special," Wiley said as his gaze zeroed in on a flash of silver under a pile of debris.

"That's an odd description coming from you. I didn't realize you and Grace had met before last night."

He could feel Steven studying him but didn't meet his brother's gaze. "We hadn't." Wiley walked forward, carefully picking his way through the mess.

He wore dark jeans and a cotton sweater plus the cowboy boots the triplets had given him for Christmas. As a confirmed city slicker, Wiley felt a little strange sporting boots, but they seemed to be expected in Texas.

He bent down and pulled a high heel from the rubble. Clearly one of Grace's shoes. The image of her unconscious on the ground flashed in his mind again, and his chest clenched in response.

"What's the deal?" Steven asked, sounding both curious and concerned. "You went to the hospital with Callum, and he said you were acting strange. Now you look like you've seen a ghost. If you and Grace don't know each other, why are you—"

"She could have died," Wiley blurted out, then rolled his lips inward. He needed to get a handle on his emotions when it came to Grace Williams. He couldn't explain to his brother the connection he felt with her. It had been immediate and intense, like a bolt of lightning slamming through him. "She was injured in a fall at our family's hotel. The hotel that Fortune Brothers Construction built. We're responsible for her, Steven."

His brother's thick brows drew together. "Are you thinking about our potential liability in the accident? Is Wiley the attorney making sure we cover our—"

They both turned when a feminine throat cleared. "Sorry to bother you, Steven." A woman walked toward them from the far side of the pool. She looked to be in her midtwenties and wore a pencil skirt and a silk blouse that made her seem a bit overdressed for a casual Sunday. "There's a reporter in the lobby asking to speak to the hotel manager." She tucked a perfect blond curl behind one ear. "If you'd like I can talk to him?"

Wiley frowned at the gleam in the woman's gaze. "Who are you?" he demanded, not bothering to gentle his tone. In the same way that he'd felt an immediate connection with Grace, he had an instant dislike of this woman.

She swallowed visibly, her gaze darting from Wiley to Steven, who'd pulled out his phone and was typing in a message.

"Jillian Steward," she said, clearing her throat. "I'm one of the management program trainees at the hotel. I have a background in public relations as well as hospitality at my last position, so I'm more than equipped to deal with the press. That's part of the role of whoever is promoted to the GM position."

Grace had mentioned something about the trainee program last night. She'd seemed worried about her job given the extent of her injuries. Did she suspect one of her coworkers was going to take advantage of her absence? Wiley didn't like the thought of that.

Steven nodded absently. "I texted Callum and Nicole, but if you want to—"

"I'll talk to the reporter," Wiley interrupted.

Jillian's lips tightened. "I don't mind."

"Someone in the family should handle the media," he said. "As hotel counsel, it makes sense that I act as spokesperson."

"Hotel counsel?" Steven whistled under his breath. "Another new development."

Wiley nodded and focused his attention on Jillian. "Would you please tell the reporter I'll be with him in a minute?"

"Sure." The woman flashed a cheery smile. "We won't let Grace's absence hold us back. If you need anything else—"

"We don't," Wiley told her.

"She's just doing her job," Steven said as Jillian disappeared into the hotel.

"It sounded to me like she was trying to encroach on Grace's role." Wiley drew in a calming breath. "I don't like the thought of someone taking advantage of the accident."

"It sounds to me like you have a lot of thoughts where Grace is concerned."

"I'm doing my job," Wiley shot back.

"As far as you being the hotel's counsel, obviously I'm all for it. You know we'd like you to stick around Rambling Rose longer. In fact, weren't you scheduled to fly back to Chicago this afternoon?"

"I changed my ticket."

"Seriously?"

"Stop studying me like I'm some puzzle to figure out," Wiley grumbled. He didn't want to think that his brother could read the feelings he was trying to hide.

He'd texted his secretary early this morning asking her to change his airline reservation to give him a few extra days in Texas, mainly because he wanted to see for himself that Grace was doing okay. He wanted more than he cared to admit to see her again. No point in sharing those details with his brother. "The Hotel Fortune is a huge deal for the rest of you. That makes it a huge deal for me."

Steven's shoulders relaxed ever so slightly. "Thanks, Wi." He clapped Wiley on the back. "Appreciate you stepping in, even if it's temporary. I know that small-town life isn't your deal."

"Yeah." Wiley massaged a hand over the back of his neck. He would have agreed 100 percent with Steven's assessment before last night. Now he couldn't say for sure how he felt. "I'm going to go deal with this reporter. He won't be the only one interested in the accident. Let's plan to meet with everyone out at the ranch later and come up with some talking points going forward."

He nodded at his brother and then headed for the front of the hotel, his mind wandering to Grace and when he might see her again.

Grace tossed her cell phone down on the hospital bed with more force than necessary. "You can't avoid me forever," she muttered, then glared at her cast leg.

She knew that everyone at the hotel was busy with preparations for the grand opening, but she'd called and texted Jillian Steward, her counterpart in the management program, a half dozen times and had yet to receive a response.

Grace and Jillian weren't the only two trainees, but they were the pair that had been singled out by the Fortunes to be considered for the promotion at the end of the six-month program. That meant Jillian was the competition, and Grace knew the woman would use every advantage she could to make herself seem more deserving of the general manger position.

And Grace was stuck in a hospital bed.

She'd received calls from a range of Fortunes since the accident, all of them conciliatory and thoughtful.

The family had sent an enormous bouquet of flowers. Grace appreciated the gesture, but when she'd asked about joining the regular Monday staff meeting by phone, Callum had told her that her only focus at the moment needed to be healing. She wondered if her mom had gotten to him.

"Who's avoiding you?"

Her gaze darted to the open door to find Wiley Fortune standing there, looking just as handsome as he had Saturday night. He wore dark jeans and a gray sweater that somehow made his brown eyes look even darker.

"No one important," she said, and offered him a weak smile, once again aware of the disparity in their appearances. She wore an old flannel shirt over her hospital gown. Although she'd managed a shower earlier with her mom's help, Grace hadn't bothered to apply makeup or do anything with her hair. She tucked a thick strand behind one ear, wishing she'd considered the possibility of a visitor she might want to impress.

"Are you up for some company?" he asked, almost hesitantly.

It was strange to see a man like Wiley appear anything but totally confident.

"I'd like that," she said, and he approached the bed. He'd been holding one hand behind his back and pulled it out to reveal an exquisite bouquet of flowers arranged in a beautiful cut-glass vase.

"These are for you." He gave a soft laugh. "Obviously."

"Thank you." She gestured him closer and sat up in the bed. "They're beautiful. Calla lilies are my favorite."

His smile widened. "You're just saying that to be nice."

"It's true," she assured him. "They remind me of summer."

"They reminded me of you," he told her. Something

in the low rumble of his voice made goose bumps erupt along her skin.

She breathed in the sweet floral scent as he held the bouquet close to her. "Mine seem a bit small in comparison." He touched a finger to the enormous arrangement on her bedside table as he placed his vase next to it.

"The hotel sent those," she said. "Along with a fruit basket."

"Thoughtful," he murmured. "Everyone is relieved that you weren't hurt worse." His gaze clouded over as it roamed over the cast. "It could have been really bad."

"If I spent my time worried about things that could have happened, I'd never have the strength to get out of bed in the morning." She squeezed her hands together and focused on staying calm. "I would have given up a long time ago."

He sat down in the chair her mother had situated next to the bed. "You can't ever give up, Grace."

"I'll keep that in mind if I can convince my parents to stop coddling me." She didn't want to sound bitter but couldn't help her frustration. "I know I'm lucky, but what good does that do me if I lose my job at the hotel?"

Wiley frowned. "You aren't going to lose your job. They'll give you time to heal. Healing is your priority."

She let out a groan of frustration. "I'm so sick of hearing that," she all but shouted, then realized how she must sound when Wiley's eyes widened in shock.

"Are you sure we hadn't met before yesterday?" She shook her head. "Because I don't normally vent to people who are practically complete strangers."

"The first time I saw you was at the party," he said, his tone gentle. "That brief introduction wasn't enough, but I thought we'd have all night to talk. Then you walked out onto the balcony and…" He ran a hand through his hair and looked away. "I wish I wouldn't have left your side."

"You couldn't have known what would happen." She reached out and covered his hand with hers before thinking about what she was doing. For several seconds, they both stared at the place where they touched. Hers was paler and looked small against his larger, golden-hued skin.

"I still regret not being able to protect you."

"But if you'd been on the balcony we both would have been hurt." Her heart beat against her rib cage, and she drew back her hand. She liked touching Wiley way too much. "I don't need to be protected and am doing my best to convince my parents of that."

"Parents worry. It's part of the job description."

Something in his tone made her wonder what he wasn't saying. "Do you…um…have kids?"

"God, no." He held up his hands in protest, like she'd just asked if he had cooties. "No wife or girlfriend, either, for the record."

She laughed softly. "Thanks for sharing."

"I'm more the uncle versus father type. Some people just aren't cut out to be a parent, you know?"

"Some aren't cut out for monogamy, either," she countered. "Unfortunately, my last boyfriend was one of those."

Wiley cringed. "Sorry."

"Me, too."

He tapped a finger on the chair's wooden armrest.

"People should know their limits. If a guy can't be committed, he shouldn't commit."

Grace wasn't sure how they'd gone down this path of conversation. But it was par for the course that she was harboring an unexpected attraction for a man who just admitted to basically being allergic to relationships.

"That's why my focus is my career," Grace said, then cleared her throat. Could she really claim a career after three months in a management training program? "My job at the hotel and the possible promotion after the grand opening. It's everything to me."

"That's right," Wiley said with a nod. "They're going to hire a general manager locally. I met someone else today who's part of the training program. Jillian something or other."

"Steward." Frustration balled in Grace's stomach. "Jillian Steward. She also wants the GM role, and I'm sure she's going to take advantage of me being on leave to ingratiate herself to everyone." She groaned out loud when Wiley shifted in his chair. "I'm sorry. I don't know why I'm sharing so many of my personal struggles with you. Jillian is a qualified candidate. Not more qualified than me, of course. Your brothers and sisters can make whatever decision they want about the promotion. I just hope I'm cleared to return to work sooner rather than later."

"My brothers and sisters think highly of you," he said with a sincere smile. "Missing a few weeks from work won't change that."

"Weeks?" She shook her head. "There's no way I'm waiting weeks. The hotel will practically be open by then. There's way too much to do and—" She paused, narrowed her eyes at Wiley. "Is that why you're here? Did they send you to tell me I can't come back until I'm done with the blasted cast? I know that's what my mom wants, but she's—"

Grace's mother entered the room, closing the door harder than she needed to. "Your mother has your well-being at the forefront of her mind. I'm sure Mr. Fortune would agree that your recovery is most important."

Wiley quickly stood and took a step away from the bed. "Most important," he repeated, and Grace felt her lips twitch at how discombobulated he looked facing down her mother.

Barbara Williams was a petite woman, several inches shorter than Grace, with a delicate frame that belied her inner strength. She worked part-time at the high school library and had since Grace and Jake went to school there. Their mother claimed it kept her busy and out of her husband's hair. Unfortunately, when she arrived at the hospital this morning, she'd also announced she was taking a few weeks of unpaid leave until Grace was up and around.

Except Grace wasn't sure how that was supposed to happen while living under her mom's overprotective thumb.

"I assume that's why you're here," Barbara said to Wiley, her tone cool. "To assure Grace she has no worries about her position since she was injured on the job."

"I stopped by to…" Wiley scrubbed a hand over his jaw, the slight scratching sound doing funny things to Grace's insides. "That is to say I'm…"

"Why are you here?" Grace frowned at how flustered Wiley seemed. She certainly hoped that didn't mean his plan had actually been to give her some bad news about her job. When he'd walked in, she'd been so darn happy to see him that she hadn't bothered to question his appearance.

She couldn't deny the connection she'd felt with him from the moment they locked eyes across the Roja banquet room. Given the invisible thread that apparently linked them together, it had seemed appropriate for him to visit her.

But her mother's skeptical gaze made Grace doubt what she felt.

If doubts were dollar bills, she'd be a millionaire.

"Your job is secure," he said, sounding less like the flirting man who'd entered her room and more like a stuffy attorney. The type of professional she'd come to distrust during her brother's fight to ensure that insurance paid his medical bills after the car accident.

Somehow those words did little to relieve her anxiety.

"Thanks for relaying that message," her mother said. "I'm sure the Fortunes who were responsible for the construction are far too busy trying to determine what went wrong to bother stopping by."

"Mom, stop. Callum called earlier and both Steven and Dillon as well as Nicole and Megan have texted. It's fine."

Her mother sniffed, then sent another glare in Wiley's direction.

"I should go," he said, offering Grace a wan smile. "I'm glad you're doing well, Grace, and hope you'll be out of the hospital soon."

"The doctor wants another round of concussion testing before she's released." Barbara flung the words at Wiley like they were a personal accusation.

"Do they suspect things are worse?"

Grace wasn't sure what to make of the concern in his gaze, but it warmed her heart. Of course, it could just be that he didn't want his family on the hook for additional medical expenses. That's what her brother would say. Somehow, she didn't believe it.

"She's fine," her mother said before Grace could answer. "But this is really a situation for the people close to her to handle. Her family."

"I understand," Wiley said with a pinched smile. "Please let me know if there's anything I…any of us at the hotel can do to help."

His gaze darted to Grace and then back to her mother before he left the room.

As soon as he disappeared, Barbara began to flit about the room, clearly filled with agitation.

"Mom, you were so rude to him." Grace wanted to go after Wiley, but she couldn't do anything stuck in this bed. The crutches a nurse had brought in rested against the wall, but it would take far too much time to manage them.

"Why was he here, Gracie?" her mother demanded, clasping her hands tight in front of her like she had to hold them together to keep in her nervous energy.

"To check on me."

"That doesn't make sense. He barely knows you."

Grace had to agree that in theory it didn't make sense, but her heart told her it was perfectly reasonable for Wiley to be at her side.

"He's being nice," she said, because explaining the

feeling of connection she had with him would be a losing argument.

"Covering his family's assets is more like it."

"You sound like Jake." Her brother had visited earlier, railing about the hotel and rumors of shoddy construction he'd heard from friends around town after reports of the balcony collapse got out. Since Rambling Rose was such a tight-knit community, word spread fast. "What happened at the hotel was a freak accident. The Fortunes are good people, Mom. They've already done so much for the town."

Barbara's mouth thinned, but she nodded. "I agree, but buildings don't just fall apart for no reason. Jake feels that there's something suspicious about the balcony collapsing the way it did."

"Jake needs more hobbies," Grace grumbled. "Or to watch less true-crime television."

Her mother's features gentled. "You have a point, but the Fortunes have had problems in the past. I remember hearing about some crazy ex-wife causing all sorts of trouble for the family. There was even talk about a kidnapping."

"Those aren't the same Fortunes." Grace closed her eyes and silently counted to ten, hoping for patience. "It was Jerome Fortune—the tech giant who reinvented himself as Gerald Robinson—whose family had those issues. He eventually found happiness, though, with his first love. And Wiley's father, David, wasn't involved in any of that. The difficulties haven't followed the Fortunes to Rambling Rose as far as I've heard."

She wanted to strangle her brother for putting these doubts into her mother's head. Barbara had always been protective, but she'd become even more of a worrier after Jake's accident. The severity of his injuries and the fear of losing him had rocked their small family to its core. Grace knew her mother's fear had seeped into her consciousness, as well. It had made Grace hesitant about taking chances, and now that she was finally getting a shot at a real career at the Hotel Fortune, she wasn't going to let unfounded rumors derail her.

"I thought they were all related in some way."

Grace opened her eyes to see her mother studying Wiley's bouquet.

"Distantly," she agreed. "But Callum and his siblings weren't close to their cousins growing up. From everything I've learned working for the hotel, they moved here from Florida with the intent to establish themselves without significant ties to the rest of the Fortune family. No one is out to get them. Why would they be?"

"These are pretty," her mother said absently. "Calla lilies are your favorite."

"I know." Warmth infused Grace's chest once more as she thought about the fact that Wiley had somehow known her preference in flowers. "Mom, tell me you believe what I'm saying. I'm not in danger working at the hotel."

"I believe the Fortunes mean well," her mother conceded. "At first, I was skeptical of the scope of their plan for the town. It felt like a bit of an invasion to those of us who grew up here and were happy with things the way they were."

"The town was dying, Mom."

"That's going a little far."

"But it's true. The Fortunes have attracted new residents and visitors from all over Texas and the surrounding states. Already-established local businesses have benefited, as well. Even the mayor agrees." Ellie Fortune Hernandez, the town's popular young mayor, had expressed doubts about Callum's plan at the start but had quickly come to be one of the Fortune family's staunchest supporters, in no small part thanks to falling in love with and ultimately marrying Steven. "And Mariana is helping with the hotel's signature restaurant. Everyone in town loves her for all those years she ran her famous market. If she's behind the project, we know it's in the town's best interest."

Her mother held up her hands, palms out. "Okay, Gracie. No need to take out a billboard to advertise all of the wonderful things the Fortunes have done in Rambling Rose. I'm glad for the town to benefit from their efforts, but my main concern is you. It's all well and good for some new-to-town family to have success, but not if my baby is at risk because of it."

Grace blew out a frustrated breath. "I'm not at risk. And I'm going back to work as soon as the doctor tells me I can. This injury won't jeopardize my future."

"I heard Wiley say your position is secure."

"My current position," Grace clarified. "He has no control over the GM role, and he already hinted that Jillian was making a play for it. If she takes over my responsibilities while I'm out as well as handling her own, she could make a strong case for why she's the best candidate."

"There are plenty of places to work that don't involve the Fortunes," her mother said, even though they both knew that wasn't true. At least not places in Rambling Rose that offered Grace the opportunities she craved.

"Mom, I'm happy to be back here." She loved Rambling Rose but hated that she'd returned on the heels of her life imploding. It was why she was so determined to earn the GM position. "But I can only stay if I can make a future for myself. I feel like the Hotel Fortune is my best chance for that. My only chance right now. I need you to support me and to make sure Dad and Jake do, too."

Her mother sniffed. "Good luck with that."

"That's what I'm afraid of." Grace leaned forward and touched her cast, blinking away tears. "Please, Mom. I know you're worried, but this is important to me. After I found out about Craig cheating and resigned from Cowboy Country, it felt like I'd never have another chance to prove myself. I don't regret coming home from college after Jake's accident, but my life veered off path after that. I want a course correction. I need it."

"Oh, Gracie." Her mother lowered herself to the edge of the bed and put her arms around Grace's shoulders. "You know I support you. Your dad and your brother, too, in their own way. We all just want what's best for you."

Sloppy tears flowed down Grace's cheeks, and she didn't try to stop them. She'd tried for the past twenty-four hours to put on a brave face, but so much felt out of her control.

After a minute, she pulled back. She hated that her mother was crying, as well. There had been so many tears during Jake's recovery. Grace didn't want to be the cause of any more. "I don't know what's best," she admitted. "But I do know what feels right, and the hotel is a big part of that for me." She wiped the cuff of her flannel shirt across her mom's cheeks, earning a watery smile. "I trust the Fortunes, especially Wiley. I can't explain it, but there's something about him."

"Well, he's quite handsome." Barbara skimmed her thumbs over Grace's cheeks. "He has a very cute butt."

"Mom." Grace laughed. "That's pretty bold."

"I might be middle-aged, but I'm not dead."

Grace hugged her mom again, then blew out a shuddery breath. "It's more than how he looks. It's how he looks at me. Like I'm special."

"You are special. But—"

"I know nothing will come of it," Grace said quickly, embarrassed that she admitted so much to her mom. "He was only in town for the birthday party, and I understand he's checking on me because he's an attorney and he's worried about the family's liability. That's how lawyers are."

A part of her hoped her mother would argue, but Barbara nodded. "Smart girl. Keep your wits about you when it comes to men who seem too good to be true. I remember how fast you fell for Craig."

Grace frowned, not sure how to explain that her connection to Wiley felt different from anything she'd experienced before. Why bother? Chances were she'd never see him again, anyway. She pressed her fingers to her chest and tried to rub away the sudden pinch.

"Will you help me convince Dad and Jake not to make trouble with the Fortunes?"

Barbara looked away for a long moment but finally

nodded. "I'm not quite convinced, but you deserve happiness. As long as you follow the doctor's orders and don't push yourself too much, I'll support you."

Grace smiled. "Thank you, Mom. I promise I'll take care."

Chapter 4

Wiley sat at the empty Roja bar the following evening, sipping a scotch as he stared out the patio doors to the rubble of the collapsed balcony. Callum's crew would begin cleanup and new construction tomorrow morning. Although the mess was both an eyesore and, more importantly, a reminder of the accident, they'd had to wait until the insurance adjuster and building inspector gave them the go-ahead.

Unfortunately, the inspector's report had been both better and worse than any of them could have imagined. Better because the man verified that the accident hadn't been a result of shoddy workmanship. Worse because his finding indicated that the support beams had possibly been tampered with, rendering them structurally unsafe and likely the cause of the collapse.

"Mind if I join you?" Nicole asked as she approached from the restaurant's kitchen. She wore a white chef's coat and dark pants, her mass of thick hair pulled back into a tight bun. The restaurant had been open on select weekends but wouldn't expand its hours until the following month when the hotel officially opened. Nicole spent as much time on-site as their brothers, working on Roja's menu and training the staff. Sometimes it still shocked Wiley to see his baby sisters functioning as capable adults. He'd left for college when the triplets were still in middle school. While he'd been home for vacations and holidays, he hadn't paid much attention to the fact that Nicole, Ashley and Megan had grown up while he was away living his life.

"It's your liquor," he told her, gesturing to the bottle.

She scrunched up her nose. "I'm going to have a glass of wine."

"I'll take a glass of what Wiley's offering." Callum appeared in the doorway, his brows drawn together and stress lines bracketing either side of his mouth.

Wiley imagined he looked just as tense. Nicole did, as well. They hadn't shared the news of potential sabotage with anyone outside the family yet, but it was only a matter of time until the information leaked. Wiley wasn't sure what made him angrier, the idea that Grace had been hurt by some unknown adversary or that other employees at the hotel might still be at risk.

"We don't have enemies," Callum said as if reading Wiley's thoughts. He took a seat on the plush leather bar stool next to Wiley, and Nicole handed him a glass. "I know the deputy raised questions based on the report, but it isn't true."

He poured himself a generous amount of scotch, then refilled Wiley's glass.

"Are you sure?" Wiley demanded.

"What other explanation could there be?" Nicole added as she came around the bar and sat on Wiley's other side.

"I don't know," Callum admitted. Wiley understood how much it took for his capable brother to say those words out loud.

"You told me that people around here weren't thrilled with your plans for the hotel." Wiley sipped the scotch, the dark liquor doing very little to warm him.

"We handled it." Callum nodded like he was trying to convince all of them. "Kane was instrumental in helping smooth things over. We got input from a whole cross section of the community and implemented their ideas into the design. As far as we've heard since then, everyone is behind the project. People understand that the hotel will benefit local businesses across the board, not just the ones we own."

Nicole twirled her wineglass between two fingers. "Do either of you think it was strange that the officer asked about the situation with Gerald Robinson and his ex-wife?"

"The evil ex-wife," Callum muttered.

"Charlotte," Wiley said. "I didn't know the details, so I did a little digging this afternoon and called Dad to see what he remembered about her case."

"Dad and I were together at the wedding when Charlotte tried to kidnap one of the guests." Callum drew in a deep breath. "That woman was definitely trouble."

Wiley wiped a droplet of condensation from the rim

of his glass. "It wasn't just the attempted kidnapping. Charlotte burned down Gerald's house and caused all kinds of trouble. She was off the rails."

"But she's in a psychiatric hospital now," Callum said.

"And why would she want to harm any of us?" Nicole asked. "Dad isn't even close to his half brothers, and we have very little contact with that branch of the family. The Austin Fortunes I've met are nice, but it's a stretch to think anyone from their world has a grudge against us."

Wiley nodded. "I agree, but it would be nice if discovering the culprit could be cut-and-dried or if we could say for certain that whatever happened with the beams was a onetime accident. At this point, the idea that someone wants to sabotage us and not knowing who or why isn't doing much for my peace of mind."

"Imagine how the rest of us feel," Callum said. "You're upset, and you don't have anything at stake in this venture. If we don't get a handle on what might be happening, I could lose everything."

Wiley's blood pressure spiked at his brother's words. He knew Callum was right in a business sense, but Wiley did have something to lose. Someone, anyway.

He'd heard that Grace had been discharged yesterday after his visit. While he was happy to know she was well enough to go home, he didn't know what to do with his strong desire to see her again. He couldn't very well just show up at her parents' house without a good reason.

He also couldn't seem to stop thinking about her. No

point in explaining the attraction to his brother when Wiley still didn't understand it himself.

"We're going to make sure that doesn't happen," he promised.

Callum gave him a curious look. "What are you planning to do from Chicago?"

"I'm actually thinking of staying on in Rambling Rose until the hotel opens next month." He said the words calmly, hoping neither of his siblings would question him.

"Wi, that would be amazing." Nicole set her wineglass on the glossy bar top and threw her arms around him. "It will be like old times with all of us together. You're the last holdout, you know."

Callum clasped his shoulder. "Are you sure?"

"I talked to the senior partner today and confirmed that I can work remotely for a few weeks. I'll still have to give time to my clients. We're working on closing a huge deal with a manufacturing company, but I should be able to manage it. That way I can also help with whatever needs to be done around here." Thinking about having a purpose made him feel calmer. "I'd like to review the employment contracts and insurance policies for the various ventures in town to make sure everything is in good shape."

"Sounds great," Callum told him.

"I'd also like to talk to some of the employees," Wiley said.

Nicole gasped softly. "You aren't suggesting that someone who works for us was involved with the balcony?" She shook her head. "This is a tight community, Wiley. It's not like the big city where people are out for themselves. Like Callum said, we got people to support the hotel. I don't want to even consider that anyone would want to do us harm."

"I hope you're right." Wiley drained his glass and then stood. "But one of your employees was injured in that balcony collapse. Grace could have died."

His sister's blue eyes filled with tears, and she glanced away. "I know."

"Don't get upset." Wiley wanted to kick himself and even more so when Callum's fingers tightened around his scotch glass. The last thing he should be doing was making his siblings feel bad. They had the best intentions when it came to their plan for Rambling Rose. He knew that.

"I don't believe for a minute that anyone working for the hotel was involved," Callum said. "Fortune Brothers Construction has never dealt with sabotage, but I know of contractors who've had their sites vandalized and projects derailed. Sometimes the motivation is as simple as someone looking for attention."

Wiley nodded. "The reporter I talked to yesterday was from the local paper, but that doesn't mean the story won't be picked up by news outlets in bigger cities around Texas if it's a slow news cycle."

"I hate having our business out there for public consumption." A muscle ticked in Callum's jaw. Wiley could feel the anger and frustration radiating from both his brother and sister. He wanted to find a way to ease their anxiety, however he could manage it.

"The paper here comes out weekly, right?"

Nicole nodded.

"Hopefully," Wiley said, clasping his hands together

in front of his chest, "this incident will have blown over by the time the story runs. We should come up with an event to bring some positive publicity to the hotel before the grand opening. Show the town that the Fortunes are here for the long haul and dedicated to doing what's right for Rambling Rose."

Callum and Nicole both expressed their agreement with his idea. Nicole pulled out her phone. "Grace would have been our go-to for a community event. She has a way with people."

The understatement of the century, as far as Wiley was concerned.

"We'll have to ask Jillian to take the lead. I can text her tonight and then schedule a meeting with her and the other trainees tomorrow for—"

"No." Wiley stepped forward quickly and held up a hand. "We should let Grace handle this if she's up for it."

He kept his features neutral as his brother and sister stared at him in disbelief.

"You must be joking," Callum said finally. "She was the one hurt in the accident. Why would we ask her to coordinate a publicity event in response?"

"She called earlier today," Nicole added, "and said that she's staying with her parents while her leg heals. They're encouraging her to rest and recuperate for at least a few weeks. Of course I told her that she can take all the time she needs, so I can't very well turn around and push her to return to work right away."

"I know what her parents want," Wiley said, thinking of Grace's distress in the hospital. "But do you think she agrees? When I talked to her, she was eager to return to work."

"When did you talk to her?" Callum's tone was suddenly suspicious.

"In the hospital," Wiley said with a wave of his hand. "You know that." He hadn't told anyone about his visit to her the previous day.

"She was loopy on pain medicine." Callum shook his head. "We can't trust anything she said that night."

"We should at least ask her." Wiley pointed at Callum. "As for why, the reason should be obvious." And it had nothing to do with Wiley's desire to spend more time with her, or at least that's what he wanted to believe. "If the employee who was injured is the one representing the hotel, that shows her faith in the family and the Hotel Fortune. You can't buy that kind of press."

"Good point," Callum agreed.

Nicole didn't look convinced, but she nodded. "I don't want to bother her at night. I'll call her in the morning and ask, but I won't pressure her."

"Let me talk to her," Wiley offered with what he hoped was a reassuring smile. "Since she was such an integral part of the team before the accident, I'd love to ask if she noticed anything suspicious before Larkin's birthday. I can mention the idea of an event and see what she thinks."

"I'm not sure," Nicole said, her tone hesitant. "She barely knows you."

Exactly, Wiley thought to himself. He needed an excuse to spend time with her. Maybe that would quench the thirst he had deep in his soul when it came to Grace. "She won't think I have an ulterior motive with regards to her job security."

Callum barked out a rough laugh. "You're an attorney. She'll think you have an ulterior motive. Your profession isn't known for rampant altruism."

"Thanks for the vote of confidence," Wiley grumbled. "Come on, Callum. I want to help while I'm here, and I'm here until all of this gets settled." He turned his attention to his sister. "I promise I'll be nice to Grace and make sure she knows her healing is our top priority. At least let me start the conversation with her. If it doesn't go well, you can take over."

Nicole looked like she wanted to argue, then glanced at Callum. "We're overextended as it is. If Wiley wants to talk to Grace, I guess that would be okay. But being nice is no joke."

"Nicole is right." Callum leveled him with a steely stare. "Don't go corporate attorney and terrify her or offend her family. The whole point of the hotel's training program is to generate goodwill within the community by offering opportunities to Rambling Rose locals, and now one of them has been hurt on the job. Any way you look at it, the situation is a PR nightmare. We have to keep Grace happy."

Wiley wasn't about to go into all the ways he wanted to keep Grace happy. "I understand," he said, hoping his expression didn't give away the anticipation building inside him now that he had a reason to visit her. "Nicole, would you text me her parents' address? I'll stop by tomorrow and then check in with you both and let you know how it went."

He said goodbye and headed for his car. All he could think about was the impending visit to Grace's house and how he couldn't wait to be near her again.

* * *

Grace sat on the overstuffed couch in her parents' cozy family room the following morning, staring at the book in her hand and realizing she'd read the same page three times. With a groan, she flung the paperback across the room. It slammed into the wall and dropped with a thud to the floor just as her mother appeared in the doorway.

"I guess you're not a fan of romance novels," Barbara said with a shake of her head. "Grace, if you're done with the outburst, you have a visitor."

"Sorry," Grace muttered. "I just hate lying around like this. I feel so useless." She raised a brow when she finally met her mother's gentle gaze. Barbara's cheeks were flushed, and she worried her hands in front of her. "What is it? Who's here, Mom?"

Her mother glanced over her shoulder in the direction of the front hall and gestured the visitor forward. "It's…um…"

"Hello, Grace." Wiley came to stand next to her mom. "I apologize for not calling first. It actually didn't cross my mind until your mom answered the door. If this isn't a good time…"

"It's… No…this is…great…fine… I'm happy to… It's fine…" She started to straighten, nervous energy scrambling her brain cells. Wiley Fortune, the man who had consumed her thoughts since he'd walked out of her hospital room two days earlier, had come to see her. He was standing in her parents' modest house, staring at her like—well, like she was someone special.

"Grace appreciates you stopping by," her mother said, the corner of her mouth twitching.

Realizing she wasn't going anywhere gracefully with the cast, Grace settled back onto the cushions and offered Wiley a friendly smile. She hoped it came off as friendly and not deranged, although he made her feel just a touch unbalanced. "What she said," Grace muttered.

Barbara picked up the book Grace had thrown against the wall and handed it to Wiley. "Have a seat," she told him. "I'll check on the two of you in a bit. Would you like a glass of iced tea, Wiley?"

"Yes, ma'am. Thank you."

Color crept up Barbara's cheeks as Wiley focused his attention on her. *See, Mom*, Grace thought. *You can be suspicious all you want, but a man that handsome is hard to resist.*

When her mother disappeared toward the kitchen, Wiley took another step into the room, glancing down at the book he held.

"Don't you dare make fun," Grace said, tugging on the hem of the Rambling Rose High School sweatshirt she wore. She hadn't dressed expecting visitors. Her parents had grabbed a random assortment of clothes from her apartment, so this morning Grace had thrown on an old high school sweatshirt and a pair of baggy sweatpants after cutting off one leg at the knee. Now she wished she'd thought to dab on a bit of lip gloss or at least a spritz of perfume.

"I wouldn't dream of it," Wiley promised. "I assume the duke mentioned in the title would be the brawny man on the cover."

"You'd assume correctly."

"I never imagined old-time aristocrats to be gym

rats—" He held up the book and tapped a finger on one of the duke's broad shoulders "—but this one is quite the impressive physical specimen."

"He fences and boxes," Grace said, hiding her smile.

"Ah." Wiley placed the book on the coffee table. "That explains it. Although not why I heard the book crashing against the wall when I arrived. Too much throwing punches and not enough wooing for your taste?"

"Plenty of wooing," she confirmed. "But I'm already sick of sitting around." She reached out a hand and brushed an invisible crumb off the cast. "I'm going to go crazy by the time my ankle heals."

Wiley offered her a smile so sweet it made her knees go weak. "We'll make sure that doesn't happen," he promised.

Grace desperately wanted to believe Wiley. Still her family's warnings ricocheted through her brain, and she told herself not to be taken in by his charm. Was that even possible? "Shouldn't you be back in Chicago?"

He lowered himself into the chair beside the couch, and she tried to see her parents' house through his eyes. It looked much the same as it had when she'd been a kid, with wood-paneled walls, bookshelves filled with family photos and her father's collection of historical nonfiction books.

"I've decided to stay in Rambling Rose until the hotel opens."

She tried to keep her features neutral even as excitement spiraled through her. Did that mean he wanted to see her more over the next few weeks? She should know better than to read too much into the way he looked at her, but she couldn't seem to stop her body's reaction to the intensity of his gaze.

"I'm sure that makes your brothers and sisters happy."

"For now." He laughed softly. "I'm going to make sure everything is in order with employment agreements and contracts for the various businesses they've gotten involved in. They'll be happy to have me here unless it makes more work for them."

"I doubt that. I can tell from seeing them interact at the hotel that your family is really close."

"They are," he murmured.

"Why doesn't it sound like you include yourself in that 'they'?"

He shrugged. "I've always been a sort of odd man out when it comes to our branch of the Fortune family. For me, it was important to feel like I'm making my own way, which is why I left Florida for college and didn't return even after law school. I wanted my life to be my own."

"I know how that feels." She swallowed back the emotion that clogged her throat. "You're lucky you've been able to accomplish it."

"Lucky," he repeated, then frowned. "I suppose you're right."

A few seconds of silence descended between them, and although it was weighted, the quiet didn't feel uncomfortable. In fact, Grace's chest loosened as she drew in air laced with Wiley's spicy scent.

She snapped back to attention at the sound of a bag crinkling. Her eyes had zeroed in on his handsome face, and she hadn't even seen the sack he held.

"I didn't come here to bore you with my family dynamics." Wiley flashed a self-deprecating smile. "I'm here to deliver a get-well care package."

"You've already brought me flowers."

One thick brow arched. "Is there a limit on the number of gifts I'm allowed to bring you?"

She wanted to laugh at the absurdity of that question. "I'm not going to put one on you." She reached for the bag he now held out. "I'm just not used to being on the receiving end of so much generosity." She inwardly cringed, embarrassed to admit she was comparing Wiley to her ex-boyfriend. Craig had been steady and reliable—or so she'd thought—but never the romantic type.

Grace had convinced herself she didn't care. She thought it was important to have a man she could build a life with, not someone who lavished her with gifts and romantic gestures. She got enough of that vicariously through books and movies.

As she peeked in the brown paper bag with the Hotel Fortune logo stamped on the outside, she tried to remember that Wiley was just being nice because she was a hotel employee. His brothers and sisters were all busy with preparations for the opening and taking care of their other businesses in town. Chances were good that they'd designated him as the family liaison for the injured employee. At least that's what Grace's brother would tell her.

She put aside thoughts of her ankle and her brother as she pulled out a stack of puzzles, a candle and a box of chocolates. "How thoughtful. I love all of it. You didn't have to..." She glanced up at him as she continued to remove items from the seemingly bottomless bag. "Did you buy one of everything in the hotel gift shop?"

Wiley scrubbed a hand over the back of his neck. "Just about. I didn't know what type of games you might like, so I got word searches, sudoku and crossword puzzles."

"I like word searches," she told him with a smile.

He nodded. "They had both dark chocolate and milk, and I can tell you my sisters are very specific with their chocolate, so I got a box of each."

"I like both." She held up two candles.

"They both smelled good," he said, sounding almost embarrassed that he'd packed so much into the bag. "But not as good as you. You smell like a spring rain shower." He gave her a sheepish smile. "Do I sound like a sad imitation of your romance duke?"

"No, but for the record I smell like water," she said with a laugh, then reached out and patted Wiley's leg when he frowned. "I'm joking. The lotion I use is actually named Rainforest Mist so you're right on the money with that."

Wiley's eyes darkened even more and the space between them seemed to shift—growing thick with a yearning that Grace didn't understand, although it sent shivers rippling along her skin.

"Thank you," she managed after a weighted moment. "I appreciate all of this and you coming to see me. I haven't reached out to many friends because I don't want to talk about the accident. People are so curious, and I just want to forget."

There was an immediate shift in Wiley, as if she'd just doused him with a bucket of icy water. "I figured people would be talking to you about the incident. In fact, a reporter came by the hotel on Sunday. The local paper is doing an article on the circumstances of the accident."

The thought of having her name associated with the event that was bringing the hotel bad publicity made Grace's stomach clench, but she nodded. "He reached out to me, as well. He wants to interview me for the story."

"Are you going to talk to him?"

She shrugged. "I guess I should, but I'm not ready yet. Don't worry, though. I'll be sure to make it clear that the hotel had nothing to do with the balcony's collapse."

"You don't have to do that. We appreciate your loyalty, Grace, but you can speak freely."

"I know," she whispered, distressed by the formality that had seeped into his tone. "But it's true. Obviously, I wish it wouldn't have happened, but the hotel isn't responsible."

His opened his mouth as if to deny her claim, then closed it again. "Speaking of the hotel…" He flashed a smile that was different from the one he'd given her before. It didn't reach his eyes. "I do have a speck of official business to discuss with you."

"Sure." Grace ignored her disappointment and reminded herself that she could read whatever she wanted into the way Wiley looked at her. That didn't make the promise in his gaze something real.

"Callum, Nicole and I talked about coordinating a small community event before the official grand opening. Nothing elaborate or time-consuming for the staff, but something that would…"

"Make people forget that I could have died in the balcony collapse?"

He blew out a shaky breath. "Yes."

She nodded, appreciating that he didn't try to sugarcoat the motivation. There was nothing wrong with what the hotel wanted to do. The Fortunes were running a business, and they needed positive PR. They couldn't run a successful hotel without paying customers. If the hotel didn't make money, Grace wouldn't have to worry whether her injury would prevent her from earning the promotion. There would be no promotion to be had.

"It's a great idea." She sat forward on the sofa, lifting her cast leg and placing her foot on the floor. The doctor had told her it was important to elevate the leg, but somehow she felt too much like a blushing maiden from one of her historical romances sprawled out on her parents' sofa as she and Wiley discussed actual business. Grace was thrilled to talk about something other than the accident, even if she wasn't officially on the clock. "I'd actually recommend focusing on other local business owners. We should also involve the spa and Provisions. Nicole and Roja can provide the food—samplings from the regular menu. I bet even the vet clinic could set up a booth in conjunction with a local animal rescue. It's important to remind the community leaders how much your family has already contributed to the town and give a glimpse of how good it's going to be. A Rambling Rose partnership would benefit everyone."

"Those are great suggestions."

Grace held up a hand. "I'm not done." She shifted again, wishing she could get up and pace as she worked through the possibilities in her head. Her crutches rested against the stone fireplace on the wall across from the seating arrangement, but she didn't want to bother with hopping over to retrieve them. Plus, she'd look like a complete fool trying to pace using crutches. For what felt like the millionth time since Saturday night, she cursed that blasted fall.

"Tell me more." Wiley reached out and squeezed her hand, as if he could sense her frustration. His touch had the immediate effect of calming her, and she drew in a breath before continuing.

"We want Rambling Rose businesess to feel connected to the hotel. Do you think your brothers and sisters would consider offering a 'locals' weekend'?"

"Um…probably."

She clapped her hands together. "I should have thought of that even before the accident. The hotel can give a discounted rate for a particular weekend, one during a slow season where occupancy would naturally be down. They'd get the great deal if they booked during the reception, and we could do a raffle for a free dinner for two at Roja." She paused and scrunched up her nose. "I keep saying 'we,' but I mean 'you' obviously. The Fortunes and the employees who are actually working. I'm sure other people will have ideas, as well." Jillian, Grace thought inwardly, would have plenty.

"Are you interested in the 'we' part?" Wiley asked

and, once more, Grace's brain seemed to short-circuit. All she could think about was a "we" that involved her and Wiley. She was interested like nobody's business.

"Yes," she managed, hoping he assumed she was talking about being engaged on a professional level.

"There's no pressure, of course." He smiled at her again, encouraging and warm, and she felt it all the way to her toes. "I'm being nice, right?"

She frowned. "Is that a trick question?"

"Nicole warned me I had to be nice," he said with another laugh. "Callum told me not to act like an attorney."

"I actually haven't been thinking about you being an attorney during this visit," she admitted. "If that helps."

"Good." He nodded. "If you think you're up for it, we'd like you to handle the reception. You can take care of a lot of the planning from here. Whatever works best for your recovery. Obviously, you're qualified based on the rush of ideas you just offered. Getting more buy-in from local business owners makes sense to me, although you'll have to run that focus by my siblings. Again, only if you feel like it wouldn't be too much."

"No." She tried to breathe around the knot that had formed in her chest. This was her dream come true as far as the scenario for the weeks of her recovery.

"No, you're not up for it?" His brows drew together.

"No, it's not too much. I'd love to be involved in any capacity. If you feel like I can handle it, then absolutely yes. I'd love it."

"Absolutely not."

At the sound of the booming male voice, Grace glanced at the door to find her father standing next to her mother, his arms crossed over his chest in a stance

Grace knew all too well. Barbara held a tray with iced tea glasses and a bowl of pretzels. The look she threw Grace was both resigned and apologetic.

This would be a battle, and it was one she didn't intend to lose.

Chapter 5

Wiley stood as Grace's father entered the room. "Hello, sir. Grace and I were just discussing—"

"She's not going back." Mike narrowed his eyes at Wiley, then switched his glare to Grace. "You aren't going back."

"Dad, I'm a grown woman." She made to stand, but her cast hit the edge of the coffee table, and she sat back down, wincing as pain radiated up her leg.

Her mother let out a gasp, and Wiley reached for her.

"Don't touch my daughter." Her father's voice seemed to reverberate through the room.

Grace felt her face color with humiliation as Wiley drew back his hand and took a step away from her. Barbara put the tray of drinks and snacks on a side table and moved closer to her husband. Grace wasn't sure if it was to lend silent support to Mike or to protect Wiley from him.

"I'm sorry, Mr. Williams. I just wanted to help."

"By putting her at risk again? Not going to happen."

"I want to work." She lifted her hands, palms up. "I can't sit around here for the next month. I'll go stir-crazy." She bit down on the inside of her cheek when her voice caught. No way was she going to start crying in front of Wiley.

"Did he tell you that someone's out to get the Fortunes?" Mike asked Grace the question but looked at Wiley as he spat out the words.

"What are you talking about?"

"Sabotage." Mike said the word like it was poison on his tongue.

"We don't know that yet," Wiley argued, then turned to Grace. "The building inspector said it's possible someone tampered with the balcony's support beams. The investigation is ongoing, but that could have contributed to the collapse."

"Definitely is more like it," her father said. "Why is someone messing with the hotel construction?" he demanded of Wiley.

"We don't know, sir." Wiley scrubbed a hand over his jaw. "But I promise you we'll get to the bottom of it."

"Not by making my daughter a potential target."

"I promise I would never—" Wiley cleared his throat. "I won't let anything happen to Grace. I'll keep her safe. You have my word." He turned to her fully, and her breath caught in her throat at the ferocity in his gaze. "I'll keep you safe."

"I know," she said softly. Somehow she had no doubt

that Wiley, a man she barely knew, would do everything
in his power to ensure her safety. It baffled her why she
felt so confident in that, but her heart remained certain.

"He's using you," her father said through clenched
teeth.

"Mike, don't." To Grace's surprise, her mother stepped
forward and placed a hand on her husband's arm. "What
happened to Grace was an accident. The Fortunes didn't
intentionally put her in danger. I agree that she should
take it easy." Barbara glanced at Grace. "You need to rest
so that your recovery isn't impacted."

Grace opened her mouth to argue, but her mother
held up a hand.

"I also understand that you're accustomed to being
busy, and your job means a lot to you." She squeezed
Mike's arm. "She's an adult capable of making her own
decisions."

"I know what I'm doing," Grace said, looking between her parents. "Going back to work will actually be
helpful to my recovery." She ignored her dad's snort of
disbelief. "I mean it. I can't do nothing for a month. If
the Fortunes are willing to let me make my own hours
and work remotely when possible—"

"We are." Wiley nodded. "Whatever you need."

"I want to try." She got to her feet again, this time
careful about her leg, and hopped the short distance to
where her parents stood. "I understand you're worried,
and I have no idea who would want to sabotage the hotel
or why. But it has nothing to do with me."

"You've got a cast on your leg that tells a different
story," Mike said, but his voice had gentled. Grace knew
he wasn't going to fight her on this any longer.

"I'll be careful."

Mike turned to Wiley. "My daughter is old enough and smart enough to make her own decisions. But I'm holding you to the promise to keep her safe. I understand you don't have skin in the game in Rambling Rose the way some of your brothers and sisters do, but consider my girl your number one priority while you're in town."

"Dad, that's ridiculous." Grace cringed even as longing threaded through her like a needle binding two pieces of fabric. What would it feel like to be a priority for Wiley? "Wiley has plenty of other—"

"Done," Wiley said, and held out a hand to Grace's father. They shook and suddenly Grace felt like some sort of Victorian spinster who'd just been promised to the roguish hero. She needed to lay off the historical romances for a while.

"Can Wiley and I have a few minutes alone?" she asked her parents. "To go over next steps."

Mike looked as though he didn't want to leave them, but Barbara tugged him toward the hall. "Let us know if you need anything. It was nice to see you again, Wiley."

"You as well, Mrs. Williams. Thank you."

When her parents were gone, Grace turned to Wiley, ready to give him a litany of excuses for her father's behavior. Instead an enormous yawn stretched her lips and exhaustion made her limbs grow heavy.

"This is too much," Wiley said without hesitation. "I promise that wasn't my intention, Grace. Or to upset your father."

She waved away his concern. "I'll be fine," she told him with a wobbly smile. "I probably need a tiny nap first. My dad's worry has more to do with what happened to my brother than this situation. Although I wish you would have told me about the possibility of the beams being tampered with."

"I'm sorry." He squeezed her fingers. "I should have brought it up right away but didn't want to upset or worry you. I meant what I said about protecting you, Grace."

"Thank you," she managed, even though her throat had gone dry. It was difficult to remember that her relationship with Wiley was only professional when he touched her with such exquisite sweetness and looked at her as though he wanted to kiss her. It had to be the exhaustion making her imagine that. "I appreciate the opportunity to coordinate an event for the hotel. I'm going to take a short rest, and then I'll put together my ideas and email them to Callum and Nicole. We can schedule a call to discuss their thoughts and go from there."

"All business," Wiley murmured, dropping his hand. If Grace didn't know better, she would have sworn she heard disappointment in his tone.

"Not all." She flashed a smile and gestured to the pile of puzzle books on the table. "You've given me a lot to keep myself busy. I appreciate it." She covered her mouth when another yawn escaped.

"We'll talk soon." Wiley stepped away from her. "Enjoy your nap, Grace. Sweet dreams."

Butterflies fluttered across her stomach as he walked away. If Wiley Fortune was a part of her dreams, they'd be sweet indeed.

"I'm still not sure why we couldn't have taken one of the ATVs," Wiley grumbled the following night as he tugged on the reins of his horse when the animal once again veered off the path to munch on a nearby bush.

"We wanted to give you the full Texas experience," Megan said, glancing over her shoulder with a wink.

"Besides, your boots are too shiny." Their cousin Kane rode up next to him on his chestnut mare. "You need some more dust to make you look like a legit cowboy."

Wiley barked out a laugh at the absurdity of that statement. "I'm nowhere near a cowboy. Attorneys aren't cowboys. It's mutually exclusive."

"Not in Texas," Megan told him. Her horse came to a stop at the edge of a low rise, the surrounding property spread out in front of them like a postcard.

"How much of this do we own?" Wiley asked, somewhat overwhelmed by the wide-open space and big sky. He knew this part of Texas was expansive, especially compared to the crowded high-rises of downtown Chicago.

"As far as the eye can see," Megan told him softly. There was something about the moment and the vista that called for quiet. Wiley suddenly understood what had drawn his siblings to this part of the country. Maybe it was something in the Fortune DNA that made Texas appeal to so many of them.

He thought Callum had lost his mind when he'd moved to Rambling Rose over a year ago and then convinced Dillon, Steven and Stephanie to go with him. By the previous spring, the triplets had joined them. Wiley had stayed in the Midwest, telling himself he was content with his big-city life far away from his family. He loved each one of them, but growing up in a house with so many kids had made him savor his independence and stake it out with all the dedication of a dogged adventurer. His career and his life belonged solely to him, and that seemed like enough.

But spending time with his siblings and the cousins he was enjoying getting to know planted tiny seeds of doubt in his mind. Although he was keeping up on his regular workload remotely, he didn't miss the bustle of the city and his busy professional life the way he assumed he would. He'd been going on full tilt for as long as he could remember, never pausing to reflect whether the path he was so intent on taking was the right one.

Of course it was right. He'd chosen it. He couldn't let a few weeks of fresh air and the sweet smile of a woman derail him. Yes, it was fun to be involved in the family business, but that didn't mean it would be better to return to the life he knew.

"I'm happy for you guys." Wiley leaned forward and patted the horse's strong neck. "You all seem to have found your place here."

"It's an easy town to call home," Megan said, a trace of wistfulness in her voice. "Also easy for some people to find love, apparently."

Kane snorted, adjusting the brim of his hat. "You don't need love to be happy."

Wiley nodded. "Amen, cousin."

"You are two peas in a pod." Megan wrinkled her nose. "What do you have against falling in love?"

"Not a thing." Kane shrugged a big shoulder. "It's just not for me."

"Me, neither, yet," Megan conceded, "but I'm not opposed to Mr. Right walking into my life. The hotel is going to open right around Valentine's Day. Wouldn't it be nice to have a romantic date with the perfect girl to share it with?"

An image of Grace popped into Wiley's brain, and he shifted in the saddle. "I think we need to keep our focus on making sure the grand opening goes off without any more problems. That's way more important than romance."

Kane nodded, a muscle ticking in his jaw. "I'd feel a lot more confident if we could get to the bottom of whether or not someone tampered with the balcony's support beams."

"I want to believe there's some explanation for the collapse." Megan blew out a frustrated sigh. "It's too scary to think that someone has it out for us or that we might be putting our employees or potential customers in danger." She adjusted one of her stirrups and glanced between Wiley and Kane. "Everything is going so well with the businesses, especially Provisions. The reservation book is filled almost every night, and the online reviews are excellent. I know Roja will be just as much of a success, assuming nothing else happens."

"It won't," Kane promised. Their cousin was taking the lead on hotel security, and Wiley had been impressed with his attention to detail.

"How do you know?"

"I met with a security company earlier today," Kane confided. "Another firm is coming in to look over the property tomorrow. I'm going to fast-track the process of getting bids so that we can have an updated system installed by the grand opening. There won't be any loose ends."

"I've started meeting with employees," Wiley said. "Everyone seems positive so far. No hint of discontent, which is good. It could be that the balcony was just a fluke or someone looking for attention."

"I hope you're right." Megan gave her horse a soft kiss, and the animal turned toward the path again. She met Wiley's gaze as she passed him, and he hated the anxiety in her cornflower blue eyes. All the brothers were protective of the triplets. He wanted his sisters to be able to focus on the positive aspects of their new business ventures without worrying about potential sabotage.

Wiley brought his horse abreast of hers. "It's going to be okay, Meggie."

"You make me believe that." She gave him a warm smile. "It's your commanding attorney presence. I was on the call with Grace this morning. We videoconferenced, and it was the first time I'd seen her since the accident. She looked good."

"What did you expect?"

"I'm not sure," she admitted. "I thought maybe she'd seem bitter or angry that she was dealing with a broken ankle."

"Grace has always struck me as a practical girl," Kane called from behind them. "All of the trainees are great, but she shines under pressure."

"Pressure is one thing," Megan answered. "Falling from the second story of the hotel is quite another."

"True," Kane admitted tightly. Wiley knew the accident weighed heavily on everyone's mind.

"How did the call go?" he asked, trying to sound casual. "I felt bad that I couldn't be a part of it, but a client meeting came up that my assistant wasn't able to reschedule."

"It's fine," Megan told him. "We appreciate you pitching in here while managing your regular life at the same time. No doubt you'll be glad when the hotel opens, and you can be rid of us and our troubles for a while."

"You aren't a trouble," he told her.

"That's nice." She laughed. "But you aren't fooling me, Wi. I remember how crazy our full house drove you when we were younger. You'd hide in the basement with the water heater just to get a little privacy."

"Nothing wrong with a teenage boy wanting privacy," he muttered, earning a loud chuckle from his cousin. He leveled a stare at Kane over his shoulder. "Not for the reasons you're thinking."

"Gross." Megan snorted. "Enough about teenage boys and privacy. The call went well. Grace put together a really comprehensive time frame and plan for a preopening reception aimed at local business leaders. We're going to suggest a Rambling Rose partnership, where restaurants, shops and other local businesses actively work to promote each other. It's a short turnaround, with her idea to put the event on the calendar for the last week of January, but it will be a perfect lead-up to the grand opening."

"Her parents are worried that she's going to do too much and compromise her recovery." A knot formed in his stomach as he recalled the look her father had given him, like Wiley was the lowest form of scum he could imagine. Wiley prided himself on his moral compass but should probably to do a little more research into the accident Grace's brother had a few years ago.

He could tell by the comments Grace made that Jake's situation had impacted everyone in the Williams family, and he wanted to understand how traumatic it had been for them.

"We won't let that happen," Megan said as the horses approached the barn at the ranch. "You won't let that happen."

He arched a brow and kept his features bland, hoping to hide the thrill of anticipation that pulsed inside him. Keeping an eye on Grace was the easiest assignment he could imagine.

"I mean it, Wiley." The three of them dismounted, and Megan wagged a finger at him. "We're counting on you to take care of her."

"Not exactly a chore," Kane said as he took the reins of Wiley's horse and started toward the barn. "Grace is fantastic."

Wiley didn't like the bolt of jealousy that zipped through him at his cousin's words. He had no reason to believe Kane had designs on Grace. They worked together, just like she and Wiley did. Ugh. That thought didn't make him feel any better.

"I'll make sure she's taken care of," he told his sister as they followed Kane into the barn, reminding himself to keep his attraction to her under control. It would be best for everyone involved—but more difficult for him than anyone would imagine.

Chapter 6

Grace sat on the porch swing looking out over her parents' front yard the next day. Her leg was elevated and her other foot bare as she swung gently in the cool afternoon air.

She'd had to put on a heavy jacket, but it was worth it to escape her mother's fussing, her father's silent admonishment and her brother's outright agitation at the fact that she was already back to work less than a week after the accident.

The doctor had told her to take recovery at her own pace, she'd reminded them, and she was being careful not to spend too much time on the phone or at the computer. She'd even napped for an hour after lunch, even though it frustrated her how weak she still felt compared to her normal energy level. Grace liked moving and working. From the time she'd gotten her first babysitting job as a teenager, the ability to make her own money and her way in the world had always appealed to her. Her parents had provided a great life for Jake and her, but finances had always been tight. As a girl, she remembered hearing her parents argue about the monthly budget. Her father had a tendency to spend beyond their means, a constant source of worry for Grace's mom.

Grace had grown up with the deep desire to never be a burden on anyone. She knew Jake felt the same, and that was part of the reason why his accident had been so difficult. His recovery had taken months and had been a challenge for every member of their close-knit family.

That didn't make it any easier to hear him degrade Wiley and the Fortunes. The hotel was one of the best things that had happened to Rambling Rose, and certainly for Grace, so she was already tired of having to defend her employer.

She blew out a breath and hit Send on the email she'd just written to Nicole, making suggestions of potential offerings for the business reception that would showcase Roja's planned menu. The Fortune triplets certainly had a way with food, and Grace envied their confidence and the bond they obviously shared. She'd met their other sister, Stephanie, as well, and although she wasn't involved in the hospitality industry, she was helping to coordinate a booth for the local vet clinic where she worked.

Grace waved as Collin Waldon walked across her lawn from his father's house next door.

"Tell me you're not posting cast selfies on social media," he called to her.

Collin was as close as Grace got to having a second brother. They had been tight friends since she could remember. Her mother loved to trot out photos of Grace and Collin playing together in the plastic baby pool in their diapers, and Grace knew that her parents and Collin's father, Sam, still held a secret hope that the two of them would eventually end up together.

The idea of a match between them was comical. It would be like dating her brother, although she couldn't deny that Collin had grown into an insanely handsome man. He was tall with a lean build, dark hair and coppery eyes with gorgeous light brown skin. As a captain in the army, he was currently stationed in Germany. His years in the military had honed his body into a network of hard planes and muscles.

"I'm working," she told him, then glanced toward the house. "As well as getting a much-needed break from my family."

"Jake said you weren't going back to the hotel." Collin climbed the porch steps two at a time.

Grace growled and made a face. "Jake is even worse than Dad right now. He's not the boss of me, and it's high time he figures that out."

"Aw, Gracie, he means well."

"Don't even go there, Collin." She wagged a finger in his direction. "You're my friend, so you have to be on my side."

"Always." He rested a hip against the porch railing. "But you can't believe that your parents and Jake aren't on your side. They love you."

"I know." She blew out a frustrated breath. As aggravated as she was by her family's fussing, she knew everything they did was motivated by love. "But I want to work, and I love my job at the hotel. I'd love it even more if they made me general manager when the hotel opens. I've worked so hard, Collin. I need a chance to prove myself."

"Even if the hotel is being targeted?" He raised a challenging brow.

"Jake needs to stop spreading rumors," she muttered.

"You could have died, Grace."

"Why does everyone keep reminding me of that?" She slammed her laptop closed, once again cursing the cast and her limited mobility. There was no way she could stomp off the way she wanted. As soon as the blasted cast was off, Grace would never take walking freely for granted again.

That thought took the wind out of her sails of righteous anger in an instant. Of course Jake and her parents were extra worried and overprotective. He'd battled back after the accident, working with physical therapists and doctors and on his own for months in order to walk again. Yes, Grace had left college and come home to help, but no one could understand what Jake had been through during that time other than him. She had no doubt the accident and the ensuing long, painful recovery and legal fight over responsibility had changed her once happy-go-lucky brother.

Now she was annoyed by not being able to walk across the front porch without her crutches. She rubbed a hand over the top of her leg and nodded at Collin. "I understand how bad the accident could have been, and I appreciate my family. But I told myself when I came back to Rambling Rose that I was going to find a way to have the life I wanted, to go after my dreams and not let anyone stand in my way."

Collin frowned. "Are you talking about your jerk-wad ex-boyfriend?"

"Maybe," Grace admitted. "We both worked at Cowboy Country, but I did my job and helped him with his. Did I tell you he got a promotion based off a marketing plan I basically wrote for him?"

"Five minutes alone in a room with him," Collin said with a dark laugh. "That's all I need."

"You sound like my brother," she told him, shaking her head.

"Great minds."

"I'm happy to be back to work, and I can't wait until I feel strong enough to go into the hotel and have my social life back, too." She held up a hand when her friend would have argued. "I'll be safe there, Collin."

He shifted to sit more fully on the porch rail. "How do you know?"

Wiley's handsome face appeared in her mind. "I just do. You should come by and check it out. The restaurant is going to be fantastic. I know you appreciate a good kitchen."

"Yeah." He nodded. "My dad doesn't exactly have gourmet tastes."

"How's he doing?" Grace knew it hadn't been Collin's plan to return to their small hometown, but when his father had taken a turn for the worse after Collin's stepmother passed away, he'd come back. Although not officially related, Grace and Collin had the family-duty gene in common.

"He seems okay since I've been here, but I've don't

have a lot of leave time. I'm still worried about how out of sorts he's been since my stepmom died."

"He loved Sharon very much," Grace said gently. "I'm sure having you here on leave helps him feel better. I only wish you could stay longer."

They both glanced toward the street as a sleek black sedan pulled up to the curb. Grace's heart fluttered against her ribs when Wiley climbed out of the vehicle. He wore a crisp white button-down shirt and dark pants with aviator sunglasses covering his brown eyes.

"What were you saying about a social life, Gracie?" Collin lifted a brow. "Because you're blushing at the stranger in the fancy clothes."

"Shut up, Collin." Grace returned the wave Wiley gave her as he approached the house. "He's not a stranger. He's a Fortune."

Collin elbowed her. "Well, isn't that interesting."

"Not to you," she muttered.

"Hello, Grace." Wiley glanced between her and Collin. "You look well."

It was kind of crazy how two words—*hello, Grace*—could cause a riot of sensation to pulse through her body every time he said them.

"I'm working." She held up her laptop. "On plans for the reception. It's coming along really well. I'm well, too, of course. Just like you said."

Collin straightened from the porch rail and leaned in. "You're babbling."

"Go away, Collin."

He threw back his head and laughed. As much as he was annoying her in this moment, it was good to hear him laugh. He'd done far too little of it since returning home.

Collin gave the swing a little push, then turned to Wiley. "Collin Waldon," he said, holding out his hand. "I'm a good friend of Grace's."

Wiley's chest expanded as he nodded. "I'm Wiley Fortune. Grace and I—"

"Are working together on the hotel event," Grace said, planting her foot on the wood porch to stop the swing. "In fact, we're discussing plans this afternoon. Collin was just leaving."

Her childhood friend grinned at her over his shoulder. "I'll talk to you later, Gracie."

She shifted on the porch swing as Collin headed back to his father's house, moving her cast leg to the ground.

"Would you like to sit down?" She patted the cushion next to her and offered a smile.

"Does he live next door?" Wiley asked as he moved toward her.

A shallow line of tension had appeared between his brows.

"Since we were babies," she confirmed. "We grew up together—best friends for as long as I can remember. Collin's in town on leave to visit his dad. He's been in the army for years."

Wiley took a seat next to her. "And now you're staying with your parents. How convenient for catching up."

She glanced at him from the corner of her eye. If Grace didn't know better, she'd think Wiley sounded jealous of Collin. A thrill passed through her at the thought of that. She really didn't want the attraction she felt for the handsome attorney to be completely one-sided.

"Collin's a good guy," she said, and maybe she kept her phrasing slightly cryptic just to gauge Wiley's reaction.

She wasn't disappointed. His jaw tightened for several seconds before he finally turned to her with a smile that was patently forced. "It's important to have good friends in your life."

"Yeah." She tried to keep her mouth from twitching in amusement, but Wiley's gaze narrowed on her.

"What's funny?"

"Nothing. I'm just happy to see you."

He visibly relaxed at her words. "I didn't really come here to discuss the hotel event. Although I'm happy to talk about it if you want. Nicole and Megan said you're doing an amazing job already."

Pride blossomed in her chest at the praise. "We're just getting started, and I still wish I was coordinating everything on-site. I hope by next week I'll feel strong enough to come to work at the hotel."

"That's great." A breeze blew a few curls across Grace's face and before she could push them away, Wiley reached out and with a gentle touch, tucked her hair behind one ear. "You have the most beautiful hair."

She swallowed back a nervous giggle. "I used to hate having wavy hair. When I was growing up, the popular style was sleek and straight. No matter how much product I used, mine would never behave. But I've gotten used to it, although it's a rat's nest when I wake up." She raised a hand to her mouth when she realized she was babbling again, but Wiley didn't seem to notice.

"I'm sure it's beautiful in the morning, too."

The rough timbre of his voice tickled her skin as she thought about waking up with a man like him next to her. Good Lord, that would be something special.

She cleared her throat and gave herself a mental "down, girl" command. "If you aren't here to talk about the event, is there something else? Do you have more information on who was behind the balcony collapse?"

"I wish I could say I did. Not yet, though. I stopped by to... I wanted to see you."

Oh.

Grace felt heat flame her cheeks. Wiley Fortune wanted to see her. She could definitely get used to that.

A tapping sound came from the house, and she turned to see her mother standing at the living room window looking out at them. Grace suddenly felt like she was a teenager again with her nosy parents trying to insert themselves into her business. Wiley waved at her mother, who returned the wave and gave him a beaming smile. At least her mother was being friendly. Grace didn't want to think about what would happen when her dad realized Wiley was here.

"Would you like to go for a drive?" She stood as she asked the question.

"Sure," he answered, quickly straightening to join her. "If you have time?"

She hopped toward the front door, laptop tucked under her arm. "All the time in the world. Just give me a minute to tell Mom I'm leaving and grab my shoes and crutches." She didn't really like using them, so she typically hopped around her parents' house.

"I'll be here."

Great. Wiley would be waiting for her.

Her mother opened the door as she reached for the handle. "Wiley is here," she stage-whispered.

"Yes, I saw you watching us from the window."

Barbara winced. "Sorry. That was too much."

"It's fine. We're going for a drive." Grace made her way past her mom and gently closed the door. "Can you grab my crutches from the family room?"

"Where are you driving to?" Her mother placed a hand on her arm. "Do you need something, sweetie? Your dad is in the garage. He'd be happy to get you—"

"Wiley came to see me." Grace covered her mother's hand with her own. "Not to talk about work or the balcony. To see me."

Her mother's mouth formed into a small O.

"Exactly." Grace bit down on her lower lip. "We're going for a drive. I don't know where." She checked her watch. "Maybe out for dinner. Maybe…it's a date."

"I'll get the crutches," her mother said with an enthusiastic nod. She gently pinched Grace's cheeks and smoothed a hand over her hair. "There now. You look so pretty with a little color in your face."

"Mom, have you become a Fortune fan?" Grace asked as she bent to retrieve her shoes—or shoe—from under the front table.

"I'm a fan of seeing my daughter happy," Barbara said. "You look happy for the first time in a while, sweetie."

"Thanks, Mom."

With a nod, her mother headed down the hall while Grace sat on the chair in the foyer and tied the laces of her sneaker. They weren't the most exciting choice in footwear, but she was still getting used to the crutches. Better to be practical than wind up on her back end in front of Wiley.

She glanced at the front door while she waited for her mom. It was probably rude to leave him standing out there, but Grace had needed a minute to compose herself. He'd said he wanted to see her. It wasn't some grand profession of devotion, despite the way her heart reacted. Other than his family, he probably didn't have many friends in town. Maybe he was just bored, and she was a distraction.

A short-term distraction, she reminded herself, even though her body ignored the warning. Her mother was right. Grace hadn't felt this excited in a long time.

Her mother returned with the crutches. "Have a good time on the drive or dinner or whatever you do."

Whatever. Grace couldn't even entertain the possibilities of "whatever." Not with her leg in a cast and her mother standing next to her. She grabbed the crutches and smiled. "I appreciate that," she told her mom, then scrunched up her nose. "I'd also appreciate if you not mention it to Dad or Jake—"

"Go have fun with your friend." Barbara reached around her to open the door. "Your dad and brother don't need any details."

Wiley turned as Grace hopped out and closed the door behind her. She arranged the crutches under her arms and started forward. "Sorry about the wait."

"No problem." He glanced between her and the porch steps. "But speaking of problems…"

"I can manage." She gave him a bright smile. Okay, so she hadn't actually dealt with steps other than when she'd returned from the hospital, but she would make it work. "I appreciate you taking me out for a bit." She got to the top step and handed him the crutches. "Could you hold these for a moment?"

"Of course. Are you sure you can manage it?"

No. "Yes."

"I could help you…"

"I've got it." Grace was probably a fool for refusing an excuse to get close to Wiley, but she wanted to prove to herself that she could handle a flight of stairs on her own—even if it was just five wooden porch steps. If she was going to head back to work the following week, she'd need to get a lot more proficient at moving around on her own.

She grabbed hold of the railing for support and hopped down each step, proud when she didn't once lose her balance. "I didn't fall," she announced with a wide smile as he returned the crutches.

"You did great." He looked at her with a huge smile.

"That was silly," she said as they started down the walk toward his car. "Maneuvering down a few steps isn't a big deal, but this is the farthest I've gone on my own since the accident. If my parents had their way, they'd encase me in Bubble Wrap for the rest of my life to make sure I stayed safe."

"It's an understandable sentiment from people who care about you."

"But not what I want."

He opened the car door for her, and she gave him the crutches to stow in the back seat. The whole process was slow and awkward. By the time Grace was buckled in next to Wiley, sweat dripped between her shoulder blades, and she felt like she'd run a marathon. How could less than a week of inactivity make her feel like such an invalid?

As if sensing her frustration, Wiley placed a gentle hand on her arm. "You've been through a lot, Grace. Your ankle and the cast are the biggest outward signs of the accident, but you fell from the second story."

She offered a wan smile. "I have the bruises to prove it."

"Give yourself a bit of…well, grace."

"I never thought of attorneys as naturally comforting people," she admitted. "But you're good at giving support."

"It's a hidden skill." He released her hand and pulled away from the curb. "We lawyers don't like to let anyone know about our human side. It ruins the reputation of being coldhearted, and then people aren't afraid of us."

"You're the opposite of scary."

"Where are we headed?" he asked when he got to the stop sign at the end of the block.

"The highway," she said without hesitation. "As much as I love Rambling Rose, I need a break. Let's get out of this town, Wiley."

Chapter 7

Wiley sensed the change in Grace as they cruised
down the open road. She'd given him directions to the
highway, and they were headed west out of Rambling
Rose, destination unknown—at least to Wiley. He liked
giving control to Grace. Wiley's life was normally a
rigid list of schedules and meetings, so the idea of not
having to worry about anything for an evening was
strangely liberating.

The sun was just beginning to set, and fluffy clouds
filled the sky overhead, swaths of cotton candy against
the blue of the sky.

He couldn't explain how right it felt to have Grace
next to him, to finally be alone with her, even on a drive
to nowhere special. He wanted to make whatever time

they spent together special. She deserved that, and he had a primal urge to be the man to give it to her.

Tiny remnants of jealousy still quivered in his stomach, out of character for him. Even when he dated, Wiley had never been the jealous type, but seeing Collin Waldon lean close to Grace had made him want to lose his mind. She'd described him as a friend, but their connection was obvious. What man in his right mind wouldn't want more from Grace?

Wiley certainly did.

"I love this time of day," she murmured, splaying her hand against the passenger window. "It's amazing how we take for granted the little things in the hustle and hurry of regular life. I never thought about it being a treat to leave the house whenever I wanted."

"I'm honored to be the one to help you escape," he told her with a wink. Open pastures and fields filled with herds of cattle glided by on either side of the highway. Similar to the trail ride with Megan and Kane, this drive gave him another glimpse into the Texas landscape, and the sheer scope and size of it gave him an unexpected sense of peace. How was it that a self-described city slicker could feel such a connection with wide-open spaces?

"You're being nice again," she said, a teasing lilt to her voice. "While I appreciate it, I'm sure you have better things you could be doing tonight than this."

"Nope." He shook his head. "Driving down the highway with you tops my list." He made the comment casually, because he didn't exactly want to share how much this moment meant to him.

"If that's the case, I bet you're champing at the bit to get back to your regular life."

"I'm enjoying the break."

"Really?" She shifted in her seat to look at him more fully. "Tell me about Chicago. The city must be so exciting. I've always wanted to visit."

"The pace is definitely different than you have around here, but not necessarily better. Just different."

"What would you be doing on a normal weekday night if you were in the city?"

He glanced at the clock on the dashboard. "Most likely I'd still be at the office."

"Describe it," she said. "Did you decorate it yourself?"

He chuckled at her attention to detail. "Not really, although I worked with the firm's interior designer to choose paint colors and a few pieces of generic art. If my diploma weren't hanging on the wall, the space could belong to anyone."

"But you spend a lot of time there. Are you part of a big firm?"

He nodded and explained how he'd interviewed with several law firms during his final semester at law school and chosen this one because of its size and the variety of clients. At the time, Wiley had been captivated by the thought of working in an office with a dozen other associates. He'd assumed he'd have the chance to work with myriad different types of clients, although in reality the work was more monotonous than varied.

As Grace peppered him with questions about his coworkers, his hobbies and his friends, he realized how one-dimensional he'd allowed his life to become. Much like a robot, he functioned on autopilot. Not that daily life in Rambling Rose was a roller coaster of excitement, but observing his siblings for the past week, he realized that they'd managed to create rich, layered lives filled with friends, new ventures and sometimes love.

He had very little to share that made his life sound fun. Hell, he'd even gotten into the habit of ordering the same rotation of meals from the carryout restaurant around the corner from his condo. He had all the freedom in the world, he realized, but took advantage of none of it.

As quickly as possible, he turned the conversation toward Grace's life. She recounted in more detail the aftermath of her brother's car accident and what it had meant for her. She didn't complain about having to leave college to help with Jake's recovery, and he admired her dedication to her family and her positive attitude.

He wanted to ask more about her time at the cowboy-themed amusement park his relatives ran in the small town of Horseback Hollow, but she suddenly sat forward in the seat. "Get off here," she told him, and he veered onto the exit ramp, although he hadn't even noticed a sign for services along the empty stretch of ranch land.

"We came here when I was a kid," she told him, looking around with a sentimental gleam in her eye.

"Where exactly is here?"

"Turn right off the exit." She pulled her phone from the purse she'd looped around her shoulder. "Shoot. I don't have service, but I'm pretty sure there's a restaurant about a mile down the road."

"In the middle of nowhere?" He grinned at her. "Should I be concerned about what they might be serving on the menu?"

"It's part of the adventure," she told him. "Let yourself go crazy, Counselor."

"So long as crazy doesn't end up with either of us hugging the porcelain throne later tonight."

She laughed at that, and the sound reverberated through him like music. He still couldn't tell what it was about Grace, but Wiley felt completely at ease with her.

The road wound in a gentle curve, grand oak trees flanking it. He liked the differences in the north Texas landscape. The way the scenery could change from wide-open fields to rows of trees standing sentry, their bare branches reaching toward the heavens.

Suddenly, a small house—or inn—appeared in a clearing. The decades-old structure was painted deep purple with a yard filled with whirligigs and metal lawn art out front.

"That's it." Grace clasped her hands together. "I remember the sculptures. I was fascinated with watching them move when we came here."

He pulled into the gravel parking lot, which was half-filled with cars. "I can't believe you found this place," he said, grinning at the happiness in Grace's blue eyes. She looked like a kid about to enter her favorite candy store.

"I can't believe it, either." She reached out and squeezed his hand. "It must be a sign."

He lifted a brow. "Of what?"

"This is the moment my luck changes. No more

cheating boyfriends or accidents or dead-end jobs. This place shows that I can find something great if I trust my instincts."

Wiley turned over his hand so their palms touched, once more amazed at how soft her skin felt against his. He wasn't certain he believed in luck or signs, but he knew enough to savor this moment and his time with Grace.

"Then let's go try your luck with the Oak Tree Inn."

By the time he pulled her crutches from the back seat and made his way around the car, Grace had climbed out, gazing at the inn's clapboard front like it was the entrance to Shangri-la.

She adjusted the crutches under her arm and started toward the building, stumbling slightly when the bottom of a crutch slipped on a large rock.

"I've got it," she said before he could offer assistance.

Her quiet independence was a new experience for Wiley. Although he kept his romantic life casual, he definitely had a type. Gorgeous, young and happy to have him take care of everything from planning dates to choosing menu items and definitely setting limits on how close he would get. He tended to go out with women whom his sisters liked to describe as damsels in distress. It wasn't as if he purposely sought out the role of "knight in shining Italian loafers" but that was often the position he found himself in.

He expected things to be the same with Grace, especially given what she'd been through. Her injuries were the perfect excuse to sit back and let him pamper her, which he would be happy to do.

But the more time he spent with her, the more he understood that making her own way was important to Grace. She didn't want to be handled or coddled, despite all the stumbling blocks life had put in her way. Her determination captivated him. Maybe that's why he found himself becoming more and more fascinated by her with every passing minute.

Grace couldn't remember a night when she'd had more fun than she had spending the evening with Wiley.

They sat near the firepit on the back deck of the cozy inn, the only two people who'd ventured out from the dining room. Dinner had been even yummier than she imagined, with the chef offering simple dishes with an Italian flair.

Her frustrations and struggles with work and her family seemed a million miles away. To her great relief, Wiley appeared just as relaxed as she felt. The inn's owner had given them a couple of thick fleece blankets to take out with them, and they sat close together on an outdoor love seat.

"This is how I want people to feel when they stay at the Hotel Fortune," she murmured, her breath catching as Wiley shifted so that their thighs pressed against each other.

"Blissed out on good food?" he asked with a wink.

"Happy," she answered simply.

Her response seemed to catch him off guard, and he gazed into the fire for several long seconds before speaking.

"I feel it, too." His voice was a quiet rumble and did funny things to Grace's insides. "Happy."

He bent forward to place his wineglass on the stamped concrete patio.

"But I think my happiness has more to do with you than this place." He gestured to the building behind him. "Or the food and drinks, although everything was fantastic."

Pleasure swirled through her at his words, because she felt the exact same way. Grace reminded herself that she not only didn't believe in love at first sight, but she wasn't interested in anything that would take her focus from her position at the hotel and the potential of earning the coveted general manager promotion.

"But if we can offer our guests—both local and out-of-town visitors—an experience that lets them forget the troubles of regular life so quickly, they'll definitely come back over and over."

Her lips tingled when he placed a gentle finger against them. "I thought we agreed no work talk tonight."

She gave a shaky nod, then wrapped her fingers around his. "Yes, but you know I'm right."

He chuckled. "You're right," he conceded without hesitation. "This night is special."

Then he leaned close and brushed his mouth over hers. It was a tentative kiss, a question of sorts. Grace couldn't tell which one of them he expected to answer. Her body had no doubt, however, and she reached up and wound her hands around his neck, needing to be close to him.

A low groan escaped Wiley's lips, and it felt like a gift that she could affect a man like him. He cupped her face between his big hands, angling her head and deepening the kiss. Their tongues met and melded, making heat shoot through Grace's body in a way that shocked and thrilled her. No simple kiss had ever stirred her in this way.

Normally, she would wait for a man to push for more, but Wiley seemed content to savor her and the moment like they had all the time in the world to discover each other. Within moments, Grace lost herself in the sensation.

After what felt like hours but was probably only minutes, Wiley pulled away. He stared into her eyes without speaking, but his gaze told her everything she needed to know. "Wow," he murmured, one side of his mouth curving.

"Exactly what I was thinking." She went to shift closer and banged her foot on the edge of the love seat, and muffled a yelp of pain. Nothing like the reminder of her injury to put a damper on the most romantic interlude she'd had in forever.

"Are you okay?" Wiley's hand immediately went to her leg, and Grace lost all ability to think coherently.

"Fine," she managed, trying not to wheeze. "But maybe you should kiss me again and make it better."

He flashed a wolfish grin and claimed her mouth again.

Grace jerked back when she heard the sound of voices headed in their direction. Two older couples were walking toward the firepit from the restaurant.

"We should probably go," Grace said, although she didn't want the moment to end. She didn't want anything about this night to end.

"Will your parents be worried?"

She shook her head. "I texted my mom while you were in the restroom so she doesn't worry. It's weird to be an adult and still check in, but she appreciates it." She stifled a yawn. "I wish I had my normal energy."

"You're overdoing it." Wiley immediately shrugged off the blanket, stood and then scooped her into his arms.

Grace sputtered out a shocked protest. "I'm not that tired."

"Could you hand me those crutches?" Wiley asked one of the men from the group that circled the other side of the firepit.

The stranger did as he was asked while the two women looked on with similar expressions of fascination. "That's so sweet," one of them told the other.

Color rushed to Grace's cheeks. "You can put me down," she said into Wiley's ear.

"Young love," the second woman responded. "If Carl tried to pick me up like that, he'd pull out his back."

The women laughed as Wiley started down the back steps and around the side of the inn. They'd already paid their bill so didn't need to return inside.

"Wiley." Grace squeezed his shoulder. "You don't need to carry me."

He paused and kissed her again. "I know you're more than capable on your own, Grace. But please let me hold you for a few minutes."

Well, when he put it like that, how could she refuse?

Reassured that he wasn't taking pity on her, she settled into his embrace for the short walk to the parking lot. He was warm and strong, and she couldn't resist tracing one finger along the strong column of his neck. His Adam's apple bobbed as he swallowed.

"You're going to cause me to stumble, and we'll both hit the ground," he said with a gruff laugh.

"I trust you."

His arms tightened around her for a few blissful seconds, and then they were at the car. He deposited her on the ground and rested her crutches against the back door.

"Thank you," he said, and pressed a gentle kiss to her forehead.

"I think I should be thanking you." She grinned. "As should those two women at the firepit. From the sound of it, you made their night with your heroics."

His gaze darkened. "I'm not a hero. I just wanted an excuse to wrap my arms around you."

"Do you need an excuse?"

He turned his head, as if he needed to look away in order to gather his thoughts. "I like you, Grace. A lot. From the moment I saw you at the birthday party, there was something…"

"I know," she said, lifting a hand to his jaw. "I felt the same thing."

He met her gaze once again. "I don't want to take advantage of you."

Please, her body screamed silently. *Take advantage*.

"I'm a big girl, Wiley."

"I'm only in town until the hotel's grand opening," he reminded her, as if she could forget.

"That gives us a few more weeks."

One side of his mouth twitched. "What exactly did you have in mind during that time?"

Heat pooled low in her belly, but there was no way she could articulate all the things she had in mind for Wiley. Her uninjured leg began to ache, an outward sign of her current limitations. The cast was going to make anything physical between them awkward at best.

Then she realized that as much as she desired the man standing in front of her, she liked talking to him and just being around him as much if not more. He made her feel smart and capable. Right now she wanted—needed—more of that in her life.

"We could hang out," she suggested. "Like tonight."

"Tonight was a date."

The words sent pleasure spiraling through her. "Then we could date more."

His thick brows drew together. "Until the opening?"

She nodded. "You're returning to Chicago, and I'm focused on my career. Neither of us has time for anything serious, but we have fun together. Right?"

"So much fun," he murmured, still teasing.

"It's a mutually beneficial arrangement." Grace held her breath as she waited for his response. In truth she barely recognized herself, suggesting a short-term fling with a man like Wiley. The brother of her bosses at the hotel.

There were so many reasons it might be a bad idea, not the least of which was the way he made her heart stutter and her body ache when he looked at her. And when he kissed her...

She couldn't focus on the risks. Grace had spent so long playing it safe. Her vow when she'd returned to Rambling Rose had been to live life to the fullest, to

push herself out of her comfort zone. This was definitely ticking off those boxes.

Wiley's dark gaze searched her face for several seconds, and then he nodded. "This is the start of a few
weeks of as much mutually beneficial fun as we can
manage."

Chapter 8

Wiley followed the sound of construction toward the hotel's back patio two days later. He'd spent most of the previous day holed up in his bedroom suite at the ranch, on a never-ending stream of calls and videoconferences. Working remotely was turning out to be more of a challenge than he'd expected, but the thought of returning to Chicago held little appeal, especially when staying in Texas meant spending time with Grace.

He'd walked her to her parents' front door after their dinner together, and the urge to kiss her again had been difficult to resist. At least until her father opened the door as they climbed the porch steps, giving Wiley a look that clearly communicated Mike's disapproval.

After taking the crutches from him with a sigh, Grace had balanced herself on her uninjured leg and leaned in for a quick peck on his cheek and a murmured thank-you before disappearing into the house.

Her father had slammed the door in Wiley's face before he'd even had a chance to say goodbye. He'd climbed in his car and started toward home, pressing two fingers to the place her lips had touched, feeling like a lovesick teenager for wanting to vow not to wash that side of his face again.

Although Grace's mother seemed to approve of their friendship, it bothered Wiley that her dad and brother clearly wanted no part of him in Grace's life. He didn't date seriously, but Wiley had met his share of parents over the years, and all of them seemed inclined to support their daughters getting serious with an attorney, especially one who came from a well-to-do family. Wiley's stepfather, David, had made a fortune in the video game industry. He and his siblings were intent on carving their own path, yet there was no doubt in anyone's mind that they came from a good family.

Wiley would have thought the Fortune name garnered extra approval in Texas, where the expanded family had such a long and illustrious history. He knew better than to take Mike's and Jake's animosity personally. The idea that someone might have sabotaged the balcony's structural beams worried him, especially given what could have happened to Grace in the fall. But he was determined to prove that he only had Grace's best interests in mind.

Callum waved to him as he stepped out into the bright sunlight of the mid-January day. Wiley glanced at the workers on ladders affixing new lumber to the hotel's exterior. Once local law enforcement and the insurance company finished their investigations, the crew had wasted no time in cleaning up the fallen balcony and starting to rebuild.

"You're making great progress," he said as he joined Callum.

His brother gave a tight nod. "We need to have the balcony reconstructed completely before the opening. I want this place to look like an accident never happened."

Wiley drew in a deep breath. Callum was right, of course. It wouldn't do them any good for the hotel's reputation to be tainted even before they had their first paying guest. Hell, that was the whole point of the event Grace was coordinating. But it bothered him that they had no idea what or who had caused the problems with the beams. Their insurance company and the police might suspect sabotage, but they couldn't prove it.

Plans for the opening were moving ahead despite the shadow of potential foul play hanging over them. The fact that Kane had already begun the process of upgrading the property's security system gave Wiley a measure of comfort. Kane was also recommending that they take increased precautions at the other businesses in town, although no one wanted to believe the balcony collapse had been personal.

"I'm not saying I want to ignore what happened to Grace," Callum said, hands on his hips. "The safety of our employees and potential guests is the first priority."

"I know," Wiley agreed. "But I don't like loose ends. If we knew for certain what had caused the accident—either way—I'd feel better."

"I feel the same, but we can't let that derail us from our goal."

They both turned as a feminine voice called a greeting. Mariana approached from the far side of the pool, her bleached blond hair pulled into a loose ponytail and reading glasses resting on top of her head. Her smile faltered slightly as she glanced up to the second floor, but it was bright once more when she returned her gaze to the brothers.

"Good morning, Fortunes," she said, holding up several brown paper bags. "I've brought lunch for your crew."

There was a resounding cheer from the men, who'd all turned to watch Mariana. The woman truly was a force of nature and well-loved in the Rambling Rose community.

"That's the best thing I've heard all day," Callum said, returning her grin as he took one of the bags. "To what do we owe the pleasure?"

She placed a bejeweled hand on his shoulder. "Ah, Callum. I'm here spreading sunshine and light in the form of my famous empanadas."

Wiley chuckled. "Food that makes everything better. That could be your new tagline." And he had no doubt it was true. Mariana had run her popular food truck for years at Mariana's Marketplace, Rambling Rose's busy flea market. Last year, she took an active role in the town's future businesses and even discovered a connection to the Fortunes through the town's old Foundling Hospital.

His brothers and sisters had been wise to involve Mariana in the hotel's development. She helped Nicole run the Roja kitchen and brought her usual enthusiasm and style to that role. Everyone on staff seemed to love her, and Wiley felt like she might give additional credibility to the venture. Not many people in town would go up against the formidable Mariana.

"How is Grace Williams?" she asked Callum.

Wiley forced himself not to answer, although his brother sent him a curious look. On the way home from dinner, Grace had told him she wanted to keep anything other than friendship strictly between them. He rubbed the heel of his hand against his chest to ease the ache that suddenly appeared there. It made no sense that he felt disappointed at the thought of not being able to publicly claim Grace as his, even temporarily.

He understood the rationale, given her position in the training program and the impending announcement about the general manager promotion. Although he would never try to influence his brothers or sisters based on his personal feelings, there was no need to in this case. After spending more time with the other trainees, particularly Jillian Steward, Wiley felt even more certain that Grace should earn the new role. Jillian rubbed him the wrong way, always trying to make it seem like she was in charge. He liked one of the other trainees, an easygoing man named Jay Cross, well enough, but Jay seemed more interested in filling in wherever needed than adept at running the entire hotel.

"From what she tells us, she's doing better." Callum nodded. "The event she's putting together is going to be a huge success. We had a phone meeting yesterday, and she's gotten the whole thing coordinated in less than a week."

"She was always such a hard worker," Mariana murmured thoughtfully. "I hope she's not overdoing it."

"Me, too."

Wiley could feel Callum's gaze on him but ignored it.

"She did look a little worn down on the call," Callum continued, turning to Mariana.

Wiley sucked in a breath. Worn down? He hadn't seen Grace since their date, but they'd been texting regularly, and he was supposed to pick her up for dinner after work tonight.

"The accident could have been so much worse," Mariana said. "She needs to make rest a priority."

Callum nodded. "Agreed, although it's hard to convince her of that. I'm going to ask Nicole or Megan to reach out, as well. We scheduled a physical therapist to work with her on any lingering soreness or potential back issues. The ankle is the most obvious injury, but she mentioned the doctor was worried about mobility and her range of motion."

"She told you that?" Wiley ran a hand through his hair and tried to mask his reaction. Grace hadn't talked to him about other injuries.

"Yeah," his brother answered. "But she hasn't returned the PT's calls. Knowing Grace, she feels like she's taking advantage since she knows we're paying for it."

"The money doesn't matter," Wiley said, realizing the harshness of his tone when both Callum and Mariana startled.

"I understand," Callum told him. "We all do. Someone just needs to convince Grace of that. I'm sure one of the triplets can—"

"I'll handle it," Wiley said.

Mariana shook her head. "Grace has always been determined to make her own way. She'd probably respond better to one of your sisters since she knows them."

"She knows me," Wiley said, making his voice gentle. "We're friends."

"Friends?" Mariana murmured while Callum shook his head.

"You don't have friends," his brother said. "You have us, coworkers and the arm candy you date."

"Wow. That's a real shot in the arm. Trust me. Grace and I are friends, and I'll convince her to work with the physical therapist." He looked between the two of them. "For the record, she's not the delicate flower that everyone around here assumes her to be. She's strong and capable, and it's about time people stop underestimating her."

When both Callum and Mariana appeared to be shocked into silence, Wiley turned and stalked away.

"You saw Wiley a couple of nights ago. I thought we were going to hang out tonight."

Grace paused in the act of applying mascara and looked at her brother in the mirror that hung above the dresser in her childhood bedroom. It still amazed her that their parents hadn't changed either her bedroom or Jake's since they'd moved out. She vaguely remembered that her mother had been planning on a whole house clean-out just before Jake's accident. Everything had been put on hold in the months after that as they all rallied around him to support his recovery.

"I know you have something better to do than watch

movies with your little sister." She pointed the mascara wand at Jake. "I heard you were becoming pretty chummy with Melissa Wagner."

Jake made a face. "Shouldn't you be busy resting and getting better? Why do you have time for petty gossip about my love life?"

"Because I've been doing very little other than resting." She placed the mascara tube on the glass charger that held her simple supply of cosmetics and turned. "I need to get out more."

"That's not true." Jake adjusted the pillow he'd propped behind his head as he sprawled across her comforter. "Mom and Dad are already worried about how much time you're devoting to this hotel event, and it's not good for anyone—especially you—to be spending time with some big-city attorney."

"We're friends." Grace hopped over to the closet to pull out a jacket, not wanting her brother to witness the heat she could feel crawling up her cheeks at the thought of Wiley. They'd agreed to keep their relationship secret, so she couldn't give her feelings away to her brother. Feelings that were probably not wise, given that Wiley was leaving town after the grand opening.

She might have suggested a short-term arrangement with her mind dizzy from his kisses, but in the past couple days she'd realized that wouldn't stop her heart from wanting more.

Jake gestured to the arrangement of flowers that sat on the taller dresser. "Why does a friend send you flowers? And cheesecake?" He snorted. "Who sends a woman cheesecake?"

"Um…you better not complain after I saw you scarf down a huge slice when Mom told you about it."

"Well, I love cheesecake."

"Me, too." Grace pulled on her jacket. "I happened to mention it to Wiley, and he told me about some bakery in New York City that makes the best."

"And then had it sent to you? Classic rich-boy move."

"Don't be a jerk, Jake. This whole business with the accident has been hard. I hate having people look at me with pity or reminding me that I'm lucky to be alive."

"Trust me, I get that."

She heard the bitterness in her brother's tone and immediately regretted her comment. "I know you do. So I hope you can also understand that I like Wiley. He's nice, and he doesn't treat me like I'm weak. He helps take my mind off of what happened."

"I get it." Jake sat up straighter with a sigh. "But that's what I'm worried about, Gracie. I don't trust the Fortunes, and especially not the attorney. Don't you think it's a little too convenient that he just happened to decide to stay in Rambling Rose after the balcony collapsed?"

"He wants to make sure everything goes smoothly with plans for the opening. He's supporting his family." She drew in a deep breath and added, "He's supporting me."

Jake studied her for several moments, and Grace decided she wasn't going to hide her emotions from her brother. She was a grown woman and could make her own choices about who she spent her time with.

"Don't let him take advantage of you," he warned,

his gentle tone almost harder to handle than the snarky remarks he'd made earlier.

"I trust him," she said, because that was the only truth that mattered to her at the moment.

The sound of the doorbell had her turning for the hallway. "Come back tomorrow night, Jake. I'll kick your butt in Scrabble."

"You wish." He climbed off her bed and followed her out of the room. "I don't suppose you want me to greet the Fortune with you?"

"Can you be nice?" she asked over her shoulder.

He pounded a fist to his chest like she'd wounded him. "Of course I can. I just prefer not to."

She smiled despite her annoyance and made her way down the hall. Once again, she'd left her crutches in the front entry. Although she didn't enjoy hopping around her parents' house, the hallway was narrow, and the rooms were filled with furniture that made it difficult to maneuver with crutches.

Her parents were in the backyard discussing plans for a garden bed her mom wanted in the spring. She desperately needed to get to the door and away from the house before they realized Wiley had arrived to pick her up. She knew her mom would be nice but couldn't say the same for her dad. He was almost as bad as Jake as far as doubting Wiley's motives. She could only imagine what they would think if they knew she was dating the handsome Fortune.

She opened the door and smiled at him, anticipation curling in her belly as she waited for his greeting.

"Hello, Grace," he said in that smooth tone, and she

felt her grin widen. Did he even realize what those two words did to her?

"Hi." She groaned in frustration when one of the crutches slipped from her hand and clattered to the floor. "I swear I'm going to get better with these before I get to the hotel."

Wiley bent and retrieved the crutch, handing it to her. "I have a better idea." He reached to one side of the door and pulled a black scooter into view. It had foam handles and a wide pad clearly meant for her injured leg. "I brought you a gift."

Grace's mouth dropped open. "Oh, my gosh. My own set of wheels?"

Wiley nodded. "I called a doctor friend, and he suggested it. Apparently, it's a lot easier to maneuver and can help with your mobility. Not that you aren't doing great with the crutches."

"I hate the crutches." She put her hands on the scooter's handle and then lifted her leg onto the long black cushion. It was so easy to push herself to the far side of the porch and then turn the scooter to head back toward Wiley. "I'm a natural on this."

When she got close to the door, she called for her brother. It didn't matter what Jake thought about Wiley. He had to see her scooter.

He appeared in the doorway a moment later. "Wow. That's cool, Gracie. Where'd you get the spankin' new ride?"

"Wiley brought it for me. It's amazing, right?"

"Yeah." Jake crossed his muscled arms over his chest as he glanced at Wiley. "Nice work, Fortune."

"Thanks," Wiley muttered.

Grace laughed at the two men, who looked equally uncomfortable exchanging even the most basic pleasantries.

"Tell Mom and Dad not to wait up," she said to her brother. "Now that I actually get around, who knows what fun we can find."

"It's Rambling Rose," Jake said with a wry laugh. "We all know there are limits to the fun you can have in this town."

"I don't know about that." Wiley lifted the scooter when Grace took hold of the staircase railing.

Grace was glad she had her back to her brother, because she couldn't prevent the wide grin at the thought of all the fun she and Wiley could have together.

Chapter 9

"I'm not sure this is such a good idea." Grace leaned forward to look at the entrance of Provisions, the farm-to-table restaurant Wiley's sisters ran in town, along with Ashley's fiancé, Rodrigo Mendoza. "I thought we agreed to keep our relationship between us."

"We're friends," Wiley assured her. "Everyone in my family likes you, and they don't need to know more than I'm helping you out with a ride. I haven't had a chance to do more than stop by the restaurant. Ashley won't quit giving me grief." He flashed what he hoped amounted to a convincing smile. "You'd be doing me a huge favor."

"I guess," she relented after a few seconds of chewing on her bottom lip. "I've wanted to eat here since they opened Provisions last year. Plus, I need to be familiar with other restaurants in town so I can make recommendations to hotel guests. Right?"

"Exactly. This is a perfect excuse for that. But if you aren't comfortable with it, we can drive out of town and—"

"Let's eat here." She reached out and squeezed his arm. "But no kissing."

He chuckled. "That's a bummer. Can we find some place to park after dinner so we can make out in my car like a couple of teenagers?"

"You joke, but I'm serious. I don't want anyone in your family to know we're dating."

"Our secret is safe with me." Wiley kept his smile on his face as he climbed out the car, ignoring the pang of disappointment that stabbed his gut knowing that Grace wanted to keep what was between them hidden. Her insistence on secrecy was an unwelcome reminder that their relationship was temporary. Of course, he knew it. After all, he'd be returning to Chicago in a matter of weeks, and Grace would be busy with the hotel. He should be feeling relief. Normally, he was the one placing parameters on his dating life about what he was and wasn't willing to offer. A few weeks was plenty of time to get a woman out of his system, but somehow Wiley knew Grace wasn't like other women.

He thought back to that moment he'd spotted her across the Roja banquet room and the word that had whispered inside him like trace of a melody he couldn't quite place. *Mine.* The idea was ridiculous, and he knew it. Grace didn't belong to anyone but herself. That didn't stop Wiley from wanting her. From wanting more.

As he retrieved the scooter from the trunk, he tried

to shake off his disturbing train of thought. Obviously, he was just reacting to being away from his regular life. He didn't have his work and his hectic schedule to keep him busy, so he had too much time to think about Grace. Once he returned to Chicago, things would get back to normal. No way was he falling under the spell of this sleepy Texas town the way his siblings had.

Grace was already standing next to the car, using the open passenger door for balance, when he got there.

She smiled up at him, a teasing light in her eyes. "You might have all the willpower, but it's going to be hard for me not to kiss you."

Just like that, every last one of Wiley's rationales about remaining distant or getting her out of his system disappeared like a puff of smoke in a brisk wind.

"Later," he promised, brushing his hand against hers. "Save that thought for later."

"Who was the first girl you kissed?" Grace asked as they made their way toward the restaurant's entrance.

"Jessica Meyer in seventh grade. We were in the same math class, and she was way smarter than me."

"You were a late bloomer," Grace said, clearly delighted. "I kissed Miles Spicaro on the playground in second grade."

"Not Collin?" Wiley asked, then regretted the question. He felt like a fool revealing how much her friendship with the boy—now man—next door bothered him.

She gave him a funny look. "Not Collin. And Miles ended up being a onetime interlude. Too much pressure for elementary school. What about this Jessica? Was it first love?"

Wiley opened the heavy wood door to Provisions and gestured Grace forward. "I've never had a first love."

"Oh." That one syllable conveyed so much about what she thought of his confession, and once more, he wished he would have kept his personal business to himself. It wasn't like him to share details about his feelings or really anything with the women he dated. He hadn't planned on not falling in love, of course. He wasn't completely coldhearted.

But love meant compromise, and Wiley valued his independence too much to give it up on any meaningful level. At least that's what he told himself.

"Hi, guys." Ashley met them at the hostess stand when they entered the restaurant. She gave Grace a one-armed hug and touched a finger to the scab that had almost completely healed on Grace's forehead. "You look amazing, and I love that scooter. How are you feeling?"

"Thank you," Grace answered almost shyly. "I'm doing better every day and looking forward to getting back to work. Wiley found the scooter, and it's a huge improvement over the crutches. I could never quite find my balance with them."

"Nice work, Wi." Ashley turned to hug him. "Did you just eat a lemon?"

He frowned at the question. "No, why?"

"Your face is all puckered. Is something wrong?"

He shook his head, willing some random alien ship to appear and beam his sister up into its depths. Grace was looking at him oddly now that Ashley had pointed out his lemon face. Even though he was certain he didn't have any kind of furrowed expression. He simply didn't want to think about what he couldn't give to a woman like Grace.

"Everything is great. We're excited for dinner." He gestured to the dining room. "You have quite a crowd."

Ashley followed his gaze to the open-concept restaurant, situated with tables filled with customers. "I hope the hotel does as well as we are. It's beyond my wildest dreams."

"We're going to make sure the hotel is a huge success," Grace offered. "Your brothers and sisters have been working so hard to get things ready."

"With your help," Ashley answered. "From what Nicole says, they miss having you at work. Not that the other trainees aren't doing a great job, but…"

Grace nodded, color blooming on her cheeks. "I can't wait to be back."

"You all need to stop pressuring her," Wiley grumbled, hating that he sounded like some kind of overprotective grandpa. But he couldn't stop himself. After speaking to Callum and Mariana about Grace not following up on the PT appointments, he wondered if anxiety about returning to work was making her sacrifice her recovery.

Were her parents actually right?

"No pressure," Ashley promised as she led them through the dining room. "You getting well is the top priority."

"I'm really feeling much better," Grace assured her, darting a quelling glance at Wiley over her shoulder.

Ashley opened the door to a private room on one side of the restaurant. "I hope it's okay with both of you, but we prepared a special tasting menu for tonight." She grinned at Wiley. "I want a chance to impress my big brother and figured you might enjoy a bit of privacy." She gave Grace a sympathetic nod. "It feels like everyone is still talking about the accident, you know?"

"I do," Grace agreed with a grateful smile. "I hate being a topic of conversation. Thank you for your thoughtfulness, Ashley. I really appreciate it."

As his sister closed the door to the private dining area, Wiley glanced around the space, pleased at how things had turned out. He'd suggested to Ashley that Grace didn't like the attention she was receiving for her injury, feeling like that was a plausible reason to request a space of their own.

The room retained the character of the grain silo that had once occupied the space, with high ceilings and painted shiplap on the walls. A white cloth covered an impeccably set table in the middle of the room. Grace wheeled the scooter slowly toward the table, taking in the flowers and candles on the sideboard. He wondered what would happen if he told her how he was truly coming to feel about her—the way his heart stammered every time he looked at her and the anticipation of seeing one of her sweet smiles. Would she admit to the same level of connection, or would he scare her away by deviating from the path they'd agreed to?

Was he brave enough to risk finding out?

Just as he was about to speak, she turned to him, and the anger flashing in her blue eyes took him by surprise.

"Do you think I need to be coddled in the same way my parents do?" she whispered, the pain in her voice cutting off all thoughts of a revelation about his feelings. Confusion filled him, and he wanted a do-over on the past few minutes. Apparently, Wiley had mis-judged her reaction to his plan for a private dinner in a monumental way.

Grace regretted the words as soon as they left her mouth. She looked away from Wiley's shocked expression and took in the beauty of the room. From the soft lighting punctuated with flickering candles to the scent of flowers perfuming the air, she couldn't have asked for a more romantic setup. Calla lilies took center stage in the flower arrangements, not a surprise since Wiley knew they were her favorite.

She had no doubt he'd orchestrated this room and the mood it set. She didn't want to consider what the attention to detail that had gone into it might reveal to the Provisions staff—and more importantly to his sister—about the nature of their relationship. She'd expect nothing less of her big-city attorney. From food to the little gifts and flowers he'd brought her, it was clear he was a master of thoughtful gestures.

As much as she appreciated being spoiled in this way, what Grace liked best about Wiley was that he'd seemed to believe in her. He hadn't treated her like a child the way her parents tended to. Despite her struggles, he never gave any indication that he thought her incapable of dealing with challenges or making her own decisions.

Until tonight.

"I don't know what you're talking about." He shook his head. "I'm not trying to coddle you, Grace."

"Then why mention to your sister how I need to make recovering my priority as if I'm not already doing that?" She moved closer to the table. "You sound like my dad or Jake. I thought you believed I could manage my own life?"

"I do."

"That's not what it sounded like." She dashed a hand across her cheek, cursing the tears that gathered in her eyes. She didn't want to cry but was working so hard to prove that she could handle everything. The truth was, sometimes she doubted herself. She felt tired and achy and like she wanted to crawl into bed, but she kept going. She wouldn't have the opportunity for the promotion at the hotel taken from her because she wasn't up to the task of it.

"Grace." He stepped closer, and she wanted to back away, but that wasn't so easy to manage with the scooter. "I know how determined you are to return to the hotel, even though you're practically managing as much as two people working remotely. But I'd be lying if I told you I wasn't worried about you."

Betrayal ripped through her, but he held up a hand before she could speak. "Tell me why you haven't contacted the physical therapist my family arranged."

"How do you know about that?" she demanded instead of answering, hating to be put on the spot in this way.

"Callum mentioned it," he said gently. "You understand that people realize how serious the fall could have been? More serious than it was." He paused, looked away for moment before his gaze returned to hers. "Deadly."

"Of course I do." She squeezed her eyes shut. "And I hate it. I hate that people are talking about me or feeling sorry for me." She slapped her hand against the scooter's metal frame. "I hate that the cast is a visible reminder of the accident. I'm forever going to be associated with this black spot that I'm sure everyone at the Hotel Fortune would like to erase."

"They don't want to erase you, sweetheart." He took her hand and lifted it to his lips, placing a kiss on each one of her knuckles.

"No kissing," she reminded him, but didn't pull away.

"You're too hard to resist." He inclined his head. "Will you make an appointment with the PT? I know how strong you are. And brave. I know that you'll work through almost anything, but that doesn't mean I don't worry." He leaned in, his forehead pressing against hers in a way that felt strangely intimate. "Not like your parents, Grace. I worry like a man who cares about a woman. The fact that I want you to take care of yourself doesn't mean I don't believe in you."

"Okay," she answered, unsure that her jumbled brain was capable of saying anything more. He cared about her. What did that mean?

Because she knew what it meant for her. It meant that her heart was happy when Wiley was around and that the depth of feeling she already had for him scared her to her core. She knew what it was like to have her heart broken, and here she was risking it with a man who'd just blithely told her he'd never been in love.

It wasn't as if she thought he was going to change for her, despite how much she might want him to try.

Yet she had to admit he was right about pushing herself. "I don't want the Fortunes to think I'm trying to take advantage of them or that I think they're responsible for me being hurt. It felt like if I worked with a physical therapist on the injuries I have unrelated to my ankle, I'd be admitting that I was hurt more seriously than people thought." She placed a finger to his lips when he would have spoken. "Which I'm not, although my back is stiff, and I probably rely on over-the-counter anti-inflammatories more often than I should."

Wiley gave a sharp shake of his head. "That's it. I'm making sure the therapist is at your house first thing Monday morning."

Grace smiled. "I'm coming into the hotel next week for a meeting about the preopening event."

"No."

She rolled her eyes at him. "Wiley."

"Grace, you just admitted you're in pain. I hate the thought of you in pain."

She leaned in and kissed him, unable to stop herself. "I appreciate that and the fact that you're concerned and not overprotective. I'll call the PT and schedule a session for Monday afternoon, but no more talk about my injuries, especially with your siblings."

He looked like he wanted to argue, so she kissed him again.

"You can't resist me, either," he said with a sexy smirk as she pulled back.

"I guess you're right." Her heart hammered in her chest at the thought of how much she was already coming to care for him. A part of her wanted to tell him, but she was too afraid of scaring him off. Instead, she moved aside the scooter and eased herself into the chair. "Let's leave talk of the hotel behind tonight. I want to enjoy every moment of this friendly dinner."

To her great relief, he nodded and sat next to her. A

discreet knock sounded on the door, and the server entered, carrying a tray filled with an assortment of appetizers that both smelled and looked divine.

Yes, Grace liked Wiley for the man he'd shown himself to be and the way he made her feel. She also appreciated that he wanted what was best for her, and tonight she was content to let herself be treated like someone special. She couldn't deny that she wanted more from him. Tomorrow she'd remind herself that her priority was proving herself at the hotel and winning the promotion. Tonight she'd let her heart lead the way.

Chapter 10

"Are you sure you don't want me to help you in?" her mother asked as they rounded the corner toward the Hotel Fortune.

Grace blew out a huff of nervous laughter. "Mom, this isn't the first day of kindergarten."

"I get it," Barbara said with a chuckle. "I know you're a capable adult, Gracie. Your father and I are proud of how you've dealt with everything life has thrown your way. A lesser woman would have let it ruin them."

"I learned my strength from you," Grace said quietly.

It was true. After Jake's car accident, her mother had never wavered in her outward confidence that her son would fully recover, despite the grueling process and all the setbacks they faced. Grace wanted to find a way to have that kind of faith in herself.

Her mother pulled to a stop at the curb in front of the hotel's main entrance. Grace smiled as she saw Jay Cross heading toward her.

"I've got this," Grace said as she opened her door, not sure who she was trying to convince.

"I love you, sweetie," Barbara said as she pushed the button to open the sedan's trunk. "I'd tell you to break a leg, but I'm afraid you might take me literally."

Grace turned to her mother with a smile. "I'll text you in a bit to let you know I'm fine."

A look of obvious relief crossed her mom's face, but she shook her head. "You don't have to, but I'd appreciate the update."

Jay had the scooter out of the trunk when Grace climbed out of the car. "Look at you, Ms. Overachiever," he said in his country drawl as she placed her purse and files in the scooter's wire basket and positioned her cast on the pad. "Are you trying to make the rest of us look like slackers?"

Excitement flooded through her as she looked at the hotel's stucco exterior. She tipped her head to the sky and said a silent thank-you for the ability to return to work and the beautiful day for it. "I'm a twenty-eight-year-old woman getting dropped off at work by my mom." She lifted a brow. "She even offered to pack lunch for me, which is sweet but also humiliating in a humbling way."

"I'll take your mom's lunch," Jay answered with a laugh, running a hand through his cropped hair.

"You'll take free food from anyone." Grace started for the hotel. "And we both know you aren't a slacker. You're just strangely tranquil."

Jay looked startled for a brief moment before his features shifted back to self-possessed. He was her favorite person in the trainee program. His easygoing attitude and willingness to pitch in made everything more fun. He definitely cared about the hotel and he worked hard, but didn't seem to have the same drive as Jillian and Grace.

"Someone needs to be tranquil with Jillian taking the lead in your absence."

Grace let out a small groan. "I was afraid of that."

"I don't think anyone is buying her 'I'm the second coming of Conrad Hilton' routine," Jay confided. "But that isn't stopping her from trying to convince them. It's like she's on a mission to suck up to every Fortune in this town."

His derision was clear, and Grace appreciated that he felt the same as she did about Jillian's attempts to cast herself in the starring role for the hotel. But she wondered if the Fortunes saw it that way.

Jillian had positive qualities. She was organized and detail-oriented, but Grace had worked in hospitality long enough to know that Jillian's snobby attitude would be a turnoff to certain guests. One of the cardinal rules about the hospitality industry was a focus on service, and in Grace's opinion, her rival still had a ways to go in learning to put the guests above her own ambition.

"I'm back," Grace murmured, unsure whether she was trying to reassure Jay or herself. "At least for a few hours every morning."

"How are you really feeling?" Jay asked, and she appreciated the concern in his voice.

"Other than the cast, I'm doing okay." She didn't

bother mentioning the aches and pains she still had every morning. True to her word to Callum, she'd left a message for the physical therapist. She hadn't expected to hear back until today, but the woman had returned her call almost immediately. So fast, in fact, that Grace wondered if the PT had been instructed to respond as soon as Grace reached out. Either way, she was coming to the house for an initial consultation that afternoon. Although she'd been assured the hotel's insurance would cover all of the expenses related to her accident, Grace still didn't feel comfortable letting the Fortunes pay for the sessions, but she'd work that part out later.

Jay opened one of the hotel's large iron doors. She wheeled through and then gasped at the crowd of her coworkers congregating in front of the reservation desk. Everyone clapped for her arrival and several people— Nicole and Ashley included—held up signs welcoming her back.

Tears sprang to Grace's eyes, and she quickly tried to blink them away. Callum stood at the back of the crowd. He gave a slow nod as their gazes met. She'd wondered if anyone would even notice her absence, but this reception made her feel like the people at the hotel were truly a part of her family.

"I wasn't the only one who missed you," Jay said as he came to stand next to her.

"Welcome back, Grace." Callum stepped forward. "It's great to have you here again."

"Thank you," Grace answered, swallowing around the emotion clogging her throat. "A lot of people would be happy for an excuse to spend a few weeks binge-watching television, but it's a testament to all of you and how amazing this hotel is going to be that I just can't stay away. The Hotel Fortune will be the crowning jewel of this town, and I'm grateful to be even a small part of our success."

Another round of applause greeted her words, and Callum's grin broadened. He was such a serious man, focused and driven, so Grace felt particularly grateful that he seemed satisfied with her impromptu speech.

"We're the ones who are grateful to you," he told her, and then stepped aside so that other employees could greet her. It was almost fifteen minutes later before Grace was alone in the lobby with just Jillian and Jay. She stifled a yawn, wondering if her mom had been right and she was taking on too much.

How could talking make her so tired? She blamed it on the emotions of the morning, from returning to the hotel to the warm welcome she received and then being asked to recount the accident for her curious coworkers.

"You're like the mayor of this hotel," Jay said with a laugh as she turned to him and Jillian.

That comment earned a scowl from Jillian. "We have a meeting with Nicole to discuss restaurant logistics for the grand opening." She eyed Grace's leg. "I'm sure it will take a while for you to get up to speed. So much has happened since you've been on vacation."

"I wouldn't call it a vacation," Grace said, forcing her tone to remain steady.

Jillian waved a hand in front of her face. "Whatever. You practically just admitted that you've been doing nothing but watching television."

"And planning the preopening event," Jay added quietly.

"Busywork," Jillian muttered.

Grace smiled. Kill them with kindness, she thought. "I appreciate the two of you taking care of things while I was recovering. If there's anything you need me to pitch in on now that I'm back—"

"Part-time." Jillian sniffed. "No, I've got it handled. In fact, our meeting with Nicole is about to start." She gave Grace a condescending smile. "I scheduled us to meet in the banquet room upstairs. You probably don't want to deal with all those steps. They're doing mainte- nance on the elevators today, so they aren't an option."

Grace's heart sank as she glanced over to the bank of windows that overlooked the lobby from Roja's private room. The staircase was just off the entrance to the res- taurant and would indeed be difficult for her to manage.

"How about if we switch the meeting to the first floor?" Jay glanced between the two women.

"There are things we need to discuss about seat- ing arrangements upstairs," Jillian insisted. "Grace can check the hotel's email inbox while we're doing the im- portant stuff. Of course, every little detail is important. You know what I mean."

Grace resisted the urge to grit her teeth. As difficult as she sometimes found it to stick up for herself, she had to start acting like a manager if that's what she wanted to be. "Jillian, I want to be part of the meeting. I'm sure Nicole will understand if we change the location."

At that moment, Nicole appeared at the Roja entrance situated off the lobby. She punched something into her cell phone, then shoved it into the back pocket of the stylish trousers she wore. "Did I hear you talking about a venue change?" she asked the three of them.

"Yes." Grace spoke before Jillian had a chance to.

"Would it be okay if we met down here so that I don't have to contend with the stairs? I have some ideas I think you'll want to hear."

"Great idea," Nicole said easily. "I want everyone to contribute."

Jillian's face went blank. "But we have seating charts to discuss so we should be upstairs if—"

"We'll manage. We can review the charts on the digital floor plan." Nicole gave a pointed look to the tablet Jillian carried. "Grace, I can't wait to hear your thoughts on plans for the grand opening. You've done such an amazing job so far with the pre-event."

"Thanks," Grace whispered. Clearly annoyed and just as clearly trying to hide it, Jillian followed Nicole into the restaurant. Jay held open the door for Grace, who wheeled forward, proud of her tiny victory in derailing Jillian's attempt at undermining her. Grace was no longer going to fade into the background for anyone.

"Thank you for the ride," Grace said later that afternoon as Wiley pulled out of the hotel's parking lot. "My mom or Jake could have picked me up."

"It's not a problem," he told her. "I'm heading back to the Fame and Fortune anyway to work on some contracts that came in for review earlier."

She rolled her head on the seat back to look at him. "It must be difficult to balance everything you've taken on at the hotel with the work from your regular job."

He shrugged. "I don't mind."

"Because it's temporary?" She couldn't help but ask, needing the reminder not to get used to Wiley's presence in her life, no matter how much she wanted to.

"Because I like the work I do at the law firm, and I enjoy helping my family."

His magnanimous answer made her feel petty and small. There was no reason to goad Wiley, especially when he'd been so kind and helpful.

"That's nice," she said when her exhausted brain couldn't come up with anything better.

"Are you okay?" He reached across the console and placed a warm hand on the top of her thigh. "Did you have a good morning at the hotel?"

She nodded. "Yes. I liked feeling productive, and it was so nice of everyone on staff to welcome me back." She stifled a yawn. "But it makes me mad to get so tired after only working a few hours. I'm used to being able to go all day and still have energy left over. Now I feel like I just ran a marathon."

"It will get better. Your body is still healing."

"I hate it," she grumbled, then blew out a breath. "I'm sorry. I know I'm not the best company right now. And the physical therapist is supposed to be at the house in an hour. All I actually want to do is take a nap and then watch movies in bed for the rest of the night." She tapped a finger to the top of Wiley's hand. "I think I might need to reschedule the PT appointment."

"Nope." He shook his head. "It's set."

"I can call her back."

"But you won't," he insisted. "The only way to get stronger is to work at it."

She folded her arms across her middle, irritation crawling through her like an army of spiders. Wiley was right, of course, but that didn't mean Grace wanted to hear it. "I think I liked you better when you were bringing me flowers and being all sweet and romantic."

"We're saving sweet and romantic for after the therapy session," he promised. "Right now, I'm being your friend."

She opened her mouth, then shut it again, his words wiping away the irritation. As much as she enjoyed the kisses they shared, the thought of being Wiley's friend was just as appealing. "Friend or drill sergeant?" she asked, not bothering to hide the sarcasm from her voice. Sarcasm was an easy mask to hide behind.

"A little of both, actually." He pulled onto her parents' street. "Text me after the PT leaves, and I'm happy to come over or pick you up." He stopped at the curb. "Or if you just want a night alone with Netflix, I understand."

She snorted softly. "If it weren't for this stupid cast, I'd be all about the Netflix and chill with you."

He laughed. "We're in no hurry."

Those words splashed cold water on the flame that ignited inside her every time she thought about being with Wiley in an intimate way. Maybe there was no hurry, but they did have a built-in end date, and she'd do well to remember that.

"Sure," she whispered.

"Grace." He took her hand, and just that gentle touch sent shivers across her skin. "I mean it. No pressure."

Oh, heavens. He thought she was upset because he might be pushing her for something she wasn't ready to handle. What would he think if he knew that without the cast, she'd be tempted to crawl over the console and attach herself to him like a barnacle? Maybe not the most romantic image, but that's how she felt.

"I appreciate it," she answered, and placed her hand on the door handle. The thought of attaching any part of herself to Wiley had her feeling a bit unhinged. She was tired. And frustrated. And she wanted him more than she cared to admit. "I should go."

Wiley looked past her out the passenger window and gave a little wave. "Your mom is coming."

All thoughts of desire vanished into thin air. Grace sighed as her mother headed down the front walk toward them. She opened her door and called out a greeting as Wiley went around to the trunk of the car to retrieve her scooter.

"How was your day?" her mother asked as Grace climbed out.

"I texted you, Mom." She tried to keep the impatience out of her voice. "It was fine."

"You look tired."

"I'm fine."

"She's tired," Wiley confirmed. "After the physical therapy appointment, she should rest. If there's anything she needs—"

"I'll ask for it," Grace said through clenched teeth. She knew he was trying to be nice and she didn't want to take his generosity for granted, but being smothered with caring chafed at her, even if it was done with the best intentions.

Barbara bestowed a beaming smile on Wiley. "I appreciate you looking out for her. It makes me feel better about her going back to work before she's fully healed."

"It's my pleasure," Wiley answered. "Everyone at the hotel was happy to see her return."

"The photos you sent were adorable," her mother told him, reaching out to pat his arm.

Grace blinked. "Wait." She looked from her mom to Wiley. "You sent photos? You're texting my mother?"

"I asked him to, sweetheart," her mom explained. "I didn't want to bother you."

"So you bothered him instead?" Grace snapped, shaking her head.

"It was my pleasure," Wiley assured her.

"Not the point." Grace placed her purse and files into the scooter's basket with more force than was probably necessary. "I'm going into the house. Thank you for the ride, Wiley. I think after my appointment, I'll rest for the night after all."

His gaze clouded. "Whatever you want."

"Other than managing my own business," she muttered, and scooted toward the house as fast as she could manage.

"Gracie, don't be mad." Her mother caught up with her in a couple of quick steps. "Wiley was only doing what I asked. I know your father and I are overprotective, but you're our daughter. Please."

The catch in her mother's voice wound its way around Grace's heart. Of course she understood why her parents worried so much, even if she didn't like it. "I know, Mom," she said softly, pausing just before the front porch. "Give me a minute out here, okay?"

Barbara nodded and waved to Wiley before heading back into the house.

Grace turned the scooter, not a graceful move by any

stretch of the imagination. As always, her breath caught at Wiley's pure physical perfection. She liked that he always dressed a touch more formally than his brothers, retaining his city polish even in Rambling Rose.

"You sent photos to my mom," she said, more a statement and less an accusation this time.

He took a step toward her and nodded.

She appreciated that he didn't try to make excuses or mansplain his behavior.

"I appreciate you looking out for me," she said quietly, looking down to the end of the block when the intensity of his gaze was too much. "But it's important to me that you understand I can take care of myself."

He moved closer slowly, as if approaching some feral creature. In truth, that's how Grace felt on the inside. Frustration and fatigue combined to sharpen her edges.

"I understand," he said. "You've proven yourself to be one of the most competent women I've ever known. You don't need my help, because you can handle anything."

"Right now it doesn't feel that way," she admitted. "It hasn't for a while. I let my prior relationship, and before that my family, dictate what I did in life. People around me were my priority, and I thought I had to put the needs of others before my own. I'm trying to change that." She reached down and massaged a hand along the top of her thigh. "Current circumstances aren't making it easy."

"I want to make it easier, Grace."

She studied him for a moment, the sophisticated attorney who seemed intent on making her feel special. It still boggled her mind that Wiley would be interested in a woman like her. In truth, that's part of why she resisted his involvement. She didn't want him to see her as a charity case.

"I don't mean to sound ungrateful." She crooked a finger, beckoning him closer. "I'm grateful for your help at the hotel. I'm grateful for you." When her voice threatened to crack, she swallowed back anything else she might say to him. Her feelings were too raw, too new at this point.

He laced their fingers together. "That goes both ways."

She felt a smile tug one corner of her mouth as butterflies fluttered across her stomach. "I want to kiss you right now, but we're standing on my parents' front lawn."

"Rain check?" he asked, leaning in close.

As an answer she brushed her lips over his, unable to resist. She drew back quickly, still cognizant of being on display for half the neighborhood. "I'll text you after my PT appointment."

The look of relief that filled his bourbon-hued gaze surprised her. It was as if he actually worried she might push him away. That he truly cared about her feelings.

He carried the scooter up the steps to the porch, and it was difficult to watch him walk toward his car again. Grace could imagine how much good it would do her exhausted spirit to spend an hour napping in Wiley's arms. But that certainly wasn't an option living with her parents.

It might be time for a change.

Chapter 11

Are you free for dinner?

Wiley blew out a relieved breath when Grace's simple text appeared on his phone screen the following afternoon. He'd gotten stuck on a series of conference calls with his Chicago colleagues that morning and then had a meeting at the county building inspector's office, so he didn't arrive at the hotel until after lunch. Grace had already left for home.

He couldn't tell why not seeing her for twenty-four hours made him feel anxious. Normally, Wiley set strict limits on his relationships so that the women he dated didn't get the wrong impression about his level of commitment.

Grace had practically accused him of trying to run

her life yesterday, a clear sign that he was in too deep with her. He never got involved with women at that level. Flowers and other gifts—like the ones he'd given her after the accident—were…well, Wiley wouldn't describe them as meaningless. But they were superficial in a way that felt comfortable. He liked boundaries and limits. He liked control, especially after feeling he had so little of it as a kid in his overlarge blended family.

But the tiny town of Rambling Rose, and Grace in particular, made him want more.

He replied to the text that he'd pick her up at her parents' around six and received an immediate response with an unfamiliar address along with a message to come hungry for pizza.

The rest of the afternoon seemed to tick by in slow motion. He resisted the urge to google the address she'd sent him to see if they were meeting at a restaurant or something that would clue him in to her plan for the night. It occurred to Wiley that he might have a bit of an issue with control if he couldn't relinquish it long enough to allow Grace to surprise him with plans for the evening.

He left the hotel after checking progress on the balcony reconstruction. The painter had put the finishing touches on it, and the structure looked as good as new. Part of why Wiley had gone to the inspector's office was to discuss the possibility of sabotage in more detail. The man had assured him that they couldn't make a definite determination on what had caused the collapse. For now they believed the accident to be just that—an accident.

Wiley breathed a little easier at that news, although

the cynic in him had a hard time totally trusting it. He would reserve judgment until the hotel opened without incident. But the relief on the faces of his brothers and sisters when he'd shared the news that the balcony may not have been tampered with made him want to believe. There was enough stress in putting the finishing touches on the hotel to have it ready for opening in less than a month. The idea that right now they wouldn't have to worry about sabotage on top of everything else clearly helped everyone. He also knew that the security system Kane had installed was top-notch. Nothing was going to get past them.

Anticipation continued to build in him as he drove to the ranch to change out of his suit and then headed back to town, following his car's GPS to the address Grace had given him. He parked in front of a nondescript brick fourplex in a residential neighborhood that he'd never been to before. Why would Grace have sent him there?

Frowning as he surveyed the block, Wiley was about to pull out his phone to text her when she called his name. He glanced toward the house to see Grace waving at him from a second-floor window.

"Come on up," she shouted. "I'll text you the code for the front door."

"How'd you get up there?" he asked as he approached the house.

She grinned, looking more relaxed than he'd seen her since that first night. "It's amazing what a girl can manage with the right motivation."

He entered the building, using the code that appeared

on his phone. The converted house had two apartments on the first floor. The staircase that led to the second floor was narrow, and he couldn't imagine how Grace would have climbed the stairs. Obviously she'd made it to the second floor somehow.

She stood in the doorway of one of the upstairs apartments, looking more beautiful than ever in a simple sweater and a pair of loose sweatpants with the right leg cut off at the knee. Her hair was down around her shoulders, and although he'd seen her almost every day for the past week, there was something different about her tonight—a light in her eye that hadn't been there before.

"Welcome to my apartment," she said, backing up the scooter to give him room to enter. "It's not fancy, but guess what?" She took his hand as he entered and drew him close for a lingering kiss. "We're alone."

The thought sent a sensation surging through him. He gave his body a silent command to settle down. Being alone with Grace didn't change anything. They were dating or friends or friends who were dating, depending on how he felt at any given moment.

"Why the change in location? Is everything okay with your family?" He squeezed her fingers. "I hope I didn't cause lingering problems between you and your mom because of updating her. Like I said—"

"Wiley, stop." She looked at him strangely, and he realized he was blathering. He wasn't a man who spoke compulsively or without prior thought. He chose his words deliberately, took action with purposeful thought. Wiley valued control above almost everything else, and suddenly one soft-spoken woman had turned everything he knew about himself on its side. "Everything is fine with my family." She shut the door behind him and released her hold on his hand, moving across the hardwood floor on the scooter toward the small kitchen positioned at the other end of the open space.

"Then why are you here?" He looked around the apartment and saw Grace's personality reflected in almost every part of it. It wasn't fancy, but from the row of bookshelves to the framed botanical posters above the slipcovered sofa, he could imagine her choosing every item with care. A complete contrast to his apartment in a sleek complex in downtown Chicago. He'd lived in his place for nearly seven years and had yet to hang a single piece of art on the walls.

The more time he spent in Rambling Rose, the more obvious it became that he was living life but hadn't created a home.

"I actually have you to thank once again," she said, grinning at him over her shoulder. "Thanks to your bullying, I didn't cancel the PT appointment yesterday."

"*Bullying* is such a harsh word," he told her with a grimace. "Can we use *support* or *encouragement*?"

"Bullying in the best way possible." She turned to him. "I needed it. You were right. Avoiding therapy wasn't going to help me heal faster or make anyone forget about the injury. The cast is kind of a giveaway, you know?"

"That doesn't explain you moving back to a second-floor apartment."

"The therapist was wonderful. She gave me some exercises to help strengthen my leg muscles for the time I'm still in the cast. I explained to her how much trouble

I'd been having with the crutches. She helped me learn to use them more effectively."

Grace pointed to the metal crutches that rested against the wall. "We even did some work on getting up and down stairs. Once I felt more confident, I knew I could move back here. I don't have to stay with my parents anymore."

"That's great." The radiant smile she gave him did funny things to his heart. "And your folks are okay with it?"

Her smile dimmed slightly. "They aren't thrilled," she admitted, "but it's not their choice. My dad picked me up from work and drove me here this afternoon while Mom did some grocery shopping, so I won't starve." She opened the refrigerator to reveal the fully stocked shelves. "Once they saw that I could manage the stairs, it made them feel better about things. I need this so badly. I need to feel like I can make it on my own."

"Of course you can," he said because even though he didn't like to think of her struggling, he knew her independence was important to who she was, and he'd never take that from her. "You know I'll help with anything you need."

"Yeah," she whispered, biting down on her lower lip. "And I do have a few places that are achy."

He immediately took a step closer. "Have you been overdoing it at the hotel?"

She chuckled and tapped a finger to her mouth. "I hurt right here," she told him with a wink. "Any chance you'll kiss it and make it better?"

Every feeling of desire Wiley had locked down came roaring back to the surface. They were alone in her apartment. The thought of what it might mean made his body grow heavy with need.

Just as he reached her, the landline phone on the counter rang.

"Hold that thought." Grace pointed at him. "I think the pizza just arrived."

Food was the last thing Wiley cared about at the moment, but he opened the door for the delivery guy after Grace buzzed him into the building. To his surprise, she'd already paid over the phone, so all that was left for Wiley to do was hand the kid a couple of dollars as a tip.

"You don't have to buy me dinner," he told her as he carried the box to the two-seater kitchen table positioned in front of a window. "I'm the man. I should pay."

He wanted to slap himself as soon as the words left his mouth, and she flat out laughed at that statement. "You need to update your thoughts about relationships," she told him as she pulled two plates from the cupboard. "As much as I appreciate your gentlemanly tendencies, I'm a modern woman."

"I'm an ass," he muttered. "My mom and my sisters would kill me if they overheard that."

"Your intentions are noble."

"That's something, I guess. Are you sure you want to put up with me?"

She laughed again. "It's only for a couple—" He watched as she closed her eyes and drew in a deep breath. There was the reminder of his dwindling time in Texas, which was beginning to feel like a specter haunting the moments he shared with Grace.

So many things would be easier once he returned to Chicago. Although Wiley was keeping up with his client load, working remotely meant everything seemed to take longer than it would if he were handling it at the main office. Despite that, he found he didn't want to think about leaving Rambling Rose or Grace. Especially Grace.

"Would you like a beer?" she asked when she met his gaze again, her eyes almost aggressively bright. "I had my mom pick up the same brand you ordered at dinner the other night."

"You're wining and dining me." He took the plates from her hand and leaned forward to kiss her neck, needing the sweet scent of her to ground him in the moment and help him forget the inevitable end to their time together. "I should push you out of your comfort zone more often."

Her shoulders relaxed, as though she appreciated his attempt to lighten the mood. "Be careful, Counselor," she warned, "or this modern woman might push your comfort zone right back."

Grace couldn't remember the last time she'd felt so content. It was nearly ten and she sat cradled in the crook of Wiley's arm as the final scene of an old sci-fi movie played on her small TV.

He was the first man she'd had in her apartment, and nerves had plagued her after she'd texted him the invitation earlier. She knew her place wasn't anything special, especially for a man who was probably used to living the high life in the city. Most of her furniture consisted of hand-me-downs from her parents or thrift-store finds. She'd shared a duplex apartment with her ex-boyfriend in Horseback Hollow and after discovering the depth of his betrayal, she'd been so intent on getting out of town, she'd simply left behind everything that wouldn't fit in her car.

It had only been a year since she'd returned to Rambling Rose, but her relationship with Craig seemed like a lifetime ago. It still amazed her how deeply she'd come to care for Wiley in such a short time. Maybe it was due to growing close to him in the aftermath of her accident, but Grace couldn't help but believe there was more to their connection.

If only she didn't keep getting the unwanted reminders that he'd be leaving sooner than later. She snuggled against him, reminding herself to stay in the moment instead of worrying about things she had no control over. That plan seemed to be serving her well as far as her job. Even though Jillian had found ways to remind Grace every day since her return about all the ways she wasn't contributing to progress toward the grand opening, Grace stayed focused on the pieces she could do. She'd invited owners of various local businesses, and plans for the Rambling Rose partnership reception were almost complete.

When the movie's credits rolled, Wiley dropped a gentle kiss on the top of her forehead. "This is nice," he said, one hand tracing lazy circles on her arm. The featherlight touch did funny things to her insides, her pulse thrumming at the thought of being truly alone with this irresistible man. Up until now, the only moments they'd had to themselves had been in his car, and there was only so much that could happen with a console separating them.

Not that a lot more could happen with her leg in the cast, but Grace tipped up her chin and trailed kisses along Wiley's strong jaw. His arms tightened around her, and he claimed her mouth, their tongues meeting as the kiss deepened. She wound her arms around his neck, reveling in the heat that surrounded her.

It felt like she could kiss him forever and never tire of it. Her body grew heavy with need and she shifted, wanting to get closer but not quite able to manage it with the cast hindering her.

"Are you okay?" he asked her when a frustrated sigh escaped her lips. "Am I hurting you? Is it your leg?"

She pulled back to gaze into his dark eyes. "I want more," she whispered. "What would the physical therapist think of me if I asked her how to manage..." She broke off and wrinkled her nose. "Being with you despite my cast."

One side of his mouth twitched. "I'm not sure, but I like the way your mind works." He smoothed a stray lock of hair from her face. "I like everything about you, Grace. So much so that I don't want to rush this."

As much as her brain appreciated his chivalry, Grace's body wasn't cooperating. "Will you stay with me tonight?" she asked, then felt heat rise to her cheeks at her own bluntness. Grace wasn't the type of woman to ask for what she wanted or take the lead in the bedroom. But it was different somehow with Wiley.

A thought wiggled its way into her mind. Maybe Wiley was being a gentleman because he didn't feel the same way about her. Although even her dad seemed to be warming to him, her brother still had suspicions about his motives. Jake still seemed to believe Wiley was protecting his family by getting close to her and sent her at least one text a day with some sort of veiled warning about not opening her heart to the Fortune attorney.

Grace didn't bother to tell Jake it was way too late for that. Her heart was already well in the mix.

She held her breath as she waited for Wiley's response. She could feel his heart beating a rapid-fire pace against his chest. "No pressure," she added when he didn't respond. "I'm not expecting anything to happen. Sleeping, of course. But otherwise—"

"Yes." He said the word with a level of reverence that sent shivers across her skin, then kissed her again.

By the time he finally pulled away, Grace felt dizzy with need.

"Don't ever doubt that I want you," he told her. "I do, Grace. So badly." He reached out and placed a hand on her leg just above the cast. "But not until you're healed totally. What I have planned for the two of us is going to be worth the wait. I promise."

"Okay," she said, her voice a squeak. How else could she answer?

She pushed away from him, needing a little bit of distance because she felt like she was in danger of spontaneously combusting. "I'm going to change into my pajamas and…" She covered her face with her hands. "This is weird, right? We're two adults—who are dating—and we're having a platonic sleepover. You must think I'm the biggest dork you've ever met."

"I think you're amazing," he assured her. He rose

from the sofa, grabbed the remote to turn off the television and then extended his hands toward her.

She allowed him to pull her to standing but shook her head when he bent as if to pick her up. "I can make it to the bedroom on my own."

"Amazing," he repeated.

She laughed at that. "It's not far."

"I'm going to text Callum," Wiley said, "and tell them not to expect me home tonight."

She made a face. "Is that going to be weird?"

"I'm a grown man," he reminded her. "They might give me a little grief, but no one will be shocked."

As she made her way to the bedroom, Grace wasn't sure whether to be comforted or terrified by Wiley's comment. Did he make a habit of spending the night away from the ranch in beds that didn't belong to him?

No reason to go looking for trouble when it had a way of finding Grace without any prompting on her part. It only took a few minutes to change into her pj's and finish her nighttime routine.

Wiley was sitting on the edge of the bed when she came out of the bathroom. He'd taken off his sweatshirt and socks and shoes but still had on a T-shirt and jeans.

Somehow the sight of his bare feet on her rug made Grace's toes curl.

"Are you planning to sleep in your clothes?" she asked, trying for a light tone.

He shrugged. "I don't want to make you uncomfortable."

She kicked out her injured leg. "The cast beat you to it. It's okay, Wiley. I know nothing is going to happen between us, but I want you to get a decent night's sleep, as well."

He rose and approached her, running his hands up and down her arms. "Even if I don't sleep a wink, it will be worth it to spend the night holding you."

Damn, the guy knew what he was doing with the smooth talk.

She reached for his belt, slowly unbuckling it as she felt him watching her. "I'm glad to hear you say that. But drop trou, Mr. Fortune. I'm ready for bed."

He grinned at her teasing, and Grace felt her heart tug once more. She liked who she was with Wiley. He seemed willing to let her be who she was in a way that most people didn't appreciate, and that gave her the confidence to explore her inner strength.

Too bad she couldn't spend the whole night exploring him.

She climbed into bed and watched him undress, forcing herself not to whimper as he tugged off his T-shirt to reveal the most perfect physique she'd ever seen in person. He was lean and muscled, hard planes and angles on display in a way that reminded her of an actual sculpture. A smattering of dark hair covered his chest.

And he was going to spend the night with her.

He joined her under the covers, and she flipped off the light, then sighed with pleasure as he pulled her close. As much as she wanted him, there was something about the comfort of his arms around her that made the fatigue she tried to keep at bay rise up like a wave inside her.

"You can sleep, Grace," he said against her hair, as

if he could sense her struggle to remain awake. "I'm not going anywhere."

She loved the sound of that, although she told herself not to forget that he meant he was with her for now. So for now she cuddled up against him and drifted off to sleep.

Chapter 12

The next week went by more quickly than Grace could have imagined. Between work at the hotel in the mornings and working at home on the business leaders' event during the afternoon hours, plus the physical therapy sessions and her time with Wiley, it felt like every minute was filled with something.

She'd never been happier.

It was strange that falling off the balcony seemed to be a catalyst for her newfound sense of confidence. Yet there was nothing like knowing she could have died to make her realize she needed to be willing to take more chances in life.

Grace had started to speak up more in meetings and insert her ideas, not only for the opening, but for how she thought things would work best in the daily running of the hotel once they were filled with guests. To her surprise, the Fortunes seemed happy to let her take the lead, and she realized that the point of the training program might have been more than simply familiarizing locals with the business model. Because they were committed to hiring most of the hotel staff locally, the Fortune family needed a way to make sure whoever they chose was going to be up for the job.

Grace and Jillian had similar backgrounds and experience in hospitality, but they had very different methods for how to deal with guests and the hotel's overall ambiance. Jillian clearly felt as though it should be an exclusive oasis that would cater to big-city guests from Houston or other parts of the state who wanted to get away from the pressures of city life but still retain the trappings of privilege. Grace saw the value in that, but because she'd grown up in Rambling Rose, she also understood what the town had to offer. Her idea was to capitalize on the community feel. Yes, the hotel was an escape but one that guests would choose in part because of the charm of the surrounding area.

It's why her Rambling Rose partnership reception felt so important. She wanted local business owners to buy in on the hotel so that when it opened and guests came to town, the community would welcome them in a way that would make people want to return over and over.

"Am I interrupting?"

The soft knock on the office door had her glancing up from her laptop. She grinned as Wiley entered, looking handsome as ever in his dark suit and crisp white tailored shirt.

"You're never an interruption," she told him, feeling the familiar rush of heat that rose to her cheeks whenever Wiley spoke to her. Since she moved back to her apartment, he'd been over almost every evening for dinner. He didn't always spend the night but stayed long enough to kiss and caress her until her body was on fire with wanting more.

"You have the office to yourself this morning?" He gestured toward the other workstations situated around the perimeter of the room. All of the employees involved with the trainee program shared this space, which would be the official management office once the hotel opened.

"Jillian and Jay are in a meeting upstairs to finalize the choice for bed linens for the guest rooms." She shrugged. "I had a call with Hailey at the spa about the giveaways for the preopening event. I figured they could handle it without me."

"Look at you delegating like you've already earned the promotion." He bent down and gave her a swift kiss. "I like watching you take control."

As much as she wanted to draw him in, Grace gave him a playful nudge instead. "You can't kiss me at work," she admonished. "People will talk."

"There's no one here."

"Still." She held up a hand. "And I'm not delegating. We're dividing and conquering."

He lifted a brow. "Own it, Grace. You want that promotion, and you're going after it."

"Yeah," she whispered, delighted that she didn't have to hide her ambition from Wiley. Her ex hadn't liked it when she tried to better herself, at least if it made her seem like she was trying to surpass him in any way. Maybe it was because Wiley was already so successful and sure of himself, but he seemed to be attracted to her even more when she stood up for herself or went after what she wanted.

It was a heady vote of confidence.

"Saturday's event is going to be great." She grinned and pushed away from her computer. "Do you know what's going to make it even better?"

Wiley tapped a finger against his chin. "The fact that every time we make eye contact you'll know that I'm thinking about kissing you senseless?"

She laughed. "No, but I'll keep that in mind. I get the cast off Friday afternoon."

His mouth dropped open and something flashed in his eyes that she didn't understand—it looked almost like dismay. "I thought you had a full month in the cast?"

"Me, too. But I saw Dr. Matthews early this morning. My mom took me in before work. He did more scans and said the fracture is healing faster than expected. The plan was to make an appointment for next week to get it off, but when I explained about the event on Saturday, he agreed to see me Friday afternoon. I'll still have to be in a walking boot for another few weeks, but…" She threw up her hands. "Walking, Wiley. Without crutches or the scooter. I'm going to almost be a normal person again."

"That's fantastic news." He continued to look shocked and definitely not thrilled the way she expected. "Are you sure you aren't pushing the recovery? What does the PT say?"

"Wow, that's not exactly the reaction I'd hoped for," Grace told him with a frown. "The doctor is okay with it, so I don't think I'm pushing anything. We already have physical therapy sessions set up for next week to start working on strengthening my ankle." She didn't bother to keep the frustration out of her voice. "This is a huge step forward—literally and figuratively—and comes at the best possible time. Not just because of work." She swallowed. "I mean you and I can...well, we'll be free to take the next step in our relationship."

He sucked in a sharp breath. "Yes. That's amazing." He waved a hand in the air, looking so discombobulated she almost felt sorry for him. "Every part of it is amazing, Grace. I'm really so happy for you. It's just a shock, you know? Because the plan changed and all."

"For the better," she reminded him.

"Of course."

Jillian entered the office in her usual flourish, then stopped when she realized Wiley was standing next to Grace's chair. "Thank God I was at that meeting."

He took a step back and ran a hand through his hair.

"Nice work with arranging the spa gift certificate," he told Grace with a perfunctory nod.

She gave him a wan smile, hoping that Jillian was fooled by his somewhat lame attempt to offer a reason for being in here with her. She wished they didn't have to keep their relationship secret, but until the promotion was announced, she wouldn't take any chances on her coworkers thinking she would be given preferential treatment during the assessment process.

Even being with him in secret felt risky, but she also

couldn't imagine not taking advantage of their time together.

"Nice to see you, Jillian," Wiley said, and for a moment Grace hoped Wiley wasn't a poker player, because the man's inability to display a convincing game face was comical.

He exited the office as Jillian took a seat at her desk.

"The linen meeting went well?" Grace asked, knowing that the other woman loved to talk about herself and hoping she'd be easily distracted from Wiley's presence in the office.

"If it weren't for me, our guests would have been sleeping on discount sheets and scratchy comforters." Jillian opened her laptop. "The bedding company sales guy was definitely trying to pull something over on us."

"What did Jay think?" Grace valued his practical opinion to balance out Jillian's tendency toward drama.

"He actually agreed with me." Jillian sounded as shocked as Grace felt. "I would not have expected Jay to be the type of man who understood the value of Egyptian cotton or a high thread count. He seems like a guy who'd change his sheets once a month and only because he got sick of crumbs in the bed."

"Yuck." Grace shook her head. "You're selling him a little short."

"He's just so regular," Jillian said with a sniff. "Nice enough but definitely not someone with my level of ambition."

Grace inclined her head. "I hate to ask where I rate on your ambition scale, but I'm curious."

Jillian steepled her hands together as she turned her

chair fully to face Grace. "Well, you take it to a whole new level."

That didn't sound like a compliment, so Grace offered her best placating smile. As much as she wanted to earn the promotion, there was no doubt that Jillian would be an asset to the hotel staff in some capacity, so Grace didn't want to be the woman's sworn enemy. "You do a great job as well," she said.

"But I don't do the boss's brother," Jillian said with a smirk. "I earn my accolades with hard work and talent."

Anger and alarm rose in Grace like two waves crashing in on each other. This was exactly why she'd been leery of dating Wiley before the grand opening. The fact that Jillian could even hint—let alone nearly accuse—Grace of being given some kind of preferential treatment pained her to the core.

"I don't know what you're talking about," she said, making sure not one bit of emotion seeped into her voice. "Wiley and I are friends. He was kind after the accident."

"I assume you repaid that kindness on your back?" Jillian asked, almost conversationally.

Grace gasped. "That's a horrible thing to say."

"But is it true?"

"No, it's not. I don't appreciate the insinuation about my character. I've earned my place at the Hotel Fortune."

"He's only friendly to you because they're afraid you're going to sue for damages or try to get some kind of settlement from the hotel."

"That's not true," Grace whispered even as her brother's words played over in her head like an annoying refrain. She reminded herself that Jillian wanted to get under her skin, and Grace had to keep it together. She knew Wiley truly cared about her. He told her as much—maybe not in so many words, but the way he held her communicated everything she needed to know.

"I overheard him talking to Callum and Nicole right after the accident." Jillian stood and moved closer to Grace's workstation. "He told them that he'd 'handle you.' We all know what that means when an attorney says those words."

"You're lying."

"I'm not. Ask him if you want. But men like Wiley Fortune don't fall for small-town girls like you, Grace. He's not even staying in Rambling Rose, so if you can't see that you're just an easy distraction with the added benefit that he protects his family, then you're even stupider than I suspected." She pressed her glossy lips together. "I feel sorry for you, actually. I have a friend who works at Cowboy Country and she told me how you were publicly humiliated by your boyfriend up there. Some people can't ever learn the lesson."

Without waiting for a response, Jillian turned and left the room.

Grace stared blankly at her computer screen as her body began to tremble. Was it possible Jillian had told her the truth? The woman was conniving and egotistical, but Grace had never once heard her lie in the months they'd worked together.

She hadn't understood Wiley's reaction to her news about the cast coming off early. Maybe he liked having an excuse not to be intimate with her. He'd given her too many reasons to believe he was a gentleman for her to doubt him on that front. It would then make sense if he was really stringing her along or getting close to her to make sure she didn't go after his family for the accident that he wouldn't want things to go too far.

As many times as Grace had warned herself not to let her feelings for him get out of control, that's exactly what had happened. She was falling for Wiley Fortune—falling in love with him. And now she feared she might end up with a broken heart and a betrayal that would hurt far worse than Craig's. If Wiley was the man Jillian claimed him to be, Grace wasn't sure if she'd ever recover.

The following morning Wiley walked toward a popular barbecue joint in downtown Austin where he was meeting his cousin Gavin for lunch. Gavin was the youngest son of Kenneth, the half brother of Wiley's dad. Similar to Wiley's branch of the clan, Gavin's was a big family who hadn't known about their connection to the famous Texas Fortunes until the past few years. Gavin and his siblings had grown up in Texas. Like Wiley, Gavin was an attorney and specialized in corporate law.

They hadn't met, but Wiley knew his cousin worked for a prominent firm out of Austin. It was Wiley's understanding that Gavin had transferred there from Denver when he decided to return permanently to Texas.

After the conversation with Grace yesterday, Wiley had reached out and asked to meet Gavin to discuss possible opportunities within his firm.

The news that Grace was getting her cast off early had been a shock, and he knew he hadn't handled it well. But that wasn't due to the reasons Grace might suspect. In truth, the thought of making love to her appealed to him more than he could say. He wanted to learn every inch of her body and how she liked to be touched, what he could do to bring her pleasure. He'd forced himself to put fantasies about the two of them to the side out of respect for her recovery. It had been an exquisite torture to kiss her and hold her in his arms each night when he stayed at her apartment and know that they couldn't go any further.

But a part of him, a tiny rational sliver of his brain, appreciated having the cast as an excuse not to take things further. Grace was different from any other woman he'd dated. He suspected that being with her intimately, instead of quenching his thirst, would only make him want her more.

The thought of taking that step and then walking away after the hotel's grand opening made a sharp ache slice across his chest. The alternative—a long-distance relationship—held no appeal, either. Because of that, Wiley had decided to think about his future in a new way.

He immediately spotted Gavin as he entered the restaurant since he'd read his cousin's bio on the firm's website. Gavin was tall and good-looking, with dark blond hair and air of confidence about him. He waved and then gave Wiley's hand a firm shake when he got to the table.

"I'm glad you called," his cousin said, and Wiley appreciated the open expression on the other man's face.

"Thanks for being willing to meet me so quickly." He took a seat, and a waitress put a glass of water and a menu in front of him. "It's strange to think our fathers are brothers but we're virtual strangers."

Gavin nodded. "My dad had a bit of struggle getting used to being part of the Fortune clan."

"I know how that goes," Wiley said with a laugh. His father had actively discouraged Callum and the rest of the siblings from getting close to their newfound relatives. "But it's a hard family to resist."

"How do you like Rambling Rose?" Gavin asked. "From everything I hear, your siblings are making quite the mark on that little town."

"It's growing on me," Wiley admitted, glancing at the menu. "Which I didn't expect."

The waitress returned to take their orders. After she'd gone, Gavin sat back in his seat with a contented sigh. "I'm familiar with that, as well. I certainly hadn't planned to end up in Texas when I came for my sister's wedding. Denver had been my home since I graduated from law school."

"So what changed?" Wiley leaned in, curious to get the insight of a man who on the surface appeared so like him. "Did the wide-open spaces of Texas call you home again?"

"Not exactly. There's plenty of space in Colorado, although it's certainly not the same. The truth is, I met a woman. It's as simple as that."

Wiley chuckled. "In my experience, women are never simple."

"The way I felt about Christine is." Gavin inclined his head. "Although it took me a bit of time to figure it out. I might be great with contract law, but I wasn't exactly a quick study when it came to love. Luckily, my firm had a Austin office, so it was easy to transfer without missing a beat. Best decision I ever made."

"I don't have your luck," Wiley told the other man, still reeling at the fact that Gavin seemed to be acting like it had been no big deal to make that kind of a move for a relationship. "How long have you and Christine been together?"

"Two years this month," Gavin told him with a smile. "Smartest thing I ever did was make her my wife. We'll be adding to our family this spring."

"Congratulations." Wiley rubbed two fingers against his chest, wondering if the emotion there that felt like jealousy could actually be that base. It wasn't as if he'd completely rejected the idea of someday getting married and having a family of his own. But having his own space and independence had always been more of a priority. As much as he appreciated the sacrifices his mom and stepdad had made, he didn't know if he was capable of being that selfless.

"It's incredible. Christine is incredible. I really am the luckiest damn man alive."

The waitress brought their food at that moment—brisket for Wiley and a pulled pork sandwich for Gavin. As they ate, Gavin asked Wiley about his work in Chicago and how he was able to balance everything remotely from Rambling Rose. They discussed Gavin's transition to Texas and what that had meant for his career and his standing in the firm.

Before this month, Wiley had never considered that he might want a change from the firm where he was on the fast track to partner. He'd made a life in Chicago that suited him, although he was quickly coming to realize his desire to stay in Rambling Rose was more than just a need for a break from the pace of city life.

He wanted a change.

As if reading his thoughts, Gavin gave him a knowing look across the table. "You've told me everything I need to know about your focus as an attorney," his distant cousin said. "Obviously you've had a lot of success in your career and from the sound of it, you have a great life in Chicago. Yet you called to discuss opportunities with my firm in Austin?"

As ridiculous as it seemed, Wiley's first instinct was to deny it. No point, since that's exactly why he had called Gavin, but saying the words out loud felt monumental, like he'd be making a huge shift from the path that had always seemed solid in front of him.

"I think it might be time to consider other opportunities," he answered slowly. "I've enjoyed reconnecting with my brothers and sisters. Somehow being part of a big family doesn't quite feel as stifling as it once did. Now it's more of a comfort, and I like the idea of being able to help out legally with what they're doing in Rambling Rose. But I'm not ready to give up corporate law. I'd like to find a way to do both."

Gavin studied him for several long beats. "You want to move to Texas permanently to be closer to your family?"

"Yes."

"That's the only reason?" Gavin prompted.

"I'm ready for a new challenge." Wiley kept his features neutral. He could tell the other man wanted something more, a revelation about love or a woman. But Wiley wasn't ready for that. The idea of taking his relationship with Grace to the next level had certainly contributed to his desire to explore new opportunities in Texas. She wasn't the type of woman he would expect to have a casual relationship.

Yes, they'd agreed to date temporarily while he was in town, but that arrangement had been made while she was at the beginning of her recovery. He hadn't expected his feelings for her to grow so deep in such a short time. The idea of making love to her and then walking away after the grand opening held no appeal. Even if he wasn't ready to talk to her yet about his emotions, he needed to be moving forward. The thought of living permanently in Texas helped him to retain some level of control.

"I'd like to set up a meeting with you and one of the senior partners," Gavin told him. "Our Austin office is continuing to expand, and it would be a huge win to attract an associate with your level of experience." He leaned forward. "Are you thinking of living in Austin, or do you want to stay close to your family in Rambling Rose?"

"Rambling Rose," Wiley said without hesitation. He knew what working at the hotel meant to Grace. Although Austin wasn't far, he'd grown accustomed to being able to see her every night. He liked having dinner with her and hearing about her day and sharing the details of his. He'd always been serious and analytical, comfortable with seeing the world through his view alone. Her mind worked in a different way than his did, and it fascinated him.

"Okay, then." Gavin nodded. "Let's see what we can do to make this happen."

Wiley released a breath he hadn't realized he was holding. Moving forward with a potential relocation to Texas permanently made him feel like he could take the next step with Grace with no reservations. And his body and his heart wanted that next step in equal measure.

Chapter 13

Grace stared at her left ankle as if she'd never seen it before. The feeling of air on her skin after so long was both strange and exhilarating. Although her uninjured leg hadn't gotten any exposure to the winter sun, the skin on her newly exposed leg looked particularly sallow and a bit pinched. It felt odd to be able to move her foot. Her entire body felt lighter without the weight of the cast.

"You're sure it's time?"

The orthopedic surgeon chuckled. "Normally my patients don't second-guess me when I remove a cast. They're too busy thanking me."

She placed a hand over her face and gave him an embarrassed smile. "I'm sorry, Doctor. Of course I trust you. You're the expert. It's just such a surprise to have it happening earlier than I expected. Now I just need a shower and to shave my legs."

"You're young and healthy," he said with a chuckle. "The body is a miraculous healer, and yours did an amazing job at it. Let's not get ahead of ourselves. You'll still need to wear the walking boot for another month. Physical therapy is going to be critical to strengthen the ankle. I know you've gone back to work, which is fine, but I don't want you to overdo it."

"I won't," she promised. "I'll be careful. I'm just so excited to not have to use the crutches or the scooter."

"I'm happy to be able to help you."

"What about driving?" Grace said, still marveling at the thrill of being able to return to a somewhat normal life.

"I would say take it slow." The doctor typed in a few notes on his laptop as he spoke. "And no standard transmission. The boot and a clutch aren't going to be a good mix. But if the car is an automatic, then I see no issue."

"I get my life back," Grace said on a happy sigh.

"Listen to your body," he advised. "If you need to rest, do that. I mean it, Grace. I know that you're driven and motivated. We want to see the progress you've made so far continue."

"Got it. Thank you so much."

They finished up the appointment, and she scheduled a follow-up with the desk. The boot was awkward, but not nearly as cumbersome as the cast had been. Grace smiled as she walked out to the reception area where her mother and brother were waiting.

"No more cast," her mother said and enveloped Grace in a tight hug. "This is fantastic, Gracie."

Jake playfully ruffled her hair. "I was getting ready to put a bell on your scooter. It slowed you down at bit."

"No more time for slow," she said, then glanced over her shoulder. She didn't need the doctor to overhear her. Of course, she wasn't going to push it, but Grace felt more than ready to get back to regular life. Especially when that involved taking her relationship with Wiley to the next level. "I even get to drive."

"You behind the wheel is scary on a good day," Jake said with a chuckle.

Grace narrowed her eyes. "Not helpful."

They walked out into the medical center parking lot. "I need to stop at the grocery store on the way home," Barbara said, turning to Grace. "Do you want to go with me? Or Jake can give you a ride to your apartment."

"I'd like to get back," Grace said. "Wiley is coming for dinner so—"

"Seriously?" Jake bit back a groan. "Isn't it time to cut the cord with that guy? You're basically healed. You don't need him keeping tabs on you anymore."

"Jake, be nice," their mother said gently.

"Or just be quiet," Grace added.

"I still don't trust him." Jake lowered his mirrored sunglasses to look at Grace. "I'm sure he'll be doing a happy dance now that you don't seem to have any long-term, potentially expensive injuries for his family to take care of."

"Wiley has been kind to your sister." Barbara smiled. "He's a good friend."

Jake sniffed but Grace held up a hand when he would have argued with their mother. "It's my life, Jake. I get to live it how I see fit. Maybe I'll go to the grocery store with Mom just so I don't have to listen to you."

"Come on, Gracie." He looped an arm around her shoulder. "Let me drive you home. I won't talk any more about the Fortunes."

"Call if you need anything," her mother said. "I expect you both at the house for Sunday supper." She patted Grace's arm. "Bring your Wiley if you'd like, sweetie. We can all get to know each other better."

"Thanks, Mom. Love you." Grace gave her mother a final hug, then followed Jake to his truck. She didn't like the tense silence that had fallen between them. She and Jake had always been close, even more so when she returned home to help after his car accident.

"Will you give Wiley a chance?" she asked softly as her brother pulled out of the medical center parking lot.

"Is it actually serious between the two of you?"

She bit down on the inside of her cheek, unsure how to answer that question. From the standpoint of her heart, it certainly felt serious. Although it had only been a few weeks since they'd met, she could hardly imagine her life before Wiley or how she'd kept herself occupied. At the same time, she knew he was leaving, so it wouldn't make sense to become too attached. The sharp ache in her heart told her it might be too late for that.

"I like him," she said, because that was the truth without revealing too much. "I'm not expecting whatever is going on between us to continue after he leaves, although I wouldn't be opposed to a long-distance relationship."

"Really?" Jake's fingers tightened on the steering

wheel. "I know I'm rough on him, Grace, but it's because I don't want to see you get hurt." He glanced over at her. "You didn't talk much about the breakup with Craig, but it obviously was hard on you."

She ran a finger along the seam of her jeans. "The hardest thing about Craig was that he cheated on me and humiliated me in front of everyone we worked with at Cowboy Country."

"Snake," Jake muttered. "I still wish you would have let me pay him a visit."

"Stop trying to sound like you're auditioning for a gangster movie," she said with an affectionate chuckle. Although she and Jake might argue, there was no doubt her brother would do anything to protect her, and she appreciated his unwavering loyalty. "Wiley isn't like Craig."

"He's an attorney," Jake said with a derisive smirk. "If you look up the word in the dictionary, there might be a picture of a snake next to the definition."

"You have to trust me. Wiley isn't like that. He's honorable. I might not be able to adequately explain our connection or how instantaneous it was, but I know it doesn't have anything to do with my injury." Her gut tightened as she remembered Jillian's nasty comments about Wiley's motivations for being with Grace. She tried to put her rival's suspicions out of her head, chalking them up to jealousy or Jillian's attempts to undermine Grace's confidence.

"I do trust you. But the verdict's still out on the Fortune."

"Jake." As he pulled in front of her apartment building, Grace reached across the console and flicked his arm the way she used to do when they were kids. "Come on. Even Dad had a civil conversation with him a few days ago."

"I'm glad you're happy, Gracie." Her brother shrugged. "Can that be enough for now?"

"For now." She opened the car door and climbed out.

"I'd ask if you need help, but I already know the answer. Call or text if that changes."

"I will." Grace turned. "You're going to come to my event tomorrow, right?"

"The one where Fortunes will be crawling all over the place?" Jake grimaced.

"The one where you'll be supporting your favorite sister," Grace countered.

Jake gave a mock shudder but nodded. "I'll be there."

Grace waved as he pulled away, then headed upstairs. She wasn't going to win any sprinting contests with the boot, but it was a lot easier to manage the staircase without crutches. She checked her watch as she let herself into her apartment. The doctor's appointment had taken longer than she expected, so she only had an hour until Wiley was scheduled to arrive.

Her plan to go to the grocery store on her own for the first time since the accident so she could make him a proper home-cooked dinner would have to be saved for another night. Once again, she put aside thoughts of how few nights they might have left together. What would Wiley think if she proposed attempting to continue their relationship across the miles?

She got undressed, undid the Velcro straps on the walking boot and climbed into the shower as she considered that option. For her, a long-distance romance wouldn't be enough, but she'd be willing to try. Anything so that Wiley could remain a part of her life. He seemed to truly enjoy Rambling Rose, and she knew he loved spending more time with his siblings, so maybe he'd be in favor of visiting Texas on a more regular basis.

Hope and trepidation battled silently inside her at the thought of what their future might hold.

Her phone pinged as she came out of the bathroom, a series of texts from Callum with a minor crisis regarding the setup for tomorrow's event. Grace didn't hesitate to begin making calls and sending off messages from her laptop to mitigate any potential issues. A few months ago, she wasn't sure she would have had the confidence to take charge without an internal panic attack plaguing her. Her time in the training program and working toward the goal of the manager promotion had taught her a lot about herself and what she was capable of handling.

Unfortunately, when the knock sounded on her apartment door, Grace realized she'd lost track of time. Instead of putting on a nice outfit and hoping to impress Wiley before a potential next step in their relationship, she made her way to the door in a fuzzy polka-dot robe with her still-damp hair loose around her shoulders. She didn't even bother to put on a dab of lip gloss. What was the point? She'd messed up this night before it even started.

Wiley sucked in a breath and tried to control his rapidly beating heart when Grace smiled at him as she opened the door to her apartment.

He wasn't sure what he'd expected, but Grace in a soft bathrobe—and possibly nothing more—with her damp hair cascading over her shoulders and a pink glow tingeing her cheeks definitely was more than he bargained for.

"Sorry," she said immediately, taking a step back to let him enter. "I had to take care of something for tomorrow and lost track of—"

She let out a small yelp when he scooped her into his arms, kicking shut the door with one foot. He claimed her mouth with an urgency he hadn't realized he felt until that moment. The entire drive back from Austin, Wiley had been weighing in his mind the pros and cons of making a permanent move to Texas.

Was it too much? Too soon? Would he lose the independence and autonomy he'd carved out in his life like he was sculpting it from precious marble if he gave up his life in Chicago?

But seeing Grace made him understand in an instant that he wouldn't be giving up anything. In fact, it felt like he'd be moving toward something, claiming a future he hadn't imagined for himself. One that now felt like it was his destiny.

He wondered if the woman in his arms might be his destiny.

"You are beautiful," he told her as he trailed kisses along her neck. She smelled clean, like soap and lemons, a combination that had his senses reeling.

"I didn't even do my hair," she said with a laugh that quickly turned into a moan as he nipped at the sensitive place under her earlobe.

"Your hair is perfect," he said, sifting his fingers

through the silky strands. "Tell me you aren't wearing anything under this robe."

He felt more than heard the hitch in her breath. "Nothing."

"Thank God," he murmured, then forced himself to pause. She wasn't trying to seduce him, he knew, or be purposely tempting the way some women would. Wiley wanted her all the more because of it.

But he also wanted to respect a pace that made her comfortable. Until he talked to his boss back in Chicago and the senior partners from Gavin's firm in Austin, he wasn't ready to discuss a potential move with her. He had to make sure everything was going to work out before he made any commitments or promises to Grace.

A little voice niggled at the corner of his mind, one that warned him love wasn't something he could control or put in a neat little box the way Wiley liked to do with the pieces of his life. But he shoved that warning into a dark corner. This was new territory for him, even being willing to consider a change in his life for another person. He wasn't quite ready to make the jump without knowing he had a solid place to land on the other side.

He would give her at least that same consideration. "Do you want to talk about the issue for tomorrow?" he asked as he put her down, then gripped her arms and shifted her away from him. The robe had loosened as they'd embraced, and he tried not to look at the expanse of soft skin he could see in the deep vee where it gaped.

She gave him a strange look, although her eyes were still cloudy with desire. "I handled it."

"Of course," he agreed. "How is your ankle?" He

leaned down to take in the black walking boot that covered her leg from midcalf to foot. "Your text said the doctor thinks everything is healing properly?"

"Properly," she repeated, and he heard something in her tone that sounded like amusement. He couldn't figure out what was funny about the struggle to be a gentleman instead of continuing to ravish her the way he wanted to.

"Are you hungry?" He glanced over her shoulder toward the kitchen. She'd mentioned making dinner, but by the looks of the clean counters it seemed as though they might be going out. That was fine. He could wait to kiss her—and more. He could wait as long as needed.

"Wiley." She reached out and cupped his cheek in her palm. He leaned in, soothed as always by her touch. "Did you hear the part where I said I'm naked under my robe?"

He swallowed and locked his knees as his legs suddenly went weak. "Yes."

"And your reaction is that you want to talk about the hotel event or my ankle or dinner?"

"I want to not take advantage of…" He licked his lips. "You lost track of time. The part about the robe… and you being…" Words abandoned him for a few moments as he struggled to retain control. "I don't want to rush you, Grace."

The corner of her mouth twitched, and he would have given anything to read her thoughts at the moment.

"I don't want to rush, either."

He felt his eyes go wide as she hooked her thumb in the robe's thick sash and undid it.

"In fact…" Her smile widened. "I hope that what comes next takes us all night." Then she pushed the robe off her shoulders.

Grace waited for Wiley's reaction to her bold move with her heart practically beating out of her chest. She wasn't normally one to make the first move—or any move—and certainly not to be assertive when it came to intimacy.

Her ex-boyfriend had been her first and only partner, and their intimacy had always been more about his pleasure than hers. She figured that was simply how it worked for a woman like her. As Craig had told her when she confronted him about his cheating, there were women men dated because they made good girlfriends and women men wanted because they were desirable.

He'd left no question that Grace fell into the former category.

But she wanted more from Wiley—with Wiley. She wanted more from herself and was quickly learning that the best way to achieve what she wanted was to take risks.

Standing naked in front of a man who looked like he belonged in some sort of catalog for genetic lottery winners, the lower part of one leg still encased in an orthopedic boot, definitely felt like a risk.

One she realized was worth it when Wiley's dark gaze traveled over her body, and his chest began to rise and fall in ragged breaths.

"I never expected…" He broke off, gave a small shake of his head and reached for her.

"Me, neither," she said against his mouth as he drew

her close, his warm hands splayed across her bare back and bottom.

He muttered a curse low in his throat as he lifted her into his arms. "I can't wait," he said. "I want you so badly, Grace. I've wanted you since that first moment I saw you at the hotel."

She wrapped her arms tight around his neck, inhaling his scent as sensation swirled through her. She should feel vulnerable. After all, she was completely exposed while he remained fully dressed. But instead, she felt powerful in a way she didn't recognize. Like she was finally claiming a part of herself that had been waiting for her to realize it was important.

Wiley gave her the confidence to step into the woman she was meant to be.

He paused when he came to the door of her bedroom.

"I want you, too," she told him, brushing a kiss over his lips. "No more waiting, Wiley. We're in this together."

"Together," he repeated on a rush of air.

He pulled down the covers and placed her on the bed with exquisite care.

But when he reached for the strap of her boot, she placed her hand over his.

"You have too many clothes on," she told him with a smile.

"Easily remedied." He stood without hesitation, loosened his tie and then unbuttoned his shirt, pausing halfway through. "My fingers are shaking," he told her with an almost shy smile. "That's what you do to me."

Heat infused every part of her body at the thought of having an effect on this man.

Then her chest tightened as he continued to divest himself of his clothes, and Grace realized that they were truly taking the next step in their relationship. Sex meant something to her, and a moment of panic broke through the desire filling her brain, at the realization that she was embarking on this act with a man who might willingly walk away from her.

As he sat on the edge of the bed and placed a gentle hand on her booted leg, she realized it didn't matter. She might want more than they'd agreed to at the beginning of their time together, but she had to believe that he wanted it, too.

There might not be words yet, but the tenderness of his touch and the intensity of his gaze on hers were enough to make her trust that she was choosing the right path.

He undid the straps of the boot and slipped it off her leg. "Is this okay?" he asked softly, then bent to place a soft kiss on the top of her knee. "I don't want to hurt you, Grace. I'd never purposely hurt you."

"It's fine," she said, surprised when emotion clogged her throat. She didn't want to read more into his words. She knew he wouldn't hurt her deliberately, but she also understood that didn't mean she wouldn't end up with a broken heart.

But as his hand moved across her skin and he kissed a path up her body, nothing else mattered. He lavished attention on all the most sensitive parts of her, like he wanted to memorize her with his tongue and fingers.

"Stay still, sweetheart," he whispered against her. "We're going to be gentle with your ankle."

Gentle was the last thing on Grace's mind, but she

did her best not to writhe under his kisses. It felt as though he was undoing her, desire thrumming through her like the crest of a wave. The pressure built inside her as he continued to explore her body, and minutes—or hours—later he drove her to the edge and over, and a cry broke from her lips.

Still it wasn't enough. As mind-blowing as her release had been, she wanted more. She wanted all of him. It might only be for now, the time he was in town, but Grace wouldn't consider that. All she knew was at this moment, they were meant to be together.

"Now, Wiley," she said. "I need you now."

"I'm here," he told her, and captured her mouth.

"More."

He pulled away and reached for his wallet on her nightstand and pulled out a condom. A few moments later he was poised between her legs, and Grace had never wanted anything more than she wanted this man inside her.

His hands were braced on either side of her head and he entered her in one long stroke. She breathed him in and then lifted her head to kiss him, needing to be joined with him as much as she could manage.

Her eyes drifted closed as the rhythm of their kiss synced with the motion of their bodies. They moved together like they were built for each other, and in some ways Grace wondered if that were the truth. Had she been made for this man? Had everything that had come before led to the moment when their eyes met across that crowded party?

Because she'd never been certain what her place in

the world was, but there was no doubt she'd found where she belonged in Wiley Fortune's arms.

He whispered little nothings into her ear between kisses, his hands holding her like she was the most precious thing in the world to him. Passion skyrocketed inside her until it felt like electricity coursed through her veins. She wasn't certain how much more pleasure she could take. The depth of it was like nothing she'd ever experienced.

And then she fell over the cliff she'd been racing toward, her body dissolving as if it were made of champagne bubbles fizzing into the air. Her body tightened around Wiley and a few seconds later, he cried out her name.

It was the most amazing thing she'd ever heard. They might not have made promises to each other with words, but Grace had no doubt that his body had just pledged something to her that guaranteed she would never be the same.

Chapter 14

"The timing couldn't be worse," Wiley muttered as he packed his suitcase the following morning.

Megan flopped onto his bed in the suite where he was staying at the ranch. He'd been as skeptical about the property as he had about his siblings settling in Rambling Rose when he'd first come to Texas. The idea of his brothers and sisters living together seemed like a recipe for disaster to Wiley, who had far too many memories of their bustling house growing up and never being able to get a moment's peace.

But the arrangement worked—surprisingly—in large part because the setup of the house allowed whoever was living there to have their own private space while still being under the same roof. He'd enjoyed reconnecting with his siblings on a daily basis, sharing coffee in the morning and whatever was on the menu for dinner.

The ranch employed a caretaker, who took care of most things, including meals, although Nicole and Megan took their turns in the kitchen because they found great pleasure in feeding the people they loved.

Wiley wondered if his memories of childhood weren't exactly accurate. Had he been the only one to feel stifled by their crowded, sometimes overbearing family? Or had he just been so committed to finding his own way and establishing an identity away from his successful stepfather and the rest of the family that he'd gone too far in the other direction?

"You'll be back for the grand opening though?" she asked, her tone sympathetic.

"Yes." He zipped shut the suitcase. "Well before that, I hope. I'm not sure exactly how the other associate botched the contract negotiations so badly. I'd given him everything he needed. Landing this client should have been a slam dunk."

"Obviously, your coworker doesn't have your level of skill," Megan said without a trace of sarcasm or irony. That was the other nice thing about family—even if they argued and teased, when the chips were down they had his back without question.

Right now he needed all the support he could get. He'd set his phone to silent when he and Grace went to bed last night and had woken this morning to a barrage of angry texts and messages from the firm's senior partner. Wiley had been leading a team over the last six months to land one of the biggest clients in their history. His extended stay in Texas had complicated the process, but he'd been diligent about conveying information to the associate who was the local point of contact in Chicago with their potential client. Much of Wiley's remote working had centered on this deal, which was set to close in two days. For some reason the client had pulled out without warning and no one at the firm could get a straight answer as to why.

He'd tried to convince his boss that he could handle the emergency from Texas, but the man gave him no choice. Hence, he was booked on a flight leaving early that afternoon.

Leaving today meant he'd miss Grace's preopening event, and he wanted to be there to watch her shine.

There had barely been time to say goodbye to her before he'd had to bolt from her apartment that morning, leaving her sleepy and rumpled in the bed. He couldn't believe how amazing it felt to finally make love to her, and he would have been happy to spend all weekend with her.

Wiley almost never spent extended periods of time with the women he dated, but as with everything, Grace broke the rules he'd set for relationships. He wanted her more for it.

He hadn't known when he'd left her that the work emergency was so dire that he'd be flying back to Chicago, and he wished he'd had time to call and explain it to her.

"I appreciate your vote of confidence," he said to his sister. "Just make sure to give my note to Grace, okay? I'm sure I'll talk to her before the reception, but I want her to have it."

Megan sat up on the bed and plucked the thin envelope from the nightstand. "I'd ask if you were with Grace last night, but she's staying at her parents', and I figure you've outgrown sneaking out of your girlfriends' windows so angry dads don't catch you."

He snorted. "Grace moved back to her apartment."

"Ah." Megan gave him a knowing smile.

"There's no 'ah,'" he muttered. "But I have to go. Just give her the note."

"I'll walk you out."

"No need."

"Sure there is." She followed him out of the room toward the front of the house. Everyone else was going about their daily business, so at least Wiley only had one sister to deal with. But one was more than enough. "You like Grace."

He tried to ignore the way his heart began to beat a staccato rhythm in his chest, telling him in no uncertain terms that he more than liked Grace.

"Everyone likes Grace. Don't you have somewhere to be?"

"Not at the moment. It's okay to fall for a woman, Wiley. Especially one as sweet as Grace Williams. You were bound to find the right one at some point. I think it's wonderful that you've found her in Rambling Rose."

He'd just gotten to the front door but paused with his hand on the knob. "It's not wonderful. I'm leaving before her big event today, and I'm going back to Chicago for good once the hotel opens." He wasn't ready to reveal his meeting with Gavin. What if things didn't work out and he disappointed his siblings as well as Grace? He looked toward his sister, figuring her pained expression mirrored his. "Tell me how that's anything but the opposite of wonderful."

"Oh, Wi."

"Why?" he repeated, purposely misinterpreting her shortening of his name. "That's exactly what I'm wondering at the moment."

"You know Chicago isn't the only city that employs attorneys," Megan told him, her voice gentle. "Even towns like Rambling Rose have need of them. You've done so much to help at the hotel so—"

"My time here is temporary." He walked out of the house and squinted against the bright light of morning. "Grace and I both know it. Hell, it's what we agreed to in the first place. I'm not even sure she'd want me for longer."

"Don't be ridiculous. Women fall all over themselves for you. They always have."

He hit the button on the key fob to open the trunk. "Grace doesn't." He couldn't help the smile that tugged at his lips thinking about the way she didn't let him off the hook about anything. "She's stronger than people give her credit for," he said as he stowed the suitcase. It was the same thing he'd told Callum and Nicole, but he'd never get sick of saying it. "Independent, too. She's already told me she wants to focus on her career."

"Here's a pro tip." Megan placed a hand on his arm. "Women can have careers and successful relationships. Look at Stephanie and Ashley. Don't sell Grace short."

"I'm not." He opened the door to the car. "I just told you I thought she was strong."

"And don't use her strength and independence as an excuse."

Wiley shook his head. "Since when did my baby sisters grow up and get so smart?"

"We've always been smart." Megan rolled her eyes. "Me in particular."

"I've got to go. Give Grace the note and please tell her I'll be thinking of her. I'll call as soon as I can."

"Have a safe trip." She blew him a kiss. "We'll expect you back here as soon as you can make it."

Grace smiled as another coworker came up and congratulated her on the success of the local business owners' reception. There was no doubt she'd exceeded everyone's expectations. She gave partial credit to the beautiful weekend weather. It was unseasonably warm for the last weekend of January, even by Texas standards, with temperatures hovering in the low seventies and a cloudless blue sky above them. Although the trees planted around the hotel's pool held no leaves, they'd been strung with party lights, giving the impression of stars twinkling when they caught the sunlight.

The other businesses owned by the Fortunes had come out in force, from Stephanie giving information on local rescue animals to the spa staff doing five-minute chair massages and offering samples of the products they used with their clients.

There had been a steady stream of local business owners who'd meandered through the booths and demonstration tents that she'd had set up along the patio's perimeter. Jillian and Jay had done a great job with the photos of the hotel's interior they'd displayed on easels. According to Jay, they'd taken over two dozen reservations for the special local employee weekend Grace had arranged, and even more people had filled out tickets for the raffle to win a romantic dinner for two at Roja. Every business owner she'd invited had agreed to be part of their local partnership.

Grace had no doubt this gesture of good will would go a long way to encouraging Rambling Rose business owners to feel a sense of pride in the hotel once it opened, which would be key to making sure that out-of-town guests had an unforgettable experience during their stay in town.

She was also happy that no one had asked her specifically about the rumor of sabotage that had initially swirled around the balcony collapse. Grace did her best to reassure people that the accident hadn't been as bad as some wanted to believe and that she'd healed without any lingering issues.

The only thing that marred her happiness was that Wiley wasn't there with her. She'd received a voice message and text from him earlier explaining that the work emergency that had forced him to rush from her apartment early this morning had turned into something even bigger and he had to return to Chicago for a few days.

The timing couldn't have been worse, and not just because it meant he was missing today's preopening reception. Last night had been one of the most amazing in Grace's life. She'd felt so close to Wiley, like their connection would last beyond his stay in town. For him to leave the way he did… Well, she didn't want to read anything into it but couldn't seem to stop herself.

He'd seemed to enjoy himself as much as she had, but in truth Grace didn't really have the experience to judge that. Was their night together a onetime thing of finally being able to scratch an itch that had plagued them both? Or could it be more? Was it the start to the next step in their relationship that she desperately wanted?

"You don't look like someone who is basking in the glow of her success."

Grace turned to find her friend Collin standing next to her. "You came," she said, and reached out to hug him. "What do you think?"

He glanced around, lifting his sunglasses from his nose so she could see his dark gaze. "I think the Fortunes are lucky to have you working for them," he said. "Everyone I've talked to is suddenly huge fans of the hotel."

"Were people not fans before today?" The suggestion genuinely confused Grace. She thought the locals had overcome their concerns about the hotel when the Fortunes had changed plans based on community feedback.

"No one was talking too publicly about your accident," he said gently. "But it's a small town. People were still talking. I get the sense that the local business leaders now see that the hotel won't just be good for the Fortunes. The fact that you're here looking happy and toeing the Fortune line gives them a lot more confidence that everything's well with the construction."

"It is," she assured him. "They still don't exactly know why the balcony collapsed. But from now on, it's going to be all good news coming from the hotel."

"Like you earning the general manager position," Collin said with a wink. "No one can hold a candle to the partnerships you're creating here, Grace."

Pride bloomed in her chest at her old friend's compliment. "Do you think so?" she asked, biting down on her lower lip. "I really want that job."

"You're going to get it." He nudged her shoulder. "I have a feeling about it."

She laughed. "Then I'm going to trust your feeling. We'll have to celebrate when you come back to town."

He crossed his arms over his broad chest. "I'm not sure your special Fortune friend would want you and me celebrating together. I could tell Wiley wasn't a fan of our friendship."

"That's not true," she argued, although she remembered Wiley's reaction to finding Collin sitting with her on her parents' porch. At the time, she'd been charmed by the fact that he might be jealous of her childhood friend. She'd wanted to believe it meant he didn't like the thought of her dating other men. Not that she and Collin were dating, but that wasn't outside the realm of possibility.

"So where is your new man?" Collin made a show of glancing around. "It seems like I can't trip without falling over a Fortune at this event, but I haven't seen Wiley."

"He's not my man," Grace clarified. "We're friends."

Collin lifted a brow. "Like you and I are friends?"

"Not exactly." She did her best not to squirm. "But he's not here. He had to fly back to Chicago for work."

"With no warning?"

"It was an emergency."

"Must have been important if he took off the morning of your moment in the spotlight."

"This partnership plan isn't about me," Grace said, forcing a neutral tone. She wasn't about to let anyone know that it hurt that Wiley wasn't here. "The point was to draw positive attention to the hotel. We did that. Joint effort."

"Grace." Collin gave her a gentle elbow jab. "We've been friends for a long time. You don't have to pretend with me."

She waved to Mariana and Jay, who were standing with Callum on the far side of the pool, then blew out a breath and turned to face Collin. "I'm upset that he had to leave, okay? Does that make you happy?"

"You know it doesn't."

"I'm sure it really was an emergency," she said, as much to convince herself as Collin. "He seemed worried about whatever was going on with his firm."

"But he didn't share details with you?"

"No," she admitted. "He called as he was getting on the airplane, but I missed it. His message didn't tell me much." She glanced up at the blue sky overhead, then checked her watch. "He's probably in the air right now."

"I hope he gets it worked out quickly. If not and he hurts you, I'll kick his butt."

"You'll have to get in line behind Jake," she said. "Please don't mention this to him. He still doesn't trust Wiley or the Fortunes, and I don't want to give him any more reason to be a jerk."

"Your brother isn't a jerk," Collin reminded her. "He cares about you. Just like I do."

"I know." Grace gave Collin a hug before he walked away.

She turned back to the crowd to see Nicole, Ashley and Megan watching her. Ashley and Megan waved, but Nicole's attention seemed to be focused on Collin's retreating back. Strange, Grace thought. She didn't think her friend knew the Fortune sisters, but she figured there were plenty of things going on that she wasn't aware of thanks to her own busy schedule.

Just as she was about to turn away, Megan called her name.

"Hey, Grace," the slender blonde said as she approached. "You've done such an amazing job today. Everyone's talking about the hotel but also about the spa and Provisions. It's like the other business owners finally see we want to work with them and they're willing to give us more of chance to prove it."

"That's great." Grace smiled again but this time noticed how the muscles in her face were beginning to feel sore. Her leg ached, and her lower back was stiff from standing for so long today. She wondered if she'd feel so tired if she had Wiley at her side, then chided herself for even feeling a hint of depending on him. She'd learned that lesson with Craig. Grace knew she could only depend on herself. She had to be her own number one priority, not expect any man to make her his.

Even if Wiley had given every impression that he was doing exactly that.

"Are you okay?" Megan asked, concern obvious in her tone.

"Of course. I'm happy today has gone so well. I know the grand opening is going to be a huge success. Every business we invited today has agreed to be part of the downtown partnership so that should garner even more positive word of mouth for the hotel. You and your siblings have done so much for Rambling Rose. I'm honored to be a part of it."

"I know we're all glad to have you on the team." Megan pulled a thin envelope out of her purse. "I'm sorry but with all the excitement today, I forgot to give this to you." She handed the envelope to Grace, who was surprised to see her name scrawled across the front.

"It's from Wiley," Megan explained. "He felt bad about having to take off this morning. I know he wanted to be here for you today."

"Oh." Grace took the envelope and held it between two fingers. The urge to tear it open was strong, but she didn't want to read the note in front of Wiley's sister. Her emotions were jumbled at the moment, and she might reveal too much about her feelings for the missing Fortune.

"Don't worry." Megan patted Grace's arm. "I told him he has to come back to help with the last-minute grand opening preparations. He's not getting off easy with us. He can go back to his fancy big-city life when the work here is done."

Grace smiled, because that's what the other woman obviously expected, but inside her heart cracked. Megan had given her exactly the reminder she needed that even if Wiley returned, his time in Rambling Rose—and with Grace—was coming to an end.

And so were Grace's secret dreams for any possible future between them.

Chapter 15

Two days later, Wiley popped the last bite of a stale turkey sandwich into his mouth and washed it down with a swig of cold coffee.

He glanced at the clock on his phone, not surprised to find that it was nearing midnight. He'd been working around-the-clock since he'd landed in Chicago on Saturday afternoon.

In almost a decade of practicing law, there had never been a deal that had gone so far south so quickly. The associate who was supposed to be managing the client while Wiley handled the bigger contract stipulations had wound up getting himself and their potential client's twenty-one-year-old son arrested in a gentleman's club Friday night. It had been a stupid, thoughtless rookie mistake, especially considering Ron Burnett, the company's CEO, had built his business on a motto of "family values." Now the entire deal was in jeopardy.

To make matters worse for Wiley, his boss had fired the associate, Jon Kirchman, after threatening to have him disbarred, and the young associate had taken every paper file he had regarding the contract with him and deleted all of the electronic correspondence and documents.

Wiley had spent the past twenty-four hours in constant contact with the firm's technology specialist in an attempt to recover the data. He'd reached out to Jon, hoping to convince him to turn over his files, but there had been no response yet.

Although no one specifically blamed Wiley for the crisis, he couldn't help but think that things wouldn't have gone so far off the rails if he hadn't been trying to manage the project remotely.

He'd never given less than 110 percent to his career but had to admit now that he'd returned to the office that the past few weeks in Rambling Rose had put that dedication to the test.

"Burning the late-night oil, I see."

Wiley stifled a yawn as Derek Curtis entered his office. Derek was a year older than Wiley, and they'd been hired with the firm at approximately the same time. Wiley respected the other man's instincts for negotiating contract transactions, although Derek had a tendency to start each week a bit slow on the uptake, often coming off a weekend of partying.

"We have a meeting with Ron Burnett and his board tomorrow. They're going to make the final vote on new corporate counsel." Wiley tapped a finger on one of the stacks of files that he and the paralegal staff had compiled. "I'm trying to make up a lot of ground from the hole Jon left us in."

"I still can't believe the guy just took off when he got fired. Who does that?"

Wiley shook his head. "Someone who isn't planning to have a law career in Chicago anytime soon."

"You need any help?" Derek lowered himself into the chair on the other side of Wiley's desk.

"I think I've done everything I can. I hope it's enough."

"This isn't your fault," Derek reminded him.

"Why does it feel that way? If I'd been here to head up the deal instead of trying to manage it from Texas..."

"Tell me about Texas." Derek sat forward. "You never explained exactly why you extended your stay. When we talked before you headed down there, you were planning on doing the family duty stuff, then heading back as soon as possible."

"It ended up being important for me to help with a few things at my family's hotel."

"A few things? Legal issues?"

Wiley shrugged. He didn't really want to share details of his life in Texas. It felt so separate from his life in the city, and he had no doubt his coworker and sometime-friend wouldn't understand the appeal. "A construction accident."

"Was anyone hurt?"

"One of the employees broke her ankle."

"Ouch." Derek whistled under his breath. "Sounds like a workers' comp lawsuit waiting to happen. You're making sure to cover your a—"

"Grace isn't going to sue the hotel," he said through clenched teeth.

"How do you know?" Derek shook his head. "I once saw a guy trip over his own two feet on a building site and then sue for six figures."

"I know her," Wiley said, then immediately regretted the words based on the smile Derek gave him.

"Is that so? Smart move, Counselor."

"It's not like that. We're friends."

Derek chuckled. "I get it."

"No, you don't." Wiley couldn't decide whether the exhaustion of working so many hours or the stress of the deal or simply missing Grace so badly was making him want to stand up and punch his colleague in the face. Maybe a combination of all those things.

"Come on, don't get bent out of shape," Derek said. "I've heard how you talk about your family, even if you don't see them a lot. We both know you're going to protect blood over some piece of—"

"Stop talking." Wiley pushed back from his desk. "Grace isn't going to come after the hotel, and I'm not friends with her for any other reason than I like spending time with her."

"But it's not serious, right?" Derek leaned back in his chair, and Wiley had the secret wish that he'd topple backward. "I know you, Wiley. You don't do serious. We're the same. Relationships are a distraction and never worth the trouble. You know that."

Wiley stared at the other attorney.

Derek gestured to the papers piled all over the desk. "If nothing else, the situation you're in now proves it. The reason you stayed in Texas was a chick, and look at what it's led to. You could lose everything you've worked for over one deal that wasn't managed right."

"I'm not going to lose anything," Wiley said, although he knew Derek was right. Wiley had taken his eye off the ball, and now he was struggling to make sure he kept it in the air.

"Let me know if you need help," Derek offered again as he rose from the chair. "My focus is right where it needs to be. Always."

"Thanks," Wiley muttered, then sank back down in his chair as the other man disappeared into the hall. He shut down his computer and began to pack up his briefcase. The rest of what needed to be reviewed before tomorrow could be handled in the morning. Right now, he needed a few hours of rest to get his head on straight again.

He didn't want to admit that Grace had been the reason he'd prolonged his stay in Rambling Rose or that his preoccupation with her had affected his work. He'd continued to manage his clients and his job from the tiny Texas town. More importantly, he'd been able to reconnect with his brothers and sisters. That was worth more than anything else.

Although perhaps not more than the career he'd dedicated the last ten years of his life to.

He had to keep focused now. Get through tomorrow and land the client, then he could think about what came next. He was supposed to meet with the senior partners at his cousin's firm in Austin in a couple of days, but Wiley wasn't even sure what he wanted now. Could he really close the biggest deal of his life and then walk away to start over halfway across the country?

His brother and sisters had made it work, but he'd always been different. The odd Fortune out, so to speak. What would happen if he tried to start over?

What would happen if he told Grace the truth about his feelings for her?

As he flipped off the light to his office, his phone buzzed with an incoming text. A message from Grace. Simple, to the point, and the words utterly gutted him.

I miss you.

How could one simple sentence possibly convey so much?

His heart seemed to skip a beat as he ran a thumb over the smooth screen, as if he could somehow reach out and touch her across the miles.

He gave his head a hard shake and pocketed the phone. As much as he wanted to respond or to call her, he'd promised himself that his focus would remain on work until he salvaged the deal with Ron and his company. The firm was counting on him, and he already felt as if he'd let them down.

Grace knew how he felt about her. She would wait. He had to take care of his current life if he was going to truly choose a future with her.

"I think we're nearly there," Nicole announced as she placed plates filled with roasted chicken and Brie over pasta on the table in front of Grace, Jillian and Jay.

"Everything we make is delicious," Mariana said with a genuine smile as she poured sparkling lemonade into their glasses.

"Some of the best food I've ever eaten." Jay scooped another huge bite of chicken into his mouth. "Seriously the best."

"Not that you probably have much to compare it to," Jillian said with a delicate sniff. "I've actually traveled to both London and Paris."

Jay gave a haughty sniff. "Well, la-di-da then," he said, his Southern accent especially thick.

Grace pressed a napkin to her mouth to hide her giggle. "I'm certain Jay has a very discriminating palate," she said, wanting to be loyal to her friend in the face of Jillian's snobbery.

"Very," he agreed with mock severity, then winked at Grace.

She grinned and took a bite of the pasta, which truly was delicious. Mariana and Nicole discussed the dish as a potential winter season special while the three trainees enjoyed their lunch.

Nicole was continuing to refine the Roja menu with the grand opening around the corner. Her attention to detail and understanding of how to meld flavors together to showcase a variety of refined but still comforting foods amazed Grace. She had no doubt that the restaurant was going to be a huge success and bolster the hotel's reputation.

Jillian and Jay continued to banter back and forth. It amused Grace to no end how much Jay seemed to enjoy irritating their uptight coworker. He might joke about his country roots while Jillian took great pleasure in giving him grief over his lack of worldliness, but there was something more to Jay Cross. Beyond his easygoing manner, Grace sensed a depth of experience he didn't want to share, so she never pushed him to reveal what had led him to Rambling Rose in the first place.

She understood the desire to make a fresh start without the past coloring every step.

Something caught her attention, and she turned in her seat to see Wiley entering the restaurant. He'd been gone almost a week. In that short time her emotions had run the gamut from disappointment to anger to heartbreak to resignation. Grace wanted to believe she'd settled on acceptance, especially when they'd barely spoken on the phone and he'd only sent a few short texts that told her no details of the emergency that forced him to leave so suddenly and when he would return.

Her brain might have taken the hint about him walking—or literally running—away the morning after making love to her, but her body hadn't gotten the message. Not when he looked as handsome as ever in a dark sweater and jeans with cowboy boots that finally appeared to be broken in. Like he belonged in Texas and in her world, although his absence this week had told her that wasn't true.

Grace had been thrown back into the same emotional turmoil she'd felt after her breakup with Craig. Of course it was different with Wiley, because he hadn't cheated on her or made her any promises about the future. Somehow that only made her heart hurt more.

She'd told herself after returning to town that she was going to focus on herself and not let anything distract her from her goals. Instead, she'd spent the past few days making excuses to go to the bathroom at the hotel and fight back tears. Everything about her daily life reminded her of Wiley. The way she'd looked forward to seeing him in the hall, to stealing kisses in the office and to spending her evenings in his arms.

The Hotel Fortune had been her chance at a brand-new life, but she couldn't even walk into the lobby without thinking of Wiley. It had gotten so bad that she'd actually considered quitting her job and leaving Rambling Rose to reinvent herself again in a place that held no emotional pull for her.

It had been Collin who'd talked her off that ledge, reminding her that this was her home and she belonged here as much as any member of the Fortune family. Everything had made sense when Wiley wasn't nearby, but watching him walk toward the table, his gaze intense on her, her thoughts and feelings scattered like dandelion fluff in a strong wind.

"You're back," Nicole called to her brother as she turned.

Grace hated the jealousy that stabbed at her heart when Nicole gave him a huge hug. Grace yearned to touch him, but she had no right. They'd agreed to date secretly—her plan—but it hadn't been nearly enough. She wanted more. More than she should and likely more than Wiley was capable of giving her. It was time to remember that.

"Something smells amazing," he said.

"Your sister has outdone herself with this dish." Mariana came to stand next to Jay's chair. "We have three discerning customers right here." She patted Jay's shoulder. "If an empty plate is any indication, Roja is ready for business."

"I have no doubt," Wiley said, offering his sister a proud smile. "Any chance you have leftovers? I haven't had a decent meal in what feels like days. I've been living off takeout the entire trip."

Grace tamped down her sympathy. Now that she looked at him more closely, she could see the lines of exhaustion fanning out from his dark eyes and bracketing his mouth. It only made her want to pull him to her and offer whatever comfort she could.

Stupid, she reminded herself. She wasn't a lovesick schoolgirl anymore. The man had made it clear where his priorities were, and she needed to do the same.

As if reading her thoughts, Nicole pushed away and wagged a finger in front of Wiley. "I shouldn't give you even a bite. I forgot that I'm mad at you. You practically ghosted us this week. We didn't even know if you were coming back before the opening."

"Of course I was coming back." He looked genuinely surprised. "I told you I'd be here to help."

"Give your brother a break," Mariana said with a gentle tsk. "He's here now." Her knowing gaze met Grace's across the table. "When the three of you are finished here, I'd love to get your thoughts on some of the grand opening events."

Grace pushed back from the table. "I actually have a meeting scheduled with Ellie to finalize plans to put a link for the hotel on the town's website."

"Smart plan." Nicole gave her an enthusiastic thumbs-up.

Jillian's lips pursed but she didn't say anything or try to one-up Grace, which made Grace suspicious. "Jay and I can take care of whatever Mariana needs," Jillian offered, then rolled her eyes when Grace gave her a shocked look.

Grace could feel Wiley's gaze on her but purposely didn't make eye contact with him. If Jillian was being nice enough to give her an out, Grace must not be doing as good a job at hiding her feelings as she hoped.

She thanked Nicole and Mariana for lunch, then hurried from the restaurant and out the hotel's front entrance, not even bothering to grab her purse from the office. She needed fresh air and a few minutes to gather her thoughts.

Wiley was back. She shouldn't be surprised. He had told her—and clearly his siblings—that he planned to return before the opening.

She just wished she could turn off her feelings for him as easily as he seemed to be able to manage it.

The afternoon was cloudy, and a brisk breeze whipped down the town's main street, making her regret the choice to rush out without a jacket. At least the cool air felt good on her heated skin.

"Grace."

Her stomach pitched and tumbled at the sound of Wiley's voice behind her. She turned, forcing a bland smile on her face as he jogged toward her.

"Hi," he said, and lifted his hand as if to reach for her but then lowered it again. He searched her face as if he couldn't quite understand why she wasn't greeting him with more enthusiasm, but Grace had finally gotten her body and heart under control, even though it felt like it was shattering inside her chest.

"How was your trip home?" She crossed her arms over her chest.

"Home," he repeated with a frown. "You mean back to Chicago?"

"Your home," she said, nodding. "I hope it was productive."

"We closed the deal. The firm is now the counsel for the largest plexiglass manufacturer in the US."

"Congratulations." Grace made a show of checking her watch. "I need to go. I don't want to be late for my appointment with Ellie."

"I'll walk with you," he offered.

"No."

His frown deepened. "What's wrong, Grace? Is it your leg? Are you doing too much? If you need a break, I can talk to—"

She held up a hand, hating that her body responded to his offer of support. Hating that she didn't trust that he wasn't being kind to make certain she didn't cause trouble for his family. As much as she wanted to deny Jake's suspicions about Wiley's motives, his lack of communication had made her doubt everything she felt for him.

"I don't need you to talk to anyone on my behalf. I can manage my life and my career on my own, Wiley. I've been handling things just fine without you here."

"I know you can manage on your own," he said gently. "But I want to help, Grace. I care about you."

"Right." She bit off the word and forced her voice not to tremble. "We're friends."

"More than friends."

"Friends," she repeated, because if she allowed herself to entertain the thought of more, she'd be a goner for sure. "That's all."

"I don't understand. I missed you, Grace. Every moment away from you was—"

"Don't." *Don't say sweet things. Don't look at me with confusion and pain in your eyes.*

She swallowed, knowing she needed to be able to mutter more than one-syllable words at him. She needed to end this. The torture of being so close and yet feeling so far away from what she wanted her life to be. "I had some time to think about the future while you were gone, Wiley. I wasn't distracted by—" she waved a hand in his general direction "—by anything. The truth is we agreed what was between us would be temporary, and it's better that it end sooner rather than later."

A muscle jumped in jaw. "Better for whom?"

"Me," she whispered. "Both of us, I'm guessing, but I have to think about myself and my future. I can't... I won't put you ahead of me. Do you understand that?"

He shook his head. "I don't understand anything apparently."

"We're friends," she repeated. "That's all we were ever meant to be."

He stared at her long and hard like he wanted to argue. A piece of her wanted him to argue. She wanted him to fight for her, but she should have known better. Grace wasn't the type of woman that men fought for. She was a woman who fit herself into the compartment the people in her life needed her to be in.

But no more.

"Welcome back, Wiley. I'm sure your brothers and sisters will be thrilled to have you here again."

Without waiting for his response, she turned and walked away.

Chapter 16

"I'm mad at you."

Wiley continued to stare at the basketball game playing on the television of the sitting room in his suite at the ranch, ignoring his sister's arrival.

"Really mad," Nicole said, walking into the room and picking up the remote from the side table. She pushed a button, and the TV went dark.

"Big brothers are supposed to make sisters mad," Wiley said. "It's part of the job description."

"Do you want to know why?" She sat on the chair next to the sofa.

"Not really." He took a long pull on the beer he'd been nursing for the past hour. "You know I was watching that game?"

"What was the score?" she demanded.

He shrugged. "One of the teams was winning."

Nicole's mouth curved into a smile. "Yeah, you were real invested in the game, Wi. Seriously, we need to talk."

"Not in the mood," he told her. Since Grace had basically broken off their temporary relationship in the middle of the street two days ago, Wiley hadn't been in the mood for anything. He'd kept himself busy and tried not to think about Grace, which was virtually impossible, especially when she seemed to be involved in almost every last-minute detail of the hotel's grand opening.

He'd found himself following her scent through an upstairs hallway yesterday until he'd heard her voice in one of the guest rooms, discussing something with Jillian and Jay. Wiley had ducked into a housekeeping closet when they came out to avoid being spotted. As he stared at shelves filled with crisp white linens and tiny bottles of toiletries, he'd realized how bad off he was with missing her.

Unlike him, Grace didn't seem the least bit affected by their breakup, if that's what he could call it. She appeared completely focused on making sure the grand opening went off without a hitch. Despite his heartache, he was so proud of her for the leadership role she'd taken on and the way her confidence had bloomed. He only wished he could share in the success with her.

"What did you do to Grace?"

Wiley sucked in a breath as he straightened. "Nothing. Not one damn thing, Nicole."

"It's obvious she's hurting."

"Not to me," he countered.

"Then you're a bigger fool than I suspected. Even

Jillian is being nice, so you know Grace must be really upset. I thought you liked her."

"I did. I do."

"Then why dump her, Wiley? Especially right before the opening. I understand that commitment isn't your thing and being back in Chicago probably had you missing the city, but—"

"You have it wrong." He pointed the tip of his bottle toward his sister. "I was the dumpee in this situation. Grace broke up with me."

"Impossible," Nicole said immediately. "Women don't break up with you."

"I guess there's a first time for everything."

"What did you do?"

He placed the beer bottle on the coffee table with distinct thud. "Nothing."

His sister's blue eyes narrowed. "Are you sure?"

"How could I have done anything?" He lifted his hands, palms up, and didn't bother to hide his frustration. "I was working around-the-clock in Chicago to salvage the deal. There was no time for anything, not that I would have wanted it, anyway. I missed her."

"Did you tell her that?"

He nodded. "Right in front of the hotel when I got back. Just before she cut me off at the knees."

"And she gave no indication of being unhappy while you were away?"

"I don't know, Nicole. I was away. Maybe her brother convinced her not to trust me. Maybe she realized she doesn't want to deal with the complications of our family."

"Grace isn't the type to shy away from things that

are hard," Nicole reminded him. "In fact, we all keep forgetting she's wearing the boot, because she doesn't let it slow her down one bit."

"She's amazing," he murmured. "Probably too smart to want something long-term with me."

"I don't believe that." Nicole tapped a finger against her chin. "You two were the worst-kept secret in town. Everyone could see she was crazy about you. Did she say anything when you talked to her during your trip that would give you a clue—"

"We didn't talk while I was gone."

Nicole's mouth dropped open. "You were in Chicago for nearly a week."

"I'm aware."

"How could you not talk to her?"

He shrugged. "It wasn't purposeful. I was busy."

"Not an excuse."

Agitation rolled through Wiley like a tidal wave. He didn't want to think that he was at fault. How could that be? No, he hadn't told Grace how he felt before he left. But she had to know, or at least have an idea. He'd never devoted so much of himself to a woman before. In fact, it had scared the hell out of him, especially when he returned to Chicago and saw the mess his firm had almost ended up in because he'd been distracted by his family and Grace while in Texas. Guilt had eaten at him, which was part of the reason he hadn't done the best job of communicating while he was away. But still...

He stood from the sofa and paced to the edge of the room. No way would he believe that he was the reason she'd broken things off. That simply couldn't be the case.

"I did call, Nicole. Or I tried." He heard the edge in his voice but regaining control was the last thing on his mind. He had to understand why she'd ended things between them. He had to know if there was a chance at winning her back. "We had trouble connecting because of how much I was at the office. It wasn't like I slept with her and then took off without a backward glance." He cringed when Nicole sucked in a harsh gasp, realizing exactly what he'd just blurted. Wiley would give anything if he could take the last ten seconds back.

"You slept with her?" Nicole moved to the edge of the seat, looking like their mother used to when she wanted to throttle one of the boys for making a stupid mistake.

"Forget I said anything." He shook his head. "I'm not thinking clearly, obviously. I shouldn't have—"

"She's our employee," Nicole reminded him through clenched teeth.

"Yours," Wiley countered. "Not mine. My relationship with her has nothing to do with the hotel."

"Does she know that?"

He opened his mouth to answer then shut it again.

Nicole's eyes widened. "Did she tell you about her ex-boyfriend?"

"The one who cheated on her?" Wiley nodded. "That has nothing to do with me, either."

"How much did she share about their breakup?"

"She didn't need to explain much. He cheated. End of story."

"Wiley."

"Stop sounding like Mom," he told her. "Your tone is freaking me out."

"I did Grace's reference check at Cowboy Country," Nicole said quietly. "The story she gave me about how things ended there was a little convoluted. I spoke with her boss in Horseback Hollow. Grace was an exemplary employee, just like she is for us. But when she discovered that her boyfriend was cheating on her with another coworker, there was a bit of a scene."

"What kind of a scene?" Wiley asked, even though he wasn't sure he wanted to know the answer.

"I only heard the details because the amusement park manager felt bad for Grace and wanted her to get the position in the training program. Apparently, the whole thing blew up at an employee picnic. The ex very loudly blamed Grace. He made it known that he was cheating because Grace lacked—" she made a face "—spark in the bedroom."

Wiley breathed out a string of curses that would have horrified his mother. "She doesn't lack spark. Grace is the sparkliest damn woman I've ever known."

"Too much information." Nicole stood, making a show of covering her ears. "I don't want to talk about you and Grace and sparks. But think of the timing, Wi. The two of you..." She shrugged. "Took things to the next level and then you left town and didn't call her."

"I called. We just didn't get to talk." He cursed again because he hated knowing that he'd made Grace doubt anything about herself. Making love to her had been the most wonderful time of his life. Not that he had any intention of discussing details with his sister.

"Maybe you should try talking to her again," Nicole suggested gently. "If you really care about her."

"I care." He ran a hand through his hair. "I more than care about her."

"You can say the word." Nicole crossed to him and patted his arm. "It won't burn your tongue to speak it out loud."

"It might," he muttered, then sighed. "I love her, Nicole. I'm *in* love with her. I didn't expect it, and I'm not sure I want it."

His sister squealed with delight. "I knew it. We all knew it. Ashley, Megan and I knew it before you did. We're so much smarter than you."

He pulled away, although he couldn't help the way his mouth curved. "Why do you all have to keep pointing it out? I should mention it's annoying. If you're finished gloating, can we talk about how I'm going to fix this?"

"Do you *want* to fix it?"

He thought about it for a long moment. Although he expected panic to rise up inside him, instead he felt a sense of peace settle in his chest. "Yes."

She inclined her head. "Why do I think there's a 'but' coming?"

"More like an 'and,'" he admitted. "I need to figure some things out. I haven't done a great job of making her feel like she's a priority for me, and Grace deserves that. I want to give her that, Nic. I don't want to mess it up."

"What if Grace says no? Will you go back to Chicago?"

He shook his head. "My time in the city is finished. No matter what happens with Grace, I'm moving to Texas. Our big, crazy family used to feel like something

I needed to escape. It didn't feel like I could have my own life when I was just one of the Fortune brothers."

"You've always been more than that," his sister said quietly.

"Took me a bit of time to realize it." He grinned at her. "It really grates on my nerves that my baby sisters are so smart, but you're right. I've had a great life in Chicago, but it's never been home. Home is where family is, and I want to put down roots in Texas. I want this place to be my home."

Grace climbed the stairs leading to Roja's banquet room on Tuesday morning, trying hard to control the nerves fluttering through her chest.

Callum had texted her last night, asking her to arrive at the hotel early the following morning for a private meeting. With less than a week until the grand opening, she couldn't imagine why the head of Fortune Brothers Construction would want to take time out of his busy schedule to meet with her, unless he'd found out about her relationship with Wiley.

After their breakup, Grace had done her best to go back to business as usual at work. It wasn't easy, because her body and her heart seemed tuned in to his presence like a radio dial. If he was anywhere nearby, awareness shivered across her skin, and it was difficult to draw a steady breath.

Yesterday she'd overheard Nicole tell Mariana that Wiley had gone to Austin for business. Of course, it was silly for Grace to be disappointed that he hadn't said goodbye to her. She'd told him she just wanted to be friends, but they both knew they couldn't go back to simple friendship after what they'd shared.

She'd walked away before she was tempted to ask Nicole how long he'd be gone and what his plans for the future were. Anything Grace heard was bound to hurt, since she understood his future wouldn't involve her.

The timing of this meeting seemed a bit of a coincidence, and part of her feared that the Fortunes would blame her for Wiley leaving again. She knew he would never try to put her in a bad position or do anything that might jeopardize her job, but after the way things ended in Horseback Hollow, it was difficult for her to trust that. She'd thought her future at Cowboy Country was secure until Craig had publicly humiliated her.

Her anxiety went into overdrive when she turned to find Callum seated at a banquet table along with Nicole and Kane. It felt like Grace was facing the Fortune tribunal.

"Good morning," she said, clearing her throat when the words came out sounding like a croak.

"Hey, Grace." Callum and his cousin stood as she approached. "How are you doing?" Callum glanced at her leg. "Damn, I'm sorry. I figured there'd be more privacy up here, but we probably should have met downstairs. I keep forgetting about your injury."

"It's fine," Grace assured him. "The walking boot makes it relatively easy to get around, and I'm slow on steps, but I can manage."

"Of course you can," Kane agreed with a chuckle. "These past few weeks have proven that you can manage just about anything."

Except holding on to Wiley, she thought to herself.

"Thanks," she answered Kane. "What can I do for all of you today?"

Nicole offered a kind smile and gestured to the seat across from them. "Let's talk for a few minutes."

Grace's heart sank, and she wanted to run in the other direction. That's exactly how the conversation with her bosses at the amusement park had begun, during which it had become painfully obvious that the best course of action for everyone would be her resignation.

She did not want to give up her future at the hotel. An image of Wiley flashed in her mind. Would she walk away from the Fortunes if it meant another chance with him? Probably, although that might make her a fool. She'd never felt anything like she did when she was with Wiley. Regret made her chest pinch, and she wondered for the millionth time if she'd given up on him too easily.

Slipping into the chair, she kept her hands clasped tightly in front of her. "Is there a problem with last-minute details for the opening?"

Nicole shook her head. "Everything is right on schedule. You, Jillian and Jay have done an incredible job."

"Far surpassed our expectations," Callum added.

"I'm glad." Grace forced a smile. "So what I am doing here?"

"The plan had been to choose the employee who would be promoted to the general manager position after the grand opening," Nicole explained. "It made sense to get through this last push and then focus on the future."

Grace nodded.

"But recent events have made us rethink the tim-

ing of our announcement." Callum inclined his head.
"We want to show stability, to make sure that people
understand we have things well under control at the
Hotel Fortune."

"We're moving forward and expecting nothing but
good things." Kane glanced behind him at the doors
that led to the balcony.

The balcony that had collapsed with Grace on it.

"Okay." Grace's cheeks started to throb as she tried
to keep her smile in place. Recent events? They had to
be talking about her accident, and it felt as though her
fall from the second floor was a metaphor for her life.
Just when she thought she had time to pause and enjoy
the view, she went tumbling off the edge. She should
have known this would happen. Of course they wouldn't
choose her for the general manager position. She was
the physical representation of a public relations nightmare. The Fortunes would be smart to promote someone who was untarnished by any scandal. Jillian fit
that bill without—

"What do you think, Grace?"

She blinked as Callum leaned forward, giving her
an odd look, and she tried to catch up with the thread
of the conversation.

"I think it's a wise decision."

His mouth twitched. "Then you're accepting the position?"

She blinked. "I think I missed something."

Nicole laughed. "He just offered you the general
manager job."

"Oh." Grace sucked in a shallow breath. "I thought

you were telling me I wasn't a fit because of the accident. I'm bad PR."

"On the contrary," Callum told her. "You've done more to bolster the hotel's image in town than we could have imagined. The partnership with the local businesses is going to be integral to our reputation as we open."

"Thank you," she whispered. "I'd be honored to accept the promotion. But…" She bit down on the inside of her cheek as she tried to determine the best way to share this next bit.

Kane sighed. "I hate a 'but.'"

"What is it?" Nicole asked gently, placing her hand on her cousin's beefy arm.

"I'm in love with your brother," she said, and Kane choked on the sip of water he'd just taken.

"Which one?"

"She's talking about our brother," Nicole clarified. "Wiley. You love Wiley."

"Yes." Grace nodded. "But we broke up."

Callum's mouth dropped open. "You were dating Wiley?"

"Get with the program," Nicole said, swatting his arm.

"What did he do?" Kane demanded. "Do I need to kill him?"

Grace almost laughed at the absurdity of that statement. "No, of course not. He didn't do anything. I just chose… My priority is the hotel. I want you to know that. I don't want there to be any doubts."

"You can have both," Callum said, as if it were the simplest thing in the world.

Grace squeezed her eyes shut for a moment, then opened them again. She could be the biggest idiot in the world for revealing all of this in a meeting where she was being offered her dream job. "That hasn't worked so well for me in the past."

"Wiley isn't him," Nicole told her with so much understanding that it felt like Grace's heart might break all over again.

"Who?" Kane and Callum asked in unison.

"I know." Grace kept her gaze focused on Wiley's sister. "I just wanted you to know where things stood. It's meant a lot to Wiley to reconnect with all of you. As much as I'm looking forward to a long career at the hotel, it won't be at the expense of his relationship with his family."

Nicole leaned forward. "Are you saying you'd give up the promotion if he wasn't comfortable with you working here?"

Was that what Grace was telling them? How was that possible? The general manager job was everything she'd wanted for her life and a vindication of what she'd been through in Horseback Hollow. Wiley hadn't given her the impression that he wanted her to forgo her dream for him. Not once. He'd only been supportive and proud as she dedicated herself to her job.

But she knew how important his family was and understood the toll that feeling distanced from them had taken on him. She wouldn't be a part of that.

"Yes." The pain she expected at saying the word didn't materialize. Instead, she felt as if her world had stopped spinning and righted itself in a way that put her exactly where she wanted to be.

"That's ridiculous." Callum shook his head. "Wiley is a grown damn man. You're important to the hotel. To our family. He'll deal."

"But if not—"

"Thank you, Grace," Nicole said. "You've proven even more why you're the right person for this job. We appreciate your loyalty and look forward to many years of you being part of Team Fortune."

"Really?" Grace swallowed. "I mean, that's what I want, as well." She pushed back from the table. "Just know that I have the best interests of the hotel at the forefront of my mind. Always."

"We know." Nicole stood and then came around the table to hug her. "And we appreciate it. We'll talk to Jillian and Jay as well and then plan to make the big announcement to the staff. Congratulations."

Chapter 17

"Oh, hell, no."

"Hi, Jake." Wiley stepped out onto the path in front of Grace's brother, ignoring his less-than-cordial greeting. "Mind if I join you?"

Jake didn't break stride as he ran past Wiley on the dirt trail that wound through one of the local parks. "If you can keep up, Wyatt."

Wiley also didn't correct the mistake of his name. He simply ran alongside the other man, grateful for his almost-daily runs along Lake Michigan when he'd lived in Chicago. Jake set one hell of a pace.

They did a fast loop around the park's perimeter, passing a few families and slower joggers. The exercise actually helped to clear Wiley's jumbled thoughts. He was clear about what he wanted, but how to convince

Grace's recalcitrant brother that his intentions were honorable was another story.

"We need to talk about your sister," Wiley said, huffing for breath, as they approached the parking lot where the trail ended.

"You hurt her," Jake said, and then bent at the waist. At least Wiley wasn't the only one sucking wind, a small consolation when it felt as though his lungs were on fire.

"I want to make it right. I love her."

Jake glanced up at him, a sneer curling one side of his mouth. "You don't have to say that. She's not going to come after your precious family and the hotel. Even if they wouldn't have handed her the promotion she—"

"Grace earning the general manager position had nothing to do with her injury." Wiley placed his hands on his hips and drew in big gulps of air, struggling to keep the temper out of his voice. He was here to win Jake over to his side, not to antagonize him further. But Wiley couldn't tolerate the suggestion that Grace had been offered the manager role at the hotel for any other reason than she deserved it.

"I know she's qualified," her brother conceded. "But even you have to admit—"

"I don't have to admit anything. Grace worked her butt off, both before and after the accident. She's a huge asset to the hotel, and everyone in my family sees that. We're not the ones selling her short."

Jake straightened. "What's that supposed to mean?"

"Why are you so hell-bent on convincing her that she can't make it on her own?"

"I'm not—"

"How do you think it makes her feel when her family is constantly telling her that the reason she's being recognized has more to do with her injury than her talent and skills?" For the moment, Wiley put aside trying to smooth the waters with Grace's brother. He couldn't stand to listen to one more suggestion that she was anything less than fully capable on her own.

"We don't do that."

"Are you sure? Because that's how it sounds to me. I fell in love with your sister and not because I was trying to protect my family or any other sort of cheap attorney tricks you might want to accuse me of. The fact is she's the most amazing woman I know. She's smart, strong and creative. She doesn't give up or give in, and we both know how big her heart is. She'd do anything for the people she loves."

Jake stared at him for several long moments, then looked away. "Did your brother or sister mention that Grace told them she wouldn't take the promotion if it upset you to have her at the hotel?"

"Yeah." Wiley kicked a small rock with the toe of one sneaker, sending it skittering across the grass. "I would never let that happen, and neither would they. I want another chance with Grace, but it's her choice. If she's truly moved on from me, I'll respect the decision. Her place at the hotel is secure, and my brothers and sisters would never treat her unfairly."

"I know."

"In fact—" Wiley broke off as he tried to digest those two words coming from Jake. He was ready to argue as long as he needed to in order to convince her brother that his family had Grace's interests at heart. "You know what?"

"I'm not fully sold on the Fortunes," Jake said, wiping a sleeve across his forehead. "Trusting people outside my close circle of friends and family...well, it's been a struggle since the accident. Grace gave up a lot to come home and help during my recovery."

"She told me about that time," Wiley said. "I know she was happy to have the chance to pitch in and remains grateful that everything turned out okay for you."

"She's the best." Jake flashed a rueful smile. "We can agree on that."

"Yeah."

"And even though you aren't the man I'd choose for her, you're the one she's chosen."

Wiley mulled that over for a few seconds, then chuckled. "I can't decide if that's a compliment or an insult."

Jake's grin widened. "We'll call it a compliment. My sister deserves to be happy more than any person I know. If you make her happy, that's good enough for me."

"I appreciate that, Jake." Wiley held out a hand, and the other man shook it. "Family is important to Grace and to me. I want us to get along. You can believe me when I tell you I'll do my best to make her happy every day if she gives me another chance."

"I believe you, Fortune." Jake nodded. "You should know that if you ever hurt her, I'll be there."

Wiley shook his head. "Don't worry about that. You'll have to get in line behind most of my siblings. But all of this is moot if I can't convince her to try again.

To be honest, I've never had to work very hard with women. That's another thing I love about your sister. She makes me want to try."

"What you need is a plan," Jake said, clapping Wiley on the shoulder as they headed toward their cars. "Grace is used to being the one to put in the effort. I think your willingness to try will go a long way."

"I hope it goes far enough," Wiley murmured, then stopped walking as an idea popped into his head. He turned to face Grace's brother, an unexpected ally but the perfect one for what Wiley wanted to accomplish. "And I hope that you'll help me make sure it does."

"Jake, are you sure we can't just get him something from the hardware store in town?" Grace drummed her fingers against her jeans and tried not to sound as impatient as she felt. Her brother had asked her to drive with him to pick up a gift for their dad's upcoming birthday.

Even though Grace had what felt like a never-ending to-do list with the opening in a few days, she'd agreed to accompany Jake on his errand. She and her brother hadn't been on the best terms lately, and she didn't want any more animosity between them.

Unfortunately, Jake hadn't mentioned that the place he was picking up some vintage baseball glove for Dad was a good half hour out of town. He'd been in a strange mood since picking her up at her apartment, uncharacteristically peppy one minute and then anxious the next.

"It's important, Gracie," he said, and gave her a bright smile. Way too bright for her to believe it was sincere. "This is going to be the best surprise ever."

"You're acting weird," she said as she looked out

the window of his truck. The last time she'd driven this stretch of highway had been with Wiley on their first date.

A dull ache filled her chest at the thought of Wiley Fortune. The past few days without him had been awful. Grace missed him like crazy, even though she saw him around the hotel almost every day. But it wasn't the same.

Jillian and Jay had taken her out for a drink to celebrate her promotion. It astounded Grace that Jillian seemed to accept the decision the Fortunes had made without complaint. Grace realized that she had Jillian to thank, in part, for the opportunity. Their rivalry had pushed Grace outside her comfort zone and motivated her to go the extra mile with every task she was assigned.

Obviously, it had paid off, but the price for her success was steep. Grace wondered if she should have given Wiley more of a chance after he returned from Chicago. She'd been hurt and felt rejected because he hadn't called while away, but part of her knew she was transferring her emotions about her last relationship onto this one. Her ex's betrayal made her so sensitive to any slight. She'd built giant walls around her heart because that had seemed like the best way to protect it.

She was coming to understand that keeping potential hurt out almost meant that the love she had to give someone was trapped inside her. Yet as much as she wanted to risk her heart for Wiley, it was difficult to imagine how much it might shatter if he didn't want to try again.

She'd told herself she would wait until after the grand

opening celebration and then reach out to him. That way she'd have the time to fall apart in a way she didn't at the moment.

"You're so quiet," Jake said as he pulled into the right-hand lane of the highway and turned on his signal to exit. "Are you tired?"

"I'm fine." She leaned forward in her seat. "Where are you going? Why are you getting off here?"

"It's our exit." He gave her a sidelong glance. "What's wrong?"

"Nothing," she lied. It was the exit for the Oak Tree Inn. As Jake turned at the end of the ramp, she realized they were going to drive right past the converted farmhouse on the way to wherever this special baseball glove was located. It shouldn't bother her to see the place that she and Wiley had shared their first kiss. She'd handled much more challenging situations than a simple driveway. So why was her heart practically beating out of her chest?

"I want you to be happy, Grace." Jake's voice held a note of tenderness she wasn't used to hearing from her tough brother. "You deserve that."

"We both do," she answered.

"Wiley made you happy."

Her mouth dropped open at those words. "I don't want another lecture about the Fortunes, especially Wiley."

"It was an observation," he countered. "Not a lecture."

She smiled despite the sadness coursing through her. "I figured the lecture was coming next."

"You have no idea what's coming next," Jake said

softly, and then shocked Grace by pulling into the parking lot of the Oak Tree Inn.

"Jake…"

"Happiness," he repeated. "You're a big girl, Gracie, and it's about time we all start treating you like one. I have a feeling I could learn something from Wiley Fortune in that regard. It's not up to me to determine what makes you happy. That's your decision. Now you just have to be brave enough to make it."

Her breath was coming out in shallow puffs. "What are you doing, Jake?"

After pulling to a stop in front of the inn, he reached over and opened the passenger-side door. "Hopefully giving you a little nudge in the right direction."

Too shocked to argue, Grace stepped out of the car. She'd barely closed the door when Jake took off, leaving her standing in the middle of nowhere in a cloud of dust.

"That wasn't exactly how he and I planned it."

She whirled around to the inn's front door to see Wiley walking toward her.

"You planned this?" Her brain felt like it was full of cotton, and her knees had gone weak. The thought that she could actually use her scooter or the crutches to help her balance almost made her smile. Almost.

"Jake agreed to bring you out here," Wiley said, his tone tentative. "I thought he was going to stay until we had a chance to talk."

"What if I don't want to talk?" she demanded, because it irritated her how good it felt to see him. She didn't want it to feel good. She wanted to stay strong and focused on the grand opening. That was her plan.

Wiley reached into the pocket of his dark jeans and pulled out a set of keys. "Take my car."

She narrowed her eyes. "So you had my brother drop me here, but you don't expect me to stay? I get that I'm tired, but I really don't understand what's going on right now."

"I should have asked Nicole or Megan for help," Wiley muttered, running an agitated hand through his hair. "They would have come up with a better plan. I'm sorry, Grace. I wanted tonight to be perfect. I thought if we were at a place that held good memories..." He gestured to the inn. "That first night we had dinner was one of the best nights of my life."

"Me, too," she whispered, suddenly nostalgic for the night when things had seemed so simple. He took a step forward, then stopped again.

"I asked your brother to help me win you back."

Grace choked back a snort. "And he agreed?"

Wiley shrugged. "He brought you to me, right?"

"I suppose he did." She glanced behind her, half expecting to see Jake come tearing back into the parking lot. "Wait." She turned back to Wiley. "You want to win me back?"

"More than anything," he confessed. "The fact is I'm miserable without you. It's like you brought the color to my life and now I'm stuck with boring black and white. I miss the color, Grace. I miss you."

She swallowed as emotion welled up in her throat. "It felt like you walked away without looking back," she told him. "You left for Chicago. You left me behind like I was nothing."

"I'm sorry." He moved closer until she could look

up into his handsome face and see the golden flecks in his eyes. Heat radiated from him, and she had to force herself not to reach for him. She needed to stay strong. "I thought about you all the time. I hated being away from you."

"Why didn't you call?"

"I'm an idiot," he said with a harsh laugh. "I felt guilty that things had gone to hell back in Chicago while I was here with you. I told myself that I needed to make it right for the firm before I left the city. I thought you knew how I felt, Grace."

She shook her head.

"I love you," he whispered. "I think I fell a little bit in love that first night. Then I almost lost you before we ever had a chance."

Hope unfurled in her chest like a flower after a rainstorm. "What do you mean left the city?" As much as Grace loved hearing those three words from him, she was having trouble following this conversation. Did Wiley really—

"I quit my job," he said. "I'm going to join a firm out of Austin. Most of the work I do will be from Rambling Rose. I want to be here with you…for you."

He held up a hand when she would have spoken, and thank heaven for that because she had no idea how to respond. "But I'm staying no matter what you decide, Grace. I love you. That won't change. But even more, I respect you. I respect your strength and your integrity and the way you never give up. I don't want to give up on us, but the choice is yours."

Hers. He was giving her the power to decide her own fate, although Grace now realized she'd had it all along. She'd just been too scared to truly claim the life she wanted. Wiley had helped her see that she deserved to do just that.

Unable to resist one more moment, she threw her arms around him and pressed her mouth to his. "I love you, Wiley," she said against his lips. "I love the man you are and the way you believe in me. I love how you make me feel like I can do anything."

"You can, sweetheart." His arms tightened around her, and she could feel his heart thumping in his chest. "You can do anything, and I'm so damn grateful that you're choosing me. I will love you for always, Grace. I'm going to spend the rest of our lives proving that I'm the man who deserves you."

"You don't have to prove anything to me." She nuzzled her face into the crook of his neck, feeling like she'd finally come home. "I love you just the way you are."

He claimed her mouth again, kissing her until they were both breathless.

"Would you like to go upstairs?" he asked as he pulled away with a sexy grin.

"Did you get us a room here?" She grinned.

"I rented out the entire inn," he told her with a wink. "The whole place is ours for the night."

"And you're mine forever," she said. Joy exploded through her entire body, and she kissed him again.

* * * * *

HARLEQUIN
Save $1.00

on the purchase of ANY Harlequin book
from the imprints below.

*Heartfelt or thrilling, passionate or
uplifting—our romances have it all.*

PRESENTS INTRIGUE

DESIRE ROMANTIC SUSPENSE SPECIAL EDITION

LOVE INSPIRED

Save $1.00

on the purchase of ANY Harlequin Presents, Intrigue, Desire,
Romantic Suspense, Special Edition or Love Inspired book.

Valid from June 1, 2023 to May 31, 2024.

52617414

5 65373 00076 2 (8100)0 12532

Canadian Retailers: Harlequin Enterprises ULC will pay the face value of this coupon plus 10.25¢ if submitted by customer for this product only. Any other use constitutes fraud. Coupon is nonassignable. Void if taxed, prohibited or restricted by law. Consumer must pay any government taxes. Void if copied. Inmar Promotional Services ("IPS") customers submit coupons and proof of sales to Harlequin Enterprises ULC, P.O. Box 31000, Scarborough, ON M1R 0E7, Canada. Non-IPS retailer—for reimbursement submit coupons and proof of sales directly to Harlequin Enterprises ULC, Retail Marketing Department, Bay Adelaide Centre, East Tower, 22 Adelaide Street West, 41st Floor, Toronto, Ontario M5H 4E3, Canada.

U.S. Retailers: Harlequin Enterprises ULC will pay the face value of this coupon plus 8¢ if submitted by customer for this product only. Any other use constitutes fraud. Coupon is nonassignable. Void if taxed, prohibited or restricted by law. Consumer must pay any government taxes. Void if copied. For reimbursement submit coupons and proof of sales directly to Harlequin Enterprises ULC 482, NCH Marketing Services, P.O. Box 880001, El Paso, TX 88588-0001, U.S.A. Cash value 1/100 cents.

© 2023 Harlequin Enterprises ULC

HSERIESCOUP0623